Three-times Golden Heart® finalist **Tina Beckett** learned to pack her suitcases almost before she learned to read. Born to a military family, she has lived in the United States, Puerto Rico, Portugal and Brazil. In addition to travelling, Tina loves to cuddle with her pug, Alex, spend time with her family, and hit the trails on her horse. Learn more about Tina from her website, or 'friend' her on Facebook.

Scarlet Wilson wrote her first story aged eight and has never stopped. She's worked in the health service for twenty years, having trained as a nurse and a health visitor. Scarlet now works in public health and lives on the West Coast of Scotland with her fiancé and their two sons. Writing medical romances and contemporary romances is a dream come true for her.

THE NURSE'S ONE-NIGHT BABY

TINA BECKETT

NURSE WITH A BILLION DOLLAR SECRET

SCARLET WILSON

MILLS & BOON

First published in Great Britain 2023
by Mills & Boon, an imprint of HarperCollins*Publishers* Ltd,
1 London Bridge Street, London, SE1 9GF

www.harpercollins.co.uk

HarperCollins*Publishers*, Macken House, 39/40 Mayor Street Upper, Dublin 1, D01 C9W8, Ireland

The Nurse's One-Night Baby © 2023 by Tina Beckett

Nurse with a Billion Dollar Secret © 2023 by Scarlet Wilson

ISBN: 978-0-263-30602-6

04/23

MIX
Paper | Supporting
responsible forestry
FSC
www.fsc.org
FSC™ C007454

This book is produced from independently certified FSC™ paper to ensure responsible forest management.
For more information visit: www.harpercollins.co.uk/green.

Printed and Bound in the UK using 100% Renewable Electricity at CPI Group (UK) Ltd, Croydon, CR0 4YY

THE NURSE'S
ONE-NIGHT BABY

TINA BECKETT

MILLS & BOON

To the nurses in my family.

Thank you for all you do.

PROLOGUE

THE STROBING LIGHTS played tricks on Serena Dias's perceptions, imbuing everything around her with a feeling of disjointed sensuality. One that came in snatches that made her see stars. And every time the flash came, the people had shifted. Moved.

Danced.

Except one couple who appeared fixed in time, straining together as the world swirled around them.

Not quite what she'd expected from her celebratory night.

She'd long since lost sight of her cousin Amilda, but then again, Ami had already warned her not to expect to leave the bar together. Serena knew her well enough to take her at her word. Which left her alone in one of the wilder parts of her hometown of Cozumel.

And yet, it was perfect. Fit her mood to a tee.

Her time in nursing school had been much like this. Not the bar itself, but the atmosphere. Her memories of the grueling process of qualifying for—and then passing—that last licensing exam came in quick, stilted vignettes that depicted the passing of time. This trip to Mexico was a celebration of finally being legally allowed to use the coveted title of Registered Nurse.

She'd worked so, so hard. Surely she deserved to cut loose for one night?

Maybe she would have been better served by staying in San Diego and going to dinner with her hunky roommate, who'd also just finished qualifying. Then, at least, she could have pretended she had someone special in her life, even though she and Avery were just good friends.

Ah, to hell with it. She could celebrate on her own just as easily as she could with Ami or Avery or anyone else. She took one last pull of her frosty margarita and set it firmly on the bar. She was here to dance, and dance she would. With or without a partner.

Her first step had a slight wobble to it, only because Ami had talked her into wearing her sky-high pumps rather than Serena's own more sensible slingbacks. By her second step, though, she'd decided she was going to own the shoes and all they stood for.

Before she could, a man crossed her path and stopped dead in his tracks, giving her a once-over and a smile that told her in no uncertain terms what he was thinking. Her chin went up, and she shook her head, moving to step past him. Except one of her heels chose just that moment to hit the floor at a wonky angle before starting to slide sideways, gaining momentum.

Oh, God. She was going to fall. In slow, strobing motion.

But something caught her from behind. Not the leering stranger, who hadn't moved. And not some*thing*.
Some*one*.
A very solid, very steady someone. His arms were

locked around her midsection, her back pressed against the entire length of him.

Oh. Wow.

She closed her eyes for a second, somehow not wanting to turn around and be disappointed by yet another leering stranger. But she owed him at least a thank-you.

Shifting, she somehow managed to tame her stilettos and get them back underneath her. She pivoted and blinked, finding a white button-down shirt. Craning her neck, her gaze followed the trail of buttons up past a tanned neck, a strong, square chin, until she met eyes that were startlingly blue.

Her mouth went dry, and she completely lost her train of thought.

"I… I… Oh…" She finally remembered what country she was in. *"Muchas gracias."*

He said something that she couldn't quite hear.

"Sorry?"

Damn. She'd done it again. She'd lived in the States so much of her life that now English came naturally, even though Spanish was her mother tongue.

"I said, 'you're welcome.'" He glanced pointedly over her shoulder before bending down. "Would you like to dance for a few minutes?"

He'd had to put his lips close to her ear to be heard over the next round of music, and the low rumble of his voice sent a shiver over her.

She realized he was trying to help her avoid an uncomfortable situation with the guy who'd stepped into her path a few seconds ago. Through the blinks of light, she studied him for a second or two before something in his face satisfied her. He really was trying to help.

She nodded and let him lead her into the throng, leaving the other guy behind.

Thank God.

Except the second she went to lay her palms on this new stranger's shoulders, they slid behind his neck instead and linked there. If he noticed, he didn't say anything, those swoon-worthy eyes of his meeting hers before he leaned closer. "How steady are you on your feet?"

Was he asking if she was drunk? Ha! Not hardly.

Her brows went up. "Steady enough." As if to demonstrate her point, she took a step back, her right hand sliding down his arm until she found his fingers, an unspoken signal for him to twirl her. And twirl he did. Thankfully, her brain managed to trick her feet into doing exactly what she wanted them to do. When the rotation was complete and she'd settled back against his chest, she looked up at him in triumph, almost shouting to be heard over the rocker on the DJ's playlist. "See? Very steady."

Just as steady as the man's hands, his gaze…his body.

"So I see." One corner of his mouth lifted, and the sheer deliciousness of the act made her insides shimmy.

They stood there for a moment or two without moving, as the lights, the music, the people continued to swirl without noticing them.

But she noticed.

And suddenly, she knew exactly the kind of celebration she wanted. The celebration she needed. She bit her lip, trying to decide just how shocked he would be if she kissed him.

Not very, she decided. He was hot. Evidently unattached…and here.

She tried to go up on tiptoe, but the shoes already had her at maximum elevation.

But somehow, he seemed to know what she wanted. Because as the lights flashed around her, his palm came up to cup her chin. He seemed to ask a question that she was only too eager to answer.

"Yes."

And then his mouth was on hers, one arm sweeping around her back to bind her to his hips. And that was all it took to seal her decision:

This man.

This venue.

This night.

CHAPTER ONE

TOBIAS RENFRO HAD made the right decision. For himself. For everyone.

Four weeks after his self-imposed honeymoon, he'd come back to the States with a renewed sense of commitment that the only thing he needed to be married to was his work. At least right now. Maybe even forever. All he lacked was a ring on his finger to seal the deal.

The fact that doubts about getting hitched had been boiling in his midsection for the past six months followed by the discovery that his fiancée Tanya had been embroiled in an affair with his best man had hammered home that he really needed to listen to his instincts.

And right now, his instincts were telling him to steer clear of women. All women, really. But especially those he worked with, like Tanya. Once had been more than enough for a lifetime.

Thank God Tanya and Cliff had decided to relocate to San Francisco so he wouldn't have to see them every day.

All in all, it was a good day. While in Mexico, he'd said his goodbyes to past mistakes in the best way possible. And vowed he wouldn't repeat them again. Ever.

Heading onto the floor to do his morning rounds, he

glanced at the nurses' station and caught sight of a quick swirl of dark hair as someone turned and rushed down the hallway at the frantic pace of someone who'd been alerted to a Code Blue. Only there'd been no announcement of one. And there was something about the way she moved that set off alarm bells of a different type in his head. His steps ground to a halt as he glanced over at Jacelyn Webber, who was entering something into a computer at the desk. He headed over to her.

"Did we get a new nurse?"

"We did. I told you about that, remember?" She looked up and glanced behind her. "Well… We did have one. Hopefully the sight of you hasn't sent her running for the hills." The charge nurse smiled to take the sting out of the words. "You can look pretty intimidating when you want to."

He could? He paused for a second and shook his head. "I don't think I've run anyone off yet."

Except maybe Tanya. He gritted his teeth. No, he hadn't run her off. She'd taken off. With Cliff.

Jacelyn's smile widened, and Toby saw why she was so popular with her grandchildren. Warm and compassionate, her ready smile was contagious, and she was also a favorite with patients on the floor. "I'm kidding." She glanced again down the hallway. "Someone must have paged her. Anyway, her name is Serena Dias, and I think she's going to make a great addition to our department. She's fresh out of nursing school and very enthusiastic."

Serena? Something crunched its way through the confines of his skull, and he struggled to drag his attention back to Jacelyn still talking about the new nurse, who was evidently brimming with new ideas.

She was responsible for hiring in their department, and she hadn't steered them wrong yet. But what if, without realizing, she'd just dragged a memory back from Cozumel? A very hot memory.

What were the odds that...?

Astronomical. Odds were good that the name and the dark-haired woman he'd glimpsed had simply struck at the memory center of his brain and made him panic for a fleeting moment.

No, she wasn't *his* mystery woman. She was miles and miles away. In Mexico.

He forced himself to relax. "Good to hear."

"Yes. She actually just got back from visiting some of her family in Cozumel. That place is on my bucket list. Serena was actually born there, lucky girl."

Every muscle that had relaxed went back on high alert. "Cozumel? Are you sure?"

"Yep. As in Mexico."

The crunching sensation grew stronger until he couldn't hear anything else. His facial muscles some-how mustered a smile. "I do know where Cozumel is." He hadn't actually told anyone where he was going a month ago, preferring that no one relate it back to his honeymoon destination. It had been hard enough to get people to drop the words of sympathy over the sudden canceling of his wedding. Their knowing that he'd taken a solo trip to his honeymoon destination was bound to bring more pity he didn't want. Hell, Toby would have felt sorry for himself. Had, in fact. Until...her.

A movement caught his eye, and he saw the woman—dressed in scrubs—trudging back down the hallway, looking like she'd rather be anywhere but here. His stomach wound tight with dread. But no amount of damning the impulses that had put them together in his hotel bed would change anything. Because despite the odds, despite his pep talk that there was no way it could be her... There evidently *was* a way. Because he remembered this woman.

In stunning detail.

From the tiny butterfly tattoo on the outside of her left breast to the way she'd jerked on her clothes not long after their time together, saying she needed to go, that her family would worry if she didn't come home tonight.

All signs that he took to mean that she actually lived in Cozumel, despite the flawless English that she'd slipped into a lot more easily than he'd expected.

She hesitated before lifting her chin and finishing her commute over to the desk. She stood next to Jacelyn, who glanced at her.

"Oh, good. I was wondering where you'd gone. Serena, I'd like you to meet one of our trauma surgeons. You'll be working pretty closely with him and his patients, since I know you spent a lot of time training in surgical procedures." She gave a half shrug. "Anyway, this is Dr. Renfro. One of our best."

Despite his best effort, his lips curved—this time of their own volition. He could tell from her face that she, too, would rather be anywhere but here. "Serena and I have already met, actually."

Her eyes went wide, and he could have sworn she shook her head, although Jacelyn wouldn't have noticed.

"You have?" The head nurse looked from one to the other.

There was another tiny hesitation before she held out her hand. "Yes. We, er, met around the time I graduated. I just didn't know he worked here. Nice to see you again, Dr. Renfro."

There'd been no doubt that her quick flight from the nurses' station had been due to her recognizing him. But if she was worried about him trumpeting about what had happened between them, she needn't. The fewer people who knew about his trip to Mexico, the better. But trying to pretend they'd never met before? It was easier just to admit it and go on. "Nice to see you as well. Is this your first day at Paz Memorial?"

He pressed her fingers to acknowledge her greeting, the contact sending him straight back to when he'd led her out onto that dance floor a month ago. Hell. Why did she have to be here, of all places?

Leonora Paz Memorial Hospital was often shortened to Paz Memorial among staff members. It had been built over thirty years ago as a memorial to the late wife of a wealthy businessman, the man having spent more than a billion dollars on the initial construction of it after her passing. The Paz family still owned the hospital today, and one of the businessman's children was the current chief executive officer.

"Yes. It's my first day."

Letting go of her hand, he kept his smile impartial,

as if touching her hadn't sent a shaft of some weird impulse through him that he'd promptly squashed.

She hadn't sent him any sultry glances or hints that she'd like to take up where they'd left off. He was grateful for that. No more hospital romances for him. The less anyone knew about their encounter the better. And from the way she'd fled the nurses' station when she'd seen him coming, he doubted there would be any danger of her starting any rumors.

Not that either of them had done anything wrong. But, hell, if he'd known who she was in that bar, things would have ended very differently.

Oh, he wouldn't have turned his back on her if the creep who'd stepped in front of her had caused trouble. But he definitely wouldn't have spent the night with her. No matter how beautiful she was. No matter how in sync her body had been with his out on that dance floor. The whole night had had a surreal aspect to it, as if it had been dredged up from a dream.

But her standing here was living proof that what had happened had been all too real.

He forced himself to speak up and end this meeting in a professional way that set the tone for any future encounters between them. "Well, I hope your time at Paz Memorial proves a good start for a long career. If you have any questions, I'm sure Jacelyn or any of the other staff members will be more than happy to answer them." He purposely left himself out of the mix.

Jacelyn gave them a smile. "Do you want to show Serena the surgical suite, Toby? We haven't gotten that far this morning. Unless you're in the middle of something…" Her head tilted as if seeing something in his face.

So much for trying to play it cool. He could just say he needed to start on his rounds, which he did. But if he acted too anxious to get away from Serena, it would make Jacelyn wonder if there'd been something more to their initial meeting than either of them had admitted.

If only she knew.

"I'd be happy to," he lied. He sent Serena a polite smile and motioned to the left. "It's just this way."

The second they turned the corner, she whispered to him, "Why did you tell her we'd met before?"

"We had. To try to pretend otherwise would only make things harder in the end." Although he was beginning to wonder. He could have pretended he was too drunk to remember anything from that night. But somewhere, somehow, one of them was bound to slip up. And if he'd been worried about rumors before, there'd be a slew of them if someone overheard the wrong thing.

"Harder for who?"

"For both of us." He stopped to face her and took in the expression on her face. "Look, I'm sorry if my admitting that made you uncomfortable."

She leaned against the wall behind her, tipping her head back to rest against the solid surface. The act made the long line of her neck visible. His eyes couldn't resist tracing it for a second, memories of pressing kisses to that soft skin making him swallow hard.

"It's more than that. I… I… I've wanted to be a nurse for as long as I can remember. I don't want anything jeopardizing that."

Her words brought him back to earth with a bump. "You think I would do that?"

"Not on purpose." Her head came away from the wall and she looked up at him. "I just would rather no one know about what happened in Cozumel."

"Believe me," he said fervently. "I'd rather no one know that I was in Mexico at all."

This time her eyes narrowed. "Why?"

There was no way he was going to admit the reason for his visit. But he also didn't want her to think he was embarrassed about being there. And something in her voice said she was wondering that exact thing.

He reached out and touched her hand. "I have my reasons. But I assure you they have nothing to do with the country or you."

She studied him for a second before nodding. "Okay. So we'll just tell people we met casually and leave it at that."

"Exactly."

She squeezed his hand and released him. "Then we'd better head on to the surgical suite before someone sees us and wonders if there's more to it than that."

She was right. Jacelyn coming down the hallway, and finding them like this would probably make her wonder. "Okay, let's go."

They headed on their way, both of them silent. He gave an internal sigh. Yes, working with her was going to be uncomfortable for a while. At least during this initial period as they struggled to find a way to deal with each other.

But those dealings would be entirely professional. At

least on his end. And he was pretty sure from her stiff posture as she walked beside him that she would be just as happy to leave things at that.

Maybe he had jinxed himself by saying today was a good day so far. Because the day had just turned upside down and proved that he was right. His dealings with women always seemed to come back and bite him in the rear.

Which was exactly why he was going to make sure his actions and behavior gave Serena no hint that he wanted to continue what they'd started in Mexico. Because to him, it hadn't been the start of anything. It had been a kiss goodbye to the past, and the signal of a new start in his quest to devote his life to his job.

At least for now. Maybe someday that would change, but Toby didn't see it happening any time soon. And definitely not with Serena or anyone else from work.

That was one vow he was not going back on. Not now. Not ever.

Toby had been nothing if not distant over this last week, ever since their unexpected meeting at the nurse's desk. Nothing like the man she'd met in that bar in Cozumel. But that was a good thing. A very good thing.

Better than his trying to sidle up to her with some kind of offer to continue what they'd started on the sly. He hadn't done that at all. But that touch in the hallway had sent her pulse skyrocketing—as had the intimacy of their conversation. Even though there'd been no hint of his wanting anything else from her than a professional relationship.

Although at that moment, if he'd leaned a little closer and just…

She shook the thought free. She didn't see him doing that. It was one of the things that had attracted her to him that night. The fact that she'd sensed that one-night stands were as foreign to him as they were to her. And that he was as anxious as she was to put it behind her. It was why Toby had been able to lead her onto the dance floor while the leering man had left her completely cold.

Fortunately, life on the surgical floor had proved too busy for her to sit there and mull over thoughts of that night. At least not much.

He'd asked her how steady on her feet she was that night. She was beginning to wonder, because she still felt unsteady any time she was around him. She'd better figure out a way to get over that, and fast.

But at least he didn't seem to have it in for her or try to subtly pressure her to quit.

Why would he do that, though? They really hadn't done anything wrong. Out of character? Maybe. At least for her. But he'd made it clear he wasn't married and wasn't in the market for a relationship, which had been perfect for her, since she wasn't either. Nursing school had consumed her life for the last several years. In fact, her last semi-serious relationship had been during her first year of college. But Parker's hint that she was too devoted to her future career had quickly extinguished her feelings for him. Her father had held her mom back from what she'd wanted in life, and her mom's resentment had been more than apparent for years. Serena never understood why she'd put up with it. She knew her mom didn't believe in divorce, but in some circumstances, Serena had to disagree.

When her dad had suddenly passed away five years ago, her mother had finally had the chance to emerge from her cocoon and fly. And fly she did. She became a writer who was both funny and poignant, and although she wrote Spanish fiction, Serena could definitely pick out the parts that touched on reality. And while she was happy for her mom, she wished her father had been more supportive of her talents while he was alive.

Serena had secretly had a butterfly tattooed in a place it wouldn't be seen to remind herself of her mom and how she needed to follow her mom's lead and transform her dreams into reality, to allow them to carry her away. And now, she was doing just that.

So she was in no hurry to link up with any man. She had a lot she wanted to accomplish in her own right. She was definitely not going to let her emotions take over the thinking center of her brain. No. If anything, she was going to overanalyze everything.

Even if Toby had tried to push her out, she wouldn't have gone down without a fight. She would not lose her career over one impulsive night. But he'd given no sign that he wanted any such thing. Which was a huge relief.

Turning the corner, she ran into the very man she'd been thinking about. Well, not literally, but they were walking toward each other. The sight of his mauve polo shirt and black pants made her tummy shift. It was different from the dark-washed jeans and button-down shirt he'd worn to the club in Cozumel. It was strange that even though he was in office attire, he looked less formal here than he had that night. Maybe because of the way he'd stared down that creep at the bar.

"Hi." Her voice came out slightly breathy, and she cringed at the sound. The last thing she wanted was for him to think she had some kind of crush on him. She didn't. Even though the time they'd spent together had taken on a dream-like quality that threatened to become entombed in her brain.

"Hello. How are you?"

"Good, thanks. Yourself?"

So far so good. This was about as impersonal as you could get.

"I'm good." He frowned slightly "Are you headed to Mabel Tucker's room, by chance?"

"I am. It's time to check her vitals and see how she's coming along after surgery." She had yet to share a surgical suite with the man, but that wasn't to say that she hadn't been in the operating room at all. She'd assisted in several procedures and found that she loved the charged atmosphere in there. She assumed that Toby had his own team that he preferred to work with.

Or maybe he didn't want to work with her at all after their last conversation.

Which suited her just fine. Although it was inevitable that they would work together, eventually. So she was just going to have to suck it up and get on with it. What she really needed to do was stop noticing every little thing about the man. Like those glacial blue eyes. And that short hair that had felt so warm and luscious that night…incredibly silky sliding through her fingers.

Oh, God.

Was that what had happened with her mom? She'd fallen in love before she'd properly gotten to know the man who would become her husband? Serena cleared her throat and realized the sound had been audible.

Toby's head tilted slightly. "Mind if I join you?"

She tensed. "Sorry?"

"Mrs. Tucker?"

Of course, that's what he meant. She needed to watch her step. If she acted put out or hesitant, he was going to pick up on it and wonder why. Except he'd been headed in the opposite direction from Mrs. Tucker's room.

The victim of a drunk driver, she'd perforated her spleen and had required emergency surgery late into the night.

"Sure. Didn't you do her surgery last night, though? I'm surprised you're here."

The half shrug he gave her was painfully familiar. He'd given her that same gesture when she'd said she had to leave his hotel room because her family would be worried. He hadn't tried to convince her to stay longer or spend the whole night with him. Kind of an "it is what it is" gesture that said it didn't matter one way or the other to him.

How could something so simple cause both relief and irritation?

Maybe because it reminded her of her mom's reaction when a teenage Serena had come across a binder of her mom's dream occupations. There'd been about twenty of them. Nurse had been at the top of the list. Serena had been shocked. She'd always thought the decision to stay at home and raise her and her brother had been her mother's choice. It was the first time she realized her dad's controlling tendencies had extended beyond her and Sergio.

When she'd gone to her mom with the binder and asked what it meant, and if she still wanted to become any of the things on that list, her mom had just lifted one shoulder and taken the book from her, carrying it back to her bedroom. She'd never seen it again. But it did cause her to pay more attention to her dad's behavior. And the little things she'd noticed bothered her more than she'd ever admitted.

"She's been in quite a bit of pain. Mrs. Tucker, that is."

He gave her a quick glance, and she tensed yet again. Of course, he knew who she was talking about. She needed to pull herself together. She'd felt slightly off today, ever since she'd woken up, and she wasn't sure why.

The surgeon pivoted, and they began walking toward the patient's room. Serena found herself hyperaware of the man. She dissected everything about him, from his clean scent to the loose, fluid way in which he moved. Honestly, it irritated her that he looked so well rested and fresh with no trace of having pulled an all-nighter. On days that she worked late, it was obvious to everyone. Her eyes became bagged down with circles and she tended to yawn incessantly.

Not this man. It was like he was perfection itself. But he wasn't. Somewhere in there were flaws. Idiosyncrasies like that half shrug. She just needed to remind herself of that fact.

They reached Mrs. Tucker's room thirty seconds later,

and Toby waited for her to go through the door first and let her take the lead once they were both inside.

A man stood almost immediately. "Hi, I'm Tom, Mabel's husband."

"Good to meet you," Serena said. "And good to see you again, Mabel. How are you feeling this morning?" They'd given her another dose of pain meds an hour ago, and Serena had been monitoring her heart rate every time she checked in at the nurse's desk. The floor was super busy today. They had two other patients from the same vehicular accident. Five others had been transferred to other hospitals.

Tom sat back down at her bedside, holding her hand.

"My stomach still hurts pretty badly. And my head." Her voice was thready and weak, and unlike for Serena, whose dark circles were caused by lack of sleep, the darkness under this young woman's eyes was caused by the trauma of the accident. She'd shared with Serena that she'd turned her head, catching sight of movement coming at her from the side just in time to be hit by another car. It had slammed her head into the driver's-side window, breaking her nose and causing a concussion. And the force of the collision had caused several internal injuries, her damaged spleen being the most critical.

It had all happened so fast that it had caused a pileup on one of the city's main thoroughfares.

"Well, I brought Dr. Renfro with me. He's going to check you over once I get your vitals."

Aware that he was watching her, Serena was glad that her hands were steadier than her nerves. She wasn't sure why she was even rattled. She'd had doctors in the

room with her before—even during nursing school—
and had done just fine.

Mabel's blood pressure was a little low and her heart
rate was up, but that made sense, since she'd lost quite
a bit of blood volume through internal bleeding.

She said all the readings aloud for Toby's benefit as
she entered them into the tablet that connected into the
hospital's mainframe.

Then she stood back so that he could move up and do
his own evaluation. Normally she would have checked
the patient's incisions and bandages, but since he would
just need to repeat all of that, she let him do it while
she observed.

He was meticulous as he checked Mabel's pupillary
responses and examined the large swelling on her forehead from where she'd hit the window. Then he moved
on to her abdomen. When she'd arrived, she'd been critical, and there'd been no time to set up the laparoscopy
equipment; they'd had to get her spleen out as fast as
they could since it was dumping blood into her abdom-
inal cavity.

"Where exactly does it hurt? Where the incision is?"

"Yes. And inside my belly." She winced as if something twinged. "Is that normal?"

He nodded. "It can be. Let me take a look. It's going
to be a little uncomfortable, but it won't last long.

Her husband leaned closer. "Squeeze my hand tight,
sweetheart." He kissed her fingers and then wrapped
his hand around them.

"Ready?"

The woman nodded, her knuckles turning white as she squeezed and squeezed.

Toby's hands were gentle as he carefully lifted her gown and peeled away the taped dressing, examining the area with those glacial blue eyes that had probably looked at thousands of incisions. The area was pink with a normal amount of puffiness. No weeping. And those stitches... They were perfection. Each suture was perfectly spaced, and the line was perfectly horizontal. Her scar would be a fine line that—barring complications—would be barely noticeable.

"Here comes the hard part. Try to relax your muscles."

Serena found herself following his instructions in a sympathetic move that made her smile.

Toby caught her, head cocking a bit in question. She quickly shook her head to indicate it was nothing.

Turning back to his patient, he pressed into the soft tissue of her belly, and Mabel groaned, her eyelids squinching tight.

"Belly is soft. No evidence of a leaking vessel."

One of the worries after internal trauma was that a bleeder would be missed or that, like dominoes falling, another system would begin to fail.

He stood straight. "All done, Mabel."

She opened her eyes and blew out a shaky breath. "Is it okay? I dreamed my stomach was filling up with blood. And when I woke up, it hurt so bad, I was afraid..."

And it actually had been when she'd arrived at the

hospital. The trauma to her mind was every bit as real as the trauma to her body.

Toby pulled the wheeled stool over and sat down next to his patient. Something pulled at Serena's insides. It would have been faster for him to stand over Mabel's bed and give her the rundown, but Serena was impressed that he clearly liked to get on the same level as his patient. Not all doctors did that.

"I'm not seeing anything that would make me think that. If there was any hint of it, I'd send you over for a CT scan. But I do want you to keep track of your pain levels and let your nurses know they can call me at any time. Day or night."

Mabel's eyes filled with tears, and her fingers loosened their grip on her husband's hand. "Thank you so much."

"You're very welcome. I'll be back to see you again before I leave for the day, okay?"

"Okay." The woman seemed to sink deeper into the mattress as her muscles loosened.

"Can I stay with her?" Tom asked.

Toby nodded. "Of course. The chair by the window folds almost flat." He smiled. "It's pretty comfortable, actually. Don't ask me how I know."

"I can get you a blanket, if you want," Serena offered.

"Thank you so much. Mabel was on the way to the airport to pick me up when the accident happened. I'm just glad she's going to be okay."

Serena smiled. "We all are. Any other questions?"

They both shook their heads.

"Well, try to get some rest. Both of you. They'll be

coming to get you up out of bed in a little while, so sleep while you can," Toby said.

They said their goodbyes, and he held the door for her to exit.

"Thanks, Toby." Too late, she realized she'd addressed him by his first name. In fact, she'd thought of him by his given name ever since their encounter that first day at the nurse's desk. After Cozumel, it seemed silly to think of him as Dr. Renfro.

But although most other staff members called each other by their first names, she'd done her damnedest to address him in more formal terms. Until now. And it was impossible to go back and undo that damage.

Only now that she'd broken that first rule, she was going to have to make sure she didn't go breaking any others. Or she'd find herself exactly where she'd been in Cozumel: in Toby's arms, doing things that drove them both wild. There could be no more of that. In Mexico, she hadn't known who Toby was, so she could give herself a pass for sleeping with him.

But now that she knew? No more excuses.

So she was going to make sure she kept any attraction she felt for the man strictly under wraps. No matter how hard that might prove to be.

CHAPTER TWO

TOBY GOT HOME and dropped into a chair, his cat curling up on his lap as he sucked down a deep breath. He was exhausted. Even more so than normal. He stroked the feline's short fur and tried to figure out what was going on.

His tiredness wasn't just because of the surgery, although he'd been up for almost twenty-four hours straight. That was nothing new for him.

So why this bone-weary fatigue that seemed to swallowed him into the very fabric of his easy chair?

It was because every time he'd seen Serena today on the floor, he seemed to tense up with memories that were best laid to rest. Except that was proving impossible. And to be in an actual exam room with her? Hell, he'd had to fight to keep his mind on his patient. And that wasn't like him. At all.

He'd always been able to compartmentalize his life. Just like his parents seemed to be experts in doing. Only their compartment for displays of affection toward their son had seemed so small as to be virtually nonexistent. So for Toby to have a hard time containing his wild sense of excitement when he'd been confronted with the fact that Serena had joined Paz Memorial was unexpected. And entirely unwelcome.

What was going to happen the first time they shared an operating room?

Nothing. Because he was going to get his act together and figure out how to work side by side with her. Without the excitement. Or clawing urge to repeat that night in Cozumel.

And that was part of the problem. It had been one night. Not even an entire night, at that.

He'd been able contain his feelings for his ex while at work, and he'd been involved with Tanya for almost three years before they'd finally gotten engaged. He'd known Serena for how long? A week?

Well…a week and part of a night. A night that dreams were made of.

But not his dreams. At least not the permanent kind. So why had she fallen so eagerly into his arms? Was that what she usually did? Pick guys up in bars for brief encounters?

No. He'd seen the flash of uneasiness in her eyes when confronted by that man who'd obviously had only one thing on his mind.

So why Toby? Why spend the night with him? Not that she had. She'd flown out of his room like a bat out of hell, nothing like that tiny butterfly tattoo on her breast that he'd traced with his lips.

And licked.

He pinched the bridge of his nose. Hell. It wasn't the only thing he'd tasted.

And that was part of the problem. Their coming together had been chaotic. So fast. And yet, every second of it was burned on his brain. Drawn with an indelible ink that he knew would mark his psyche for a long time to come.

But he wasn't sure how to separate that night from the days he was going to spend working with her.

There would be a lot of those days. They stretched out as far as the eye could see. And knowing he was never going to be able to touch her again like he had that night...

Well, hell, it shouldn't be as hard as it was.

Somehow he was going to have to figure it out, and fast. But for now, he decided he was too tired to move. Too tired to shower. Too tired to watch television.

And hopefully too tired to picture any more scenes that had Serena as the star.

Instead, he was going to let himself do something he almost never allowed himself to do. And it didn't involve sex. Or tattoos. Or heavy drinking.

He was going to put his thoughts on hold and allow himself to fall asleep in his chair. With his cat. And hope to hell that when he woke up, a solution had magically slid into his skull and made itself known.

Seriously?

He was pretty sure all that was going to happen was that he'd wake up cranky and sore and wishing he'd taken the time to stretch out in his own bed.

But it was what it was. And for tonight, he was going to be okay with it staying like that.

For a brief second after she hoisted herself out of bed and her feet touched the ground, the world spun at a crazy angle. It righted itself almost immediately, but it startled her. She blinked and stood there with an out-stretched hand, waiting for the sensation to come again.

It had to be that crazy dream.

That stupid strobe light at the bar from Cozumel had visited her last night. And not in an erotic, sexy way either. Not that that would have been any better. No. She'd been running for her life. Fleeing from something that was just behind her but that remained unseen. Every time she'd turned to look, nothing was there but a shadow.

She blew out a breath and let herself take a tentative step toward her bathroom.

Still steady.

Okay—that's all it had been. The remnants of a nightmare she was glad was over. Time to get ready for work.

A sense of anticipation slid over her that hadn't been there yesterday. Maybe because the reality of working with Toby hadn't been quite as traumatic as it could have been.

He was just a regular guy. Right? One that was crazy sexy and a little intense, but a lot of surgeons were like that. It also explained the precision in the way he'd kept her on the razor edge of climax in Cozumel. Time and time again, he'd brought her almost there only to pull back at the last minute. A shiver of heat went through her.

Oh, God.

She could hear Avery, her roommate, in the kitchen. Cutlery was clanging, and it gave her a sense of normalcy. Serena had needed someone to help split expenses in nursing school, and finding him had been a godsend. They got along like a dream, in a purely platonic way, which had helped her survive the frantic pace of school. They'd each known when to tiptoe around the other, and Serena had poured her heart out to him one time when she'd been so frustrated with one of her courses that she'd considered dropping out of the program. He'd talked her down from the ledge, and for that she owed him a huge debt of gratitude. Because she was finally where she needed to be.

Avery had had a secret of his own that he'd wanted kept from the school, and especially Paz Memorial, where he also worked. He didn't want any special favors or treatment. And Serena respected the hell out of him for that.

Grabbing a quick shower, she toweled off and got dressed, putting a quick coating of mascara on her lashes and dabbing some clear lip balm on her mouth. She let her hair down from the clip and allowed the waves to fall around her face. The humid days of summer made it impractical to try to straighten the thick tresses. They would just go back to their crazy, untamed state. Her ex, Parker, had said the thing he loved most about her was her hair.

She didn't get it. At all. But because of how strong his personality had been, she'd found herself subconsciously trying to please him until she'd realized with horror that it was becoming a habit. A dangerous one. One that she imagined her mother had once played when dating Serena's dad. For her mom, it had signaled the loss of autonomy and independence. So maintaining her independence was something that was now super important to Serena.

Once she'd realized she was falling into a vat of complacency with Parker, she'd found herself fighting the curls, straightening and straightening them until she'd worn out her flat iron. She went to the store and stared at a replacement iron for a long time before putting it back on the shelf. It wasn't worth it. *He* wasn't worth it. No one was.

She'd ended the relationship not long after that. She wasn't sure why, except that she didn't want to be with someone who'd made her feel she had to fight to maintain her sense of self. Parker hadn't meant to make her feel that way. But some of the little things he'd said and done had reminded her a little too much of her dad. Hypersensitive? Yes. She could admit it. And until she could figure things out, she didn't need to be in any kind of relationship.

She needed to work on what was most important to her: her career.

Her time with Toby in Cozumel had been perfect in that she now knew she could sleep with someone without feeling forever tied to them. Not that she was going to start clubbing any time soon. But knowing she could cut loose and have fun and then snip whatever thin thread that bound them together and go on her merry way was relieving in a way she didn't quite understand.

But then again, she'd never expected to see the person she'd done that with again. And she was finding it harder to deal with than she'd expected.

Sliding her comfy shoes on, she exited her bedroom

and found Avery with a sizzling pan filled with a tantalizing scent. "What is that?"

"Omelet. There's more than enough to share."

Her nose twitched, feeling slightly guilty. "Are you sure?"

"Positive. Besides, I've barely seen you all week. It'll be good to have a few minutes doing something normal. Something that isn't life-or-death."

"I agree." She dropped into a chair and watched as he used a spatula to divide the eggs and slid her half onto a plate. "Tell me I shouldn't expect you to do this every day. Despite the fact that I may or may not have heard someone call you Mr. Sunshine at work."

He made a face. "Yeah, I have no idea where that came from. And don't worry." He motioned to the skillet. "I don't even do this for *me* every day.

"I hear you. I take it cardiac care is as crazy busy as we are on the surgical floor?"

"Let's see." Avery swallowed his first bite of egg. "Do you sit down for meals?"

"Not so far. You?"

"Same."

She blew out a breath. That was why Paz Memorial was such a popular hospital. It had an impeccable reputation for top-quality care. "How's it going, other than that?"

He stared at his plate for a minute before glancing back up at her with a shrug. "Okay. A couple of bumps in the road, but nothing I can't handle. You?"

"A couple of bumps for me too." She started to echo his thought that it wasn't anything she couldn't handle, but in truth, she wasn't sure yet. She'd hoped at some point to transfer to the ICU after getting her nursing legs under her. But so far, she'd loved her time on the surgical floor more than she'd expected. Whether she was still just in the honeymoon phase of the job or if it was love at first sight, she wasn't sure. But having Toby working there too threw a kink in the works. A big one.

She was about halfway through devouring her breakfast when her jaws quit moving. That weird sensation spiraled through her again, this time with a hint of something crawling through her belly.

"Hey, are you okay?"

She started chewing again as the elusive feeling vanished. "Yeah. Just tired."

He dropped his fork onto his now empty plate. "You have a day off coming up, don't you? Make sure you sleep in."

"I plan to."

He took his plate to the sink and started to rinse it for the dishwasher. "Leave it, Avery," Serena said. "You cooked, so the least I can do is load them in. Besides, I don't have to be at work for another hour."

And in truth, it would keep her from thinking too much about things…or Toby. Avery was right. They were just bumps in the road. Once she got past them, surely things would smooth out, and she'd find herself in a routine. In the meantime, she'd make sure she didn't give off any hints that their night in Cozumel was still hovering in her head.

She definitely wasn't going to lapse into Spanish around him, since he'd seemed to like it when she'd done it that night. She didn't do it nearly as much any-more, anyway. And she didn't really see any reason why she would, unless she had to translate for a patient at some point. So far, no one had asked her to.

"Are you sure you don't mind?"

Her roommate's voice pulled her from her thoughts. "Yep. It's kind of nice to do something that doesn't re-quire quick thinking."

"I get it. Okay, I'm off then. See you."

"Yep. Have a good day. And don't speed over those bumps."

"I don't plan on it."

He closed the front door with a soft click, and she could hear his key locking it behind him.

She got up gingerly, hoping she wasn't coming down with something. That was all she needed. But nothing happened. She felt fine and the omelet had actually been delicious. Piling all of the dishes in the sink, she gave them a quick rinse and stacked them in the dishwasher. She'd just finished when her cell phone went off. Glanc-ing at the readout and hoping it wasn't the hospital al-ready, she relaxed when she saw it was her mom.

"Hola, Mamá. Cómo estás?"

Listening with one ear while her mom recounted her research trip to Greece, she found herself smiling. She was in the planning stages of her latest book, and Ser-ena loved hearing her talk about it. The passion in her voice was evident, and Serena could picture the shine in her eyes, the way she would twirl her hair around one of her fingers, something Serena did as well.

Fifteen minutes later, the call ended. Not because

they didn't have anything left to talk about, but because this had grown to be their pattern. They chatted most days. Her mom knew how busy her life had gotten since she'd started nursing school and said she didn't want to monopolize her time. She never did. But her mom had always been someone who showed she cared by subsuming her own wants and needs and taking care of others. It was the one thing that she and Serena actually argued about. But at least she was living her life fully now. So it was hard to argue with that.

Sliding her cell phone in her pocket, she grabbed her keys and followed the path Avery had taken forty-five minutes earlier. She hoped today would be a good day. She *needed* it to be a good day.

He was struggling.

The patient's husband was trying to explain something to him, but Toby's Spanish wasn't the greatest. Especially when the other person seemed to be talking at a hundred miles an hour. The unconscious woman had come through the emergency department and had been sent straight back to surgery after a knife she'd been using to pry frozen fish apart had slipped and sliced open her arm, cutting through skin and muscle alike. He wasn't sure if she'd passed out from the sight of her own blood or if she had some kind of preexisting condition.

He was waiting on the hospital translator, who was currently helping someone else. If she didn't get here soon, Toby was going to have to trust his own instincts and start treatment.

He caught sight of Jacelyn, who was motioning for

Serena to come forward. The nurse took a deep breath and moved toward him.

Was she that reluctant to work with him? If so, they were going to need to sit down and hash this out. He couldn't risk patient care just because they had some personal baggage that needed—

"Serena speaks Spanish. Maybe she can help."

Of course. He'd almost forgotten.

Well. No, he hadn't. Some of those little words and phrases she'd murmured so fluidly had slid over him like silk.

Not the time, Toby.

Without addressing him, Serena turned to the man and began talking, nodding and replying in turn before finally turning back to Toby. "His wife was mugged several years ago and stabbed. When she cut herself, he thinks it brought back those terrible memories. For him too. He heard her scream, and by the time he made it to the kitchen, she was on the floor and there was blood everywhere."

That made more sense. "Ask him if she has any medical conditions we should know about."

She repeated the question to him.

The man nodded. *"Lucinda está embarazada."*

That was one phrase he understood. The man's wife was pregnant. He tensed.

"I understood that. Anything else?"

The answer to allergies or other conditions was met with a shake of the man's head. But he evidently asked if the baby was okay.

"Jacelyn, would you mind paging Gary from Obstetrics?"

"I'll do it right now."

He would have asked Serena to do it, but he needed her to stay with him in case he had more questions for the patient. And he was grateful for her help. He glanced at her with real relief sliding through his veins. "Thanks. Seriously."

"You're welcome. Seriously." The tiny smile that played around her lips made him swallow. But at least some of the tension seemed to have left her.

"Can you get him to sign a consent form and explain that we'll have to take her into surgery to repair the arm? It doesn't look like there's nerve or tendon involvement, so it should be straightforward. I just want Gary to take a quick look at her too."

"Is he an OB-GYN?"

"Yes."

Serena turned back to the man, whose name was Pedro, and explained what was happening while Toby placed another layer of gauze on the wound to absorb the bleeding.

Consent forms were signed just as Gary arrived wheeling a portable ultrasound machine. He smiled at Pedro and introduced himself, switching over to Spanish with ease. Toby really did need to put some more effort into learning the language. Pedro and Serena laughed at something the other man said.

It made Toby feel like an outsider. Something that shouldn't bother him, but it did. Maybe because he'd felt that way in his childhood home a lot of the time. His parents probably hadn't realized what they'd done—they probably still didn't, but it had made it all the more attractive to be somewhere other than home.

Lucinda moaned, and her eyelids fluttered. Pedro gripped her uninjured hand and smoothed her hair back from her face, talking to her in low tones. Her eyes found his.

"El bebé?"

Gary said something to her and then pulled the ultrasound machine to the bed and set it up. They soon found the baby's heartbeat, and he reassured both of them that the little guy was still okay. Of course, he had to translate everything back into English for Toby's sake.

But at least everything was normal. They could give her a light sedation, do the repair to her arm without needing to go all the way to general anesthesia. Because of the trauma she'd experienced before, he'd rather not try it with just a local anesthetic.

"Can you assist with the surgery?" he asked Serena. Because of the translation issue, he'd rather keep everything as consistent as possible, and having Serena in the room would help Toby avoid getting messages secondhand. It would be their first time together in surgery. In reality, he hadn't tried to keep her off his cases. They'd just fallen that way.

"Oh… Of course."

But something in her voice didn't sound super thrilled. Which he understood. He was also less than thrilled with the whole situation, but they were going to have to get through it somehow. And it couldn't be any harder than those last days of working with his ex after discovering what she'd done with his best man.

Jacelyn came back over. "Room one is set up for you."

They got her into the room and found that the team

was already there waiting for them. Sedation was a breeze, and Toby made sure they knew she was pregnant, as that could sometimes affect choices in medication.

They carefully peeled back the layers of bloody gauze and found a jagged, ugly wound on an arm that looked none too happy about what had happened.

"Let's get this irrigated so I can take a closer look at what needs to be done." He pulled his loupes onto the bridge of his nose. Serena seemed to anticipate what he wanted almost before he asked. He was impressed. Especially since she didn't have nearly the experience of most of the other nurses on the floor.

She was also obviously interested in everything that went on in the room. Another thing that showed everything was still new and fascinating to her. He wished he still had that sense of wonder.

But he also knew that what was fascinating to him was often someone else's heartache, so he tried to keep that in mind whenever he treated a patient. Especially someone like Lucinda. She had a husband who was very worried about her. And she carried some terrible memories inside of her.

"I'm going to stitch in layers," he explained to Serena. "Fortunately, the wound isn't on an area that has a lot of movement. So it should heal pretty well."

The woman's vitals blipping across the screen to his right were steady. Blood pressure was holding.

He sensed more than saw Serena standing there watching him, surgical instruments neatly laid out on the tray in front of her. "If this were a straight-line slice,

I might go with deep dermal sutures or use a set-back suture. But because it's jagged and there is a large span between sides, I'm going to use four-zero VICRYL absorbables on the muscle tissue and the same weight nylon on the dermal layers."

Glancing over, he saw her nod. "Got it. I've heard of set-back sutures in class but have never seen it done in real life."

There was a sense of wistfulness in her words that could have been his imagination. Then again, maybe it wasn't.

"How about I call you in if I ever have a case where I'm going to use it?" He had no idea why he'd offered that, other than the fact that he had a lifelong love of learning and teaching others.

"That would be great."

Serena's hair was all pulled up into a surgical cap, but he knew from his time in Mexico that when set free, her curls were lustrous, beautiful things that framed her face. A painter would have found her fascinating. Not just because of her looks. But because of the way her face moved when she talked, highlighting every single one of her emotions.

Like it had that night in Cozumel.

Right now, he sensed a mixture of interest and nerves coming from her that was understandable. But those nerves didn't get the best of her. Her hands were steady, and she followed his requests without hesitation. Under different circumstances, he might have found himself enjoying working with her.

Actually, he was still enjoying it, and that set him on edge.

She was gorgeous, but hell, he did not want to be attracted to her. Not after what had happened with Tanya. She'd already been working at the hospital when Toby had come on board, transferring from a smaller hospital in Lancaster. Back then everything had seemed so easy, uncomplicated…convenient, even. They'd started dating. That had turned into commuting to work together, since their apartments were near each other. Then they'd gotten engaged and moved in together. They'd been in sync about waiting a few years to have children, which had more than suited Toby, who wasn't at all in a rush. At least, they had been for the first couple of months. Then Tanya had mentioned kids unexpectedly at dinner one night while talking about a girlfriend who'd just had a baby. Those mentions had happened more and more frequently until impending fatherhood seemed to play in his head like a litany. At thirty-five, though, she'd pointed out, he was already older than most fathers she knew.

At the time, it had come across as an accusation.

Toby hadn't been completely sure about having kids at all because he wasn't positive, with his own strange, stilted childhood as his only example, that he actually had what it took to nurture anyone. Much less a child. After the argument with Tanya about his age, he'd found himself avoiding those uncomfortable conversations. That had turned into avoiding most conversations with her at all. Especially ones that might trigger talks about having kids.

It was at that point that his best friend—who was also to be his best man—had come to town for a visit and stayed in their spare room. Toby had been in the middle of a complicated case at work, and so Tanya had offered to show Cliff the sights.

Evidently, one thing had led to another, and things had unraveled pretty quickly.

So no. Attracted to a colleague or not, he'd learned from his mistake. And it was honestly a relief to have fatherhood taken off the table for good.

Besides, he had his cat, Porkchop, the one residual of his relationship that he'd kept. That feline was the closest thing to a kid he was likely to have. And it was enough for him.

He pulled his attention back to the procedure at hand and realized Serena was looking at him funny. "Sorry. Did you say something?"

"Nothing important. I asked if you did set-back sutures often."

"Not terribly often. But there are situations where I feel they work better for gaping wounds. They take longer to heal, and getting the stitch tension right is important."

A half hour later, they were done, and Lucinda was waking up from her sedation. Her first question was about her baby, and sure enough, Serena had to translate. Her second question was a little harder. She asked if the hospital had a counselor who could help her work through what had happened with the mugging, so that she didn't have the same reaction if, say, her child was cut by something at some point.

"Tell her I'll look into it. If not, I might have a name for her." He handed Lucinda one of his business cards. "Call me later today and I'll let you know."

He'd actually gone and talked to someone right after his breakup with Tanya, and her advice had been to not make any major decisions for the next year. He'd vowed to make it five years instead. He had four years and nine months left to go to make that goal.

Ha! Falling into bed with Serena probably wasn't what his counselor had had in mind. But hopefully, that was a blip that wouldn't be repeated.

He changed the word *hopefully* to one that had a little more oomph to it.

So no. Not hopefully. Definitely.

That night with Serena would *definitely* not be repeated.

CHAPTER THREE

SERENA HAD WORKED two more surgeries with Toby over the next couple of days, and unlike with Lucinda's, where he'd seemed happy to answer her questions and had even offered to let her see a specialized suture procedure, he'd been reserved. Quiet. He answered questions when she asked but didn't offer anything more.

She'd been surprised when he had the name of a counselor on his phone, but she wasn't sure why. She shouldn't be curious about it.

But she was.

She went over to the nurse's desk after checking on a patient to find Toby there talking to Jacelyn. She got there in time to hear the woman say to him, "Just a heads-up, Toby. Tanya stopped by this morning. Said she was visiting HR to pick up a letter of recommendation." Jacelyn's lips tightened. "She asked about you, Toby."

His eyes met Serena's before moving back to the other nurse. She could have sworn there was a quick flash of guilt in his glance. "Okay, thanks."

That was it. He moved away and headed on his way without another glance in her direction.

Before she could stop herself, she asked, "Who's Tanya?"

It wasn't a totally unprofessional question, right? But

what if this woman had been fired because of something Toby had reported her for? In this day and age of mass shootings, it was better to be prepared in case a disgruntled employee decided to seek revenge.

What she wasn't prepared for, however, was Jacelyn's answer.

"Toby's fiancée." Her nose wrinkled in distaste. "I should say ex-fiancée. She cheated on him and ran off with his best man."

Shock went through her. For some reason, she couldn't picture the surgeon being engaged. He seemed totally at home with being single. And he didn't seem the type given to big displays of emotion.

Of course, he'd been different in Mexico. More open. More spontaneous. Maybe that was the side of him that his ex had usually seen.

She couldn't think of anything to say, except for, "How awful."

"Yes. I'm just hoping she hasn't realized her mistake and decided to come sniffing around here again. They were supposed to honeymoon in Mexico."

Mexico.

With a voice filled with dread, she asked. "When was the wedding supposed to be?"

"About a month ago."

A pang of nausea went through her. A month ago. That was when she had found out she'd passed all of her exams and landed the job at Paz Memorial. When she'd gone to Cozumel to celebrate. When she'd met Toby.

God. Had she been a stand-in for this Tanya person?

She didn't know why, but the thought filled her with a sense of horror.

"What does Tanya look like?"

"Pretty. Dark hair…a little like yours. But definitely not a nice person."

Somehow, she got through the rest of the conversation, quickly changing the subject to something work related. But that didn't mean her mind had stopped mulling over what she'd just learned.

Had he seen a counselor after his fiancée cheated on him? Was sleeping with Serena his own form of revenge?

Except he would have been more likely to do that under her nose, wouldn't he?

Shake it off, Serena. You won't know for sure unless you ask him.

Yeah, she was never, ever, ever going to do that. Not only because he didn't seem anxious to talk about their night together, but because she might be mortified by his answer. Not that she would have wanted him to express his undying love for her. No. Her climb up the nursing ladder was best done while single. Maybe once she'd been here for a couple of years she might start dating again. That was a big maybe. Right now, marriage and children were kind of nebulous things that she might decide she wanted one day. But not now. Not when she still had so much to learn about herself and her own ambitions.

And if the time came to start a family and she wasn't with anyone? Well, you didn't have to be in a relationship nowadays to have babies.

Thank God.

But it could wait a few more years.

With that thought in mind, she pushed the queasiness of her discovery about Toby out of her head and got back to work.

Jacelyn found her a few minutes later. "Hey. Mabel Tucker is asking to see you."

Their splenectomy patient. "Is she okay?"

"Yep. They're looking to maybe release her earlier than expected since she's been working hard at rehab. She wanted to make sure she saw you before she went home."

"That is great news." Especially since Mabel had not been in good shape when she'd arrived at the hospital. "I'll head over there, if there isn't anything you need me to do before that."

Lucinda would be back on Monday to have her stitches removed. One thing that surprised Serena was how quickly you could get attached to certain patients. She could see why nursing school had needed to drill it into their heads that they had to remain objective.

She was following that protocol in that she wasn't emotional during treatment. But surely it was natural to be happy about positive outcomes, wasn't it? She wasn't sure. But Jacelyn hadn't seemed peeved that a patient had asked for her.

"Nope. Why don't you head to lunch after you've seen her? It's been kind of a crazy morning."

Yes, it had been. She'd assisted with three surgeries since she'd arrived this morning. One appendectomy, a patient who'd come in with a partially amputated foot and a drunk driver with a brain bleed.

It was interesting working with different doctors as well. And seeing so many different types of injuries. But it was also mentally taxing, and she found she was already dragging with exhaustion, and it was barely noon.

"Thanks. I will."

She arrived at Mabel Tucker's room and dredged up a smile before going inside. Her patient was sitting up in bed, the bruising around her eyes starting to turn the slightest bit yellow around the edges, a good sign that there was healing going on just below the surface. "I hear you're getting sprung today. I'm sorry I didn't make it over sooner. How are you doing?"

"It's okay. And better, actually. The pain meds are finally making some headway."

Serena nodded. "I think your body is doing its part too."

"I hope so. I'm still pretty sore, but I actually told Tom to go back to work today." She laughed. "And then they told me I was going to get to go home, so he'll have to get off early anyway."

"I can't think of any better reason to have to leave work." She moved closer and squeezed Mabel's hand. "I'm so happy for you."

"Me too. We've been talking about… Well, thinking about starting a family. We've been married five years and have been waiting for the perfect time. But after the accident…" Her chin wobbled for a second before she continued. "Is there ever an ideal time? You never know what life is going to throw at you."

"No, you don't." A wave of compassion went through her, not to mention an unexpected pang of longing. Hadn't she just been thinking about her career and how she wanted to get settled before making any kind of decisions about having kids? But what would happen if at each milestone she convinced herself to wait a little longer? And then a little longer after that? Mabel was younger than she was.

Even so, Serena wasn't an old maid, by any means.

"Do you think I'm crazy?" Mabel asked.

"No. Not at all. I always think it's good to evaluate what's important to you at regular intervals."

"Will not having a spleen affect my chances of carrying a baby to term?"

She hesitated. She didn't want to give Mabel incorrect information. "Let me put a quick call in to your surgeon and see if he's available."

Taking out her cell phone, she called Jacelyn. "Is Dr. Renfro in surgery?"

There was a pause. "No, I'm not seeing one listed. Do you need him?"

A moment of shock went through her followed by the realization that the other nurse was only asking if she needed him in a professional sense. God, she needed to get herself together. "I'm here with Mabel Tucker, and she has a question about getting pregnant since she no longer has a spleen."

"Ah, I see. Let me page him. Or you can."

Gah! She didn't want to. Not this soon after starting her job.

"Would you mind? He can call me directly, if he wants to."

"Yep, I will. I'll let you know if he's not available for some reason."

"Thank you."

She hung up and then looked at Mabel. "She's paging him to see if he's available. Has he been in to see you yet today?"

"No. But I assumed maybe before I left he'd come in."

"Yes, I'm sure he will. But it can't hurt just to double-check. He would be the one releasing you, anyway."

Less than a minute later, her phone rang, and she swallowed when she saw the hospital's name displayed. "Serena Dias here."

"Serena, it's Toby. Are you with her now?"

"I am."

"I was headed that way. Be there in a minute."

With that, the line went silent.

Okay, then. She'd gotten no indication of whether he was peeved that she'd had him tracked down. But then again, he'd made it sound like he'd been on his way, anyway.

He also hadn't told her whether he wanted her to stay there or not, so she was hesitant. But it didn't feel right to just suddenly tell Mabel she was leaving. So she made herself busy, taking vitals to be ready with them in case he asked.

She'd just finished when he pushed through the door. His eyes were on Mabel and not her, although why would he look at her?

He smiled. "You're looking even better than you were

yesterday. I was on the fence about releasing you then or today, but I thought you might benefit from another day of being waited on hand and foot."

Mabel laughed. "I'm going to say, your menu could use a little work."

"So I've heard."

He finally acknowledged Serena. "You can reach me on my cell anytime, you know."

That made her gulp.

"Okay, thanks. Mabel was asking about pregnancy following a splenectomy."

He sat on the stool and wheeled himself over to the bed. "You should be able to get pregnant, but we would want to follow you carefully. There are some elevated risks, but most of them can be managed." He paused. "We definitely would like you to receive some additional immunizations for pneumonia and flu fairly soon."

He talked to her about the spleen acting as a filter for the vascular system to catch microbes and debris before things could spiral out of control. "The liver will take over some of the spleen's duties. But we still worry about infections."

"For how long?"

"You'll have to keep on top of it for the rest of your life."

Mabel seemed to sink deeper into her pillow. "Better that than the alternative, right?"

"That's my thinking. I want you to know I would not have removed your spleen unless I thought it was absolutely necessary for saving your life."

"I know that. And I appreciate it. I'll do whatever I need to do. But I can get pregnant?"

"I don't see any reason why not. I'd like to get our OB-GYN in on the conversation, though, before you make any of those decisions. Would you like to talk to him before you're released?"

She nodded. "Yes, please. I'd prefer to wait until Tom gets here, though. I want him to hear whatever the other doctor has to say."

"I completely understand. I'll arrange for a consult. If there's a problem with getting it before you're released, I'll make sure he's available when you come back in for a recheck. Does that help?"

"Yes, thank you."

"I'll get back to you as soon as I hear from him. Can I check you over while I'm here?"

"Of course."

Toby was just as thorough with this evaluation as he'd been with that first postsurgical exam. When he finished he said, "Everything looks great. You're a model patient. We're going to try to keep you headed in that direction."

"I can't thank you enough. You saved my life."

"Believe it or not, you had a lot to do with that. You're young and strong and your body was fighting hard to keep you alive until the EMTs got you to the hospital."

He might have been brusque with Serena on the phone, but his bedside manner was actually pretty damned outstanding. He was direct rather than patronizing, but he wasn't impatient. And he was an excellent surgeon. If she had to have surgery, she would trust him implicitly.

"Before you're actually released, I'll come in and go over everything later this afternoon. And I'll want to see you in a couple of days to get your sutures out. I don't want you around a lot of people until you've had a chance to have some booster shots. And unfortunately, you'll need to wear a medical alert bracelet for the rest of your life to let first responders know you've had your spleen out."

"Wow. And all of this because of a drunk driver."

"I know. I'm sorry." He gave her hand a quick squeeze. "Don't hesitate to let Serena or one of the other nurses know if you or your husband have any other questions before I come back."

"Thank you again."

"You're very welcome."

Serena nodded to him and waited a minute or two after he left before saying her own goodbye to Mabel. Not because she was afraid to be around him, but just because she didn't want to look like she was angling for some extra chitchat.

Once out of the room, she headed for the hospital cafeteria, opting for a sandwich and salad and then deciding she wanted to eat outside in the garden area of the hospital rather than being stuck inside.

As soon as she stepped into the heat of the outdoors, she breathed a sigh of relief. While she liked air conditioning as well as anyone, it was always nice to be out in what she called "real air" for a while. Especially since it was so chilly inside sometimes.

The clay-tiled area had lush greenery meandering down the center of the space, and various concrete tables and benches were scattered around the open areas. Her eyes traveled the perimeter for a second before stopping dead.

Okay, she hadn't expected Toby to be out here. He had a cup of coffee and was looking at something on his phone. She started to take a step backward, thinking maybe she'd go back inside after all. Except right at that exact moment, as if sensing some kind of movement, his eyes came up and caught her midstep. He looked at her for a moment.

"Want to join me?" His low voice carried across the empty space.

What could she say? No? That would seem rather rude at this point, since it was obvious she was on her lunch break.

So she forced her legs to move toward his table and lowered herself onto the bench across from him. She really didn't want to have to eat in front of him. For some reason, she was suddenly self-conscious. She didn't like it at all.

Shades of her time with Parker.

So she tilted her chin and pulled back the cellophane cover on her egg salad sandwich.

She could feel him watching her for a second before he said, "Most people don't venture out here this time of year. They can't take the heat."

Serena swallowed. Right now, she was having a little trouble taking the heat too. But it was more from the heat generated from the churning of her innards rather than the balmy air. "I'm from Mexico, so it kind of feels like home to me."

Damn. She hadn't meant to mention her home country in front of him. It wasn't that she was trying to hide where she was from—after all, he knew that. It was more like she was trying to hide from what their time together had been like while there. She also didn't want him to know that Jacelyn had told her why he'd been in Mexico that fateful day.

"Yes. The heat there was…unexpected."

His words drove the breath from her lungs. She stared at him. When he tilted his head with a frown, she realized he was talking about the temperature and not their night together.

Dios. She needed to be careful. The last thing she wanted was for him to figure out that everything he said was viewed through the filter of that one hot, passionate night they'd spent together. Especially when something inside of her was whispering to her that she could have that again, if she just let herself.

No. It wasn't smart to even let herself think that way. And just because she was looking through some distorted filter, that didn't mean that he had the same view. In fact, it was pretty obvious he didn't. Instead, she was seeing special inflections in his words that weren't there. Like the ones about the heat being unexpected.

She took a bite of her sandwich and swallowed before changing the subject completely. "Mrs. Tucker seems to be taking everything remarkably well."

"Yes. Maybe a little too well. Used to be that a splenectomy was done a lot more than it is now. But we've discovered that removing the spleen brings a whole set of complications with it."

"I actually did some more reading on it, since it's the first case I've been involved with that's had one."

"And what did your research say?"

Was he being sarcastic for how she'd turned to Dr. Google? She searched his face but found only genuine curiosity.

"I didn't think to look for pregnancy-related issues, but I did find that there's a much higher chance of vascular events like blood clots in those with a splenectomy, and like you'd said, the risk of serious illness. And that some people actually have a second spleen that can take over if the first one is injured."

"I'm impressed. Unfortunately, Mabel isn't one of the ones with an accessory spleen."

"I figured you would have said something to her if she were." Serena realized her elbows were on the table and that she'd leaned toward him as she was speaking. She made a conscious move to sit back and took another bite to prevent herself from running away with another tidbit from her research.

"She will need to be monitored for a while, and she needs to make all of her doctors aware that she's had her spleen removed. But other than that, with some care, she can lead a normal life. Have kids. *If* that's what she really wants to do."

Her brows went up. "You say that as if having children would be something bad."

"Not bad. No. It's just not for everyone."

He made it sound like he was one of those people. Had he and Tanya disagreed on having children?

"Are you talking in general terms? Or personal

ones?" Why had she asked that? It was really none of her business.

"Mostly general. But I don't really see children in my future either. You?"

Touché, Dr. Renfro.

She'd had no business asking him anything so personal. He had every right to turn it back around on her.

"I think I might like kids at some point, yes. Although not for a while. And I'm thinking that maybe it's something I'd rather do on my own. Relationships are…complicated."

Putting his coffee cup to his lips, he drank before setting the empty cup back on the table. "That they are. Whether they're years long or only last a single night. Kind of like Mabel's splenectomy, they bring with them their own list of repercussions."

This time, there was no doubt he was talking about their time in Cozumel. They stared across the table at each other.

She bit her lip. The man really was very attractive. With his electric-blue eyes, and stubbled jaw, she could imagine he got second glances wherever he went. But it wasn't just his looks. It was something inside of him that superseded his physical attributes. It was a dangerous combination.

He could probably have a new hookup or date every week if he wanted one. Except it appeared that he agreed with her that involvements weren't the simple things they were made out to be.

Before she had a chance to comment back, he glanced

away and stood. "Well, I should get back. I've spent longer out here than I should."

Spent too long eating lunch? Or with her?

But there was no way she was going to ask. So she nodded and said, "Thanks for letting me join you."

"Not a problem."

But she felt like it was, and she wasn't sure what to do about it.

He headed for the door, and she knew this particular conversation was a closed book. And she, for one, didn't want to reopen it, because she would twist his words one way and then another, trying to find some hidden meaning in them. Even as she thought it, her stomach clenched, and the egg salad she'd just eaten gathered at the bottom of it, forming a rock. A kind of queasy, greasy rock that never quite stayed still, reminding her of that feeling of unsteadiness she'd felt over the last several days.

For the second or third time, she hoped she wasn't coming down with something.

But whatever it was, from now on she was going to avoid personal subjects with her coworkers whenever possible.

And especially with one Tobias Renfro.

CHAPTER FOUR

TOBY WASN'T SURE how the subject of children or relationships had come up, but they were definitely not things he wanted to tackle. With anyone.

Especially not someone he'd slept with. It made him uneasy in a weird kind of way. He was sure Serena wasn't angling for anything; it had just been an innocent conversation she might have had with anyone, but for some reason it had struck a raw nerve. Maybe because of Tanya showing up unexpectedly, followed by Mabel asking about getting pregnant.

They said things came in threes, didn't they? Well, as long as the whole pregnancy thing didn't come after him, it didn't matter.

He'd used protection when they were together. In fact, when they'd crashed into that hotel room and fallen onto the bed, she'd specifically asked if he had some. So he was pretty sure she wouldn't have asked if she'd been planning on using him as some kind of sperm donor. Although she had mentioned wanting to go it on her own when she eventually did have kids.

Ridiculous. She'd *asked* him to use a condom, which he'd already planned on doing.

But he could see how if a woman wanted to have a

baby and didn't want a relationship, that was one easy way to get what you wanted. Except Toby would never be irresponsible enough to not use protection. Unless she asked him not to and said she'd taken care of it. And probably not even then. Because he didn't believe in shirking his responsibilities. If he got someone pregnant, and the woman chose to carry the pregnancy to term, he would feel obligated to provide in some way for that child.

Obligated to provide…

Something in his gut roiled in protest. He could envision his parents saying something very similar to one another. Although they'd never voiced that in front of him. But providing for his physical needs had seemed to be paramount on their list of things to do for their child. Emotional needs, not so much. Even now that he was an adult, there were no chatty phone calls. Just birthday cards and the perfunctory call at Christmas.

And if his attitude really was all about obligations like theirs was, he couldn't envision himself having anything positive to add to a child's life.

He brooded over it in his office for a half hour after he'd shared that table with Serena before finally switching off those thoughts. Not that it was an easy task. It seemed everything was coming up babies right now.

And then, there was Tanya. Why come to the hospital in person? And why was she suddenly looking for a letter of recommendation? Was she not happy with her life in San Francisco? Her life with Cliff? Hell, he hoped she was, hoped she didn't have any ideas of trying to get back together with him, because that had ended the second she'd confessed that she'd slept with his best friend. His love had died a quick, hard death—actually, it had been on life support even before that moment. No extraordinary measures would bring it back to life now.

The arguments over children and his eventual regrets over getting engaged to her in the first place just added to that sense of his not having what it took to sustain a relationship. Like there was some personality flaw that wouldn't allow him to form lasting emotional attachments. Did he really want to raise a child, if so? Did he want to parent a baby the way he'd been parented?

No.

But it was a moot point. Things with Tanya were over. Forever. So hopefully she'd gone back to San Francisco with her letter and that would be the last he ever saw of her.

Right now, he needed to get thoughts of Tanya and Serena out of his head and put his attention back on getting Mabel Tucker's discharge instructions together like he'd promised he would. He would worry about the rest of it later.

And only if it became necessary.

Serena loved Balboa Park. It was one of her favorite spots in all of San Diego. She came here every morning for a yoga class that was held in an area shaded by majestic palm trees. Unrolling her mat, she joined the other people who were already doing some gentle stretching in preparation for the half-hour-long session. She could just as easily do the moves in her apartment, but motivation was the problem. It was easier to find things to clean than to spend time on herself. And there was just something about sharing the experience with others that couldn't be beat.

Their instructor, Veronica, had a portable sound system that was just loud enough to be heard over the soothing sounds of a nearby fountain. When the instructor was ready, she took the group through a preplanned series of stretches that started off easy and moved into some of the more difficult poses. The pull of Serena's muscles and tendons as she worked through the routine felt good. She'd been wound up tight this week, and her stomach was still somewhat messed up. She'd thrown some menstrual products in her bag, thinking maybe that was part of her problem, although she'd never been particularly regular.

They got through the hardest portion of the routine and then entered a cooldown phase. She never had time to run back by the apartment afterward, but the park was close to the hospital, so she would just wear her yoga pants and T-shirt and walk to work, switching to her scrubs in the staff changing area.

Feeling more rejuvenated than she had felt for the last two weeks, she determined today was going to be a better day. She had the power to shape her attitude, and today she was going to try not to let anything get to her. Including Tobias Renfro. Her encounter with him at lunch had been unsettling, to say the least. One minute he was talking about not wanting kids, and the next he was making a veiled reference to their night together. Unless she was reading more into his words than the situation warranted. Which was a very real possibility.

As was the worry that she might be developing an unhealthy obsession with the man.

The class ended, and she rolled her mat back up, tucking it into the beach bag she'd brought with her. She exchanged some small talk with a couple of regulars to the class and then headed on her way, taking one of the main paths, staying to the side so runners could get past her.

She had a spring in her step that she allowed to remain as she took in the beauty of the park. Although she'd relocated to the city to go to nursing school, she'd fallen in love with San Diego and had decided to stay here. She was glad she had. This place had it all. Beaches, parks and a great nightlife. And she wouldn't trade her friendship with Avery for anything.

He'd been a big part of her life for the last several years, and although their schedules were a little different now than they'd been during their classes and they saw less of each other, she knew she could tell her friend anything and it wouldn't go any further. Although she hadn't told him about that night in Cozumel yet. Not because she was embarrassed about it, but it was just nice to have a tiny area of her life that no one knew about other than her. And there'd been no real reason to tell him.

She'd been doubly glad she hadn't told him when she realized she'd be working with the very person she'd slept with.

Maybe she needed to get back on birth control. Fortunately, Toby had taken care of that aspect of their being together that night, and she would never have unprotected sex, but it wouldn't hurt to have an IUD put in as an extra safeguard. The pill had not been her friend when she and Parker were together, but he hadn't been interested in taking on any of that part of their relationship. In fact, she halfway got the feeling that he would have been happy if she'd gotten pregnant. The better to control her with? More and more, as she looked back at that relationship, she realized she'd probably dodged a bullet. There'd been warning signs that she'd probably ignored, thinking she was overreacting. But the last straw had been his intimation that he'd rather she not be as dedicated to her career path as she'd been. It's probably what had happened with Mom and Dad.

Heavens, she hadn't thought about Parker in a while. And as soon as she'd broken up with him and left their apartment, she'd put an ad up looking for a new place so she wouldn't be tempted to go back to him. When Avery had immediately responded offering a room at his place, she'd initially been hesitant about sharing a space with another man. But he'd quickly put her at ease, and she hadn't regretted the decision for even an instant.

She was so lost in her thoughts that when a jogger pulled up beside her, it took her a second to realize they'd altered their pace on purpose. Glancing to the side to see Toby, she closed her eyes for a quick second. So much for the resetting that her yoga class had done.

Toby was dressed in running gear, and sweat streamed down his temples and darkened the chest of his gray T-shirt. The sleeves of the tee had been cut off and showed off his tanned arms and the curve of his biceps.

Ugh! He was even more gorgeous when he was hot

and sweaty than he was in his casual hospital clothes. The word *steamy* took on a whole new meaning.

She gritted her teeth, managing to get out, "I didn't know you ran in the park."

What else could she say? It was true. And if she had known, she might have been a little less inclined to do her yoga classes here.

No. She was not going to do that. Not going to change her routine just to make it more convenient for him to run here.

Except he hadn't asked her to. She was being ridiculous!

"And I didn't know you...walked here?"

That made her smile. He'd had no idea what she'd been doing here. "Yoga. They teach classes here."

"Ah. I see."

But she didn't think he did, and she felt a little defensive. "It's a bit harder than it sounds."

"I wasn't saying it's not. I just didn't realize they had yoga classes in the park."

"You should try it sometime. Several of the people that come use it to warm up before running."

Her mouth snapped shut. Why on earth had she said that? The last thing she wanted was for Toby to show up at one of her classes and disrupt her chi.

"Seriously?"

Okay, now that was the last straw. "Yes, seriously. You should try it before you laugh something off."

He frowned. "I actually wasn't laughing it off. I just didn't know that runners often used that technique. When are your classes?"

Wow, she was taking everything he said and twisting it into something negative. And she wasn't quite sure why.

"They're every day at 6 a.m."

Maybe she'd jumped to conclusions because he made her, well, jumpy. And because Parker had pooh-poohed yoga as being nothing but fluff. And because of that, she'd basically just taunted Toby into taking one of her classes.

Parker had seemed so charming and accommodating at first. After a month of dating, he'd encouraged her to move in with him, saying it would help both of them with expenses. But once she was installed in the apartment, his demeanor had changed subtly. Good-natured coaxing had shifted to guilting her into things. Including sex. By the time she recognized that she was falling into the same patterns as her mom had with her dad, they'd been together almost six months. The relationship had become stifling, and she'd known she had to break it off.

It was easy to paint anyone with alpha characteristics with the same brush, but she knew it wasn't fair to do so. Toby had stood up to the creep at the bar, but he hadn't pressured her to do anything. In fact, if she'd shunned his help, she had no doubts that he would have backed off immediately. He was a leader. But he didn't turn that natural ability into an abuse of power. It was why everyone she'd met so far respected him.

Actually, she did too, if she were honest with herself. What harm could it do if he joined her class? Maybe it would help her see another side of him that would make her respect him even more.

Was that such a good idea, though? Couldn't respect turn into other things?

Not if she didn't let it.

"How long are the sessions, and is this okay to wear?" Toby held his arms out as if to let her look at his attire. And she did. But it also gave her a reason to remember exactly what that body had looked like without any clothing at all. The side of her breast tingled as a memory swept over her, and she pressed her arm hard against the area to keep the sensation from spreading. Her malleable bra was great for yoga, but not so great when it came to hiding erect nipples.

"It's fine." She jerked her eyes away from him. "Classes are a half hour. Most runners just wear whatever they're going to run in afterward."

"But you don't."

"Sorry?" She shifted her glance back to him.

"You don't run afterward?"

"No. I mean, I've competed in a couple of half-marathons, but running tends to be a solitary endeavor, and I like having company. So the yoga classes are perfect."

"What time do you have to be at work tomorrow?"

She blinked. "My shift starts at nine, but I like to go straight there after yoga. It's a short walk and I can change and get my mind where it needs to be before I start my workday."

"I'll tell you what. I'll come to yoga class if you'll come running with me afterward. I can see if yoga works for me. And you can experience running with someone else. It can be a one-time thing, so no one feels pressured to continue."

What? He was asking her to run with him?

Why?

Ha! Maybe because she'd suggested he try her class. If she refused, wouldn't she be guilty of exactly what she thought he'd been doing?

"You've got yourself a deal." On impulse, she stuck her hand out to shake on it.

He accepted her offer and gripped her hand. His fingers were cool against her skin, and yet, his touch burned her in a way that said her bra was definitely going to fail her. Sure enough, she felt it happen…

She swallowed and their eyes met. And she could tell he knew. God! He knew exactly what she was feeling.

But he didn't let go. And neither did she. They stood there for a long moment while the skin of her arms prickled as if wanting his palm to slide down them too.

Strands of her hair slid across her cheeks in the warm breeze, just as his gaze dipped to her mouth. It finally woke her up to the fact that she *wanted* him to kiss her. The way that he had in Cozumel.

That would be a total disaster. For both of them.

As if reading her thoughts, he released her hand and turned to walk again. "Well, I have surgery in a half hour. Would you mind if I went ahead and finished my run?"

Mind? No. She'd be relieved. The last thing she wanted was for them to walk the whole way there or arrive at the hospital together. She was having enough trouble being around him without worrying about gossip.

"Of course not. Go ahead."

"Okay. See you over there."

"See you."

With that, he began running again, giving her a fantastic view of his strong back and even stronger glutes, which flexed and released with each step he took. And since he couldn't see her staring at him, she drank in the sight, knowing that was all she was going to do. Maybe she should call off running with him.

But if he showed up for her class and she suddenly said, *Sorry, I'm not going with you*, she'd have to come up with some kind of excuse that didn't include phrases like, *Would you like to fall into bed in a sweaty heap with me after this?* Or, *Hey, want to share a shower stall?*

Ugh. That was what had gotten her into this mess in the first place. Letting her id go wild that night in the club.

It only went to show you that letting your impulses run amok was not such a good idea.

But at least it hadn't been her suggestion that they exercise together. Or had it? She'd kind of been the one to get that ball rolling. And now it was racing down the hill and probably getting ready to smash against the nearest obstacle.

God, those thoughts were starting to whip her stomach into a frenzy again. It had been a week, and she'd had no other symptoms, so it was doubtful she was catching a cold or the flu or even COVID-19. So what else could it be?

Nerves?

Her period getting ready to start?

How long before Cozumel had she had her period? Maybe a couple of weeks? She didn't tend to track it because of how inconsistent her cycle was. So, two weeks before Cozumel. Then four weeks had passed before she'd started at the hospital. And she'd been at Paz Memorial just over two weeks, so she did some quick addition... Two plus four plus two equaled—eight.

Eight weeks since her last cycle. Had she ever been that late before?

She didn't think so. Five or six? Yes. That happened all the time. But eight?

The products in her bag seemed to taunt her. She'd slept with Toby six weeks ago.

No, no, no...

It couldn't be that. It would be unimaginable. Horrifying, even. She hadn't gotten pregnant with Parker the whole time they'd been together. There'd never even been the slightest hint that she might be. And she'd never worried much about it, because her irregular cycles had always been *normal*. She'd always taken care of protection, and since they were exclusive and clean, Parker hadn't used a condom. Hadn't wanted to.

But Toby had. There was no way he would have purposely done something to put her at risk. Especially not after his comment about kids.

A trickle of panic went through her. She didn't think she'd ever gone eight weeks without having a period.

She stopped at the entrance to the park as her legs started shaking and her chi deserted her completely. Making her way to the nearest bench, she lowered herself onto it and bent forward, taking slow, deep breaths. Partly to control the sudden nausea that threatened to overwhelm her and partly to slow her racing heart.

How on earth was she going to face Toby at work today? Or, worse, tomorrow morning, when he showed up for yoga class?

She needed to do a pregnancy test to put her mind at ease. But not tonight. Not when she knew she was going to have to speak to him tomorrow morning. He'd see the truth on her face.

Wasn't he going to see it anyway, though?

"Okay, okay. Think about it for a second, Serena," she muttered to herself. "He doesn't have to know about any of this. Even if it turns out you are pregnant, you could let him go on not knowing he'd fathered a child."

Could she do that? Was it even moral to do that? Was she stupid enough to think he wouldn't figure it out?

She didn't know anything. Right now, all she could do was sit here on a park bench and breathe and breathe and breathe.

CHAPTER FIVE

SERENA STARED AT the little stick on the counter the following morning, unable to tear her eyes away as a hundred fears swirled around her, gathering more friends as they went. Pregnant.

She stared at herself in the mirror. How could she be pregnant? It had only been one time. One. Time.

How many women had asked themselves this very same thing? One time was all it took.

Except, they'd taken precautions.

But she knew even the best contraceptives failed from time to time.

After all the times she and Parker had been together, it still made no sense to her that a one-night stand had made the unthinkable happen.

She tore her eyes away from the test results that now seemed to be swaying from side to side and bent over to lay her head on the cool granite countertop. Toby had mentioned that even one night could have repercussions. But she'd never even dreamed that this could be one of them.

She could get rid of it. He'd never know. Never *need* to know. Her fight-or-flight instincts were telling her to run from the situation as far and as fast as she could.

Gulping back a renewed sense of nausea and wondering how in the world she was going to face Toby later that morning at that damned yoga class, she forced herself to shower and get dressed as if it were any other day.

Only it wasn't. But she couldn't hide out in her bathroom forever. Avery was waiting in the other room to hear what the test had revealed. And if she thought it was hard going out there and admitting she was pregnant to him, she could only imagine what it would be like to tell Toby.

She wasn't sure she could do it.

But she had to move. Do something. Maybe her roommate would have some nugget of wisdom that would break through the ice that was beginning to thicken the blood in her veins.

Taking a deep breath and leaving the test on the counter of her ensuite, she opened the door and headed out of her bedroom.

Avery searched her face for a minute before saving her the trouble of getting the word past the lump in her throat. "It was positive, wasn't it?"

Serena nodded and dropped onto the chair across from where Avery sat on the sofa. She'd come home with a pregnancy test last night and told him her fears, leaving out the *who* and *where* of the situation. She'd wanted to do the test right then and there, but he'd convinced her to wait until morning when it would be most accurate. And even though he didn't need to be at work until nine, he'd gotten up at the crack of dawn to hear the results.

"It was. What a nightmare." Even Mr. Sunshine couldn't make her see the positive side of this situation.

"I'm not going to ask you if you're sure, because there's no way in hell you haven't been staring at that stick in shock for the last fifteen minutes. What are you going to do?"

"I have no idea."

"You know who the father is, though."

She gave a choked laugh. She guessed someone at the hospital was going to know about her time with Toby after all. But Avery would keep her secret. Just like she'd kept his.

"Would you believe me if I told you I spent a wild night in Cozumel with one of the trauma surgeons at the hospital?"

"Reginald Miller?" One corner of his mouth curved up in a way that made her burst out laughing.

Maybe Avery could work his magic after all. Dr. Miller was sixty-five and was due to retire in a few months.

"Jerk. Not that Dr. Miller isn't a silver fox. But no, it's not him. It's Toby Renfro."

"Whoa. I never saw that coming."

"I know. I met him in the park yesterday morning and basically accused him of being too macho to participate in my yoga class."

He propped an ankle on his knee. "Not a smart move, Dias."

Avery called her by her last name most of the time. And Serena liked it. It kind of sealed their friendship.

"I know that. Now. But I wasn't thinking clearly. And I think I see the reason for that now. When it's too late."

It also explained why she'd felt off balance a couple of times when standing quickly and why her stomach had been so wonky the last couple of weeks.

"Are you going to tell him?"

"I don't know if I can. He as much as said he doesn't want kids."

"Really?"

She shook her head. "He told me over lunch when we were talking about a splenectomy patient we'd had who now wants to get pregnant that he didn't see children in his future."

"Sometimes people change their mind."

She squinched her nose at him. "I can't really see him doing that." She twirled a strand of hair around her finger as a renewed feeling of despair went through her.

"In the end, it doesn't matter what he wants or what he doesn't. What do *you* want?"

She twirled her thoughts like she'd done her hair. She knew what she *could* do. What she probably *ought* to do. But what if this was a sign from the universe that now was the time to do this? Mabel Tucker's words came back to her.

Is there ever an ideal time? You never know what life is going to throw at you.

It was very true. Serena didn't see herself putting her career or life on hold in order to have a child. But she'd toyed with eventually including a pregnancy in her life. She wouldn't necessarily have to halt everything for nine months or more. She could work almost up to her due date and then take six weeks off work after she'd given birth.

And then what? How was she going to support them both on her salary? What would she do for childcare when she was at work?

She swallowed. But wouldn't she always wonder those things? She'd already told Toby this might well be something she did on her own.

But how likely was it that she was going to run to the nearest fertility clinic and start the complicated process of artificial insemination or in vitro?

She was already pregnant. Couldn't she somehow make it work? Single mothers did all the time.

And she respected Toby. A lot. There were worse things out there than having a child that would remind her of a fun time in her life. A time of crazy, once-in-a-lifetime spontaneity.

She finally responded to Avery's question. "I think I'm going to have this baby."

There was a long pause while he studied her face before smiling. "I think you are too. Congratulations. You're going to be a great mom."

"I sure hope so." Serena blew out a breath as the reality of the situation swept over her. "Keep this just between us for now, okay?"

"No worries on that front. I would never betray your trust."

"I know you wouldn't." She bit her lip before asking the question running through her mind. "If you were Toby… Would you want to know?"

He sighed and let his foot slide back to the floor,

leaning forward in his seat. "I'm not Toby, though. And I'm not you, so I can't tell you what to do. But if it *were* me… Yes, I'd want to know."

"Even after saying you didn't want to have kids?"

Avery nodded. "That's a hard one. Maybe he'll make it easy and say he doesn't want to be involved."

"And maybe he'll ask me to get an abortion."

"Do you really think he'd do that?"

She thought about it for a minute. "No, I don't." That was the problem. But she could see him secretly wishing she'd get one, though. And since part of the baby's DNA would be his, would it be right to have it even if she knew it was against his wishes?

She had no idea. But what she did think was that Avery was absolutely right. Toby did have a right to know and decide for himself what he wanted to do about it. Should she tell him after the yoga class today? Just thinking about that made her put the back of her hand to her mouth to hold back the sensation of nausea.

She'd have to see if there was an opening to say something. The last thing she wanted to do was blurt it out without having a chance to measure her words.

Maybe he would just do what Avery said and leave it all to her. She already knew she wouldn't challenge him or ask him for any kind of support. Having this baby was all her decision. And she was perfectly willing to shoulder all the consequences of that decision.

Alone.

Even if it was the hardest thing she'd ever done.

Okay, so Serena was right. Yoga was a lot harder than it looked. Suddenly, he felt every one of his thirty-five years.

But he gritted his teeth and allowed the moves to burn through him. He could see why runners might want to use this before workouts to prevent sports injuries. But he could also see how his pride might force him to push harder than he should to...

Show off?

Hell, no. At least, that shouldn't be his motivation.

He watched Serena out of the corner of her eye as she lay on her stomach and did something the instructor had called the bow pose, bending her legs at the knees while she arched up and caught her ankles with her hands. Hell. He got as far as bending his knees and arching his back, but the whole hand-to-ankle thing? No can do.

"Only do what feels good." The words came from the front of the class. "Your flexibility will increase."

Was she talking to him? He glanced around the area and saw that no, it wasn't just him. Around fifty percent of the group had perfected the move, like Serena, but not everyone. Okay. That made him feel less conspicuous and out of place.

Serena, on the other hand, seemed to have trouble meeting his eyes today.

Was it because of that prolonged handshake yesterday? He hadn't meant that to happen. Had somehow just lost track of where he was. And he'd been pretty sure that in that moment, Serena had too. She'd moistened her lips, and he could have sworn she'd reacted to his touch, although he'd done his damnedest not to let his gaze drift to where he knew that little butterfly lay hidden.

Today, with her sleeveless tank on, he'd caught tantalizing glimpses of it as she'd stretched her body to the side. She probably wasn't even aware that it could be seen. So he'd opted to stare straight ahead and not let his peripheral vision have access to what she was doing. Although it was damned hard.

"Let's move onto our left sides." The instructor's voice was soothing, waiting as they all moved to follow her instructions.

The position had him facing Serena's back. How glad was he that none of the yoga moves had them pairing up?

Very glad. Because even facing this side of Serena was a dangerous proposition. He was very glad when the next set of instructions had them slowly twist their upper torsos until their shoulders were pressed to the ground, arms out to form a T.

There was another pause. "Now turn your head to the right and feel the stretch in your side increase."

And increase it did. But it was a good stretch. And one that was easier than the bow thingamajig.

They switched to the other side and repeated the stretch. Toby closed his eyes and concentrated on what his body was feeling.

This really was nice. He might have to come again sometime. But he wasn't sure he could handle sharing this space every day with Serena. Ever since yesterday, he'd been far too aware of her, moments from their night together sliding through him unexpectedly and putting him off his game. Running would be easier. It was harder to think when you were panting and trying to push through the burn. At least, he hoped it was.

"Okay. Good job, everyone. Lie there until you're ready to get up. No hurry, as always. And hopefully, I'll see you again tomorrow."

Hmm. She'd probably have one less participant to-morrow. He could always find another place where he could do yoga. But how likely was it that it would be at a park where he could run afterward? Serena was right. This really was the best of both worlds.

He got up slowly and waited as Serena did the same. She rolled up the thin mat she'd brought with her. He'd opted to just do the moves directly on the ground. Carry-ing gear wasn't a great way to run, and he'd left a change of clothes in his locker at work. Serena didn't have the bag with her that she'd had yesterday, but what was she going to do with…? She went up to the instructor and said something to her before handing her the mat. Okay. Well, that was different.

When she got back, he asked, "She's going to hold onto that for you until tomorrow?"

"No, she brings extras that you can borrow for fifty cents. She charges just because it costs her something to sanitize them."

"But yesterday you had your own, didn't you?"

"Yes. But yesterday I wasn't going on a run, like I am today." She seemed to hesitate, chewing a corner of her lip before saying, "Are you ready?"

So despite her kind of quiet attitude this morning, she wasn't bailing on him. "Aren't you going to ask me what I thought of yoga?"

She seemed to relax, as if relieved about something. "Of course. What did you think?"

"Surprisingly, I like it. It's not something I pictured myself doing, but…" He shrugged. "Maybe those are the very things you should try."

She got a funny look on her face, and she stared at him for a long moment before looking away. "And sometimes it depends on what it is."

"Yes. Sometimes." He had no idea what she was talking about, but what else could he say? "Well, you asked if I was ready, so you're up for a run?"

"I'll give it a try. How far are we going?"

"Ten miles?"

When her eyes turned into saucers, he laughed. "I'm kidding. Let's go by time rather than distance. A half hour, say? Same as your yoga class?"

She blew out a breath. "That sounds much more doable for a newbie."

They started out at a slow jog, before she glanced at him. "If you're slowing your pace because of me, don't. I'll tell you if you're going too fast."

And those words transported him right back to Cozumel and her frantically whispered words.

Too fast. God, I don't want this to end. Not yet.

He'd immediately slowed his pace, despite the fact that his body had been screaming at him to end it. To cross that finish line. Except Serena had been right. Delaying their gratification had been so very right.

And had made it that much harder to forget.

Pushing those thoughts to the back of his head, he picked up the pace and saw her follow right along. He wasn't a sprinter; he preferred to run at a moderate pace. Just enough to let his muscles know they'd been well worked.

Like they'd been that night?

No. Not thinking about that right now.

Ten minutes later, she panted, "Okay, I have a stitch in my side, so I'm going to slow down, but you can keep going."

"Nope." He slowed his footfalls. "You said you didn't like running because you have to do it alone. I'm not going to be the one who makes you do that."

She didn't say anything, and when he glanced over at her, he noticed her arm was draped across her stomach, although she didn't seem to be in distress.

Still… "Hey, are you okay?"

She nodded, still not saying anything, and he swore he saw her chin wobble. He reached out and gripped her wrist, slowing to a stop and pulling her to a halt too. Turning to face her, he touched her cheek. "Serena, what is it?"

A tear slipped free, trickling down her cheek. He was right. Something was definitely wrong.

"Is it your stomach?"

She closed her eyes, and a squeaked laugh came out. "No. Yes. No."

Okay, that made no sense whatsoever.

"Is it something I can help with?" He used his thumb to wipe away the tear, the moisture pulling at something in his gut.

Her eyes popped open in an instant. "No. Please don't ask me anything else. Not right now. I'm just— trying to absorb some news… There's a decision I need to make."

Okay, so she'd gotten bad news. Or maybe she'd decided something. A thought hit him. "Are you quitting? I know you said not to ask you anything else, but—"

"No, I'm not quitting." She met his gaze. "It has nothing to do with work, I promise. Just something personal."

He studied her for a second before deciding he wasn't going to press her for more answers when it was obvious she didn't want to talk about it. But why had it suddenly been so important to him to know whether or not she was leaving Paz Memorial?

"Got it." He paused. "Well, I hope whatever decision you have to make works out for the best for all involved."

"Yeah. Me too." She released an audible breath. "Do you mind going on without me? Thanks for coming to yoga with me. It's not the running. Or you."

There was a sincerity in her voice that sent a shard through his chest. He wanted to help. But if she wanted him to know whatever it was that had upset her, she would tell him. And although he was loath to leave her standing there, he was pretty sure she wanted to be alone right now, so he took her at her word. "Rain check?"

That made her smile, a look of relief on her face. "You can count on it."

"Okay, see you at work." With those words, he turned and started running again, heading away from Serena and whatever her problem was.

Because really, if she didn't want to tell him, it was none of his business.

Soon, Toby was caught up in his own little world, back to his normal pace that put him in the zone, all the while thinking to himself that Serena might just have been right. That running was better when you had someone next to you.

* * *

They had another surgery together that afternoon, and Serena seemed completely recovered from whatever had been wrong this morning. She was professional but not standoffish. "Four-zero nylon suture, please."

She handed him a pre-threaded needle with the perfect amount of suture material running through it. A lacerated liver due to a fall from a ladder had taken some finagling to close, and surgery was already at the three-hour mark. But he wanted to make sure nothing would open up again once he placed the final suture.

Taking his time closing the skin, he kept an eye on the man's blood pressure readings, as any drastic change in it could indicate a complication of both the initial injury and surgery itself. So far, they had held steady, though. He glanced around the room at his team. The people who shared every victory with him. And mourned every loss. He was really lucky to be where he was, with this incredible team. He had never doubted that Paz Memorial was the place for him. From the moment he'd stepped onto the surgical floor, something had clicked into place. Even that mess with Tanya and Cliff hadn't made him doubt that this was where he belonged, and he'd never been tempted to transfer. Even if Tanya had stayed, he would have somehow figured out a way to work with her. The same way that he and Serena had figured out a way to work together after that initial shock of seeing each other again.

They'd even spent a little time together away from work—not that it was a habit he wanted to get into.

Wiping that tear away this morning had forged some kind of emotional bond that he was struggling to break free from. He needed to just keep sawing away at it, no matter how long it took. He still didn't believe that workplace romances were a good idea. For him, anyway. He would never put those rules on anyone else. But he'd seen firsthand the heartache it could cause all involved.

He also knew that he shared a part of the blame for what had happened with Tanya. Her sudden interest in having a child had caused him to pull away from her. Emotional withdrawal seemed to be a remnant of his childhood that had carried over to his adult life. So he was more than surprised by the pull he felt toward Serena. Was it just due to that night in Mexico? Or was it something else? One thing he knew was that he didn't trust himself to hold steady in any relationship.

Giving an internal sigh, he placed the last suture and checked everything once and then again.

"You used set-back sutures."

Her observation startled him for a second.

He looked at the incision line. Yes, he had. He'd done so without thinking. And he was surprised she'd even noticed. Or remembered them talking about that particular technique. He smiled at her. "So I did. I guess you finally got to see them done."

"I'm glad I did. Watching a video isn't quite the same as seeing someone do them live."

"You're right."

The interest and sparkle were back in her eyes,

and he found himself glad of it for some weird reason. He didn't want to know her personal problems. But he did like it when someone was excited about their work. It energized him. Made him glad he was a surgeon. Especially on cases like this or like Mabel Tucker when life-or-death situations ended with a good prognosis.

"Speaking of sutures, Mabel Tucker is due to come back into hospital right before five to have her sutures out. Do you want to assist?"

She hesitated, biting her lip. "It kind of depends on how busy my day is. Can I let you know a little closer to the time?"

"Sure."

And just like that, she was back to that quiet, pensive person she'd been during their jog. And he found he wasn't happy with the regression. Despite the fact that she'd said it had nothing to do with him. Well, she'd actually said it had nothing to do with work, not him personally. But since he was part of her work, wasn't it the same thing?

He wasn't quite sure. And now was not the time to ask, especially since she'd been pretty clear about not wanting him to pressure her into talking about whatever it was.

He'd convinced himself he didn't want to know. But now, he was not so sure.

He was sure of one thing, though. It wasn't just a general sense of malaise. There was a specific reason behind her weepiness of this morning. She'd as much as admitted it.

But unless she wanted to tell him what it was, he was going to have to be satisfied with not knowing.

No matter how hard that might be.

CHAPTER SIX

"Do they have these luncheons all the time?"

Serena had spotted Avery across the room at the buffet line and headed over to him, glad to see a familiar face.

One face she hadn't seen here was Toby's. It had been a couple of days since he'd been at her yoga class. He hadn't appeared at the park since then. At least, not that she'd seen. She hadn't even caught sight of him jogging after her class. It made her feel worse somehow. Maybe he was afraid of her having another breakdown like the one during their run.

If it was true and he was avoiding her because of that, how would he react if she told him she was pregnant? God! She didn't even want to think about it.

She hadn't meant to cry. Especially not in front of him, but when she'd said she needed to slow down and he'd said what he had, it had hit her right in the midsection.

You said you didn't like running because you have to do it alone. I'm not going to be the one who makes you do that.

Emotion had boiled over that had nothing to do with the slight nausea she'd been dealing with at the time.

Even now, the memory of the way he'd said that—the way he'd brushed her tear away—had the power to make her to cry all over again.

Because the reality was, she wanted someone there with her. Both during her pregnancy and beyond.

She *didn't* like running on her own. And she actually thought she could raise a baby on her own?

Now Avery was looking at her funny.

"What?"

"I answered your question."

She blew air into her cheeks letting them puff out as she wracked her brain. "Sorry, Ave. What was the question again?"

One of his brows went up. "About the luncheons. And whether they have these all the time?"

She laughed. "Of course. Ugh. My brain isn't quite working like it should be nowadays."

"I've noticed. Any luck with that…decision to tell a certain person something?"

"No. But I'll need to figure it out soon. He's already guessed something is wrong."

Avery's glance went past her before coming back. "Speaking of which. He's here."

There was no need to ask who *he* was. She didn't look. "Any chance I can slide out of here without him noticing?"

"Since he's looking right at us, I would say no."

She glanced up and saw Toby was indeed looking at her. In fact, he'd started heading their way.

"Do you want me to stick around?"

"No, it's okay. Maybe I need to make that decision now."

"Okay, Dias. Good luck. And whatever happens, you'll be okay." He smiled. "Just remember, you're not alone."

"And Mr. Sunshine makes another appearance. I can see why that nickname is gaining traction." Her smile started off bright, but just as suddenly, her eyes watered, and she reached for his hand and squeezed it before going up on tiptoe and kissing his cheek. "Thank you, Avery. You are a good, good friend. The best."

"Don't forget that. I'm here to help."

And then he was gone. Just as Toby arrived. He looked at her for a second. "Someone special?"

"What?"

"The guy you were talking to."

Her brain felt full of cotton wool. "Oh." She glanced at where Avery was already talking to someone else, his ready smile in evidence. "Yes, Avery is pretty special. We went through nursing school together. He's talked me down from a couple of ledges."

His jaw tightened. "I see."

He might, but she sure didn't. He looked almost angry about something. "Is there something you wanted to talk to me about?"

He glanced across the room for a minute toward where Avery had gone before looking back at her. "You forgot to text me about Mabel."

Damn. She had. She'd told him she would check with him when the time got closer. Only she'd forgotten. Or maybe blocked it out in her desperation not to have to talk about anything that didn't have to do with work.

Maybe she didn't want to look for an opening to tell him. Maybe that's what it boiled down to.

Maybe she needed to just get this over with.

"You're right. I did. Did she already come by?"

"She did. She's doing really well. She wanted me to let you know that she and Tom have decided to start a family as soon as she's cleared to do so."

It seemed like ages since that talk about timing and how it was never perfect. How crazy was it that Serena had been the one to get pregnant before their patient? And the timing certainly wasn't perfect.

But maybe there was something to what Mabel had said. There would never be a perfect time to get pregnant. Nor would there be a perfect time to tell Toby about the pregnancy. Or not tell him. But one way or the other, she needed to make that decision.

She searched her soul. Could she live with herself for trying to keep him in the dark? For keeping her baby in the dark? If she stayed at Paz Memorial, he was going to put two and two together anyway and would eventually ask her what was going on. And if she left?

Other problems would arise that would be just as hard to deal with.

Her baby would grow up and eventually ask about their father. And it would happen. What would she tell them? She couldn't see a scenario where that question wouldn't arise. And for Toby to have a twenty-year-old young adult appear out of nowhere and say, *Hey Dad, you never knew about me, but I'm your kid.*

She cringed. No. Toby would have every right to hate her for depriving him of his child, or at least for depriving him of the right to decide whether or not he wanted to be involved in that child's life. So leaving Paz Memorial wasn't going to solve her problems. And the truth was, she didn't want to leave.

Realizing he was still standing there looking at her, she blurted out, "That's great about Mabel." She paused. "Hey, can I talk to you? In private?"

"Sure. How about in my office?"

"Perfect. Thank you."

Even though this was her choice, each step felt like it was leading her closer and closer to disaster. Mainly because she had no idea how he was going to react.

But really? It wasn't like she had set out to get pregnant. And she wasn't alone in the getting there.

He bore every bit as much responsibility as she did.

Except he wouldn't be the one ultimately deciding what happened from here. That was all on her. Despite what he'd said during their run, she was alone in that sense. And she alone would bear the consequences for that decision.

They reached his office, and he unlocked the door, letting her go in ahead of him.

Without asking, she locked the door so they wouldn't be interrupted, and then because her legs felt like gelatin, she dropped into the nearest chair and waited for him to round his desk. But he didn't. Instead he pulled out the chair next to hers and sat in it.

He didn't give her a chance to speak first. "I'm feeling a little sucker punched right now, I have to admit."

God! He did not look happy. Had he already figured it out? Or been told by someone? No. The only other person on the planet who knew about the pregnancy was Avery, and there was no way he would have said anything.

She swallowed. "Sucker punched?"

He sat back in his chair and regarded her for a moment before blowing out a rough breath. "I didn't realize you were involved with someone when I met you at the bar in Cozumel."

Shock took all of her thoughts away for a few seconds. "Involved?"

"Serena. Really?"

"I have no idea what you're talking about. If you're referring to that jerk in the bar, I didn't even know him."

His brows came together. "No. Not him. The guy from the luncheon just now. The one you admitted you were involved with."

"I never..." She realized he had taken her words completely out of context. "You mean when I said he was special? He is. But we're not involved romantically. We're roommates. Only roommates. And really good friends."

Her world pieced itself together enough that a thread of anger came through. "You actually thought I'd sleep with you if I were involved with someone else?"

"It's not like it never happens."

Jacelyn's comments about his fiancée cheating on him came rushing back, and a stream of compassion went through her. She reached out and grabbed his hand. "It might. But it's not something I would do. I'd never cheat on someone."

His fingers squeezed around hers, his gaze steady on

hers for a moment. "No, I don't think you would. I'm sorry for even thinking it."

"I can see how it might have come across." And she understood why he had jumped to that conclusion. And she ached for him. What would it be like to have someone you trusted betray you so horribly? Parker may have been a lot of things, but at least he'd never cheated on her.

He let go of her hand. "So what you wanted to talk about, does it have something to do with why you were so upset at the park?"

And here they went. She'd thought and thought, but the right words just wouldn't come. "This would be so much easier if neither of us remembered the other from that night in Cozumel." She closed her eyes and whispered. "*So* much easier. For both of us."

The room seemed to shift for a second as he continued to process the fact that she hadn't cheated on him. When she'd first said that Avery was someone special to her, he'd been angry. Furious, even, that she would use him to cheat on her significant other. It had brought back the memory of finding out how Tanya had behaved with his best man.

Only it had somehow hit him so much harder thinking that Serena had cheated on someone with him, and he had no idea why.

And now she was acting like Cozumel had had so little impact that they might have forgotten the other existed?

He stared at her. Then one side of his mouth unexpectedly went up. "You think I could *ever* forget that night? Or you?"

"Oh." Her teeth came down on her lip. "I—I didn't quite mean—"

"I remember everything. Every. Little. Thing. Including a certain little butterfly." Right on cue, his body responded to the memory. When he'd seen her with that other guy at the luncheon, he'd been so sure they were lovers. The hand touch, the steady way they looked at each other. The kiss. The thought of that man kissing her tiny tattoo had made something in his stomach drop.

He'd decided then and there that the man had something to do with what she'd said at the park that day. With her teary request that he not ask her anything else about it.

The relief he felt in discovering they were just friends was way out of proportion to the situation. Why should it matter to him at all?

He leaned forward and cupped her cheek.

All common sense seemed to retreat to the back of his brain and cower in a corner as a sudden need began to thrum through him, and the blood coursing through his veins began to pick up speed.

Because dammit all. It was true. He remembered everything about that night, including the wild satisfaction of feeling her flesh close around his and grip tightly until he… He wanted that again. Wanted to lay her on his desk and make her feel what she'd made him feel that night.

Her lips parted, the tiniest bit.

Her hair was in wild disarray, like it was on most

days. But it was sexy. So, so sexy. Bedroom hair. And the feeling as he'd gathered all those luxurious silky locks together and…

"Toby…"

He wasn't sure if it was a question or a plea, but the shaky longing in her whisper swept through him like a typhoon, hurling away everything in its path. Their chairs were on wheels, and he yanked hers closer in a rush, his knees pushing between hers in a way that made his breath seize in his chest.

Her mouth was inches from his, and he hesitated a fraction of a second. Just long enough to make the first touch that much sweeter before giving in to his body's demands. His hands gripped the arms of her chair as hot coals licked at his innards, igniting an inferno of lust. The touch of her tongue at the corner of his mouth was his final undoing. His hands left the arms of the chair and slid around her hips to cup her butt. With a single hard movement, he hauled her onto his lap, relishing the tiny moan she gave as she came fully against him.

Yes.

He hid his face in her neck, the wild beat of her pulse against his lips, making him want to throw caution to the wind, as if there'd been any other option.

This was the woman she'd been in Mexico: fueled by the evidence of his neediness. Desperate to touch and be touched.

His hands buried themselves in her heavy hair, his mouth going back to hers. His tongue didn't hesitate. It dove inside her mouth, that first plunge sending him to hell and back. He wanted her.

Needed her.

No matter what the cost.

As if sensing his thoughts, she eased her mouth from his and went up on her knees, and he gripped her hips to help her keep her balance. She slowly slid her white gauzy skirt up her thighs, her hair dancing around her face as she looked down at him.

He swallowed. "Damn, Serena. You are so beautiful."

"I could say the same about you." Biting her lip in that seductive way she had, she murmured. "Undo your zipper, and I'll let you see my butterfly." The slow swirl of her hips made him think the words had more than one meaning.

He pulled her forward and kissed her stomach, then said, "Give me a sec."

He barely had enough room to get his hand into his back pocket to get his wallet out and remove something from it. Then he undid his zipper and freed himself. One hand slid under her blouse and found her breast, squeezing and stroking. Her eyes fluttered shut. He lifted the condom packet he'd taken out to his mouth with his free hand and tore it open, somehow managing to roll it down himself.

With that done, he slid his hands up her back and carried her shirt over her head.

Lacy bra. Covering what he wanted to see. He undid it and let it fall free.

There.

His fingertips touched the wing of the tiny creature decorating her breast. Palming her back, he eased her forward until he could reach it. The tip of his tongue slowly traced over the tattoo, his arm going around her bottom and pressing her against his chest as his mouth shifted from the butterfly to her nipple. The first suck was so satisfying. So sexy. And those damned sounds she was making was going to make him come apart long before he was ready. His hands went to her hips and urged her to straddle him again, until all that was between them was her panties.

She rocked against him, making his world go multicolored as he used his tongue, his lips, his teeth to bring her as much pleasure as she was bringing him. Her arms went around his head, holding him to her breast. Not that he was planning on going anywhere.

But he wanted more. Wanted it all. Sliding the elastic on her remaining undergarment to the side, he pressed his fingers against her pubic bone as his thumb touched her most intimate area, before moving deeper, finding heat. Moist, sexy heat. He wanted to sink deep into her and lose himself in a rush. But he remembered exactly how satisfying it had been to hold himself on the brink. To force himself to wait. And wait. And wait.

The crazy intimacy of their position… He groaned. They were close. So close that touching her meant he was touching himself too.

And it was hotter than anything he'd ever done with a woman.

"Dios… Ahora, Tobias… Ahora."

His whispered name came out in accented Spanish, and instinctively he knew exactly what she meant. Taking himself in hand, he positioned himself, but she wasn't waiting. As soon as she felt him, she pushed down, hard, her hands gripping his shoulders, head thrown back.

He filled his hands with her curves, matching his rhythm to hers, driving up each time she came down.

"*Tobias…*"

Her movements grew more frantic, and with each movement she pushed him closer to a cliff. One that he wanted and yet didn't want to leap off.

Then she seated herself fully. "Ahh!"

He felt it. The desperate, squeezing pulse that did what he'd been trying to avoid. Holding her against him, he thrust and thrust until the ecstasy ripped everything from him, leaving him vulnerable and exposed. Yet he kept moving, each stroke a little slower, a little more replete. And then he was still, his breathing unsteady, brain in a whirl.

It took him a second to realize she was leaning back looking at him and had said something.

And she was staring at him in a way that made tension gather in his loose muscles. A strange tension that said something was about to change forever.

Serena waited for him to say something. To respond to what she'd just told him. She was horrified that she'd sat here in his office and had sex with him instead of having the hard conversation she'd come here to have. But she never quite thought straight when she was around him. And to have blurted out that she was pregnant so soon after making love with him again… None of this was happening the way she'd wanted it to.

But now that she'd said it, she couldn't take the words back.

He blinked as if not quite sure what to say. "Sorry?" He shifted her on his legs, easing out of her.

She hated the feeling but understood that he was probably in shock. Maybe she should backtrack and try this again.

"I… I…" She took a deep breath. "I haven't been feeling quite right for the last couple of weeks, and I couldn't figure out why."

"You didn't look like you felt at all well when we were running. And add that to what you said before we parted ways…"

Her teeth scraped against each other a couple of times as she tried to drum up the courage to say again what she needed to say. "I couldn't get up the nerve to tell you what was wrong that day."

"And now you want to."

He looked confused. Maybe Toby hadn't actually heard what she'd said a minute ago. She hadn't exactly shouted out the news. "Yes. As I said, I wasn't feeling well and realized my cycle was later than it had ever been. So… I decided to take a pregnancy test."

"I see."

He was calm. Too calm.

A sense of horror and foreboding rushed over her. "I'm pregnant. And as you now know, Avery is not the father. Although I'm sure you might wish he were."

"You're pregnant?"

The words were said with that same strange calmness

even as her brain was still busy staggering back to its feet after what they'd just done together.

Why was he staring at her as if he still didn't understand what she was saying?

He repeated the words once again before he blinked. "Oh, hell. *I'm* the father?"

This time his voice wasn't monotone, and although he hadn't shouted it at her, his words nevertheless struck her with the force of a sledgehammer.

She scrambled off him. "I'm so sorry. I just thought you should know." She licked her lips as she stood there in complete disarray, the fact that she was naked from the waist up barely registering with her. "I should never have…" She motioned at the chair he still sat in.

Should never have what? Let him make love to her?

Yes. Exactly that. Except she'd been so caught up in his words as he said he could never forget that night, or her, that she couldn't think clearly. She'd been bewitched by him. Just like she had been at the bar in Cozumel. Only none of that was his fault. She never should have let him make love to her before he knew the truth about why she'd wanted to speak to him.

But there was no going back now.

Even though he'd made it more than clear before this that he didn't want to be a father. At least not at this point in his life.

And maybe not ever.

Toby stared at her as he tried to clear his head. He didn't want to be a father. Didn't want to be involved with anyone. Didn't feel he was capable of sustaining any kind of relationship, much less that of father and child. And yet, he'd just…

With quick jerky movements, she righted her panties and skirt and pulled on her bra and shirt. Parts of his body that had gone numb, twitched for a second before he got them back under control.

Dammit! Say something!

But there were no words he could think of to say. And as much as he wanted to wish this away, he couldn't. It was real.

Serena seemed to give up on him having any other response, because she ran her palms down her skirt. "Even though I felt you should know, please believe me when I say that I don't expect anything from you. Don't want anything from you. I am fully prepared to—I *want* to do this on my own."

Her reasons for not liking to run alone came back to him vividly, and yet, he still had no idea what to say to her. He couldn't even believe this was happening. The words that finally came out of his mouth were insane. And totally insulting.

"I know you said you and Avery aren't together, but was there no one else? You're sure it's mine?"

She should have slapped him. Screamed at him. Called him all manner of names. But she didn't. She just stood there for a minute and stared at him.

Her question, when it came, was so quiet he almost missed it. "What do you think?"

Remorse clawed through his conscience until he couldn't stand it any longer. "I don't know why I said that. I have no excuse other than being caught off guard."

"Don't worry about it." She walked over to the door before looking back. "And we never have to talk about any of this again."

She motioned to the chairs. "Not about what happened in this room. Or what happened in Cozumel. Or what is going to happen from here on."

With that, she headed out of the room, closing the door behind her.

Was the pain of that last encounter ever going to fade? She was on day three since their encounter in his office, and it was still there. Still churning in her stomach every time she thought about what had happened.

She'd toyed with the idea of resigning and trying to find a nursing position somewhere else, but how would she explain to a prospective employer that she'd quit less than a month after being hired? It didn't look very good. And by the time she found something else, she'd be even further along in her pregnancy.

Paz Memorial was her dream job. But right now, she couldn't imagine working with Toby day in and day out. She loved working the trauma cases, loved watching Toby's expertise and skill. But in her head, she could still hear the shock in his voice as he asked her if she was sure the baby was his. It hadn't been a question, exactly. And yet, it was obvious a sliver of doubt was there.

Because he didn't want it to be his.

That's what it boiled down to. She hadn't expected him to be overcome with happiness and start picking out baby names. But even without meaning to, he'd wounded her deeply with his words, and she wasn't sure she could get over it.

Maybe the best course of action would be to wait until the baby was born, then give her notice and start looking for another job. But that was something she could do after having some more time to think. Because today, she just felt tired and sad and out of sorts.

But she would get through it.

To his credit, Toby didn't ask what she was going to do, although he'd probably realized by her coming to him that she was going to keep the baby. Talking about how she was going to do it on her own had made it pretty clear. And if she'd been going to have an abortion, she wouldn't have even told him about the pregnancy.

Toby hadn't shown up for work yesterday or today. The thought that maybe he was going to be the one to quit zipped through her system. That was probably part of her sadness. She didn't want that either. He belonged here. It was clear he was well loved and highly respected.

She'd finished working out her shift after they'd had sex and then had gone home and cried on Avery's shoulder. She couldn't even remember what he'd said to her, but she'd finally stumbled to her feet and fallen into bed. The next morning, she'd been a little more clearheaded and thought she might go back and reassure Toby yet again that he didn't have anything to worry about. That she knew he didn't want children and had no intention of trying to saddle him with one.

But how could she explain the sex to him when she couldn't even explain it to herself? When he'd reached for her in his office, she'd been so relieved that he wanted her that she'd let her emotions take over. Maybe part of her obliviousness had been born out of some dreamland that wanted everyone to live happily ever after.

Well, her mom hadn't gotten that kind of ending, so why would she expect to? Yet she wouldn't be really going it completely on her own, no matter what happened. She had her mom and some good friends, including Avery. She would need their love and support now more than ever. They would be the safety net she had when things got tough. In fact, when she'd called her mom and told her about the baby, her mom had been both thrilled and sympathetic. "I could relocate to San Diego if you want, Serena. I can write anywhere."

She'd reassured her mom that she would call on her if she needed her but that there was no need to move. If anyone would be relocating, it would be Serena. But that was a decision she could make further down the line. Who knew? She might even miscarry, although even the thought had her laying a protective hand over her belly.

It might solve a whole lot of problems, but she definitely did not want to lose this baby. Instead, she found herself already imagining what the baby would look like. How it would feel to hold them in her arms...

She finished checking on her patients and then headed back to the nurses' station to catch up on some paperwork while she could.

Shuffling through a couple of computer screens to find the one she wanted, she glanced up when she heard the elevator ping. The doors opened and Toby got off. He looked at her, and at first, she thought he was going to walk right past her without saying anything, but then he moved toward the desk.

"When you get a chance, could I have a quick word?"

She gulped back a queasy sensation of panic.

"Um, yes. As soon as Jacelyn comes back from break. Do you want me to come by your office?"

His jaw went tight for a minute before he shook his head. "Can you text me when you're free and meet me down in the courtyard?"

Did he think she was going to jump him in his office…again?

No, of course he didn't. She was being ridiculous. And she shouldn't want to meet him in a private place either, after what had happened last time. Although from the look on his face, the last thing he wanted from her was sex.

"Yes, I will."

"Thanks."

Lord, he had this defeated look on his face that made her cringe. It brought the hurt roaring back to life. Or maybe she was projecting her own feelings onto him.

Except she suddenly didn't feel defeated. She was having a baby. One that was going to be loved and wanted, if only by her and a handful of her family and friends. But that was enough.

She'd done the right thing in telling Toby and had tried her best to reassure him that she didn't want anything from him. She couldn't help it that he didn't want the baby.

Of course, she hadn't wanted a positive pregnancy test either. At first. But now?

Yes, she was happy. Not about the way that it had happened, but that the decision about the "right time" had been taken out of her hands. Because left to her own devices, she might never have taken the leap on her own.

Jacelyn came back a half hour later and told her to go ahead and take off. Serena had made an appointment with the OB-GYN she'd met the day of Lucinda's arm gash, Gary Rollings. She'd really liked him. She'd thought about going to an outside hospital to have more privacy, but really, what was the point? It was going to become obvious pretty quickly that she was pregnant. She already had an answer ready for anyone who might ask about the father: he wasn't in the picture.

Because it was true. And actually, that was okay. To try and force a relationship for the sake of a baby usually only ended in disaster. And the last thing she wanted was for Toby to try to "do the right thing by her." Because it wasn't the right thing. For either of them.

So why had she had sex with him again with such eagerness?

She had a ready answer for that too: he was good at it. And maybe it had felt like they had unfinished business from Cozumel. Well, that business was good and done now.

She smiled. He'd made it sound like she was unforgettable. That was probably at the crux of why she'd fallen back into his arms.

She typed a message on her phone.

On my way to the courtyard.

A second later, he texted that he would be down in a minute.

Once she got there, all she could do was wait.

CHAPTER SEVEN

TOBY HAD NEEDED a couple of days to think about things. And it had boiled down to some pretty basic facts.

Fact one: he didn't want to be a father.

Fact two: he was going to be a father whether he wanted to be one or not.

Fact three: none of this was Serena's or the baby's fault.

Fact four: he was not going to make Serena do this on her own.

That last one was the key and the one he wanted to talk about. None of the rest of it mattered. What mattered was what he was going to do from here. If she would even hear him out.

If she refused... Well, he couldn't force her to accept his help, but he did want to offer it up in a way that was sincere and honest. So he hoped to hell he didn't make as big a mess out of this as he had the last time they'd talked.

It was part of the reason he wanted the meeting to happen in a public place. The woman did something to his head and reached into places he'd thought he'd closed and locked. Well, he'd now reinforced those locks and had learned some valuable lessons in the process.

Getting off the elevator, he grabbed a coffee from the cafeteria, taking a chance and getting a decaf for her, picking up all kinds of packets and flavorings and hoping that she'd like something in the bag of stuff.

When he pushed through the doors and entered the San Diego heat, he spotted her immediately. And in front of her was a paper coffee cup.

That made him smile. Maybe he hadn't been as far off as he'd thought.

He made his way over to her and sat down on the curved bench in front of her, a sense of déjà vu coming over him. How long ago had they sat here and eaten lunch? Not all that long, but right now it seemed like forever ago.

"Hi. I brought you something, but I see you've already got some coffee."

"How did you know how I like it?"

His smiled widened. "Well…" He dumped out his bag of offerings.

"Oh, my." Her brows went up. "I don't put *quite* that much stuff in it."

"Let me hazard a guess." He separated out sugar packets and vanilla creamer and slid them toward her. "Right?"

"Wrong." She pushed the items back into the pile, and her fingers swirled around the choices for a few seconds before she shrugged and brought her hand back to her coffee, fingers curling around the cup.

"I didn't see any other—"

"That's because there isn't anything else to put in it. Because I like it black."

That shouldn't have surprised him, but it did. Hell, did he stereotype yoga practitioners? That stuff had been pretty damned difficult to do. A lot harder than plunking one foot in front of the other for an hour, like he did with running.

He held his hands up palms out. "Okay, you got me. Caffeinated or decaf?"

"Normally I like full test, but things have changed on my end. I still like the taste, though."

"At least I got that part right." Leaning forward, he looked at her. "I want you to know that I realize I handled things poorly the other day."

"No, you didn't. I'm pretty sure this was an outcome neither of us expected. Both in Cozumel and in your office. I meant it when I said I don't expect anything from you. And while I in no way planned to get pregnant, I can't bring myself to regret it." There was a moment of hesitation before she continued. "I should have come out with it right when we got to your office. Before things got out of hand."

"I don't think either one of us expected what happened in that office." His smile was a little weaker as he weighed his next words. "I'm here to ask how I can help."

"Help?"

"I want to be there for you. For the baby. We can take turns with parenting duties and—"

"Absolutely not."

Shock held him silent for a second. "I'm sorry?"

"You made it pretty clear how you felt about having kids the last time we were in this courtyard. And your reaction in your office only reaffirmed my suspicions." She shrugged. "My telling you had nothing to do with expecting you to take on any parenting duties. I just didn't feel right about keeping it a secret from you. Someday, they might want to know who their father is. Better for you to be shocked now than to be shocked then."

He frowned. "And you think it's okay to tell that child about a parent who played no role in their upbringing, who thinks he didn't...want...them?"

"Well, you don't, so—"

"You're right, Serena. I didn't want or expect to have a child. Not right now, anyway, if ever. But I am having one." He paused to suck down a breath. "The same way you didn't expect to have a baby, but you are *choosing* to have this child rather than terminating the pregnancy. In the same way that I am *choosing*—for lack of a better term—to have a role in the child's life. It's not out of duty or obligation. I want to be there."

She didn't say anything for a long, long moment. "What if you change your mind?"

"I won't. You'll find I'm a pretty black-and-white kind of guy. I don't want to be in a relationship. I can't offer you that. But I would like to be a father to this child."

"I never expected us to be in a relationship. I don't want that either. My mom and dad didn't have a good marriage, and I'd honestly rather be on my own than risk getting involved for the wrong reasons. Or with the wrong person."

"I agree with you. I've been there too, and it wasn't

the greatest experience." He gave a pained laugh. "Cozumel was supposed to be my honeymoon, actually."

"I'd heard. I'm so sorry."

His mouth cocked to the side. "I should have figured someone would tell you. Anyway, I went there for the purpose of committing my life to my job and nothing else."

"And then you met me." Her eyes went big, and she stuttered for a second before saying, "I'm talking about the pregnancy, not about us being involved romantically."

"I got it."

"I never did get a chance to thank you for stepping in between me and that guy in the bar."

"No thanks were needed." He smiled at her. "So can we try to figure out how this is going to work?"

"Yes... But I'd really rather no one at the hospital know who the father is right away. If I miscarry, it could make it even more awkward than it's eventually going to be."

He frowned. "Have you been having any symptoms that might suggest a miscarriage?"

"No. I didn't mean that. Just that some pregnancies don't make it for one reason or another. There are no guarantees."

The thought of her losing the baby bothered him on a level that surprised him. "Have you seen a doctor yet?"

"No, but I've made an appointment with Gary Rollings. It's a couple of weeks away."

"Gary's a pretty discreet guy. I'd like to come with

you to that appointment. But I'll understand if you'd rather I didn't."

Serena looked surprised. "Can I think about it?"

"Of course. Take all the time you need." He couldn't blame her. It was one thing to let him be a part of their child's life. But he understood that she needed to mark out some boundary lines and stick to them.

"I do have a question. I wasn't going to ask, but since you're here…" She shook her head. "Is there any genetic stuff from your side of the family that I should know about?"

That hadn't dawned on him. But then again, neither had a lot of things. "I had an aunt with early-onset breast cancer, but it's the only thing I can think of right now."

"Okay, thanks."

"Anything else?" He wanted to know if she had any other reservations or questions. He was a little worried that this meeting had gone better than he'd expected it to. Was halfway expecting the bottom to drop out at any moment.

"Just one thing."

He tensed. And here it came. "Okay."

"I would like to pick the baby's name."

It was so far from what he'd expected her to say that it made him laugh. The tension drained from his body. "Well as long as you don't choose something like Fig or Tree, I don't think we have a problem."

She smiled back at him. "I think I can work within those parameters."

The next three days seemed to go pretty well. Even though she hadn't asked the question she'd really wanted to ask him out on that terrace. She'd actually chickened out and blurted the wanting-to-pick-the-name thing when what she'd really wanted to ask was whether or not he felt like they could continue working together under the circumstances.

But he'd given no indication that he couldn't. She'd shared an operating room with him twice since he'd been back, and he'd been courteous and respectful, if a little bit stiff.

She couldn't blame him. They'd had sex in his office, for heaven's sake, and they were having a child together. Yet looking at it through objective eyes, they really didn't know each other all that well.

But then, had she really known Parker either? Oh, she'd thought she had, but it turned out she had had a romanticized view of him that hadn't held up to scrutiny. He'd probably felt the same way about her.

She also needed to decide whether she wanted Toby there for her appointments or not. Her gut feeling was to hold that part of herself aside. Letting him be there…

It felt possibly a little too intimate, despite the fact that they'd had sex twice. Sex, though, was different from intimacy, as she'd learned from her relationship with Parker.

Plus, it would be much easier to keep her secret if no one, not even the OB-GYN, knew the truth other than her and Toby. Well, aside from Avery.

She hadn't actually told Toby that Avery knew either. But he did know that they were close friends, so surely he would figure it out.

Right now, though, she couldn't worry about any

of that. She needed to concentrate on staying well and healthy. So far, her morning sickness had been fairly mild. Just that occasional queasiness that left as quickly as it came. It was one of the reasons she hadn't realized she was pregnant until she'd started counting the days.

Her phone buzzed on her hip. Glancing at the screen, she frowned. It was Toby.

Uh-oh.

"Hello?"

"Hey, are you still on duty?"

She hesitated. "Yes, but I'm getting ready to leave. Is there an emergency?"

"No emergency. I was just headed for the beach and thought you might like to join me."

She was surprised by the invitation, actually, and an alarm went off inside of her. Maybe he'd changed his mind about the whole thing. "Any particular reason?"

"Friday is just normally my beach day. I like to sit and listen to the surf. It's something I thought I might like to do with the baby. I'll understand if you'd rather not come, though."

"Actually, that sounds pretty good. It's been a rough day."

There was a pause. "Everything okay?"

She mentally filled in the blanks, since the word *miscarriage* had previously been mentioned. She was actually touched that he sounded a little concerned. "Yep, it was just a busy day."

"Got it. Meet you at the door to the parking garage?"

"No bathing suits needed, right?"

"Are you suggesting what I think you're suggesting?"

The obviousness of his comment made her laugh for what felt like the first time since their talk in the courtyard. "I'm not suggesting anything of the sort. Give me about fifteen minutes, okay?"

"You got it."

She disconnected, feeling a relief that bordered on giddiness. Maybe this would all work out after all.

Twenty minutes later, they were in Toby's SUV, navigating the streets of San Diego. "You really go to the beach every Friday?"

He nodded. "I think it's my yoga."

"Not quite the same thing, but I get it. It's how you recharge."

"Exactly."

She halfway expected him to press her for answers about going to the doctor together, but he didn't. Instead, they talked about cases. Some that they'd worked together and some separate. It almost felt like what she and Avery did on occasion. Except this man definitely wasn't Avery.

Whereas she felt she could be totally herself with her roommate, she didn't have that same easy relationship with Toby. And maybe that was because of Cozumel. What she'd thought had been a fun, no-strings-attached romp in a hotel room had turned into something more complicated than anything she could imagine.

It was confusing. And scary in a way she didn't understand.

She'd talked to her mom about it, although she hadn't given any names. But her mom's only advice had been to follow her heart. Then again, her mom had done that too, and it hadn't exactly ended well. But her mom was wiser now. She hadn't jumped back into a relationship, and it had been five years since Serena's dad had died.

Maybe she no longer trusted her instincts.

Kind of like Serena? While Parker hadn't scarred her for life, it had made her wary of what lay just beneath the surface in any man that might have caught her interest.

Including Toby. He'd been a study in contradictions in some ways. And yet, he seemed to be as steady as a rock when it came to his job. But, like her, he already had one failed relationship in his past.

She blew out a silent breath. She just couldn't think about this right now.

"Almost there."

Maybe her sigh hadn't been as quiet as she'd thought. "It's fine. I'm still not sure why you invited me to come."

"I thought it might be good if we got to know each other a little better, since we'll be seeing quite a bit of each other outside of work."

She wasn't sure that completely answered her question, but she could hazard a guess. "Because of the baby."

"Yes. And I'd like you to know what kind of man I am outside of work."

Okay, so this was more about reassuring her that he was no serial killer? She had to remember that he had no interest in her personally. That circumstances had dragged them together, and he was trying to make the best of things. So the least she could do was try to meet him halfway and do the same.

She glanced at him. "So tell me something I don't know about you."

"Hmm… I, um, have a cat."

"Seriously?"

"Seriously, although I kind of inherited her."

Before she could think of a response to that, he tossed the same question back at her.

She grinned at him. "I like country music. And line dancing."

His brows went up. "I find that more surprising than the yoga."

A laugh squeaked out before she could stop it. "Are you saying you're not a fan?"

"Not saying that. I like all kinds of music." He pulled into one of the area parking lots and found a spot.

Nice. She couldn't have picked a better place.

"I love Mission Beach." It was one of the larger beaches in the area, with a long stretch of sand. Since he'd said he liked to come and sit near the ocean, she figured he wasn't into the rich nightlife that the area also offered. She wasn't either. So it made it even funnier that both of them had wound up in a strobe-lit bar in Mexico.

"It's my favorite spot."

They made their way past the boardwalk and onto the beach. It was still pretty early, but some of the sun worshippers were starting to gather their things, so it wasn't hard to find a spot on the sand.

They didn't have towels, but it was okay. There was something warm and grounding about sitting on actual sand. "I don't get to come out here very much anymore," she murmured, half to herself.

"I finally had to decide I was going to make an effort to drive out here. Otherwise, things get crowded out by all the noise of life."

She could understand that. She'd done that very thing, which was why when she'd realized she was pregnant, she'd had to look at her life and decide what was really important. Mabel's words had come back to her, and she realized she could do this. She could be a mom. And that now was as good a time as any.

"So what's your cat's name?"

"Porkchop."

She stared at him, trying to decide if he was telling the truth.

He smiled. "It really is. It was the name she came with."

"Came with? From where? A pig farm?"

His chuckle washed over her like one of the waves that lapped against the shore. She found that she liked the sound of it.

"No, she came from a shelter. I think maybe it was partly a joke. She has a tan spot on her side that kind of looks like a, well, a pork chop."

"Too funny."

They sat there for a few minutes without speaking, and as the sounds of the surf continued to rumble, Serena could feel her muscles unwinding. Maybe this really was like yoga, only without the physical effort. She flopped back onto the sand and closed her eyes for a few minutes, just listening. Absorbing what was around her.

There was music and human interaction. The squawking of gulls as they flew overhead. The ocean as it pushed forward and then retreated.

She opened her eyes and turned to her head to find Toby watching her.

"What?"

He didn't say anything for a minute, just reached over and brushed a strand of hair from her forehead. The act made her shiver.

Then he said, "Thanks for telling me."

She knew what he was talking about. And those simple words pulled at something deep inside of her, threatening to call up feelings that she'd rather stayed buried deep. Threatened to forge new brain pathways that she definitely couldn't cope with right now. Rather than examine any of that, she just looked back at him and said, "You're welcome."

A sharp cry came from the boardwalk area behind them.

Serena sat up in a rush to find that Toby was already on his feet. "Where's it coming from?"

The scream came again.

"Up there." They ran to the boardwalk access and found an elderly man lying on the asphalt surface with people already gathering around him.

"Call 911." Toby pushed through, telling people he was a doctor, while Serena dialed emergency services.

By the time she joined him, he was already examining an area on the gentleman's head that was bleeding profusely. He glanced at her. "He tried to step out of the way of someone on rollerblades and lost his balance. He hit his head on the concrete wall."

She winced as she looked at the thick concrete that separated the boardwalk from the beach.

He had his phone out and turned on the flashlight setting as he peered into the man's eyes. He swore softly.

"One of his pupils is blown." He looked around the crowd. "Does anyone know him?"

There were head shakes indicating those nearby didn't know who he was, and no one stepped forward with any information until someone finally said, "I think he's homeless. I've seen him walking down here before."

Serena's heart ached, as she heard the faint sound of a siren in the distance.

Careful not to move him, Toby patted the man's pockets, probably hoping to find some ID, but he looked at her and shook his head. She moved next to him and monitored his pulse while Toby went to flag down the paramedics. They were there in minutes, bringing a gurney while Toby explained that he thought the man had a skull fracture.

Together, they put a neck brace on him, carefully slid a backboard underneath him and loaded him into the back of the vehicle.

It all happened so fast that Serena wasn't even sure it actually *had* happened. One minute they were on the beach and the next they were in emergency mode. "Do you want to follow them in?"

"No. They've already called the hospital and will have a trauma team waiting for him. We'll be five steps behind."

She shivered, wrapping her arms around herself. "I hate that he was all alone." He'd looked so small lying there. So frail.

"So do I." He glanced at her. "No one should ever have to feel that way."

Was he still talking about the injured man? Or about their own situation. Serena was suddenly bone-weary. So much had happened over the last several weeks. So many changes to her life that it was overwhelming.

"Do you mind if we go back to the hospital?"

"Are you okay?"

"Yeah. I think so. Just tired. I think I'm going to get in my car and call it a night."

Not that night had even officially darkened the sky. But right now, she felt like she could sleep for a week. There'd been something so vulnerable looking in Toby's face as he'd leaned over her, thanking her for telling him about the pregnancy.

She'd never quite seen that in him before, and she wasn't sure how to deal with it. Because somehow, he'd succeeded in tunneling into her heart when she wasn't paying attention and was now taking up residence there.

She needed to do one of two things: Either send him an eviction notice and kick him out. Or somehow learn to make peace with his presence.

CHAPTER EIGHT

HE HADN'T EXPECTED the man from the boardwalk to make it, but when Toby arrived at work the next morning and asked at the nurse's desk, he'd been told the man was in ICU but very much alive.

He decided to head over there and check on him, since his floor was quiet at the moment.

The second he stepped through the doors, he was struck by the difference between the surgical area and these rooms. Surgery could be loud or not so loud, but there was always a lot of movement, with staff leaning over beds and fighting to save lives.

ICU was quiet. So quiet, it was eerie. This was also a place where the fight to save lives happened, but it was a completely different type of fight.

He went to the desk and was told they were calling him Patient Doe for the moment. So far, no one was looking for him. At least not that they knew of. And he'd had no ID at all on him. The nurse nodded at the room number. "He's a popular guy today."

Toby frowned but went into the room.

Serena sat on a chair beside the bed. He shouldn't have been overly surprised that she'd beaten him to the punch. "I should have known."

She turned around and looked at him. "I had to check. They said no one has come forward yet."

"I'm sure they're checking some of the local services to see if anyone knows him. But at least he's still fighting. And social services will be called in to assess him if he really is alone."

"Are you working today?"

"Yep. You?"

"I'm actually off." She glanced at him. "Oh, and if you want to go with me to my first OB-GYN appointment, you can. If you're free, that is."

What had made her change her mind? He'd been almost positive she'd been going to tell him no. "Text me the day and time when you get a chance, and I'll put in on my calendar."

Even if he had to move things around, he was going to do his damnedest to be there.

"Okay, I will. Will you let me know if there's any change in his condition?"

Serena had come in on her day off just to check on their John Doe. She could have called, but instead, she'd come in person. Something shifted inside of him without warning and got lodged somewhere in his chest. "I will. Hopefully he'll pull through."

"Yes. Hopefully." She glanced up at him. "How's Porkchop?"

"She's fine."

She smiled. "I halfway thought you were pulling my leg yesterday."

"Nope, I wasn't." He pulled his phone out and scrolled

through some pictures until he got to an image of his cat. He turned it around so she could see.

"Oh, my gosh. She really does have a marking. And it looks exactly like a pork chop."

"Told you."

"Well, on that note, I think I'll head home. I'll text you that date."

He nodded. "Appreciate it."

As he watched her walk away, hips swaying slightly under the same gauzy skirt she'd worn that day in his office, he glanced at the picture of the cat—his only current commitment—and hoped to hell he was doing the right thing in agreeing to take on a child.

These were real lives. Lives that could be hurt. Or disappointed. He'd already disappointed one woman. He sure as hell didn't want to be responsible for disappointing another one, because this one came with consequences that were a lot weightier than falling in or out of love.

This was a child's future. And somehow, he was going to have figure out how to balance it gingerly in his hands and keep on doing it for the next eighteen years and beyond.

Almost as soon as he digested that fact, his phone pinged, and he glanced down at it. It was a notation with the time and date of Serena's appointment with Gary Rollings at his private practice. Counting down the numbers in his head, he realized it was only a week and a half away. Even as he thought it, an internal clock began some kind of countdown, clicking off seconds and pushing them behind him. Forever. One after the other.

This was real. Far too real. He lowered himself into the chair and stared at John Doe's silent form for several seconds, wondering exactly how he was going to father a child when he had no idea how to do that.

Serena came in to work the next day and stopped at the desk on the surgical floor to see if there was anything critical that needed her attention. It was still quiet. She was a few minutes early, so she was going down to check on the elderly man they'd helped on the boardwalk. Just as she started to turn back toward the elevators, Toby appeared from the hallway where his office was.

"Hey, I was just getting ready to go down to see if—"

She stopped when he shook his head, the look on his face making her blink. "What?"

"He didn't make it."

"What? What happened?"

He took a step closer. "He had a massive brain bleed."

"But he was stable when I left."

"I know. I was still in the room with him when he coded."

"You mean last night? How long were you there?"

"Just a little while. There was nothing that could be done."

A little white speck of energy slid up her spine and lodged in her neck. "You said you'd let me know if there was any change."

"I know I did. But there was nothing you could do. And you were probably still on your way home."

The energy expanded and circled a nerve center, setting it off. "I wouldn't have asked you to contact me if I didn't want to know." She worked to keep those words low and even.

His head tilted, probably not sure why she was so upset.

In truth, she wasn't sure why she was either. Was it about the man's passing? Or about Toby's circumventing her wishes?

"I understand that. Which is why I waited for you to come in this morning to tell you in person. I didn't want the news to come from a text or a phone call."

Her anger fizzled away in a rush. Okay, so she'd guessed wrong about his motivation. "Sorry."

He waited as if expecting some further explanation. But what could she say? *I thought you were acting like my father?*

He hadn't been. But she'd expected him to on some level. Maybe because Parker had displayed some of those same characteristics once they'd moved in together. But it didn't mean that Toby was the same kind of person.

She turned around and leaned a hip against the nurse's desk, which was empty at the moment. They were probably doing last-minute checks before the shift change. "I really wanted him to make it."

"I know. So did I." He glanced at her clothes. "No yoga today?"

She couldn't prevent a smile from forming, despite the lump of sadness in her throat. "Already went. I just changed into work clothes before coming up. No running?"

"Same."

"Looks like we're creatures of habit."

She wasn't sure that was a good thing.

He joined her at the desk, crossing his arms over his chest. "Looks that way."

"Did they ever find out his identity?"

"No. They didn't."

Somehow, that was even sadder than his passing. It was like he'd slid from the world and disappeared without leaving a trace.

She touched her stomach. Was that part of what having kids was about? It wasn't just loving them and raising them. Maybe it was about making sure there was someone who kept the previous generation's memories alive.

Shaking off the morbid thought, she glanced at him. "So what's on the docket today?"

"Our liver laceration patient is being released this afternoon, so that's good news."

"Any more word on Mabel Tucker?"

He nodded. "She has an appointment tomorrow for a routine follow-up. She was supposed to get a couple of immunizations this past week. And her medical alert bracelet should arrive next week."

It was hard to believe she was the first patient they'd seen together. It seemed like ages ago. Maybe because so much had happened since then.

"All good news."

His blue eyes caught hers, and her tummy shivered the way it always did when he looked at her.

Someone called her name, and she turned away from Toby in time to see her mom get off the elevator and start walking toward them. Oh, God. That was all she needed.

Her mom knew about the pregnancy, but Serena hadn't told her specifically about Toby yet, and she wasn't sure why. Hurrying over, she rattled off a string of Spanish asking when she'd arrived. And why.

Her mom glanced at Toby and then answered her in English. "Since when do I need a reason to visit my only daughter?"

Leave it to her mom to lay on the guilt. "You don't, of course. I just could have left a key to the apartment for you."

"I actually was in the area on the way to research a nearby town and thought I'd drop in." She glanced at Toby again. "Aren't you going to introduce me?"

"Oh, of course." She headed toward the desk, her mom close behind. "Toby Renfro, this is my mom, Gracia Dias." It was virtually impossible to say her mom's name without pronouncing it in Spanish. "Toby is a trauma surgeon here at the hospital."

Her mom gave her a long, searching look. "Is he now?"

Toby, evidently unaware of the unspoken messages being sent back and forth between mother and daughter, held out his hand. "I actually do work here at the hospital. Serena told me you're a writer?"

Oh, no. He was just going to add fuel to her mom's speculation.

Serena quickly added, "I've told a lot of people that."

Toby frowned, and she couldn't blame him. She was

being ridiculous. Why was she avoiding telling her mom who he was?

Because she didn't want to get hurt.

More than that, she didn't want to give her mom any reason to hope that she and Toby might get together romantically. Because they weren't going to. She'd eventually explain it to her, but not here. Not at the hospital.

"I'm just starting my shift, Mom, so I'm sorry I can't take you back to the apartment." She pulled her keys from her pocket and took the one to her apartment off the ring. "I'm not sure if Avery will be there or not when you get there, so just ring the bell rather than go right in." She didn't think he'd be walking around in the nude or anything, but since he thought she was at work...

"Well, I'll make you dinner, then. What time do you get off?"

"Five."

"And what time do you get off?" She fixed Toby with look. Serena could swear her mom had already guessed. How? They hadn't made googly eyes at each other, or even been standing that close together. But she had been thinking about how his blue eyes did it for her. Right as her mom got off the elevator.

"Mom, Toby doesn't want to eat with us."

"Actually, I wouldn't mind." His slow smile would have melted butter. "That is, if it's okay with you, Serena."

Oh, he was going to pay for that.

"Perfect. Then, it's settled. Dinner will be at seven, but come over whenever you get off work." Her mom didn't bother waiting for Serena to answer Toby's question about whether or not it was okay.

Was this the same woman who'd let herself get pushed around when Serena and Sergio were kids? She'd definitely come into her own. Serena couldn't be mad at her for that. And she wasn't. She was proud of her mom.

So very, very proud. And if that meant she cooked a meal for Toby and interrogated Serena without end, so be it. Serena wouldn't have it any other way.

She finally put her mom back in the elevator and told her to call when she got to the apartment, just as Jacelyn rounded the corner with a smile. "You got here early, Serena."

Yes, she had, and she was already exhausted from that scene with her mother. But since the other nurse was here, she couldn't grumble at Toby for letting himself get roped into dinner with them. If she knew her mom, it would be complete with candles and all the works.

"Well, I guess I'm going to go on rounds and check on a few patients." He gave her a wicked smile. "See you later."

Jacelyn waved at him while Serena sent him a glare, although she wasn't really mad. Just exasperated. The last thing she wanted to deal with today was having her mom and Toby in the same room.

But it looked like that was exactly what she was going to get, whether she wanted it or not.

Toby arrived at the house to find Serena's roommate heading out the door. "Dr. Renfro?"

"Yes. And you must be Avery."

"I am. Go on in. I'm actually headed to the hospital. But enjoy your dinner. It smells pretty great."

"Thanks."

Whether the other man knew about him or not was up in the air. But he was beginning to regret his impulse to tease Serena by allowing himself to be invited to dinner. She obviously hadn't told her mom about him. But he assumed she knew about the pregnancy. And if he had to guess, that was what had brought Gracia Dias to San Diego—not research. She probably wanted to see for herself that her daughter was okay. Who could blame her for that? It was so not like his parents, though. They'd given their son almost complete autonomy by the time he'd reached his teenage years. Curfews were never voiced, and Toby never once remembered his parents peeking in his room to make sure he was there.

He could see that was not how Serena was raised, and it made him tense. Was he sure he could do this? And he didn't just mean dinner.

He went through the open door in time to hear Serena talking to her mom in heated tones. The conversation was in Spanish, but he heard Gracia say his name a couple of times. Yep. This had definitely been a mistake.

He entered the room, making his presence known sooner rather than later by clearing his throat.

Serena saw him first, and her eyes widened. *"Mamá!"*

Her mom didn't look the slightest bit embarrassed. She just came over and stood on tiptoe, kissing him on the cheek.

"It's a custom." The words came from Serena, but she didn't need to explain.

"It's fine." He smiled at her mom, feeling warmed by the gesture, despite the fact that it was probably nothing more than a formality. "Nice to see you again. Thanks so much for inviting me."

"You're very welcome." She sent Serena a knowing smile.

Avery was right. The apartment smelled amazing. And the table was set with care. Long red tapers perched in the middle of it, along with a fresh bouquet of flowers. It was a mixture of daisies and roses.

"Go sit with Serena, while I finish a few things."

Serena sent him a look as she led him over to a couch, before mouthing *Sorry.*

"It's fine." He looked at her carefully. "Does she know about me?"

"Yep. And I didn't even tell her. But to deny it would have meant lying, and I couldn't bring myself to do that. She already knew about the pregnancy. Just not the rest."

"And Avery?"

"He knows too. I'm sorry. Here I am saying I want to keep it quiet, and I'm the one who's letting the cat out of the bag."

"If you trust Avery, then I do too. And your mom doesn't travel in the same circles as we do." He frowned as a thought came to him. "Were you going to tell her about me at all?"

She glanced away, telling him all he needed to know.

"So you weren't."

"Not right away. My mom, she's just…" She gave a small laugh. "A hopeless romantic."

"So the candles and the flowers…"

"Not meant to woo you, I promise. Not yet, anyway. She just likes to set a beautiful table. And daisies are my favorite flower, so she almost always gets some when she knows I'll be home."

"I didn't know they were your favorite flower."

She shrugged. "It's not something I go around telling everyone."

He tucked that piece of information away, not sure why, other than he didn't know a whole lot about her favorite things. He knew that she liked Mission Beach. And yoga. And that she drank her coffee black. And that she could mourn the death of someone she didn't even know.

Actually, there was a lot to like about Serena Dias.

"I think we are ready." Gracia came back into the room.

Toby got up and went over to the table with Serena, waiting for her to tell him where to sit. She must have noticed because she motioned to the chairs. "It doesn't matter. Avery and I rarely have time to eat together, so there aren't any assigned seats."

He opted for one of the plates in the middle of the table. Since there were four places, Gracia had evidently expected Avery to stay. "I passed your roommate in the hallway."

"Yes, he had to work. My mom's saving him enough food for tomorrow and probably several more days."

Her conspiratorial tones made him smile.

Gracia remained standing and served their plates. Serena was right. It was a huge meal, and he had no idea how she'd accomplished so much in so little time.

There were enchiladas, beans and rice, guacamole with salad greens and tomatoes and a couple of side dishes he didn't recognize.

Serena gave a low groan. "I don't think I'll be doing yoga tomorrow after this meal."

"There's always running."

She made a face at him.

He liked this side of Serena. It was playful and just a tiny bit snarky. And it fit her to a tee. Strangely enough, despite her mom's vivid personality, Toby felt more relaxed than he'd felt in a long time. Maybe a little too relaxed.

As they ate, Gracia asked him about his work and what he liked about it and what he didn't.

"I was very proud of Serena for following her dream. I used to want to be a nurse. But..." She shrugged in a way that made him glance to his right at her daughter.

"But you followed another dream, *Mamá*."

"Yes, and I love it."

There was a brief lull in the conversation while they ate, before Gracia glanced at Serena. "Are you choosing baby names yet?"

"It's still too early. We'll, er, I'll do that later."

"Too early? Never. I had your name picked out before you were even conceived. I always knew your name would be Serena. It means *serene*. It fits her, no?"

He was pretty sure Serena was not feeling like her name right now. If anything, she looked flustered and maybe a little dismayed.

His own parents would never have made a dinner and invited his friends to join them. It wasn't that they didn't care. His physical needs had always been met. But now that he was grown, he realized not all needs were physical. Some of his emotional needs had fallen by the wayside. It had instilled a fierce independence in him. To rely on someone else to meet his needs was a foreign concept to him. And the opposite was true as well. It made it hard for him to meet someone else's emotional needs. Because he wasn't always sure what they were. What he did know was that he didn't want his child to grow up thinking he didn't care about them. What kind of parent would he end up being? Warm and gracious and a bit of a bulldozer like Gracia? Or cool and reserved and completely hands-off like his own parents had been?

Shouldn't he be thinking about things like that? Whether or not he'd let his child pick out their own clothes. Or whether or not he'd make them eat their vegetables.

Like Serena said. It was still early. But in his head, he could still hear that *tick, tick, tick* of the seconds passing by.

She hasn't even had her first doctor's appointment yet.

So yes. Still very early days.

"Where do your parents live, Toby?"

"They're actually in Lancaster, where I'm from originally."

She offered him more food, but he shook his head. "I'm completely full, but thank you."

"You saved room for flan, I hope."

For some reason, he didn't think there was a choice involved. Serena gave him a quick shrug.

A minute later, Gracia was back with a picture-perfect dessert in a deep rounded plate. She cut slices with precision, spooning a golden sauce over them before passing them around. Toby's first bite melted in his mouth, the caramelized sugar the perfect foil for the rich custardy base.

When he'd finished, he waved off anything else. He couldn't remember the last time he'd eaten so much.

"I am wrapping some up for you take home."

"That's not necessary."

Her mom smiled. "Maybe not, but I would still like to."

Toby was kind of surprised that she hadn't mentioned the baby beyond asking if they'd picked out names or not. Nor was there anything more said about his being the father. Then again, he wasn't out the door yet.

He glanced at his watch, surprised to find it was almost nine o'clock. "I need to head home pretty soon. I have an early morning."

Serena looked relieved. By the fact that he was leaving?

Gracia returned with a large bag. "This is for your lunch tomorrow." Then she kissed him on the cheek again.

"Thank you." To turn it down would seem ungrateful, and somehow he wondered if he'd be allowed to even leave the apartment without the bag of goodies.

Serena said in low tones, "I'll walk you to the door."

When they got there, he looked at her. "Well, that was

a lot less painful than it could have been. She didn't ask any difficult questions."

There was a long pause before she finally responded. "Yeah, I noticed that. And to be honest, it kind of has me worried."

CHAPTER NINE

TOBY MET HER in Gary's office. He was right. The OB-GYN was discreet. When she'd told him that Toby would be joining her at the appointment, he'd arranged for them to come in another entrance at the building where his private practice was located and to wait in one of the exam rooms.

She was grateful. She knew there were Lamaze classes and so forth that she'd have to go through, and while Toby was coming to this appointment, she was reserving judgment about his being her birthing partner.

She didn't even know if he'd accept the role anyway.

She hadn't wanted to rock the boat, because things between them were actually not so bad right now. But she had a feeling it was because they were both on their best behavior. Kind of like Parker had been during the early days of their courtship.

Why had she thought of that? She and Toby weren't dating or even in a relationship.

But they were having a baby together.

She glanced at him to find he was staring at something on the wall. When she looked over there, she spied a large baby-development poster that showed the stages of pregnancy. There was a tension in him that made her uneasy. One that she hadn't sensed at dinner with her mom. Was he having second thoughts about all of this?

"You don't have to be here, you know."

He was the one who'd asked to come, but maybe this was all happening too fast for him. It wasn't like she could slow the process down, though. But his tension was spreading to her, and Serena wasn't sure she wanted to go through this with each and every appointment.

"I know."

Not quite the reassuring words she might have hoped for, like *I'm here because I want to be here*. Maybe she needed to talk to him afterward.

And tell him what? That he needed to shape up and act happy or he couldn't come anymore?

The last thing she wanted from him was an act. She'd already experienced that before, and she could really do without it. She wanted her pregnancy to be a thing of wonder, where she anticipated each new stage—just like on that poster, where the mother-to-be was smiling—she'd rather it not be a stressful mess of wondering if Toby was regretting his decision to be a part of this. And she wondered about that each and every day. Today, he was giving her even more reason to wonder.

He could be funny and charming. But he could also be distant and hard to communicate with. Like right now.

He could be sexy as hell, and he could also shut down with a speed that made her head spin.

Wasn't she like that as well?

Maybe. But not about this. She was anxious to see what the appointment would bring. She wanted to know everything. The baby's size. How they were doing. If the baby was developing normally.

And she wanted to know the gender as soon as they could tell.

Did he?

She decided to tackle that question first, because Gary would eventually ask them. "Do you want to know if it's a boy or a girl when it comes time to find out?"

He glanced at her and then right back at the wall. The foot he had propped on his knee twitched a couple of times before quieting back down. "Whatever you think."

She blinked. What did he mean by that?

God, she was over thinking everything. But it felt like he was sucking every bit of joy out of the room. Out of her.

She decided not to ask him anything else. Maybe once Gary came in, he'd perk up.

Or maybe he wouldn't. But right now, she was regretting letting him come to the appointment at all.

A nurse came into the room, took her vitals and walked her down the hallway to weigh her. Toby opted to stay in the room, not even offering to accompany her. Which made sense, since they were trying to keep things quiet. But she halfway expected to find him gone when she reentered the space.

But he was still there. Still kind of broody, although he did send her a half-hearted smile, while his foot continued to bounce up and down on its perch. She could feel her heart rate speeding up to match its rhythm.

By the time Gary got there, she was a mass of conflicted feelings. Maybe she wasn't doing the right thing by having this baby. Maybe she should…

No. This was the right thing. For *her*. But maybe it wasn't for Toby. They hadn't really talked about the appointment over the last week and a half, and honestly he'd seemed fine about it. Until now.

Gary came in the room, took one look at Toby and said, "Everything okay?"

So she wasn't the only one who'd noticed it. She was glad, and yet, she wasn't. She'd kind of hoped she *was* being overly sensitive.

"Yep." He stood and shook the other man's hand. "Thanks for letting us come in the other entrance."

Serena felt herself shrink back in her chair. Was that it? Was he embarrassed that she was carrying his child? Despite the fact that she'd been as eager as he was to not let everyone know he was the father—at least not right away—this felt different somehow.

"Not a problem."

Gary turned to Serena as Toby took his seat again, crossing his leg and bouncing that damned foot again. She finally reached over and touched it. "Could you not do that, please? You're making me nervous."

"Got it." He uncrossed his legs and sat forward in his chair, elbows propped on his knees.

Well, hell. That wasn't any better.

She decided to ignore him.

"You ready to see what's happening with this little one?" Gary asked.

"Yes. More than ready." She forced a smile. Right

now, she was just ready to get this over with and get out of this room. Away from Toby.

"Hop up on the table for me." She was already dressed in the hospital gown they'd given her when she'd first stepped foot in the room. And she'd never been so glad for the curtain that curved near the door and blocked Toby's view of her disrobing, which was ridiculous. But she was self-conscious all of a sudden, and she wasn't sure why.

She slid onto the table and somehow made it through the pelvic exam, feeling more and more regretful of Toby's presence in the room. He wasn't trying to be negative. He was just…quiet. Too quiet.

She missed the fun of the yoga class they'd taken together, missed the time they'd spent sitting on the beach—where the quiet had been a good thing, not this excruciating sensation that he'd rather be anywhere else in the world than here.

His words came back to her about not seeing himself having kids in the future. Well, the future was already here, and it was too late now. His world had been turned upside down in an instant.

"Okay, I'm going to do a sonogram, even though we won't be able to see a whole lot at this early stage. Certainly not enough to be able to see the baby's genitals, if you decide you want to know the sex.

Whatever you think.

That was just it. It wasn't whatever she thought. If he wanted to be involved in their child's life, she wanted his input. Not just about this, but about a lot of things. To have him sitting there, present and yet not present, was an awful sensation. One she didn't want their child experiencing.

Gary squirted warmed lubricating jelly on her lower abdomen and then placed the scanner in the middle of the stuff. She immediately heard sounds of static from the wand being drawn across her belly. She was afraid to even look at Toby, afraid he'd still be staring at that poster on the wall and wishing he was anywhere but here.

"Okay, here we go."

Serena turned her attention to the screen, where she saw a black circle. In the middle of that dark space was a curved little creature. She immediately recognized the head. The tiny limbs that were starting to form. And she stopped dead when a distinct sound filled the room.

Blub-blub, blub-blub, blub-blub.

Just like the bounce of Toby's foot.

"We have a strong heartbeat." Gary glanced down at her with a smile.

Suddenly, she didn't care what Toby felt or didn't feel. An overwhelming sense of love filled her, growing to encompass this tiny start of life. But it didn't stop there—it soon spread outside of her belly and expanded its reach to include...

Toby.

Her eyes widened for a second. No, it was just the wonder of seeing their baby for the first time. Of course she'd feel love for anyone in this room.

But she didn't love Gary Rollings. At least not in that way.

Something in her heart said the love she felt for Toby

was different than what she felt for their baby. And that it was something that had been growing as irrevocably as the tiny scrap of life inside of her.

She kept her eyes on the screen, even as her heart wept over the impossibility of the situation. She wanted this baby.

But she also wanted him.

But he'd been clear. Very, very clear. While he was willing to entertain the idea of being a dad—something he might very well be rethinking right now—he'd made it clear that he didn't want anything more than that.

He'd even said he couldn't offer her a relationship. And she'd reassured him that that was okay. That she didn't expect one or want one either.

It hadn't been a lie. At the time. But it might very well be one now.

"Do you want me to print off an image? The 3D ultrasounds make it nice. You'll eventually be able to really see the baby's face."

"I would like one, thanks." She didn't ask Toby if he wanted one, and neither did Gary. It was pretty clear that he was either shell-shocked or…something else.

She was pretty shell-shocked herself. Not by the pregnancy. But by the discovery that she was in love with him.

And she had absolutely no idea what to do about it. One thing was for sure. She was not going to sit him down like she'd done with the pregnancy and tell him. She also wasn't sure she could sit here in an exam room month after month and try to hide her feelings from him.

On the surgical floor, it was one thing. Things were busy and there wasn't a whole lot of time for introspection.

But here… Watching the growing development of her baby, she was afraid of seeing that mirrored in her feelings for him.

Maybe she needed to set up some boundaries and to cut off any time spent together outside of work and pre-natal appointments.

That meant no more trips to Mission Beach. And that made her sad in a way she didn't understand.

"Do you know the due date, so I can try to arrange my schedule?"

Those were the first words out of Toby's mouth since they'd started the ultrasound. And the words had been a clinical dissection that cut to the heart of what was important to him: rearranging his schedule.

It should have made her happy that he seemed to con-firm he still wanted to be a part of their baby's life. But she'd hoped for some kind of emotional response from him rather than something so detached.

"So conception… Do you know an exact day?"

Toby answered without hesitation. "May sixteenth."

Wow. She hadn't expected him to come up with the date that fast. And of course her brain was already put-ting all kinds of spin on that information. Was it that memorable? Was it a day he was hoping he could wish away?

She wouldn't know unless she asked. And she couldn't do that. Wouldn't do that. Not with the way she was feeling right now.

Gary checked something and then marked sections

on the ultrasound. "That lines up with the size of the fetus. That puts you right around February sixth for a due date."

February sixth. Wow. It all of a sudden seemed right around the corner.

She finally chanced a glance at Toby and found him looking at his phone, tapping on the screen. Had he even looked at the ultrasound?

Surely…?

A sick sensation began crawling up her stomach. This wasn't right. She knew with a sinking heart that she couldn't go through this again.

It was obvious Toby was not happy being in this room. And right now, she'd rather he be anywhere but this room too.

She was not going to do this. Not this way.

It wasn't even like she'd asked him to come. He was the one who'd asked her if he could.

People change. Remember?

As if realizing something was wrong, Gary added, "Delivery times aren't set in stone, though. They're just a guideline."

They finished up the exam, which seemed to take forever. All she wanted to do was get out of this room. Get away from him. And do some heavy thinking. She would never take the baby away from Toby if he truly wanted to be a part of their life. But she would take anything involving her off the table.

Seeing as she was currently sitting on an exam table, that suddenly struck her as hilarious. And she giggled, the giggle changing to a laugh that lasted a few seconds too long. Toby and Gary were both looking at her like she'd lost her mind.

"Sorry. Something just struck me as funny."

Except it wasn't funny. Not right now, anyway. And she couldn't see the two of them laughing over this in the near future either.

So she'd just pull herself together and leave this room with all the dignity she could muster.

Toby had never had a panic attack before. But as he'd sat in that exam room with Serena yesterday, he'd come very close to having one. The walls had seemed to close in around him, the poster on the wall just making that sensation of time ticking by even stronger. February suddenly seemed right around the corner.

And he wasn't ready for this. Any of it.

He should probably go talk to Serena about it. He'd hoped she hadn't noticed anything was wrong, but there was no way she hadn't. He'd barely said two words. And when Gary had printed off one ultrasound image and handed it to Serena, he hadn't asked for one as well.

The images on that wall were burned into his head. The baby was chugging right along and would soon pass through all of those stages. And then things would no longer be hypothetical and abstract. They would be concrete, as in a living human being would settle into Gary's waiting hands.

And then Toby's entire life would change in ways he probably couldn't even imagine.

Ways that he'd tried to avoid.

Every visit to this office would drive that point home. Over and over and over.

Yet the alternative was unacceptable. That he would take the selfish way out and keep living just for himself.

Things weren't really all that cut and dried, but he tended to make them that way.

To top things off, Tanya had called him yesterday evening to tell him she was pregnant as well. Except she'd assured him it was Cliff's baby and not his. In case he heard about it through the grapevine. He had no idea which one that would be. Because while Paz Memorial had its own gossip chain, it didn't normally extend to neighboring hospitals, much less ones that were in other cities.

He'd told her he was happy for her. And he was. Her life seemed to have come together in a way that his hadn't. She was evidently in a loving relationship, which probably made things easier.

He was pretty sure if he'd offered marriage or some other form of commitment to Serena, she'd have cut him off.

She'd barely let him come to her appointment. And the thought of going to the next one… Well, it sent that crushing weight back to his stomach where it settled in for the foreseeable future.

He didn't think he could do it. Being a running companion was one thing. But being a parenting companion was another.

He was going to have to tell her. Or at least try to explain why he'd acted the way he had at her appointment. Gary asking if everything was okay pretty much told him that his panic had been just as noticeable as he'd thought it had been.

He just wasn't sure exactly how he was going to tell her. About any of it. The ball of fear that hung over him. The realization that he was right about fatherhood: he wasn't ready for it in the slightest.

But it was coming. Whether he was ready or not.

And somehow, he was going to have to figure out a way to come to terms with it.

Surgery on Monday morning was routine. A biker had laid his motorcycle down on the road and sustained an open fracture to his femur. And yet, as Serena handed Toby surgical instruments, it was anything but routine. She felt like she was standing over herself watching the surgery unfold without really being a part of it.

She realized then that was probably how Toby had felt at that appointment. That he'd been there, and yet, he hadn't been.

That made her sad and worried. She didn't want the man "going through the motions" when it came to his child's life. She wanted someone who was fully invested. Someone who felt they had skin in the game. Although the word *game* made her cringe. None of this was a game. It was very real. And far too important to take chances with.

So she was going to ask him to sit out for a couple of months from having anything to do with the pregnancy and then reevaluate how he felt afterward. If, at the end of that period, he felt relief, then she was going to do him a favor and ask him to step away from the situation, period—reassure him that she would be fine. She'd started off expecting to raise the baby on her own and had been reassured by both her mom and Avery that she wouldn't really be alone. There were people who wanted to help. Who really wanted to be there for her. And that's who she wanted gathered around her as she went through this process. Not someone who would come to resent everything to do with her and her baby.

She somehow got through the rest of the surgery and then slid away as soon as it was over to do a little thinking. She could do that while she saw to the patients and went about her day. She would have one final surgery at the end of the day, but it wasn't with Toby. It was with one of the orthopedists who had a specialized hand surgery coming up. Something that was new to Serena. Normally, she welcomed those kinds of cases—looked forward to them, since she learned so much from them.

But this time she wasn't. She kind of felt like she was in limbo, stuck between two worlds and trying to decide which one she wanted to choose. Which one she needed to choose.

Having this baby drag Toby along for the ride, or asking her mom to come and walk through the process with her.

She knew which one she wanted. But she didn't want it to involve an individual who said he'd be there but, in his heart of hearts, didn't really want to be there.

So after she was done with her final surgery, she was going to call him and ask to meet. And lay things out so there'd be no misunderstandings. On anyone's part.

* * *

Toby went to the beach. He'd needed the sounds of the ocean to lull him back to a place that wasn't so fraught with tension.

Except, when he got there, all he could remember were the cries for help and that elderly man lying broken on the boardwalk.

He sat there for a few minutes before getting up and walking over to the spot where the man had lain. Rollerbladers and pedestrians streamed around him, most of them probably oblivious to what had happened there a little over a week ago. The man was long forgotten.

But not by him. And not by Serena either.

These days of her pregnancy would be forgotten too, eventually. And yet, right now, they were incredibly painful and drew up every insecurity he'd ever had. If it had been planned, maybe he'd feel differently. And yet, Serena seemed totally at ease with her decision.

So why wasn't he?

Checking his pocket for his phone, he realized he'd left it at home. That put an end to his plans for figuring this thing out. He needed to get home and make sure there were no emergencies that needed his attention.

So he got in his car and drove back to his apartment. The second he arrived, Porkchop greeted him at the door, winding around his ankles and begging for food. Not that he hadn't already fed her. She tended to beg no matter how many tidbits she received throughout the day.

"Wait a second, girl. I have to check something first."

He got his phone off the desk and scrolled through

several messages before he realized his brain had skipped over one of them.

Backing up, he saw it there in red font. He'd missed a call from Serena. Two calls, actually, an hour apart.

Hell! Was there something wrong with her? With the baby?

Ignoring his cat for the moment, he pressed redial and waited as the phone on the other end rang once, twice, before a shaky voice responded with a single word.

"Hello?"

CHAPTER TEN

SHE MET HIM at the beach the following day, telling him she would drive separately. She couldn't see him wanting to take her home after she'd said what she had to say, although honestly, she thought some part of him would be relieved.

The thought of meeting at the hospital, even in the courtyard area, was unbearable. Even being the surgical nurse for his cases was hard right now. It brought back the fact that she cared about him in a way that had nothing to do with their being work colleagues. He'd been honest and told her the truth about how he felt, and she respected him for that. She wouldn't have wanted him to lie.

The weirdest thing was that she'd expected him to act one way, but then he'd acted in completely the opposite way—and it bothered her. Whereas Parker and her dad had a tendency to state what they wanted in no uncertain terms, Toby had expressed no interest whatsoever while they were at the doctor's office. In anything. Even when she'd joked that she wanted to be the one to choose the baby's name, he'd been fine with it.

He hadn't wanted a copy of the ultrasound. And while he'd programmed the delivery date into his phone, it was done as if it were simply another business appointment. The number of "not interested" signs was piling up fast. And she couldn't push through and pretend it didn't matter when he was right there beside her making it obvious that he'd prefer a token involvement rather than a real one.

But their child deserved more from him than that. And she would accept nothing less than true commitment.

This time, she brought a towel and sat on it as she waited for Toby to arrive. He wasn't late; she was early. But she'd wanted to make sure she was as composed as possible. She even had a cheat sheet tucked in her purse if she needed it that she could use to get all her points across. Although she couldn't see him arguing with anything she suggested.

Going back to work would be hard. The impulse to immediately quit and go somewhere else was still strong. Really strong. But she'd already been through that and decided she wasn't going to make any decisions until after the baby was born. To do anything else would be to act like her mom had with her dad—changing her plans because of something he wanted or didn't want instead of sticking to what she wanted.

She'd managed to work with Toby after sleeping with him. This would be no different, right?

Toby found her five minutes later studying her notes, which she quickly shoved into her pocketbook.

He dropped onto the sand beside her and looked at her. "Why couldn't you tell me whatever this is about over the phone?"

"Because I think it's better done in person." She realized she was using the same argument Toby had used about not telling her about Patient Doe's death over the phone. He'd been right, she thought now. About that, at least.

"Okay." He drew the word out in a way that said he didn't agree.

But it didn't matter if he agreed. She'd already made the decision. And she was going to make this about her rather than about what he had and hadn't done.

"I think I'd like to go to the rest of my doctor's appointments by myself."

He closed his eyes for a second before looking at her again. And yes, she could swear that was relief in expression. "Any particular reason?"

"Lots of them. But they all lead to the same place. That it's uncomfortable for me to have you there." She left out the part about its being due to his stilted behavior.

"I'm sorry if I've—"

"I think I would have felt the same way no matter what."

He waited a long time. "And the baby. Are you still going to let me into their life?"

"We—meaning both you and I together—can decide that after the baby gets here. In the meantime, I want you to think long and hard about what you want, because there won't be any fence-sitters. I don't have an option about being a parent—well, I do, but it's not one I want to explore. You can choose though. I know you said you wanted to be involved, but by not coming to my appointments, it'll give you a chance to reexamine your motivations for wanting to be involved. Whatever they are, don't let it be out of guilt. Because that isn't fair to the baby."

He didn't interrupt her. Didn't correct her. He just let her keep on talking until she was all done.

Then he nodded. "So let me see if I've got this straight. You don't want me at your appointments. And you want me to use the time to figure out if I really want to be involved in the baby's life or not."

"Yes."

"You're still coming to work. Is that correct?"

She looked at him. "Is that a problem for you?"

"No. But you're making it sound like you don't want us to be around each other until after the baby is born, and maybe not even then."

"We don't see each other all the time at work. So I don't have any plans to go anywhere."

His brows came together. "I don't remember asking you to."

"Okay. Just making sure." She paused. "Do you have anything to say?"

If she'd been hoping for him to argue with her, to say that's not what he wanted at all, she was sorely disappointed. Because his only comment was, "You'll let me know how things are going?"

"I think it'll be best if we don't talk about the baby at work at all."

"So I'm just to assume that no news means that everything is going as expected?"

She hesitated. "If I…lose the baby…" She almost couldn't get those words out. "I'll let you know."

She wasn't sure, but she thought he might have gone pale at her words. But that didn't make any sense. She'd made peace with their not being together—at least she hoped to hell she had—but she had to accept that, just like folks who were divorced with kids, they would always be in each other's lives in some way, shape or form because of this baby.

Unless he decided he didn't want to be involved in any way. A part of her hoped that would be the case. Because then she could stay or leave the hospital and even the city without giving any thought to him or his access to his child.

He'd been looking out to sea, but when she said that, he turned to look at her, his eyes intent on hers. "I want to let you know that whatever happens, I don't want you to lose this baby. I want this little one to be healthy and have a happy life. I'm just not…"

He didn't finish his sentence, but it didn't matter. None of the myriad combination of words would make whatever his thought was into something positive. But at least she was finally getting some honesty out of him. And, whatever it was, *not* was at the center of it.

Not…good father material.

Not…prepared to father a child.

Not…willing to be involved.

They all basically meant the same thing.

"It's okay, Toby. Which is why it's better this way. You let me know when you've made a decision one way or the other."

"I told you that you wouldn't have to go through this alone."

The words were like a spear that hit her midchest. She'd thought about that, but that first appointment had made her take a closer look at his offer. "Sometimes you're alone, even when there are other people around."

He averted his gaze, looking out over the water. "I'm sorry if you felt that way."

She shrugged. "It's just easier to go it alone than…" Than worry about whether the other person is dreading being there. But she left that part unsaid. He'd gotten her point. It was better to leave it at that.

With that, she stood and shook her towel out. "Well, that's all I wanted to say. I'll see you at work."

"Yes."

He didn't get up or offer to walk with her back to her car, just sat there looking straight ahead.

It was easier this way. There was no need to confess her feelings or pressure him to keep coming to her appointments. The first one was too awful. Too painful. It reminded her of all she wanted but couldn't have.

She walked away, heading toward her car. Her vision was blurred, and her head suddenly was stuffed full of second thoughts and wishes that there'd been another way.

There hadn't been. And he'd seemed to confirm that by his response.

He was relieved. Even if she was anything but.

She was true to her word. Serena saw him at work but made no effort to engage in small talk. She treated him like any other doctor she'd worked with. Maybe even a little more formally. Because he noticed she did engage in chit chat with other doctors. With Toby, though, she normally just nodded and did her job, keeping her head down whenever possible.

And she rarely looked him in the eye. He found he missed that the most.

Hell, he shouldn't have cared. She'd made it pretty clear that she didn't want him involved in her life. At all. She'd said it was up to him, but she sure hadn't made it sound that way. So he was bracing for her to shut him out of her life completely. Including out of his child's life.

He'd thought that was what he'd wanted as well when he'd sat there in that exam room. But a hard ball of bile had sat at the back of his throat for a week now. A week since they'd talked on the beach. A week and two days since her initial doctor's appointment.

Mabel Tucker was due to come in today for her third and final follow-up. He didn't call Serena and let her know, because, well, she didn't want to be around him. She'd made that very clear. So he doubted she would want to be there for anything involving him. Even for a patient she liked.

He sat in his office, looking at the chair they'd made love in. He'd had it professionally cleaned, saying he wanted to start doing that periodically. But it didn't matter how many steamers came in. He would always picture her kneeling over him, her butterfly tattoo clearly visible.

Maybe he'd have to throw those ones out and get some new chairs. Chairs that didn't remind him of her.

Sometimes you're alone, even when there are other people around.

He hadn't understood what she'd meant. Until now. Until he'd stood in a surgical suite with her nearby and felt totally disconnected from her. Totally alone. Just like he had felt during his childhood. And he'd realized how very much he'd missed out on growing up.

The old man from the boardwalk came to mind. He'd had a crowd gathered around him. And yet, he'd been totally and utterly alone. Unknown by any one of those people. Unknown by him. By Serena.

Was that really who he wanted to be? Someone people recognized but didn't really know?

There was a knock at the door and his heart sped up for a second only to thud to nothing when he opened the door and found Mabel and Tom standing there.

There must have been something in his face, because Tom spoke up. "Did we have the right time?"

"Yes, of course. Sorry."

Had he really expected Serena to be there, telling him she was sorry and that she really wanted him to come to her appointments after all?

A little flicker of shock lit up inside of him. He kind of had. Why else would his heart have reacted the way it had?

He was an idiot. He was the one who should be going to her and asking for her forgiveness rather than the other way around. It was because of him that she'd felt alone and unsupported. Maybe after this appointment, he'd go find her and see if he couldn't somehow make this right.

He ushered the couple into his office, and they sat in the chairs across from his desk, making him swallow.

"I have a new piece of bling." Mabel shook her wrist and a silver bracelet jingled there. Holding it out, she let him look at it.

"This is a fancy one."

It was a medical alert bracelet, but the links and attachment were swirled and decorative, the nameplate looking more like an oval piece of silver than the utilitarian versions he'd seen in the past.

"I love bracelets, so I researched them."

He read the inscription on the plate, and it had all the pertinent information in clear lettering, so he couldn't complain about it. Not that he would, unless he felt it wouldn't be clearly seen by emergency services.

"It's very nice. And I'm glad to see you wearing it." It had been more than four weeks since her surgery. "How are you feeling?"

"A lot better than last week. I feel like I've finally made it over the hump."

"You might still feel better, but it's easy to overdo it, so take it easy for a couple more weeks.

"I'm trying. But it's not easy."

"Did you get the immunizations we talked about?" She nodded. "Yep. Last week. But..."

"But?"

"Are we cleared to, um, resume relations?"

"Yes, as long as you're not having pain." He paused. "I know you guys talked about wanting to start a family, but I'd like you to hold off for a month or two until we see how your body adjusts to life without a spleen."

"We weren't planning to start trying right away. The thought of having someone push on my stomach during an exam is still a little daunting."

"I know. Fortunately, we won't have to do that today, unless you're noticing anything abnormal."

"No. Nothing. The scar is starting to turn white, though. It's been bloodred ever since it was done."

"That's good news, actually."

Tom took her hand and squeezed. "I'm just glad she's here, alive and well."

"So am I." Mabel's eyes were no longer black, and looking at her, you would have never guessed that she'd been on the brink of death from a car accident just over a month ago. She was very lucky.

And lucky she didn't have to go through her recovery alone, without emotional support.

His gut spasmed.

Yes, she was very lucky. Because unlike that man on the boardwalk, she had someone who made sure of that. Someone who hadn't left her side and had been there in ways that went beyond the physical. Something Toby hadn't done for Serena. Or her baby.

Why?

He blinked, suddenly realizing why. Because he'd fallen in love with her. And being around her made him want things he'd said he'd never want again: companionship...a family.

Was that why he'd been so struck by the stuff he'd seen in the waiting room? By the picture of developing babies that reminded him that even if he was there for the baby, Serena probably didn't want him around her?

Hell, she'd made that pretty clear on the beach.

But maybe that had had more to do with his attitude than hers. She'd been happy enough to have him there, until she'd actually experienced his being there. He'd been an idiot at Gary's office, to be honest. He'd been uncommunicative to the point of being rude. He hadn't been present. Not in an emotional way. Instead, he'd held himself apart.

To protect himself from being hurt?

Maybe. That and out of fear, for sure. The thought of becoming a father like his own still terrified him.

Was it because he was afraid Serena would take off on him, like Tanya had done? Or was it more about his fear of becoming the kind of parent that made you feel alone, even when they were there? Like Serena had mentioned on the beach.

Well, his fear had made that a self-fulfilling prophesy. He was afraid. So he'd held himself back. Until he hadn't been there at all. He wouldn't blame Serena for wanting him out of there.

And if he'd participated in that appointment?

He was pretty sure that things would be different now. Serena was not Tanya. She was the type to stay in there and gut it out. As long as she knew the other person would do the same.

Would he?

Tom was looking at him, and he realized he'd missed something they'd said.

"Sorry, I was thinking of another case. What did you say?"

"I asked if there was anything else we should be looking for from here on out."

"Gotcha. Like I said before, just be careful of exposing yourself to communicable illnesses. And wait at least a month or so before trying to start a family."

"That sounds easy enough."

Didn't it, though? Lots of challenges could be solved by a simple set of steps. People just weren't always willing to do the work.

Like him?

Yep. Just like him.

And what was the work?

To tell Serena that he cared about her. That he cared about the baby. And then wait and see how she reacted.

Could he do it?

The question wasn't *could*. It was *would*. *Would* he do it?

He and the Tuckers said their goodbyes, and the couple headed out the door, hand in hand. Maybe Toby needed to be brave enough to face life head on, like Mabel and Tom. To do that, he needed to go find Serena and...

Do what?

He wasn't sure. But he hoped he would know as soon as he set eyes on her.

Closing the door to his office, he headed down the hallway toward the nurses' station only to spy a figure rushing toward him. Serena. Her face was streaked with tears, making a chill go through him. He quickened his step, and when he reached her, he took hold of her arms.

"What is it?"

She sobbed, putting a hand to her mouth. "Toby, I—I think I might be losing the baby."

CHAPTER ELEVEN

THE TRIP TO Gary's office was made in complete silence as Toby gripped the wheel and dodged traffic for the two blocks that it took to reach the private practice. His heart was stuffed with regret over all the things he hadn't said. The things that might be too late to say now.

This time, Toby didn't worry about going in any back entrance, just gripped her hand and rushed her into the building.

As soon as the receptionist saw his face, she picked up her phone and called someone. A few seconds later, a nurse motioned them to come through the door, bypassing everyone else in the waiting room.

Gary appeared, his face showing concern. "I know this isn't a social visit, so tell me what's going on."

"I'm bleeding. And I'm afraid—"

"How much blood?"

"Not a ton, but—"

"Let's get you into a gown and on the table. If I even suspect something is happening, you're going right back to the hospital."

He looked at Toby, who nodded, feeling numb with fear.

"Understood," he said.

Gary left the room and Toby helped her undress and get into the fabric gown, seeing for himself that there was blood in her panties. He swallowed a lump, wanting to say so much yet knowing now was not the time.

The exam was quick and involved a physical exam, where Gary pronounced that the cervix looked intact, although there was a hint of bloody discharge. "It's not necessarily indicative of a miscarriage. Sometimes there is a little spotting, but I want to do another sonogram and make sure everything looks okay inside."

A nurse came in and got things ready, and then the wand moved over Serena's bare abdomen.

This time, when Toby heard the baby's heartbeat, a sense of overwhelming relief washed over him like a tsunami, completely different from the fear he'd felt last time in this room.

"How is everything?" The words came out before he could stop them.

"Everything looks good. The baby's heart rate is right on track."

"Thank God." He couldn't stop himself from dropping into a chair and putting his head between his hands. He took a moment or two to calm his erratic breathing, the adrenaline that had gotten him here deserting him completely. His legs felt like blocks of cement, and he wasn't sure how he was going to get them to carry him out of this room.

Serena's voice came to him. "So I'm not miscarrying?"

That made his head come back up as he waited for Gary to make his pronouncement.

"There's no sign of that. Sometimes, especially with first pregnancies, we see a little bit of spotting and never discover any real reason for it. We'll culture a swab and make sure there's no sign of infection, but there's no more active bleeding, so we're going to assume all is well. I want you to go home and put your feet up and let me know if it comes back."

"Thank you. I don't know what I'd do if…" The shaking of her voice got Toby staggering up out of his chair, and he gripped her hand hard.

Serena looked up in his face with a look of confusion. He couldn't blame her. He'd been a complete jerk the last time they were in this room. But he wanted to change that as soon as they got out of here.

Gary shook both of their hands and told them to call him if there was any more bleeding. Toby promised they would.

They.

As in both of them.

Because he hoped to hell she would be willing to give him a chance to explain. To say that he'd come to a decision. That he wanted to be involved in not only the baby's life, but also in hers.

"I'll take you home."

She nodded, getting dressed quickly. "I feel so stupid."

"Don't. Gary didn't treat this lightly, so that should tell you something. I was just so glad to hear that heartbeat."

"You were?" She stopped and looked at him again.

"I was, and I—"

His phone rang and when he glanced down at the readout, he saw that it was the hospital.

"It's okay. Answer it. We can talk later."

He pressed a button. "Renfro here."

He listened as one of the ER doctors asked where he was and if he could make it back to the hospital as soon as possible. They had an emergency, and he was the only on-call trauma specialist scheduled for this afternoon.

He glanced at Serena, who must have seen something in his face.

"Go. I told Avery what was happening, and he was supposed to meet me here. I didn't even think to call him back and tell him that you'd decided to come with me. He can take me home."

Said as if she hadn't expected him to even offer. Hell, he had so much to apologize for. But it had to wait.

"Are you sure?" He told the hospital he would be there in five minutes, then hung up.

"Yes. Absolutely."

He gripped her hand and gave it a squeeze. "I'd like to talk to you, but since it's already four o'clock, I have a feeling it won't be until tomorrow now. I want you to rest this evening and get a good night's sleep. Can you promise to call me if you need me?"

"I will."

He carried her hand to his mouth and kissed her palm. "Then how about we meet up at your yoga spot in the morning?"

She nodded. "I'd like that. Now go, so you can take care of that emergency."

With his heart feeling just a little bit lighter that it had all week, he headed out the door.

Daisies lined the perimeter of the little area of Balboa Park.

Had last night been a dream? Toby had seemed so different. Had said he wanted to talk to her. And when he'd kissed her palm, she'd almost hoped...

Well, she hadn't been able to stop thinking about that all night. And she was horrified by how hard she'd been wishing that there was more to that kiss than met the eye.

But now, there was no sign of him. Although this spot didn't look the same. Nor was there any sign of a yoga class being set up. Serena stopped, her beach bag with her yoga mat and change of clothes over her shoulder. She must have stopped at the wrong place.

She backed out of the area and glanced around at the nearby benches. Yes, this was the right spot. She and Toby had jogged out of here as soon as they'd finished doing the class that day.

Had they discontinued the classes? Surely Veronica would have sent her a text saying so if that were the case.

Besides, Toby had asked her to meet her here. Had he changed his mind?

She went back into the little cut back area and looked again. Still no sign of anyone. And although Serena tended to run early, she'd never gotten here before the instructor.

And although there were always palm trees, the pots

of daisies were new, unless they were planning on planting some in the area.

She stood there for a minute longer before realizing someone was behind her. Whirling around, she saw Toby standing there, another basket of daisies in the crook of his arm.

"W-where's my yoga class?"

"It's still meeting. Just a few yards away. What I have to say, I want to say to you alone."

She took a small step backward in confusion.

His finger circled her wrist. "Stay. Please." His touch was warm and soft, the slide of his thumb on her inner wrist making her pulse jump all over again.

She glanced at the potted plant in his hands. "Are you responsible for the flowers?"

"You said they were your favorite."

So he'd had all of these brought in? Had asked the yoga class to meet somewhere else? She swallowed. He surely hadn't done this for the benefit of the instructor or the other students. He'd done it for…her?

Why? Unless…

That kiss on her palm.

No. That couldn't be right.

"What's this about, Toby?" Her voice shook, but there was nothing she could do about that right now. God. She didn't want him to say anything if it wasn't what she was beginning to hope for.

"This is about me. Apologizing. And hoping you'll forgive me."

"Because of yesterday?"

"Yes, but not because you thought you were losing

the baby. I met with Mabel and Tom yesterday afternoon and had already decided to go look for you and apologize." His eyes closed for a second. "And then you came running down the hall, and I thought my whole world was ending."

"You did?"

He nodded and then pulled in a deep breath. "The first time I sat in that doctor's office, I kept thinking about all the reasons I couldn't have a family. Why I'd make such a horrible dad. And it became this huge macabre ghost that I couldn't see past."

"But why did you feel like that?"

"My parents are nothing like your mom, Serena. They're—it's hard to explain. They're not demonstrative people. And I sometimes find myself being like that too. Having a hard time calling up my feelings and letting them out."

"I noticed that in Gary's office the first time. I sensed you didn't want to be there. But yesterday…"

"Yesterday, that all changed. And not just because I thought you were losing the baby. I realized I didn't want to lose *you*."

"And so…?"

"I realized at Mabel Tucker's appointment yesterday that I want what she and her husband have. The companionship that means they don't have to experience being alone even when other people are around."

"But you can only have what they have if you—"

"Love each other? Yes. And I understood right then… I love you, Serena. I love this baby—even though I'm scared out of my wits that I won't be good at being a father."

"Are you saying all of this because you think it's what I want to hear?"

He shook his head. "I'm saying it because it's true." The fingers still encircling her wrist moved down, sliding over her palm in a way that half tickled, half aroused her, reminding her of the firm lips he'd pressed to it yesterday.

Could this really be happening? She hadn't wanted to see him anymore, because she'd also realized she loved him and that it was an impossible situation.

And yet, he'd been the first person she'd run to when she thought she was losing the baby. Because she loved him too.

She looked around the space. Hundreds of baskets of her favorite flower. "How did you even get these all here?"

"I rented a van yesterday afternoon and went to a flower market."

"Seriously?" She tried to picture him walking around and searching the place for daisies. Her heart swelled to bursting. Because she really could see him doing that. At least, the Toby from yesterday at the doctor's office. "What are you planning to do with them all afterward?"

"I'm donating them to the park to be planted around this area. I want them to be a permanent reminder of how I feel about you every time we come here to do yoga."

"We?"

He nodded. "If you want me there." He took a step

closer and cupped her chin. "Because I want to be there. I want to be there for all of it. Your prenatal appointments. Your cravings—if you even get those."

"Oh, I do. Believe me."

"I want to be there for this baby's birth and for every event thereafter. But most of all, I want to be there for you. I realized that I didn't want to be John Doe, standing alone in the midst of a crowd."

She nodded. "I thought the same thing about John Doe. It was one of the reasons I didn't want you at my appointments. I decided I wanted to forge meaningful relationships, like the one I have with Avery and my mom and brother. And when I thought you weren't able or willing to give me that... I couldn't bear to see you there month after month just going through the motions."

"And now? Do you think you can forge a meaningful relationship with me?"

Her fingers came up to touch his face. "I do. But only if you truly mean it."

"I've never meant anything more in my life."

He took her yoga mat out of her bag and laid it on the ground. Then he coaxed her to sit down next to him.

Daisies surrounded them. Beautiful. Meaningful. And Toby had done it all for her.

He kissed her. "I love you, Serena."

"I love you too, Toby. So very much."

His fingers sifted through her hair. "Can I come to the appointments again?"

"Yes. As long as you're serious about them not bothering you."

"I can't promise they won't affect me. But I imagine that's going to be in good ways from here on out."

"Does this mean I have to go jogging with you too?"

"Only if you want to."

She grinned. "I think I'm going to like it a whole lot better now."

"If they can't find John Doe's family, I'd like to unofficially adopt him as ours. To see that he gets a decent burial with a marker."

"I'd love that." She hesitated for a minute. "And I'd like to name our baby Faith. Because it's going to take a lot of faith to get us where we're going."

"Faith. I like that. But what if it's a boy?"

"We'll cross that bridge when we come to it. But we'll do it together."

He set his daisies down next to the mat and gently leaned in to kiss her. Her insides quivered as his lips skimmed over hers again and again. Thank God this was a private—

"Excuse me. Do you know where they moved the yoga class to?"

The voice caused them to shoot apart. Serena laughed when she saw the woman's befuddled glance as she looked around the space.

"I'll take you to it," Toby offered.

After going with Toby to lead the woman to the day's temporary yoga space, Serena smiled at the other people who were already working on their poses. Several of them stopped to clap when they saw her. One said, "Will you be joining us?"

"Not today, ladies. I've got some other things to do."

She glanced behind her to find that Toby had followed her over. "And they include this guy here. But I'll be back."

His brows went up, probably at her public acknowledgment of their relationship. But right now, she wanted the whole world to know. She loved him. And he'd said he loved her.

They left the yoga class to its own devices and wandered past the other spot hand in hand. "Oh, wait," she said. She zipped in and picked up her yoga mat and the one pot of daisies that Toby had been carrying.

"What's that for?"

"It's a memory of today. So that in the morning, I don't wake up and wonder if it really happened."

"You'll remember, Serena. Because I plan to wake up next to you tomorrow. And every other day. For the rest of our lives. If you'll let me."

"Oh, yes, I'll let you," she breathed. "I'll let you do that, and so much more."

This time when they kissed, it was a pledge that they would indeed be there for each other. And the promise that neither of them would ever have to be alone again.

EPILOGUE

SERENA'S MOM FIDDLED with her veil and then gave her a peck on the cheek. She then bent over to kiss the fluff of hair on the head that peeked out of the baby wrap carrier Serena had strapped to her chest.

She and Toby had decided they didn't need a traditional wedding—not all of it, anyway. So they'd opted to wait for Faith to be born and to make her a part of the ceremony. Instead of a maid of honor, Serena had asked Avery to be a *person* of honor instead. And her mother would walk her down the aisle.

It was perfect. Every little bit of it.

She and Toby had both had to make personal sacrifices to make their relationship work. He was fully committed to her and the baby—something he proved daily through his actions. And he claimed it was not a sacrifice at all. She and Toby had both gone through counseling and had learned to listen and communicate, to make sure they each had the other's best interests at heart. They were still learning. But it was working for them.

"Are you ready?" her mom asked.

"More than ready. We'd better do this while she's still sleeping."

Gracia adjusted the train of Serena's wedding gown

and snugged the baby a little more firmly in the white knit carrier that had been trimmed with some of the lace from her veil.

Then she opened the doors to the hospital chapel, and they stepped into the tiny anteroom.

Toby was at the front, looking dazzling in his black tux. He was accompanied by Paz Memorial's chaplain and Avery, and they were chatting with each other and hadn't yet seen her. A handful of friends and family, including his parents and Serena's brother, were scattered in the chapel's seating area, while daisies filled the space. It reminded her of when she'd arrived at yoga class to find he'd tucked pots of the flowers among the greenery, making it a place of wonder. And love.

Toby noticed her first.

Holding the baby against her with one arm and gripping her mom's hand with the other, they slowly made their way down the center of the chapel as the music played. Toby's incredible eyes locked on hers, and he mouthed *I love you* as they drew near. She smiled at him, happiness filling her to overflowing.

It was beautiful and small and serene, just like she'd wanted.

Arriving at the front, he came down the step to stand beside her, waiting there while Gracia kissed them both. Serena handed her daisy bouquet, made by her mom, to Avery, who nodded his approval.

"Do you have the rings?"

Avery reached in his pocket and withdrew two rings. One a solid black band and one in silver set with emeralds. While the chaplain read the words of their vows and waited as they each repeated them back to him, Serena could barely believe this was happening. But it was. She was the luckiest girl on the planet. She'd expected to have a baby and raise it on her own. She would have been grateful for just that. But she'd gotten so much more. She'd gained a partner who would make sure she didn't run this particular race on her own. He'd be right there with every footfall, through happiness and exhaustion, through frustration and joy. And Serena wouldn't have it any other way.

"By the power vested in me by the State of California, I pronounce you husband and wife. You may kiss each other."

Toby wrapped his arms around her and the baby and held them for a long, long time, whispering how happy she'd made him. How he hadn't known what he truly wanted in life until he'd almost lost it. Then, and only then, did he kiss her softly on the mouth, taking his time and making heat simmer in her belly.

Avery handed Serena's flowers back to Toby, since she didn't have enough hands to juggle everything, and they turned and faced their family and friends, who cheered and called for them to kiss again. Serena was happy to oblige, letting go of his hand so she could pull his head down. She put everything in that kiss—all of her love, hope and dreams.

They would quietly go back to Toby's apartment and feed Porkchop and start living the life they'd dreamed of. No honeymoon. They'd already kind of, sort of, had one of those in Mexico almost ten months ago. Right now, all they needed was each other.

Walking down the aisle, they were showered by rose petals from those in attendance. And Faith chose that moment to give a chirping cry, stirring in the carrier. Her blue eyes, so like her daddy's, blinked open, and she fixed her mommy with a look that said they didn't have much time. And feeding her in this gown might prove challenging.

It was okay. Life itself was challenging. But it was also good. So very good.

Serena planned to spend every day focusing on that. And Toby would be right there with her. Each and every day—as far into the future as she could see.

His arm tightened around her, and he swept her out of the chapel, out of the hospital and into the wide, wide world. Where anything was possible. And where love was everything.

* * * * *

NURSE WITH A BILLION DOLLAR SECRET

SCARLET WILSON

MILLS & BOON

This book is dedicated to my fellow nurses
all over the world, on International Nurses Day.

Thank you for the job that you do.

CHAPTER ONE

THE DAY WASN'T supposed to start out like this. It just wasn't. Dr Robyn Callaghan pushed her hair out of her face for around the twentieth time and wondered why the air-conditioned hospital seemed to be keeping everyone cool but her.

She could feel a horrible trickle down her spine as she climbed the stairs—two at a time—to answer her sixth page of the morning. Her breakfast/lunch was still sitting on the cafeteria table, next to her coffee. There hadn't been time to eat it. She'd need to remind herself about the solitary banana in her pocket whenever she finally got a minute.

She pushed open the doors to the cardiac floor and made it three steps before the arrest page sounded. No. Not again. She didn't even listen to the rest of the message.

She looked up as she heard the echo of a similar page nearby and started running to the coronary care unit. She'd already attended two arrests in the unit that morning.

A large guy barrelled out of the door to her left and almost straight into her. Thankfully, his broad frame was deceiving; this guy could move like a dancer, as he dodged around her and gave her a half-amused smile. 'Wrong way,' he said as the rest of the arrest message was repeated.

'Cardiac arrest. Main door, front entrance.'

Robyn nearly swore out loud. She spun around and darted after Mr Light-on-his-Feet as he disappeared through the door to the stairway. If the page had only gone off three minutes earlier, she would have saved herself a stair climb.

Her heart thudded as she tried to keep up with her athletic colleague. As he reached the ground floor he paused for a moment and held the door open for her.

'Thanks,' she breathed as she ran through and straight along the corridor to the main entrance. She could already see the commotion in front of them. A man in a suit was lying on the ground, a few people on their knees around him.

As she got closer she realised a nurse was already performing CPR on him. 'I'll get the cart,' she said, darting to the right, where the outpatient department was based.

The bright red emergency trolley was fully stocked and sitting directly outside one of the consulting rooms. Robyn grabbed it and ran back to the main entrance, her brain going into automatic pilot. She lifted the defibrillator from the trolley, peeling the labels from the two pads, and positioned herself above the person doing cardiac massage.

The nurse stopped massage for a few seconds, and opened the man's shirt, allowing Robyn to slap the pads onto his chest. It only took the machine a few seconds to read his heart rhythm.

The man from the cardiac unit grabbed a bag and mask from the cart, positioned it appropriately and started to bag air into the guy's lungs. It was clear from his colour he wasn't breathing for himself.

All eyes were fixed on the monitor. Two seconds later it went dead.

Robyn leaned over and gave it a knock. She'd never seen a defib turn itself off. The nurse in pale pink scrubs on the floor seemed stunned. But the guy—the dancer—in the green scrubs of the cardiac unit raised his eyebrows and got to his feet. 'First time for everything. I'll get another.'

He took off at a run, leaving Robyn and the outpatient nurse staring in dismay at each other. A little light flicked in Robyn's brain. If she told her medic friends this at a later date they would all shake their heads in horror. But Robyn refused to let panic anywhere near her. While a defib was now considered an essential part of a hospital's equipment, at some stage they hadn't existed. 'You bag, I'll do massage,' Robyn said to the nurse, hoping to kick-start her natural instincts again.

In an ideal world, she'd be trying to get venous access by inserting a cannula—but right now, that would have to wait. Come to think of it—where was the anaesthetist? There was usually one who responded swiftly to an arrest page, but, no matter how hard she strained her ears, she couldn't hear the sound of any other pairs of running feet.

One of the hospital porters came out of a nearby room, blinked twice, then leaned over. 'Shall I get you guys a trolley?'

They both nodded, Robyn as she started chest compressions, and the nurse, who inserted an airway and started bagging the patient.

'Do you know anything about this man?' Robyn asked the nurse.

She shook her head and gave a half-smile. 'I was just going on my break.' She glanced over her shoulder. The doors to Outpatients were closed behind her. 'They'll think I'm in the canteen.'

'Robyn Callaghan,' Robyn said quickly. 'Just started my cardiac rotation here.'

'Monica Garske,' said the nurse. 'Been in Outpatients

for twenty years and never had a cardiac arrest.' She smiled nervously.

A firm hand landed on her shoulder. 'And you're doing a great job.' The guy in the green scrubs dropped to his knees. He had another defib in his hands and swopped the pads over in a virtually seamless motion. He pressed the button on the machine as an older man appeared, slightly sweaty, and stared down at them. The anaesthetist had finally arrived.

'Tell me we can get this guy a little higher. I don't think my back can take it.'

'Don't worry, Joel,' said Mr Green Scrubs smoothly. 'Ardo is on his way with a trolley. I'll get him up for you.'

Robyn's eyes were on the monitor again. 'Ventricular fibrillation,' she said, perfectly in time with her green-scrubs-wearing counterpart. Their eyes locked for a moment and her breath caught somewhere at the back of her throat. He might have been kneeling next to her, but she hadn't really looked at him yet. Not properly.

And now was certainly not the time.

If she had the time, she might consider that the green of his scrubs definitely brought out the green in his eyes. His tanned skin and slightly longer dark hair made him resemble that Italian male model from years ago who had appeared out of water in very tight white trunks, advertising aftershave.

If she'd had the time, she might have lingered on all of that. But the human brain was amazing, and all that flitted through her mind in the literal blink of an eye.

'Charging,' she said, leaning forward, pressing the button and sweeping her gaze around. 'Clear, everyone.'

Hands were lifted and everyone stepped back. The man's body shuddered but the heart rate remained unchanged.

A trolley rolled next to them, and a plastic sliding mat appeared in the corner of her eye. Five seconds. That was all it took to slide the flexible plastic mat under the man and lift him up onto the trolley, the defib being lifted second and placed next to his chest.

'Clear,' Robyn said again, as if this were the most regular thing in the world. In an ideal world, she would have had the time to take him into a suitable room and do a proper assessment. But cardiac arrests were pesky. They didn't give anyone time. In fact, they were the direct enemy of time. And she knew the sooner they could shock him out of this rhythm, the better.

'Clear,' she said as she pressed the button again and electric charge was applied directly to the gelled pads on his chest.

Again, there was no response. She flicked the switch to turn up the joules. As she turned back she saw that the older anaesthetist was checking the patient's airway, and Mr Green Scrubs was tapping his arm, ready to slide a cannula in place to give them venous access. She might not know either of these individuals yet, but everyone clearly knew their job.

She waited the few seconds it took for the cannula to slide into the vein and be secured and tried not to be put out. Sometimes siting a cannula was a pain in the neck. Lots of patients had tricky veins, small and delicate, that would collapse as soon as anyone tried to get access. But her colleague had slid it into place as if it were the easiest thing in the world.

The defib showed it was ready and she checked again.

'Clear,' she announced, giving a nod when everyone had lifted their hands from the patient.

His body arched and after an ominous pause the heart tracing changed, giving a few spread-out beeps. Robyn held her breath. 'Sinus rhythm, bradycardic,' she said.

'ER or Coronary Care?' asked the anaesthetist.

'ER,' said Mr Green Scrubs, just as she said, 'Coronary Care.'

She stared at him, hard. She was the physician leading the crash team. This should be her call.

'No beds in Coronary Care,' he said with an apologetic smile. 'ER for now, and I'll go up and clear a bed for you once we have this man stabilised.'

He was annoying her now. 'And you are?'

There it was again. That tiny quirk of the eyebrow. She was being rude, and she knew it. But he hadn't introduced himself.

'Avery Smith, Coronary Care Unit.' He had a broad smile on his face. And it didn't help. Because this guy was more handsome than was healthy for a work environment.

'Robyn Callaghan, I'm your new doctor,' she said briskly.

A figure appeared next to her, pulling up the side rail and clipping it into place. 'ER it is,' said the porter and started wheeling the trolley.

Avery kept pace, automatically clipping his side rail into place and talking to the anaesthetist. 'Didn't think you had the page today, Joel.'

'I didn't, but Emmanuel's wife decided to go into early labour. He had to leave.'

Avery's face instantly creased. 'Gemma's okay, though? What is she—three weeks early?'

Joel gave him a knowing smile and nodded. 'You remember everything, and yes. There's no big problem, though. Her waters broke earlier, and she started to labour, so called Emmanuel to tell him she was heading in. I've never seen anyone happier.'

'So why the long face?' asked Avery. 'Did you really not want to carry the page that much?' His voice held a hint of teasing in it.

Joel shook his head. 'No, but it means I've lost the theatre wager on the baby's date of birth.'

Avery let out a laugh as the automatic doors to the ER opened and they rolled the trolley down towards the resus rooms. A harassed-looking woman with messy blonde hair frowned at them. 'What's this?'

Robyn bristled at the woman's tone, about to reply, but Avery got in there first. 'This…' he paused at the word, making a point, but in a much smoother way than she would have '…is a gentleman who had a cardiac arrest at the front door. I haven't managed to get his wallet out yet because we've had to shock him three times to get him back into sinus rhythm. Coronary Care is full, so could you give us some space so our doctor, Robyn—' he said her name as if they were best friends '—can stabilise our man, while I go up and free up a bed for him upstairs?'

The woman rolled her eyes and let out a sigh. 'Fine.' She gestured with her head sideways. 'In there. But don't be long. This place has been hectic all day.' She gave Robyn a stern glance. 'And I can't free you up a nurse.'

This time Robyn couldn't help herself. 'If he'd collapsed in the entrance way of your ER, could you have freed me up a nurse then?'

She could almost see the cogs and wheels of the woman's brain turning. Robyn's Scottish accent always got stronger when she was annoyed, and right now she was distinctly irritated. It took a few seconds for her counterpart to make sense of what she had said.

'Fine.' The woman turned to face Avery. 'But I need my room back in an hour.' She turned and headed out of the door.

'Is everyone here always this friendly?' muttered Robyn under her breath as her patient groaned. She moved forward and talked slowly. 'Hi there, I'm Robyn. You're at Leanora Paz Memorial Hospital. I'm one of the doctors. Do you remember anything at all?'

The man took a few moments, then shook his head, confusion all over his face. Avery moved into full charm mode on the other side of him. 'I'm Avery, one of the nursing staff. You're in the ER. Can I just check inside your jacket pocket? We want to get your name and details.'

The man gave a brief nod, and Avery slid his hand inside, pulling out a wallet he flipped open. 'Hal Delaney?'

The man gave another nod, and Avery turned the driver's licence to a colleague behind him to take some details. 'Can I let someone know you are here?'

Hal sighed, clearly still confused, and patted his trouser pockets. After a few seconds, he realised his shirt was wide open and there were pads on his chest. 'What happened…?' he asked.

Robyn wasn't happy. She wanted to look after her patient properly, and the noisy ER wasn't ideal. She gently peeled the defib pads from Hal's chest and put on some electrodes from a nearby cardiac monitor, fastening a blood-pressure cuff to his arm.

'Hal,' she said in a low voice. 'We need to have a chat. Your heart wasn't beating properly. You collapsed in the en-

trance way of the hospital. We had to give you some electric shocks.'

Hal's eyes widened. He looked terrified.

She kept her voice steady. 'Did you come here to visit
someone? Or did you come to the hospital because you
weren't feeling well?'

He shook his head. 'No,' he said. 'I had an appointment.'

'At Outpatients?' asked Robyn.

Hal shook his head again. 'With Mr Paz.'

It was only for a split second, but Robyn noticed it. Avery
froze. It was as if he'd been caught in a set of headlights.

Robyn was new here. But she knew the hospital had
been built as a memorial to the wife of a wealthy billionaire
businessman, who had died years earlier. The Paz surname
was apparently synonymous with wealth beyond measure
in the San Diego area. She was sure that the Mr Paz he was
meeting wasn't the original Mr Paz, but maybe it was his
son, or grandson?

She pretended not to notice Avery's frozen position and
turned to the nursing assistant behind her. 'Can you dial
up to the office of Mr Paz and let the secretary know that
Mr Delaney has taken unwell, and is currently in the ER?'

The nursing assistant beamed, delighted to have such an
important job. Avery, on the other hand, was doing his best
to look composed. 'I'll go and clear a bed for you upstairs,'
he said smoothly. 'I'll phone down when it's free and we
can arrange to transfer Mr Delaney upstairs.'

Robyn wanted to pay more attention to her brand-new
colleague's hasty departure. But her head was full of ECG
tracings, ordering blood tests, a possible chest X-ray, and
administering some medicines to Mr Delaney. Whatever
was going on with Avery would have to wait.

'Fine,' she murmured, averting her gaze back to dealing with her patient as Avery hurried off down the corridor. She ordered some tests, and sat down next to Hal, ready to take his history. Her stomach growled loudly, and she remembered the breakfast/lunch still at the cafeteria that she'd never get back to.

Hal was starting to get a little more colour in his cheeks now. He pressed a hand to his chest. 'Ouch,' he said. 'It's sore.'

Robyn nodded. 'Chest compressions. Don't worry—we'll check to make sure you have no broken ribs. You managed to catch everyone's attention today.' She clocked the blood-pressure reading on the monitor. It was surprisingly low.

'Have you been feeling unwell at all?'

She ran through the usual questions quickly, trying to build a picture as to why Hal had collapsed today inside the hospital entrance. Before she had a chance to complete her history-taking, a tall, broad-shouldered man appeared in the doorway, obviously not waiting for any kind of permission to enter. 'Hal, how are you?'

Robyn was a little taken aback. She stood swiftly. 'I'm afraid Mr Delaney isn't fit for visitors right now.'

It was as if she hadn't spoken at all. The man ignored her and walked around to clasp Hal's hand in both of his. 'This is a fine way to get out of a business meeting.'

'I'm sorry,' said Robyn quickly. 'But I'm in the middle of a consultation. You'll have to wait outside.'

The ER manager appeared in the doorway looking instantly flustered. He was usually as cool as a cucumber, but today was practically flapping.

He gave Robyn a quick anxious glance. She could tell he wasn't delighted that she was the doctor in the resus room.

'Jon,' she said stiffly, 'I've just resuscitated Mr Delaney at the front door. I need time to assess and treat him. Could you escort this visitor out, so I can take care of my patient?'

There was an uneasy silence. A long, long silence.

Jon gave a nervous laugh. 'Robyn, Dr Callaghan, let me introduce you to Mr Paz, our hospital chief executive.'

Robyn blinked. She nodded. 'Pleased to meet you. I'm sure you understand that, right now, it's essential I provide the best care to your friend. In order to do that, I need to take a full history, order some more tests and do a full assessment.'

She could swear Jon had just turned five shades paler than white. Mr Paz was clearly the main man around here. But she was a doctor. Should she just stop treating a patient to let a business friend interrupt what could be critical care? As the thought formed in her brain, her body moved automatically to get between Mr Paz and her patient. 'Why don't you let me call you back when I'm finished? As soon as our tests are completed and Mr Delaney is stable, we will be moving him up to the coronary care unit. I'm sure you can visit him there.'

There was a not so friendly smile on her face, and every muscle in her body was tensed.

It wasn't that Robyn didn't like rich people. It was just their sense of entitlement she didn't like. Growing up in a poverty-stricken part of Glasgow, Robyn had been luckier than most. She'd done well at school and had interviewed successfully enough to get a place at medical school. While the fees were covered, the food, lodgings and placements at hospitals around Scotland weren't. Some grants had helped, along with the biggest variety of part-time jobs. She'd delivered pizzas, worked in a nursing home, a supermarket, a library, a gym, and a bar.

She'd trained alongside some others from rich families. While she'd worked back-breaking hours over and above her studies and placements just to survive, they'd swanned around in their flash cars, showed off their apartments and all their latest technology. Robyn could have lived with all that.

What she hadn't liked—or stood for—was some of the entitled attitudes the rich had towards those less fortunate than themselves. It made her blood boil. So, any time she was around someone who was clearly richer than King Midas, it made her twitchy.

It hadn't helped that the one time she'd risked dating someone in the richer-than-rich category, it hadn't taken all that long to realise he wasn't with her because he actually wanted to have a relationship with her. He was there because she was smarter than him and could help him with his studies. Finding out he'd only been amusing himself with her, until he could find a wealthier replacement with better connections, who could help him with his longer-term career prospects, had been a bitter sting. It had made her resentment against inherited wealth and the entitlement of the richer classes, and her strong desire to work herself out of poverty, even stronger.

There was a good thing about being a stubborn Scots girl. She didn't feel obliged to fill the silence. She just let her words sit with Mr Paz. Robyn was also a master at staring out people. She'd learned that in her days as a steward at the football stadium for one of the two rival teams in Glasgow, when she'd had to deal with sometimes drunk, troublesome fans. It had stood her in good stead.

Jon coughed. It suddenly struck her that she might not be doing herself any favours. She was new here. She'd only met the head of the ER briefly in passing. She'd certainly never met the chief executive of the hospital.

'Mr Paz, shall we give Dr Callaghan some time to finish with your friend?' Jon suggested, breaking the standoff.

Mr Paz gave his friend's hand another squeeze. 'I'll see you upstairs, Hal, and I'll make sure our top cardiac physician takes care of you.' He gave Robyn a hard stare and left the room. Jon moved to follow but Robyn switched on a bright smile.

'Can you spare me a nurse? I've got a few things still to complete, and it will go quicker if I have someone familiar with everything.'

Jon looked as if he wanted to say a whole lot more, but his gaze fixed on Mr Paz's retreating back and he flinched. 'Fine,' he muttered as he walked out of the door.

Five hours later Robyn was knackered. She'd accompanied Hal up in the elevator, helped him transfer into the coronary care bed, given a rundown to his assigned nurse, and talked over the tests, results and findings with the stern-faced senior physician.

She'd done a good job. She always did. But she couldn't help wondering if she'd just done herself no favours in her new work environment.

By the time she headed out to the nursing station she could have easily sat in a chair and cried. That, or mugged someone for any single snippet of food they might have on their person.

She finished inputting some final details into a chart and looked around. Nurses' stations were usually a mecca for food. But this station was pristine. Not the usual ramshackle collection of half-chewed pens left by drug reps, or scraps of paper with indistinguishable notes. Not even a half-opened packet of biscuits. This was the poorest excuse for a nurses' station she'd ever visited.

Robyn sighed and walked towards the treatment room. She could hear the murmur of voices. 'We've got Dr Grumpy covering for us for the next six months.'

'Which one is Dr Grumpy?'

'The girl with red hair. She's Scottish. Pale skinned. I suppose she's pretty enough.'

Robyn stopped walking.

'So how did she earn the nickname of Dr Grumpy already? She hasn't been here long.'

'My friend works in the cath lab. She was apparently quite nervous when she started. Bumped a tray in the cath lab when observing an angiogram and put the whole procedure back. Apparently she's been walking about scowling ever since.'

'Who was doing the angio?'

'Raul Hempur.'

'Dracula? Oh, no. Making a mistake around him would be my worst nightmare.'

'Well, apparently it was hers.'

There was some laughter and a rustle of something that sounded suspiciously like a packet of sweets. Robyn had started to take a few backward steps, deciding it was definitely time to retreat, but just as she lifted her head Avery Smith came walking out of a patient's room.

This time it was Robyn's turn to freeze and cringe all at once.

This cannot be happening.

'Dr Callaghan? Everything okay?'

Humiliation for Beginners was not a class she intended attending today. She shook her head and strode forward into the treatment room and looked the three staff in the eye. 'Dr Grumpy at your service! I don't suppose you've got any food around here? Cafeteria's closed and I'm afraid I'm absolutely starving. I haven't eaten today yet.'

There it was again. The three brains having to process what she'd said, because she was annoyed so was speaking quicker, with a strong accent. This was going to get old very quickly.

She could sense Avery's presence at her back. Three sets of eyes were squirming in front of her as they finally deciphered what she'd said. One was a nurse, one a physio and one a cardiac tech. It was the tech that handed over a half-empty packet of sweets, with an apologetic shrug. 'Here you go.'

'Thanks. And it's Robyn, by the way.'

A light hand touched her shoulder. 'Why don't I show you where the staffroom is? You can have a seat for five minutes and take a break.'

She bristled, about to tell Avery Smith she didn't need a break. She knew he was trying to be a peacekeeper. But he added, 'We have a coffee machine,' and the magic words made her instantly more pliable.

She didn't look back at the other three staff, just made her way out of the door. 'I hope it's good coffee,' she said. He nodded and led her further down the corridor and into a medium-sized room with a small table and chairs, some cupboards, a sink, microwave, comfortable chairs and, yes, a coffee machine, which was bubbling and sending off delicious aromas in her direction.

Robyn didn't wait to be shown what to do. She'd been first a medical student, and then a doctor too long. She moved over, opened a cupboard to grab a mug, and poured herself some coffee from the jug. She reached into her pocket for some artificial sweetener, popped two in and stood back for a moment with the mug in her hands, just letting the smell drift around her. She closed her eyes and breathed.

She was aware of the silence and eventually opened her eyes again. Avery Smith was staring straight at her with an amused expression on his face. Now she was finally getting a chance to get a better look at this guy. If he could stare at her, she could stare at him.

He definitely looked like the brother of the aftershave model. His scrubs showcased his broad shoulders, sculpted chest and long limbs. But the clear green eyes were his most distinguishable feature. They were still staring at her.

'Sorry, was I supposed to pour you a cup too?'

He laughed and shook his head, ignoring her slightly sarcastic remark, and got himself a cup, pouring coffee and then reaching down into a refrigerator next to the sink. She'd missed that. He smelled the milk, checked the date, before pouring it into his mug. 'Milk?' he asked.

She couldn't help but finally smile. 'The familiar actions of someone who's worked in a hospital too long.' She held out her mug for him to add a splash of milk.

He tapped a sign on the front of the refrigerator. 'Some desperate soul actually put a note up here, trying to get people to put the freshest milk at the back of the fridge to make sure things rotated.'

Now Robyn laughed. 'Fool. Did they actually expect that to work?'

She reached into the packet of sweets—it was actually

chocolate-covered biscuits, but they would do—and pulled out two before flopping onto one of the old comfy chairs.

She took a sip of her coffee, a bite of one of the biscuits as her stomach grumbled loudly. Avery laughed as heat rushed into her cheeks.

She owned it, and patted her stomach. 'Haven't eaten properly since last night. I did buy food in the cafeteria earlier, but the arrest page went off before I had a chance to eat it.'

He gave her a curious look. 'How many times has that page gone today?'

She raised her eyebrows. 'Don't you know the rules? We don't talk about fight club.'

His smile broadened at her movie joke. In Robyn's experience, as soon as you talked about the arrest page, you cursed yourself, and it would usually go off in the next few minutes.

'I'll give you that one,' he agreed.

She took another bite of the biscuit. 'Six is the answer.'

'That many?' He sat forward. 'I took the page when I came on duty this morning. The arrest at the main door was my first.'

She frowned. 'I thought the nursing staff started at six?'

He sighed. 'We do. It's officially my day off. I'm supposed to be working at the free clinic in the heart of the city, but someone here called in sick.' He leaned back again. 'Or maybe they went home sick after so many calls.' He held up his hands. 'Who knows? I didn't really have time to ask. I'd just come on duty, saw the unit was full, and took the page before it went off.'

He settled back into the chair a bit more. 'And don't mind

what the others were saying back there. They give everyone nicknames.'

'Really? What's yours?'

He shifted, his comfortable chair obviously becoming uncomfortable—then pulled a face. 'Mr Sunshine,' he admitted.

She groaned and closed her eyes. 'You have got to be kidding me! So, you're Mr Sunshine, and I'm Dr Grumpy? No way.'

He waved his hand. 'You've just got here. They don't know you yet.'

She raised one eyebrow. 'Well, just wait until they know me. My nickname will be ten times worse than Dr Grumpy.' She wrinkled her nose. 'And who will cover your shift at the free clinic if you're here?'

He sipped his coffee. 'I swapped it with a friend. I'll work this Sunday instead. I wouldn't let them down. Now, tell me a bit about yourself. I love your accent.'

Robyn tried not to avert her gaze. She hated personal questions and tried to give away as little as possible about herself. 'You first,' she challenged.

He licked his lips for a second, then nodded. 'Well, I'm Avery Smith, I'm twenty-six. Trained as nurse. Born and brought up in San Diego. Chose to work in the cardiac unit because I just love everything about the science. I love the transplant work, the surgeries, the implantable defibs, the pacing wires, the management of the heart failure patients, the angiograms, the MI work.' He waved his hand. 'I could go on and on.'

She gave a small smile. 'So, it's where your heart is?'

'Exactly.' He grinned at her very poor joke. 'If you do a surgical rotation, you might meet my best friend. Serena

Dias works in Critical Care. We did our training together and shared an apartment for a while.' He gave a mild shake of his head. 'That was before, of course, she met the love of her life, Toby Renfro. He's one of the surgeons here, and they've just moved in together.'

'So, you've been left high and dry?' Robyn quipped.

He shrugged. 'You could say that.' He leaned forward, putting his elbows on his knees. 'Or you could say that I'm delighted that my best friend has found her happy ever after. She deserves it.'

'Sunshine by name, sunshine by nature? Do you ever get grumpy?'

He finished his coffee. 'I try not to. Life's too short. Now, don't think you're getting away with not telling me more about yourself. Play fair.'

Robyn forced a smile. 'So, I did my medical training in Glasgow, I was born and brought up there. Did my first year in a hospital in Aberdeen, then joined a new programme where you traded places with someone from another country, in an already established programme there.' She held up her hands. 'I ended up here.'

'You didn't choose here?' Avery seemed surprised.

'You only get to choose the country, not the actual hospital. I did a placement in Germany first, and this time in the US.'

She tried to work out the expression on his face. 'Most doctors or trainees who come here have gone through rigorous selection procedures. Paz Memorial is renowned for its cardiology department, its surgeons and its techniques. Some people try for years to get a job here,' he said.

The implication was clear. He didn't approve of her. She wasn't good enough. He might be Mr Sunshine for the rest of the world. But he didn't look remotely sunny from where Robyn was sitting.

'Like you?' she said, letting the sarcasm drip from her tone.

It was almost as if he'd switched off, being so focused on how elite this hospital was. 'Only a few from my nursing class were successful in getting jobs here.'

'Did you have to go through a rigorous selection process?' She was getting angry now. Was he doing this deliberately?

'Four interviews,' he said without hesitation.

She leaned forward, into a similar position as he'd adopted. 'And what makes you think for a second that I didn't?'

He blinked. She let him process that for a few seconds.

'The international programme had seventy thousand worldwide applicants. They picked one hundred.' She stood up. 'Sadly, I wasn't their number one pick, but I was the number two.' She watched his eyes widen at her statement. 'So, I more than earned my place here. But don't try and talk to me about selection processes. I've spent my life seeing how unfair some selection processes can be—unless, of course, you have a large bank balance.'

He blanched, then quickly stood up too. 'What's that supposed to mean?'

'I mean that often those from the wealthiest families get the best placements, or the settings that they want. It was certainly like that for me when I was back in medical school. The selection process for this programme was the first time I felt as if things were fundamentally fair. I actually had a fighting chance to be picked because of my scores and not my bank balance.'

Avery was looking at her with a deep frown in his forehead, as if he didn't quite know what to say to that.

The door opened and another nurse walked in, took one look at them both, turned on her heel and walked back out.

Robyn felt exasperated. She waved her hand. 'Might as well earn my new nickname.'

She watched as Avery took a few long, calming breaths, wondering what on earth she'd said that had set him off. He raised his eyes to hers. 'I think we got off on the wrong foot.' He put his hand on his chest. 'I love this place. I'm passionate about it. Paz Memorial has a great reputation and it matters to me—' he shook his head '—for reasons I can't really explain. I didn't know about your programme. Most doctors have to apply or specially request to continue their training here. Competition is tough.' He hesitated for a second, 'And I'm sure bank balance doesn't matter in the selection process. But I'm sorry, I didn't mean to sound defensive.'

'I think we did get off on the wrong foot,' replied Robyn quickly, turning his explanation over in her head. What reasons could he not explain? 'But then, you did abandon me down in the ER earlier.' She put her hands on her hips.

'I did not.'

'Oh, own it, Avery. As soon as that hospital CEO appeared, you practically broke the record for the four-minute mile. What was that all about?'

She saw something flash across his eyes. Anger? Annoyance? Fear? She couldn't quite put her finger on it.

'I did not,' he said defensively. 'I'd just started work and already knew the unit had no free space. The most useful thing I could do for you was to come up here and clear a bed for you, so Mr Delaney could get the expert care that he needs.'

'Sounds like you read that straight from the brochure,' she said sarcastically.

He shook his head.

'So, you really think the best thing you can do, the first time you meet a new doctor, carrying the arrest page, is to leave her in an unfamiliar environment, with staff she doesn't know, and procedures she's not used to?'

She saw his jaw clench. 'I might not have met you before, but I had no idea you'd never been inside the ER before. I'm not responsible for the induction of new staff. That should have been covered before you started. You should know all the procedures by now and you were with the head of the ER; you couldn't have been in better hands.'

Robyn hadn't moved her hands from her hips. Six months. That was how long she was going to be here. She wanted to learn everything that she could from all members of the team. Why did she have to get stuck with this guy? He was clearly a fake. Everyone else called him Mr Sunshine. But she wasn't fooled for a second.

Her back ached. She hadn't slept the last two nights because the room the hospital had given her backed onto the kitchens, where deliveries seemed to come all hours of the night. She was tired. She was still hungry. And some of the staff here were already talking about her snidely.

Robyn might excel at all things medical, but she readily admitted that her people skills were always a little trickier to negotiate.

She sighed. 'From my perspective, you practically raced out of the ER. You weren't even sure our patient was stable enough to leave. One thing you will learn about me, Avery, is that I call things the way I see them.'

He frowned and held out his arm. 'Did I clear a bed for you?'

She gritted her teeth but nodded.

'And is the cardiac unit the best place for Mr Delaney right now?'

She nodded again.

'Then, things have happened the way they should. You're imagining things. Maybe you're tired. Maybe you need to sit down, take a break, and get a proper meal. It's overwhelming coming to a new place. And as for the procedures, I can take some time to go over them with you if you want. All the staff here are willing to help our new doctors. All you have to do is ask.'

'It's hard to ask when they're too busy gossiping and name-calling.'

Avery drew in a deep breath, gave a conciliatory nod and lifted his left hand. 'You're right. I'm sorry about that. I'll talk to them. That's not the kind of unit that we run.'

He was being nice now. But it wasn't helping.

'I'm a big girl,' she said as she raised her chin. 'I don't need your pity.'

She turned and headed to the door, her stomach growling again. Her footsteps slowed and she reached back and picked up what was left of the chocolate biscuits, aware that his green eyes were still on her.

She gave a toss of her hair and walked out of the room, glancing at her watch and heading to the nurses' station. She was due off duty and she couldn't wait to hand over this page and get out of here.

Maybe coming to San Diego hadn't been such a good idea after all.

CHAPTER TWO

'YOU DID WHAT?' Serena threw back her head and laughed.

Avery groaned as he sipped his coffee. 'Stop, you're not helping. I can't remember ever making such a bad impression on someone before.'

'No, you're just used to charming your way around this place with a big grin on your face. She might have the nickname of grumpy, but maybe she's just the one girl that will make you work harder to prove yourself.'

He set down his spoon and stared at his friend. 'Why would you say something like that?'

Serena started dissecting the plum and apple she'd bought in the cafeteria. They were sitting outside the main eating area in the central courtyard—usually a suntrap, but today was warm but cloudy. It was away from the throng of the main cafeteria and offered a little more privacy, with tables and benches, a winding path, and plenty of greenery around.

She grinned at him. She hadn't even answered yet and he was already shaking his head. 'You're in that crazy-in-love stage. You want to imagine pairing up everyone round about you into couples and happy families. Believe me, our Scots girl is more likely to chase me with an axe than anything else.'

Serena leaned her head in one hand and looked a bit dreamy. 'There's nothing wrong with a bit of happiness.'

He gave a conciliatory nod. They'd shared an apartment for over three years. He knew Serena better than anyone, and he'd never seen her so happy since she'd got together with Toby.

'Guess what happened now you've moved out?'

'What?'

'The dishwasher broke. I swear it always worked perfectly for you, and never for me. Now that it knows you're gone—it's decided to go on strike.'

She laughed. 'You just don't talk nice to it, that's what's wrong.' Serena gave a wicked grin. 'But then it seems like you don't talk nice to other people too.'

Avery groaned and put his head in his hands. 'I tried my best.' He took a deep breath. 'It didn't help that the patient we'd resuscitated had a special visitor in the ER.'

Serena took a bite of her plum. 'Oh, who?'

'Leo Paz.'

She stopped chewing, her eyes widening. 'No.'

'Yes.'

'Did your uncle recognise you?'

'He didn't get a chance. I was out of there in a flash— another reason Robyn was sore at me. She accused me of abandoning her.'

'Well, did you?'

Avery cringed and looked upwards. 'No, yes, maybe....'

'Mr Paz.' Serena shook her head. 'I have never seen him the whole time I've been here.'

'Neither have I. Or, at least, I hadn't.'

Serena gave him a curious look. 'What do you think he would have said to you if he had recognised you?'

Avery actually felt sick. 'I don't know. There was such bad blood between him and my mother. If she were still alive, I definitely wouldn't be working here. She would have hated it.'

'I'm not sure she would. Your mother had a good relationship with your grandparents. It's only her siblings that caused trouble.'

Avery smiled. 'Well, she did go out and fall pregnant to a married man. Scandalous behaviour. My uncle told her that every time he saw her.'

'But, at the end of the day, it was none of his business. You always said your grandparents never said a bad word about your father. It was just a shame that he died when you were so young.'

Avery sighed. 'Money and families complicate everything.' He held up his hands. 'Part of this place is mine since my mother died. But I keep myself hidden for a reason. The rest of the family know I exist, but they have no idea I'm still in San Diego, or that I'm a nurse.'

Serena put her hand over Avery's. 'But your mom had such good care at this hospital. Doesn't working here ever stir up memories for you?'

He looked off into the distance. 'Yes, and no. I'm never in the cancer unit, and her sudden onset leukaemia came on so quickly.' He sighed. 'There are still some things we can't cure. And we all have to live with that. But working here—for me—it helps me honour the memory of my grandparents and mother. My uncle didn't take over as CEO until after my mother died, and I was still young then. I always guessed he just bullied his way into it, like he did with other things in life. Changing my name and keeping away from my uncles and aunts was done at my attorney's advice. He didn't want me to work here. He thought it was too risky. But the last time my uncle saw me I was a young teenager.

He certainly wasn't around when my mother got sick, and she was furious at the way her brother steamrollered the rest of the family over the running of the hospital. She didn't want me to have to deal with any of that. She wanted me to be free of all the family drama.'

Serena bit her lip. 'But you trained as a nurse for a reason. You love cardiology. It's natural you want to work in the place that's renowned the world over.' She took a drink from her water bottle. 'It's not your fault this place is named after your grandmother. Maybe if your grandfather was still alive, things would be different.'

He rolled his eyes. 'If my grandfather was still alive, he would be over a hundred.'

Serena gave a soft smile. 'We've had hundred-year-old patients before.' She reached her hand over and squeezed Avery's. 'You've always known that at some point your colleagues might find out your name is Paz and not Smith. There's still a chance you will run into your uncle and he'll recognise you. You need to have a contingency plan in place.'

He finished his coffee. 'Well, I guess I've just ruled running away to Scotland out of the equation. What about France? Or Hawaii? I've always wanted to work there.'

'Are you purposely picking places I'll need to fly to with a baby if I want to visit?'

'You'll be visiting me?

'*We'll* be visiting you. Me, baby and Toby. Stop trying to get away from us. You will still be required to be our babysitter on occasion. No matter where you try to go to.'

Avery squeezed her hand back. 'And I'll be honoured. But in the first instance, I need to try and make up with my department's new doctor.'

Serena frowned. 'Just how grumpy is she?'

He held his hand out and wiggled it. 'I'm not sure. Is she even grumpy? Or is she just bolshie? If what she told me about her selection process is true, then she must be a very good doctor. I think she might just be a straight talker.' He ran his fingers through his dark hair. 'My trouble is, when she starts talking quickly, I struggle to catch everything she says—her accent is really strong—and somehow I know that's not going to help matters.'

'Well, you know how to solve that one, don't you?'

He shook his head, leaning over, grabbing her apple and taking a bite. 'No, how?'

'Hoi.' She slapped his hand away from her apple. 'Stay away from a pregnant woman's food. You're taking your life into your hands here.' She fixed him with a hard stare. 'We're talking about this new doctor quite a lot. What does she look like?'

'What does that have to do with anything?'

'Interesting,' said Serena, looking amused. 'Instantly defensive. Now, tell me what she looks like.'

He made a throwaway gesture with his hand. 'Red hair, but more the brown kind than the ginger kind. Blue eyes. About the same size as yourself.' He rolled his eyes. 'Without the pregnant stomach.' Then he looked thoughtful. 'Or maybe she does have one. But if she does—it's not obvious.'

Serena tilted her head. 'That's a lot of detail. You noticed her eye colour? I'm impressed. And the particular shade of red her hair is? What's happened to you?'

Avery was indignant. 'I'm a nurse. I'm meant to be observant. Have you forgotten that?'

The smile that spread across Serena's face made him want to rapidly change the subject. He knew she would spend the rest of the time teasing him. She tapped her fingers on the table. 'I think it's something else.' Her words had that kind of sing-song tone and he groaned and held up his hand.

'Stop. Let's go back. How do I solve the problem with the accent?'

'Oh, that's easy. The way to get used to her accent is to be around her more. It's simple. You'll get used to it. Just make sure that you spend as much time with her as possible. Oh, and *don't* make her mad.'

'Oh, I don't intend to. Remember that phrase—what was it? *You wouldn't like me when I'm angry.* Said by everybody's favourite green superhero. I think that might apply to her too.'

'You're tough on her,' said Serena with interest. 'Does Mr Sunshine want to spread some of his bright light?'

Avery shook his head at his nickname. 'I can't help the fact I'm a happy individual,' he said. 'My mother says I was born smiling.'

Serena put her hand on her small stomach. 'Well, feel free to spread the sunshine to this one. I would love a happy baby.'

They sat in comfortable silence for a few moments, Avery's mind going back to the recent events with Robyn.

After a few minutes he leaned back from the table, stretching out his back and arms. They were aching. The hospital seemed to be going through a spell of cardiac arrests. Dealing with prolonged arrests was tiring for all involved. 'Six,' he murmured.

'Six what?'

'Arrest calls. That's how many Robyn dealt with on her first shift.'

'No way. What on earth was happening?'

'I don't know.'

'Well, surely that would make anyone grumpy?' Serena looked quite indignant.

'Why do I get the feeling you're going to be *#Team-Robyn*?'

'Because I'm just naturally *#TeamGirl*. But imagine having a day like that, getting deserted in the ER, then going upstairs and hearing the petty nickname you've been given. If it had been me, I would have been wearing the Dr Grumpy nickname with pride.'

Avery let out a slow breath. 'I get it. Plus, it's a new city, a new hospital.' He leaned his head on his hand. 'And I really didn't help things. I was on edge when I saw my uncle and then I think I might have misinterpreted something that she said, and that made me even more defensive.'

Serena took a breath. 'I meant what I said about you needing a contingency plan for if the truth comes out. Particularly if there's a chance you might run into your uncle again.'

Avery sighed. 'I know it. I'm an adult, not a young teenager any more. And I have a stake here—financial and emotional—in this place that I love.' He looked around the courtyard. 'I just don't know if I'm ready to reveal myself. Ready to step up to being a Paz.'

Serena pressed her hand into his shoulder. 'Well, I can't tell you how to deal with your family. But I can give you a hint about Robyn.'

'Go on, then.'

'You need to buy her dessert. Cake. Chocolate. Candies. What do they eat in Scotland?'

'I don't know.'

Serena stood up. 'Well, find out. It's time to start making amends with Dr Grumpy.'

* * *

Robyn had spent the last hour trying not to cry. She wouldn't. She just wouldn't. But every time the noisy delivery trucks broke her sleep again, her mind drifted back to a few days ago and the staff in the cardiac unit gossiping about her. As for the disagreement with Avery Smith, her brain wouldn't even let her go there.

She'd messaged her friend, Genevieve, who was working back in Scotland. Ginny always had her back—no matter what else was going on—and Robyn was grateful for the support.

Her placement in Germany had been easier than this. At least she could sleep there. The hospital had put everyone up in studio flats, a five-minute walk from the hospital. All the other doctors had started on the same day as her, and there was a certain camaraderie when everyone learned at the same time.

Here—she'd started a few weeks later than the others due to a mix-up with her working visa. It had been an admin error by the hospital, and Robyn wasn't penalised for it. But it meant the others had already made friends, scored the best rooms, and found their way around the city.

As the beep-beep of yet another van backing up started to sound, she finally gave up on sleep and flung the pillow she'd had over her head away. Nothing could deaden the noise around her. She wasn't even supposed to be working until later.

She showered and grabbed some clothes, tying her long hair up. She had no idea where she was going, but maybe if she went for a jog she could familiarise herself with the city and grab some breakfast.

Paz Memorial wasn't quite on the waterfront of the bay,

but it was close enough for Robyn to see the naval boats and head in that direction. It wasn't even six a.m., but she could see a number of early-morning joggers running along the edge of the marina. The paved path was broad and the morning was light and bright. Robyn took it easy, only covering a couple of kilometres before changing direction to run through some of the streets. The Gaslamp district was nearby and Robyn was relieved to see some of the stores were already open. It didn't take her long to inhale the scents of a bakery and join the short line outside. After the last few days she didn't hesitate in ordering two of the wonderful-smelling coffees and three of the mini pastries.

By the time she finished the five-minute walk back to the hospital, one of the coffees was finished, and the three mini pastries were gone. Like all hospitals, Paz Memorial was never quiet. As she walked back through the glass-fronted lobby there were a number of staff all arriving for their shifts. She didn't recognise any of them.

Her heart gave a little pang. This was a big place. With over six hundred beds, and designated Level Two trauma centre for the area. She knew there would be a myriad people working here, would she even have time to make friends?

She paused for a moment, watching the world go by. Her room was too small to spread out comfortably. She'd shower again and head for the library. There were plenty of procedures and protocols she could study before reporting for duty. She might even take a look at some of the listings for apartments nearby. The hospital admin staff were usually good at pointing new staff in the right direction—steering them away from any undesirable areas, or places where transport could be an issue.

Feeling a little more heartened, she turned around and

took a step—just as someone collided with her. Her coffee shot up into the air, then down all around her. Robyn let out a gasp as the other person dropped a large white box on the floor with an ominous splat.

'Sorry,' she breathed quickly as the now not so hot coffee dripped from her running gear.

A mild expletive came from the person next to her. Avery Smith had been wearing a white shirt and blue jeans. She doubted that shirt would ever be white again.

Not only had he been doused in coffee, he also had an interesting array of bright red, brown and pink splotches decorating his shirt. She tilted her head. 'What on earth were you carrying?' she asked.

'Dessert,' he said glumly as he picked up the barely together white box and lifted the lid.

Robyn peered inside. 'Yikes.' The jam doughnuts had exploded, and the apple pie had merged into the chocolate cake. 'Is it someone's birthday?'

He shook his head. 'I was just bringing in some cakes.' He hesitated for a brief second. 'I do that sometimes.'

There was something about the way he said it that was off. She didn't doubt he sometimes brought in cakes for his colleagues, but for some reason she didn't quite believe him.

He held up the box again. 'How about we find some cutlery and just eat what's left?'

Robyn shook her head. 'No. Not for me, thanks. I just had breakfast and am heading to the library before I'm on duty.' She pulled a face. 'Sorry about your clothes.'

Avery shook his head. 'It's fine. I need to put on a uniform anyway.' He gave a small smile at the mangled box. 'See you in the unit later.' There was something resigned about his tone. Was he sorry she was working today? Maybe he didn't want to work with her at all.

Robyn felt instantly defensive. Every part of her prickly. She couldn't find any other words, so she just turned and walked away.

Just over an hour later, Avery was still trying to find a way to make amends with Robyn. In theory, she should also now be trying to make amends with him, but somehow he knew her brain didn't work that way. The doughnuts had been a bust. He couldn't even admit he'd been bringing them in for her as way of an apology—it had just seemed stupid at the time. So now he was back to square one.

He'd walked through the whole unit twice. The cardiac beds, the day beds, the intensive cardiac care unit, the angiograph unit, and the cardiac rehab dept. Robyn was nowhere.

'Anyone know where our new doc is?' he asked a few of the staff at the nurses' station.

'Dr Grumpy?' asked one of the physios.

'Dr Callaghan,' Avery said pointedly.

But this point was lost on the physio. 'She's down in the ER seeing a teenager with potential cardiac issues. I don't think the paediatrician wanted to admit him, but she's having none of it. Last I heard she was trying to page Dr Anker to back her up.'

'Dr Anker?' Avery's eyebrows shot upwards. He let out a groan. Everyone knew that he was the most difficult of their consultants. 'Why would she pick him?'

'Because she has a penchant for tragedy?' suggested the physio, with a shrug.

Of course, he went down to the ER. He didn't even pretend it was for any other reason than to help out their new doctor. One person nodded in solidarity, but another rolled their eyes.

The ER was strangely chaotic for the middle of the week. He saw a nurse colleague and went up alongside him. 'Michael, is there a party and you didn't tell me?'

Michael was loading supplies into his own arms. He turned and automatically loaded some into Avery's. 'We've got a pile-up on the freeway plus a nursing home with norovirus. A medical doctor and an ER doctor off sick, and referrals backed way up. You here to help?'

'I was here to find my new doctor.' He started walking alongside Michael, to wherever the supplies were needed. 'But I can call upstairs and tell them you need some help for an hour.'

Michael nodded. 'Great. Your girl is in cubicle seven with a kid. Her and the paediatrician have fallen out.' He gave Avery a sideways glance. 'I like her. She's smart. She's also offered to see a few patients for us. Didn't hesitate to throw her hat into the ring. Not like other disciplines I can mention.' He scowled at one of the surgical doctors who was practically sprinting out of the department.

He ducked behind some curtains, dumped his supplies and motioned to Avery to put his on a nearby trolley. 'Help is appreciated. Go to the whiteboard and take anything that seems reasonable to you. Shout if you need help.'

Avery swallowed. He was always happy to help, but was aware of his own limitations. He was relatively newly qualified. Most people who worked down in the pit—as they called the ER—had a few years under their belt. But Avery knew he could see a few patients. The elderly with norovirus would likely be dehydrated. He could draw bloods, give anti-emetics, put up IV lines and keep them comfortable.

Cardiac patients were his speciality, but Avery was always prepared to help out when things were busy. And apparently so was Robyn.

He was a little intrigued. The fleeing surgeon was not unique. Once most doctors moved to their specialist areas, they didn't like to cross into any other territory.

He moved over to cubicle seven. He could hear Robyn's Scottish accent immediately. He moved his head to see through the gap in the curtains. She'd obviously changed out of her running clothes from earlier and was wearing a knee-length shirt-style red dress, belted at the waist, and flat black shoes. The colour surprised him, but looked good on her. His brain instantly told him that it was ridiculous to think people with red hair wouldn't wear red clothes. Her hair was pulled back from her face with a black headband. Her traditional white coat was nowhere in sight.

She was pointing to the screen of the ultrasound machine. 'This shows the flow of blood through your heart.' He could see exactly what she was focusing on—one of the heart valves.

'Tell me exactly when you've felt short of breath,' she asked the young man.

He squirmed a little. 'I've put on some weight. I'm not sure why. I'm still playing basketball. But I just don't have the same energy. I feel short of breath after ten minutes of play.'

Robyn spoke. 'You can come in,' she said in a low voice without turning her head from her patient.

Avery gave a small start—embarrassed that she'd realised he was there. He stepped in through the curtains and gave a nod to the young man. 'Hi there, I'm Avery Smith, one of the nurses from the cardiac unit.' He turned to Robyn. 'I came down from the unit to see if you needed any help.'

She gave him a slightly nervous smile. 'I paged Dr Anker. Can you check if he's answered and he's on his way?'

Avery nodded and headed back out to the nurses' station, in time to see Dr Anker—in his golf clothes—walking from the opposite direction. He'd seen this irritated face on a few occasions. Dr Anker was a good cardiologist, but was an older man, and there was no getting away from the fact he could be chauvinistic at times.

He nodded at Avery. 'Good, finally someone with sense. Did you tell her she shouldn't page me?'

Avery straightened up. 'Actually, I think you'll be interested in the patient. He looks as if he has valve disease. It's a good catch by our new doctor.'

Dr Anker gave Avery a hard stare for a few moments. Avery could swear he could almost hear the man's brain ticking.

Avery was sure about what he'd seen on the screen in the cubicle—just as he was sure Robyn had been. She'd been right to argue with Paediatrics about not discharging this young man.

Dr Anker drew in a deep breath and gave a nod. 'In that case, let me see.'

Avery led him down the corridor. As they approached they could hear Robyn talking to someone else. 'Was Simon ever sick as a child?' she was asking.

Dr Anker drew back the curtain and frowned. Robyn was video-calling an adult on a phone. Avery guessed it was Simon's mom.

She waited until she got an affirmative reply, then turned at the noise. Her cheeks flushed, and Avery could see her starting to get nervous. She handed over an electronic chart to Dr Anker.

'Simon, this is Dr Anker, the specialist doctor I told you I'd called. He'll check you over and will likely want to talk to your mom too.'

Dr Anker was already flicking through the electronic report. 'Chest X-ray, blood work, ECG.' He looked up sharply. 'Where's his echocardiogram?'

'I've just completed it,' Robyn said quickly. 'I've not reported it yet, but the recording is here for you to view.'

Dr Anker pulled his stethoscope from his neck. 'In a second.' His slightly gruff manner disappeared and he turned to his patient, an old-time charm appearing. Within a few minutes he'd listened to Simon's heart, lungs and reviewed his echocardiogram, before going on to ask Robyn to call Simon's mother back.

Avery gave Robyn a reassuring smile. Was that a slight tremor in her hand?

She'd done everything right. She shouldn't be worried at all.

Dr Anker turned to her, as if he'd read Avery's mind. 'Good catch, Dr Callaghan. I can see that the other doctor was prepared to send Simon home without carrying out so many investigations. Cardiac conditions can easily be missed in teenagers.'

He turned on a dazzling smile to Simon's mother. 'You're on your way in? Good. I'm going to arrange for Simon to come upstairs to our specialist unit. I have some staff who specialise in teenagers and I'll assign one of them to Simon's care.'

He made a few scrawls with an electronic pen on Simon's chart, then gave a few other brief instructions.

Robyn stepped outside after Dr Anker to get some final details and scribble some quick notes. Dr Anker disappeared fairly quickly and Avery looked at Robyn. 'Paeds really wanted to discharge him?'

She nodded. 'They said the shortness of breath was due to his weight.'

Avery tried not to look surprised. 'Wow. They didn't look past that? They didn't consider anything else?'

She shook her head. 'I came down for something else and just heard them chatting about Simon. His report of his sudden weight gain seemed odd to me. As was his sudden shortness of breath.' She lowered her voice. 'I didn't get as much time as I'd have liked on his echocardiogram, but his heart valve is diseased. I'm guessing undiagnosed rheumatic fever.'

Avery nodded. 'I think you're right. We've had a few adults in their mid-twenties with rheumatic fever in the unit.'

Robyn seemed to be calming down. 'Okay,' she said, as if she was reassuring herself. She closed her eyes for a second. 'Everyone told me not to page Dr Anker. But it was the only way I could persuade the ER doc that Simon should stay. As for the paediatrician, I don't think he'll talk to me again.'

'Don't worry about that,' said Avery. 'You did a good job.'

She nodded her head then looked at Avery for a moment and finally smiled. 'Thank you,' she said. 'I'll call up to the unit to arrange to transfer Simon up. Unless you can take him?'

He went to answer but she jumped back in. 'Sorry, I didn't mean it like that. I'd take him up myself, but I said I'd stay and give them a hand down here.'

He gave her a smile. 'Me too.'

'Oh.' She looked surprised, and then almost laughed and shook her head. 'I'll make that call, then.'

Avery was painfully aware of where Robyn was for the next few hours. Every flash of red hair or red dress seemed to imprint on his brain. She was like the ultimate distraction and he couldn't entirely work out why. One hour inevitably turned into two, then almost three.

He looked after seven elderly patients from the care home, all dehydrated, some confused, but he took bloods, a history where he could, put up IV lines, and rolled endless commodes in and out of the cubicle curtains. Norovirus was never pleasant, and was highly infectious. Avery was careful to ensure he wore protective clothing and equipment that he changed between every patient. It was hot and uncomfortable down in the ER, and the protective equipment made that even worse. He found water jugs and glasses for all seven of the older patients and took the time to make sure they were all sipping water on a regular basis.

As he was finishing all his notes one of the elderly women started to cry out. She reached towards Avery. 'Paul,' she murmured. 'Paul, where have you been?' Her voice was weak and crackly. Avery knew she was confused by the dehydration, and by the urinary tract infection she also had. He sat down next to her, lifting a glass with water, and putting in a straw and holding it up to her mouth.

'I'm here now,' he said quietly. 'Take a sip of water.'

She obeyed and settled down, holding one of his hands and stroking it. Avery knew it would only cause her more distress if he told her he wasn't the Paul she thought he was. So, he sat with her and talked softly. Listening to her stories and nodding in agreement. After a while she laid her head back on the pillow and went to sleep.

At one point, he thought he saw a flash of a red dress again and wondered if Robyn had finished with her patient. But he didn't want to move from his position until he was sure that his elderly lady was completely asleep. Avery took another few moments, going back around checking all the other patients he'd looked after, making sure they were comfortable. By the time he'd finished all the charting, Michael appeared behind him.

'You've been an angel today,' he said quickly. 'I can't tell you how much I appreciate it. A lot of people would have been reluctant to help—particularly with anything that can be infectious.'

Avery held up his hands. 'All of them are really quite sick. I was happy to help. Is there anything else you want me to do?'

Michael shook his head. 'We've taken enough of your time. Your doctor too—she's been amazing. She can certainly fly through the patients, can't she?'

Avery's skin prickled a little. Some people would see that as a compliment. But others? They might see it as a sign of shoddy or careless work.

'I'll just go and check on her,' he said distractedly, his eyes going to the whiteboard to see which patient she was examining.

As he walked along the corridor towards her, things immediately got more complicated. She was talking to a disdainful-looking young man, a notebook in hand, a stethoscope around his neck, and a pristine white coat. A clear sign of a medical student. There was something about him that Avery couldn't quite put his finger on. He gave the student a nod as he approached. 'Avery Smith,' he said as introduction.

The student gave him a half-hearted glance but didn't reply. Robyn continued. 'Let's go over the details again.'

The medical student appeared confident. 'The ER manager told us that around thirty per cent of people who attend shouldn't be at an ER. It costs millions of dollars every year. We need to filter them out.'

Avery saw Robyn's eyes light up with interest. 'Go on,' she said. There was something in her voice, in the tone, that the medical student didn't catch. But Avery did. He wanted to warn the young man to tread very carefully. But it was already too late.

'I checked over Mr Runo's symptoms. They were vague. He just said he didn't feel right. His right eyelid was a little droopy. But it wasn't pronounced. He had full movement in his right hand, arm and leg. Nothing to indicate he'd had a stroke, or even a trans ischaemic attack. His blood pressure and heart rate were both slightly raised, but not clinically worrying. He said something about his face not sweating— but how could he even know that? There's air conditioning in the ER. There was no confusion. He's orientated to time and place. No headache, no nausea. No signs of anything else. It all just seemed—' he threw up his hands '—a whole lot of nothing.'

Avery was already reaching into his pocket for his pen torch as Robyn spoke the very telling words. 'Were his pupils equal and reactive?' She made the question sound normal.

The student looked momentarily surprised. He patted his pockets, clearly realising he didn't have a pen torch. Avery handed over his own. 'I didn't check,' said the student.

'Could you check now?' asked Robyn. The edge to her voice was becoming very distinct.

The student disappeared behind the set of curtains. Avery gave Robyn a careful glance. 'We were all students once,' he said quietly.

'Were we all complete tools too?' she replied.

Avery frowned, trying to make sense of the words. 'So, in Scotland, if someone is a "tool"—that means?'

'Insert the word of your choice,' she said briskly. 'Fool. Prat. Imbecile.'

Avery held up his hand. 'Tough crowd.'

Robyn stared impatiently at the curtains, waiting for the student to emerge again. 'What are you doing here anyway?'

'I came to see if you needed a hand with anything,' he said, giving her a bright smile. 'You know, after you told me I abandoned you here the last time.' He looked at the curtains too. 'But it seems as if I should stay as a protective shield for the medical student whose name I don't even know yet.'

Robyn gave him a dirty look. 'I've waited long enough.' She swept the curtains aside and stepped inside the cubicle.

'How are Mr Runo's eyes?' she asked.

The student turned round. His earlier cocky demeanour had vanished. He wasn't looking quite so confident now. It was clear he was feeling defensive.

'Well, it's hard to tell. But one of his pupils might be slightly constricted.'

'I see. Can you think of any conditions that you can link the symptoms to that you've found today?'

He blinked. His opened then closed his mouth as if trying to find an answer, but he shook his head. 'Nothing seems clear enough to make a definitive diagnosis.'

Avery saw something flash across her eyes. She took a deep

breath and pulled her own pen torch out of her pocket. 'Watch, and learn,' she said as she walked through the curtains.

Avery followed after the student. He couldn't fault Robyn's handling of Mr Runo. She was pleasant and professional. She asked questions without causing alarm, specifying symptoms and their length, and gathering as much history as she could. Once she'd examined Mr Runo herself, she sat in a chair at the edge of the bed.

'Mr Runo, you've got a fairly unusual condition. It has a couple of names. One is Horner's Syndrome, the other is oculo-sympathetic paresis.' She gave him a smile. 'Yes, I know, it's a confusing name. What it really means is that one of the nerves that feeds into your face is being affected somehow. That's why your eyelid is drooping, your pupil is constricted, and you're not sweating on one side of your face.' She took out a mirror and gave him a few moments to look at his own pupil. 'I'm glad you came in today,' she said reassuringly. 'My job, as your doctor, is to carry out some tests to find out why your nerve is affected. Once we know, we can look at getting some treatment for you.'

She gave him a gentle pat on the hand. 'You'll need to stay a few days. Can we contact someone for you?'

Avery whipped out a pen and took a note of the name and number Mr Runo said while Robyn kept talking.

They left the cubicle a few minutes later and Robyn walked the student into one of the nearby treatment rooms. 'Tell me what you know about Horner's Syndrome.'

'Never heard of it,' said the student bluntly. 'Just know what you said to the patient.'

Robyn nodded her head slowly. 'What do you think could cause an issue with a facial nerve, then?'

'A disc problem. Swelling. An injury.' It was clear he was

grasping at straws. 'It seems minor. The symptoms were difficult to spot.'

Avery felt his stomach clench. Paz Memorial was a renowned teaching hospital. They were used to students here—from all disciplines. Most were keen, pleasant and anxious to learn. Only occasionally did they get a few that were on the arrogant side who secretly thought they knew best. And weren't particularly prepared to learn. Avery could also sense an element of chauvinism from this student. His body language towards Robyn was causing small alarm bells to ring for Avery. He clearly didn't like being taught by a woman.

Avery might only have been around Robyn a few days, but he knew this was unlikely to end well—not with this straight-talking doctor.

'Let's be really clear,' she said, her accent strong. 'You potentially could have sent Mr Runo home. If you had, you should know that his Horner's Syndrome could be caused by a variety of tumours, a carotid artery dissection, or encephalitis—to name just a few.' She held up the electronic chart. 'If you had, the physical findings that you recorded, but missed the importance of, could have caused you to spend a long time in court, and risk the medical licence you are hoping to gain.'

Silence. Avery was thankful.

'Who is your supervisor?'

'You're only covering down here. I shouldn't even be working alongside you.' The words were spat out with unhidden indignance. Avery winced.

Robyn held up her hand. 'Stop. Now.' Her voice was very firm, very clear.

'I was going to suggest to your supervisor that you use

Mr Runo as one of your patient cases and follow through on his investigations and treatment. Horner's Syndrome is rare. There is much to learn here. Most of your student colleagues would have been jealous that you've seen a case and, potentially, got to write it up as one of your learning achievements.' She put one hand on her hip. 'But it seems I'll be having an alternative conversation with your supervisor about your attitude.'

The medical student seemed to realise his mistake. But instead of immediately apologising, he maintained his superior demeanour and shook his head. 'Robyn,' he said condescendingly, as if he actually knew her, 'I think you've misunderstood.'

Avery stepped between the two. 'I don't think there has been any misunderstanding. In order to do well at Paz Memorial, you have to want to learn—and you have to show respect to your patients, and your colleagues. It's time for you to stop talking. Go to the library. You have some reading to do. I'll speak to the ER manager and let him know where you are.'

The disdain on the student's face was clear. 'You can't tell me what to do. You're just a *nurse*.' He spat the word out as if it were unpleasant.

Avery kept calm. He'd dealt with angry patients and relatives in the past—they didn't faze him. He'd also dealt with similar students. Sometimes arrogance was a front. Sometimes people who seemed disdainful were anxious, or worried. Avery was always painfully aware he didn't know what lives people lived away from the hospital. And yet he couldn't shake the feeling of just…something familiar about this student.

The student was clutching his ID badge in his hand but

Avery couldn't make out the name. 'You need to leave,' Avery said firmly. He was at least four inches taller than the student, and while he'd never use his size to intimidate someone, it also didn't hurt that he went to the gym a few times a week.

The student turned abruptly and strode down the corridor. There was purpose to his steps. 'He's going to complain about us,' said Avery matter-of-factly.

'He'll have to be fast to beat me,' said Robyn. She turned on her heel, striding down the corridor to the ER manager's office.

She knocked once and entered. The timing could be better. Last thing a manager wanted to hear when a place was extremely busy was that they had a student who could be trouble.

Avery waited outside. He wasn't the type to get involved in any kind of pile-on, but he would support a colleague if asked to give his version of events.

He could hear low voices inside. Two minutes later Jon stuck his head out of the door, starting when he saw Avery waiting. 'Perfect, you're still here, Avery—did the student miss the diagnosis?'

Avery nodded.

'Was he rude?'

'Definitely.'

Jon sighed and ran his hand through his hair. 'Do I need to take him off the floor?'

Avery shook his head. 'If he has the capacity, he should learn from his counterparts. But he needs proper supervision. I know you're busy, and I know he would have run his findings past another doctor before discharging the patient, but...' Avery stopped. 'No. Actually, I'm not sure he would have done that. He was over-confident. He also has a lack of respect for nursing and female medical staff.' He put a hand on Jon's shoulder. 'Good luck with that one.'

'So, Dr Callaghan isn't overreacting?'

Avery shook his head. 'No. She's definitely not.'

Jon lowered his head and put his hand on his hips. 'And it would have to be him, wouldn't it?'

Robyn walked out of the door beside them both. 'Who?' she asked.

Jon lifted his hand. 'Nothing. It doesn't matter.' He gave them both a resigned look. 'Thanks for letting me know. I'll deal with him.'

As they walked back down the corridor, Robyn looked at Avery. 'Do you get the feeling Jon didn't tell us everything?'

Avery sighed. 'I'm not sure. Maybe he's just tired or over-whelmed by the rush today.' He looked sideways at Robyn. 'Let's grab some food before we go back upstairs. We'll have missed the roster for breaks and I don't want to go all day without eating.'

'Me either,' she agreed.

As they walked through the corridors to the cafeteria he could see the serious expression on her face. Robyn was pretty, but her face was often marred by a frown. He knew better than to tell a woman to smile—not if he wanted to see another day—so he took the conversation another way.

'It was nice that you offered to help out in the ER today. Not many would have done that. You had two really good catches today. The teenager, and the Horner's Syndrome. Not everyone would have picked up on those—particularly when it's not your speciality.'

Now she did smile as they pushed open the cafeteria doors. 'I told you. I'm smart. Didn't you believe me?'

He thought back to her story about how many applicants there had been to her programme. He had actually believed her, because Robyn Callaghan gave him the distinct impression that she was an entirely truthful human being—she wouldn't waste time with lies.

'I did believe you,' he admitted, 'but sometimes believing something and witnessing it with your own eyes are two entirely different things.'

She was still smiling as they approached the counter and grabbed a tray. She selected a diet drink, a tuna-fish salad and, after much deliberation, a chocolate bar. She sighed. 'I miss my UK chocolate. Things just don't taste the same over here.'

Avery kept pace with her, picking up a bottle of water, then letting out a groan and grabbing a grilled-cheese sandwich from a fresh tray one of the staff had just put on the serving plates. Robyn gave him a smile. 'It's the one food you can eat the whole world over.'

He nodded, looking at her salad. 'I should get the same as you, but one whiff of the grilled cheese and I knew I was gone.'

They paid for their food and sat down at a table facing out onto the courtyard.

A small gust of air breezed by them and he got a hint of something spicy with hints of orange. It must have been her perfume—and he didn't recognise it.

'Did you get to finish all your notes on the Horner's case?'

Robyn nodded. 'I was recording as I went along and I'd already sent a handover note to both physicians who'll be taking over his care.' She took a forkful of her salad. 'But I'll go back and chase both. Our boy Simon will be easy to follow up, because he'll be in our unit.' She paused for a moment. 'Think I've made an enemy of Dr Anker?'

Avery pulled a face. 'Honestly? It's hard to say. He's a bit of a Jekyll and Hyde character, and you never know which one you're going to get. Most of the nurses in the unit try and go on a break when it's time for him to do his rounds.' He gave her a broad smile. 'But the most important rule is never to page him when he's playing golf—even if he is the senior doctor on call.'

Robyn groaned. 'Well, that's strike one against me already, then.'

Avery held up a hand. 'It could go two ways. He might be impressed you stood your ground with the paediatrician, and picked up a condition in a teenage boy that means he can be treated. There is a chance he could like that about you.'

'Or...?' She said the word because there were clearly unanswered elements hanging in the air.

Avery finished chewing part of his grilled cheese sandwich. 'Or he'll just remember you as the pesky doc who ruined his best game of golf ever. You'll get all the grunt work to do for the rest of your time here.'

Robyn leaned her head on one hand. She tapped her fingers on the table. 'I can live with grunt work. That's not so bad.'

Avery laughed. 'Oh, no. Dr Anker's grunt work is legendary. He once made a doctor who'd annoyed him pull five hundred random case notes of past patients to audit the medicines used.'

'Was it for a study?'

Avery shook his head.

'Because, if it was for a study, about finding best outcomes after procedures, that would be good. It could be written up as a research paper.'

'Stop trying to make things seem better. There was no research paper. You'll just need to wait to see what personality he's wearing later today or tomorrow.'

She gave a sad kind of smile. 'Medicine would be great, if it wasn't for people.'

'You sound like my old charge nurse.'

Robyn looked up. Her blue eyes meeting his. It was the first time he'd got a real look at her. Her dark red hair was smooth and shiny, her pale skin, with a few fine freckles on her nose, and dark blue eyes complemented her tones. There were no lines on her skin yet. She wore a little make-up, including striking red lipstick that matched her dress.

If he'd seen her someplace else, he'd have thought she was some kind of actress or model. But no, she was here, in Paz Memorial, in his home town.

Her accent was lilting to listen to. He still had to concentrate on occasion to understand every word, but he loved that everyone knew exactly where she came from, as soon as she opened her mouth.

'What did your old charge nurse say?' she asked.

'Oh, Marie said that work was great—apart from managing staff. She said there was always drama, always infighting, and holiday squabbles. Marie hated that it got in the way of patient care. She ended up retiring early.'

Robyn looked thoughtful. 'Was that good, or bad?'

It was an interesting question. Had Marie been too jaded to do her job well?

'Both,' he admitted. 'Bad, in that Marie was a wonderful nurse, great with relatives and patients, and I learned a lot from her. Her teaching skills were impeccable. But good in that a disgruntled staff member complained about her. Went to HR because Marie wasn't sympathetic to her apparent health issues.'

'Did she have health issues?'

'Not that anyone knew of. Plus, this woman had a history of moving from place to place and causing trouble. But for Marie, it was the last straw.'

'And how is she?'

Avery sat back. 'What makes you think I know?'

Robyn shook her head, pushing her salad away and unwrapping her chocolate bar. 'Because you do, don't you? You just spoke about a colleague you like and admired. It's clear you think she was shafted in some way. So, now she's retired, how is she?'

Avery nodded. 'She makes a great Sunday dinner. She helps out at a soup kitchen with me a couple of times a month, and at the free clinic. And she looks ten years younger.'

'I knew it.' Robyn looked triumphant. Avery leaned over and snapped off a square of her chocolate. 'Hey!' She wrinkled her nose. 'Why do I think you make a habit of this?'

Avery shrugged. 'I have no idea.'

Robyn looked at him curiously. 'You mentioned me helping out in the ER today. But you came down and helped out too. I saw you with some of those elderly patients.'

He wondered what else she was going to say. He gave a shake of his head. 'Of course, I helped out. The place was going crazy.' He decided to be truthful. 'I have some experience with surgical patients, and I did spend some time in the ER, theatres, general medical unit and care of elderly when I was doing my nurse training. But I'm no expert. When I offer to help I'm always careful not to step outside of what I know. Today, I knew I could take care of the elderly patients, do bloods, put up IVs, run tests, and make sure they were comfortable.'

'I saw you sitting with one of them for a while. Talking to her, telling her a story, and holding her hand.'

Avery nodded in acknowledgement. It *had* been Robyn that had walked past when he'd been looking after the elderly patient. 'She was upset. She has dementia. She thought I was her husband.' He drew in a long breath. 'Of course, I was going to spend time with her. The ER is overwhelming. Her confusion was heightened with the dehydration and infection she was suffering from. It was nice to take a bit of time with her. You don't always get that opportunity when places are so busy.'

Robyn gave him a contemplative look. 'Maybe you shouldn't have specialised in cardiac, maybe you should have considered care of the elderly.'

Something flashed through his brain. 'I'm not built for it. I find it difficult enough helping at the free clinic, and at the soup kitchen. With the older folk? I get too attached, and too frustrated with the lack of investment in services for our older patients, aids to keep them safely at home, in an environment they are familiar with, and even more exasperated by the "granny dumping".'

Robyn gave a shudder, clearly in sympathy. The act of an older relative being left at an ER by other members of the family, who didn't stay, was not entirely unusual to either of them. 'It's not so bad back in the UK, but it does still happen. Although healthcare is free, social care carries a cost. Some local authorities struggle to provide packages of care to keep people at home, usually due to a high turnover of staff, so, on occasion, it happens there too.'

He shook his head. 'And that's why I couldn't consider elderly care. I'd get too angry. Plus, the cardiac stuff always fascinated me. There's so much to learn, so many developments, and new techniques and drugs all the time. It's definitely the right place to be. And Paz Memorial is world-renowned as a centre of excellence. Why would I want to be anywhere else?'

Robyn leaned back and stifled a yawn. 'Sorry,' she said quickly. 'I haven't had a proper night's sleep since I got here.'

He was curious. 'Is something wrong with your accommodation?'

Robyn held up her hands. 'I started a little later than everyone else. There was a mix-up with my working visa, and by the time I got here all the rooms had been assigned except the one I got. It's right above the back entrance to the kitchen. I can tell you that the milk gets delivered at three a.m., the farm supplies get delivered around four a.m., and the baked goods around five a.m. If I'm hot and open my window it just amplifies the noise of all the delivery trucks. If I don't get some sleep soon, I'm likely to kill someone.' She must have caught his expression because she quickly added, 'Not because of bad medical practice. Just because sleep deprivation makes me decidedly cranky. I'll probably fight someone to the death over the last bar of chocolate.'

He tried not to smile too widely. 'Heaven help the person that gets between you and your chocolate.'

Robyn picked up the bar and held it to her chest. 'Don't you know it?' She glanced at the clock. 'We'd better get back to work.' She shot him a sideways glance as they headed to the exit. 'Don't want to get labelled a slacker as well as grumpy.' There was a twinkle in her eye.

She headed up the stairs before him and he made sure to fix his gaze on her shoes rather than anywhere far more distracting. Robyn Callaghan was proving more than a little interesting and he had a horrible feeling that his friend Serena knew him better than he knew himself.

CHAPTER THREE

'HOW ON EARTH can a medical student get away with that?'

It was a few days later and Robyn was finally getting the hang of all the processes in the cardiac department. While she was always confident in her medical skills, learning the processes somewhere new always took time. She often found herself lying in bed at night wondering if she'd ticked all the boxes on a handwritten bloodwork form, or if she'd pressed the final electronic button on an order for a test. Last thing she wanted was for a patient's care to be delayed or compromised because she hadn't managed to find her way around all the systems.

She hated to admit it, but Avery had been more than helpful. He'd gone through all the electronic processes with her and even given her a checklist for her pocket. She was quite sure the folks around here were still calling her Dr Grumpy, but Robyn was concentrating on the medicine, not the people skills.

She walked over to join the staff gossiping. Lia, one of the nurses, was rolling her eyes. 'No one's said anything, but I guess it's got something to do with who he actually is.'

'You mean how much money his family's got and who he knows on the board,' another nurse wisecracked as she walked by.

Robyn couldn't help but be intrigued, clearly a mistake

as Lia turned to her. 'You know all about it, Robyn. Tell us more.'

'More about what?'

'The medical student who messed up in the ER, but is still walking around telling everyone that he requires minimal supervision and that no one will stifle his learning.'

Robyn waited a few seconds for the rage to rise, then fall again. 'I imagine he can say whatever he wants. All medical students will mess up at some point. It's normal.' She licked her lips and connected with Lia's inquisitive gaze. 'It's what they learn from their mistakes that makes or breaks them as a doctor.'

Lia nodded. 'But your guy is telling all the other students that he was initially told he required supervision but his uncle has intervened.'

'Who's his uncle?'

Everyone stared at her. 'What?' she said. 'What have I missed?'

Lia patted her arm gently. 'His uncle is our chief executive, Mr Paz.'

Her stomach did a skydive, then a somersault, then a backflip, but she refused to let anyone know. Robyn was an expert at the deadpan face.

'It doesn't matter who his uncle is. He's a medical student and they all need supervision—whether he likes it or not. I've never met a programme director who would let the overall basis of their programme be compromised by any kind of influence like nepotism—' she glanced at the other wisecracking nurse who'd stopped walking '—or money.'

Robyn gave a shrug. 'Paz Memorial has a great reputation as a teaching hospital. That won't be risked.' She shook her head. 'He'll just be shooting his mouth off because someone found out what happened down there.' She raised her eyebrows. 'I haven't discussed it with anyone. I'd never do that. I'd never gossip about a student when I know they are working in our hospital.'

She witnessed a few embarrassed exchanges of glances, along with some hostile glares. 'I'm going to get a coffee. Anyone want one?'

She wasn't normally so hospitable, but she was trying to make a point. There was a general shake of heads and Robyn started to walk back to the staffroom, but changed her mind and descended the stairs to the machine in the cafeteria. They had a coffee bar and she ordered a skimmed extra-shot latte. Her heart was already racing, so an extra shot of coffee wouldn't make much difference.

Robyn climbed the stairs again and nestled herself in one of the offices, reviewing some patient notes and ordering some extra tests. Once she had finished, she exited the hospital programme, and surfed the Internet looking for a little more about the Paz family.

It was a large family, with lots of branches, and she couldn't quite work out where the medical student potentially could fit. Maybe it was just hospital gossip.

Her heart had finally stilled to a dull roar. She'd already caught the attention of Mr Paz by throwing him out of a cubicle in the ER. Now, if his relative complained that she'd highlighted him to his programme supervisor, she could find herself on a shaky peg.

The anger that she'd found so easy to quell earlier started to bubble again. Robyn had always been quick to flare with temper, but that was rarely visible to anyone else. She usually controlled it well. The only time it threatened to bubble over was when money and privilege were involved. Living on the wrong side of financial privilege for most of her life had given her what some might consider a skewed view on the unfairness of it all—one that she'd never been shy about vocalising.

Too many students from private schools were regularly reported as getting into medical schools—even when students from public schools had scored the same results in their exams. They had lower acceptance rates that a variety of excuses were made around.

Robyn had worked exceptionally hard to get where she was—despite her address in one of the most deprived areas of Scotland. She'd tried hard not to be envious of her fellow students who'd attended university with huge trust funds that had meant they had the best accommodation and didn't have to worry about eating or paying any bills.

Robyn had spent most of her life going without, so it had been nothing new to her. It was her normal. When she'd got a job doing late nights at a pub a few miles away from the university, she'd lived in constant fear of someone recognising her, and reporting her. The university had a rule that none of their students could take part-time jobs while studying. And while it was a nice idea that students could spend all their time and effort studying, the sad fact of life was that not everyone could afford to live that lifestyle.

'Hey,' a voice came from the door. 'Could you have a look at Mr Burns for me? He's getting tachycardic and his oxygen sats have gone down.'

Robyn was on her feet in an instant, already unwinding her stethoscope from her neck. She followed the worried nurse through to the cardiac unit where Mr Burns was situated. She'd read his notes. He'd had a whole host of cardiac issues for the last few years and had been admitted to the unit on multiple occasions.

The nurse was right. His colour was slightly off. Not blue. Not deathly pale. But definitely the start of something.

She glanced at the monitor. Heart rate one hundred and ten. Oxygen level ninety-one.

Avery appeared at her side. 'What's happening?'

She knew that he was familiar with Mr Burns and had looked after him on many occasions. He stepped around to the other side of the bed, and automatically helped Mr Burns to sit up, allowing Robyn to sound his chest and back.

She gave a slight nod when she was finished, and adjusted the pillows to let Mr Burns settle in a more upright position.

'Let's order a chest X-ray and get some bloods,' she said with a nod to the other nurse.

'Don't worry, Mr Burns, we'll look after you.'

She scribbled some notes and moved over to the nurses' station, asking for the phone. Avery appeared beside her as she paged Mr Burns' regular cardiologist.

He raised his eyebrows at her and she pulled a pad from her pocket, writing him a cryptic note: PE? He groaned and nodded. It wasn't uncommon for people with cardiac conditions to throw off a clot due to the fact their heart wasn't pumping blood around the body quite the way it should. Clots could form anywhere, but in this case Robyn suspected it was in the branch of one of his lungs, meaning that now they were compromised, and couldn't absorb oxygen properly.

She spoke in a low voice to Mr Burns' regular doctor, telling him her findings, the tests she'd already ordered and asking whether he would prefer a pulmonary angiogram, a CT or VQ scan. All could play a role in diagnosing a pul-

monary embolism, and Robyn didn't know these doctors
well enough to know what their preferences would be.

He surprised her, telling her he would attend himself and
decide at that point. Some of the specialists rarely attended
in an emergency, but it appeared that Dr Shad was different.

'Have you met him yet?' asked Avery as she replaced
the receiver.

She shook her head, wondering if she should even ask
the question of what he was like.

But it was as if someone read her mind. 'The man's a
dream,' came a voice at the other side of her. Rue, one of
the physios, was smiling. 'Always pleasant, always put his
patients first.' She put her hand on her chest. 'If I ever end
up in here, that man *better* be my doctor.'

'Can't get a better recommendation than that,' Robyn
said, smiling. And it was true. Doctors and nurses were the
same the world over. They could list who they did and they
didn't want to take care of them, in any place they'd worked.

Robyn looked around, suddenly self-conscious. Once
they got to know her, would any of the staff here want her
to be their doctor in case of emergency? She swallowed, her
throat dry. She'd like to think so, but she honestly wasn't
sure. Avery, meantime, was already talking to a patient
who'd just pushed their buzzer. He had his trademark wide
smile on his face. Mr Sunshine. It seemed to be his natural instinct.

Robyn had been told before that she had a resting bitch
face. Charming. It was the same person who'd first tried to
charm her by telling her she looked like a famous cartoon
princess, and then tried to come on to her. When she'd been
unimpressed, she'd then received the ultimate compliment

regarding her normal expression. She'd been self-conscious about it ever since. And that was so not like her.

She watched Avery for a few minutes because she just couldn't help it. He was so comfortable in his own skin. If he knew how handsome he was, he certainly didn't play on it. Avery was very down-to-earth and went out of his way to take the time to talk to people. She hadn't heard another member of staff say a bad word about him.

In a way he kind of unnerved her. Too good-looking. Too friendly. Too sexy. Too easy to chat to. Too nice. Too much fun. She really needed to get a life.

Robyn sighed. She glanced at the clock. She was due to be off duty, and she really, really wanted to get to sleep. But there was no way she was leaving now she knew one of the senior doctors was coming.

'I'm going to do some checks on other patients,' she told the charge nurse, 'Can you give me a shout when Dr Shad appears?'

The nurse nodded and Robyn went to follow up on some other test results, and to check in on Hal Delaney, the man who'd had a cardiac arrest at the front door.

He was in a luxury private room in a special part of the unit, with his own private nurses and his own chef. It was likely that he only wanted his specialist doctor to see him, but Robyn always liked to check up on any patient she'd been involved with.

She knocked on the door and went in. 'Hi, Mr Delaney. I'm Robyn Callaghan, one of the doctors who looked after you downstairs. I came in to see how you were doing.'

The man was reading an old-fashioned newspaper. They were nowhere near as popular as they used to be, with most people reading their news online now.

He looked up and put his paper down on his bed sheets. His head tilted slightly to the side, then she could see the recognition in his face. He let out a hearty laugh. 'The red-haired fire demon. I wondered if I'd actually imagined you.'

Robyn blinked. She'd been called an angel before, but demon was a first.

But now Hal Delaney was wagging his finger. 'It's the accent. It imprinted in my brain.' He held out his hand towards her. 'Whereabouts in Scotland are you from?'

'Near Glasgow,' she said, shaking his hand gently.

'Scotland.' He sighed, putting his hands up in the air. 'I think someone bought me a peerage there as a birthday gift. Beautiful country.'

All the hairs on her neck stood on end. She'd known Mr Delaney was likely to be rich from his private room and service. But now she knew for sure. Maybe she was supposed to be amused by that anecdote, but, funnily enough, some rich man buying a peerage in her country as a kind of joke did nothing for her.

'I'm glad to hear that you're doing well, Mr Delaney. How much longer do you expect to be in?'

She hadn't looked at his notes—not quite sure what the etiquette was in the hospital for patients who were being cared for in a different way.

He didn't answer, just rested back against his pillows, and kept smiling at her, shaking his head. His monitor was to his side and she could see his heart rate and last blood-pressure recording. If she was asked to place a bet, she'd say that Mr Delaney would be getting a pacemaker sometime soon.

'I'm just excited to meet someone who had the nerve to tell Leo Paz to get out the room. Most people are terrified of him.'

'They are?' Robyn tried to hide the most enormous gulp.

'Oh, yes, even though I was sick, I was delighted you had the balls to tell him off.'

The door opened and a support worker came in with a large carafe of coffee. 'Is that decaf?' Robyn couldn't help but ask the question.

The support worker shook their head. So, Robyn shook hers. 'Bring back some decaf, please.'

Mr Delaney started to object but Robyn moved closer to his bed and pointed to his monitor. 'Your heart rate is tachycardic but irregular. You must feel the palpitations?'

He frowned, but nodded.

'Did your doctor suggest modifications to your diet until he has things stable?'

Mr Delaney's frown deepened but he nodded again. 'But I pay my own chef.'

She bristled at the entitlement and the fact he'd ignored the instructions given by his doctor. But decided to tackle this a different way.

Robyn gave him a smile. 'So, just like I had the balls to tell Mr Paz to leave while I treated you, I have the balls to tell you to spend the next few days following the instructions of your doctor.' She tapped the monitor. 'Your heart rate is very irregular. You're going to need this treated. I really don't want to have to answer an arrest page for you again.'

She paused, looking at him to let the words sink in, then taking another breath. She could frame this as a challenge. 'There's lots of great decaf versions out there—and I'm sure you're happy to pay for the best. Why don't you sample a few versions to see if you can find one that tastes just as good as the brand you normally drink?'

He mumbled under his breath, clearly used to getting his own way unchallenged.

The support worker came back in with another large pot of coffee. It smelled just as good as the last.

'Thank you,' said Robyn as they set it down then left again.

Mr Delaney was giving her a hard stare through heavy lids. She folded her arms across her chest. 'I want you to know that as a child I was unmatched in stare-out duels.'

He blinked and let out a snort. 'Are all Scots women like you?'

'You should know. Don't you own a peerage?' she shot back without hesitation.

He poured his coffee into what she assumed was a fine bone-china teacup and plate. 'I like you,' he said.

'You should. I helped save your life. Take care of it, Mr Delaney. I want to hear that you've lived a long, happy and healthy life.'

She gave him a wave and exited the room, just as the support worker appeared with a plate full of delicious, clearly freshly baked cakes. Robyn sighed and plucked the top one from the plate with a wink, and the startled support worker stared at her. 'I'm helping with his diet,' Robyn explained as she walked back down the corridor nibbling the delicious raspberry and coconut sponge.

It seemed that the rumours were true. Dr Shad was a de-light and gave Robyn faith that not all senior doctors were fierce and a bit conceited. By the time she was finished on the unit, all she really wanted to do was lie down in her bed.

But the muggy evening air was too warm, so she changed into shorts and flowery top and took a walk down along the front, staring at the giant naval vessels, then working her way across and into the Gaslamp district. It really was one of her favourite parts of San Diego. The atmosphere was always friendly. People seemed relaxed. Music drifted out from a few of the bars. Several of the restaurants had tables outside and the smells were nothing short of tantalising.

Robyn considered her bank balance. While she was surviving, she would never describe her bank balance as healthy. She lived pay cheque to pay cheque. She constantly had to help out her parents back at home—neither of them had ever held down regular jobs. Both just seemed to drift from one low-paying job to another, with no built-in benefits and frequently being laid off at short notice.

She glanced at a few menus on the restaurant windows. She had no qualms about going in and eating on her own— she was quite comfortable doing that. It was the dollar signs that were signalling in her brain. She could have a beer. A cold beer on a night like this would be nice.

Robyn moved further along the street to a bar that seemed not too busy but had the sounds of a mix of jazz and soul drifting out onto the street. The worker on the door gave her a nod and waved her in, and as she entered she was hit by the smell of food. Spicy chicken, garlic and other spices, and that well-known smell of good old mashed potatoes and gravy.

Her stomach gave a low grumble as she headed to the bar and bought a bottle of cold beer. Conscious of the fact she didn't want to sit on one of the high bar stools, she made her way to the far wall and slid into one of the wooden booths. The lights were dimmer here, and it gave her a chance to study the menu and the prices.

She'd almost talked herself out of it when a figure slid into the opposite side of the booth.

She started, ready to tell the stranger she didn't want to share, but instead she was met with a wide grin of perfect white teeth, and a set of gorgeous green eyes. Avery slid another bottle of beer across the table to her.

'Where did you come from?'

He nodded backwards, 'I was at a table with some of the theatre technicians. I saw you come in.'

She looked around self-consciously, but couldn't see the people he was referring to. She glanced at the beer again, noticing it was the same as the one she was drinking.

He was wearing a white T-shirt and blue jeans. Perfectly casual with his dark hair looking more ruffled than usual. And as soon as he'd sat down, she got that little whiff of his aftershave. Or maybe it was just his anti-perspirant, or his washing powder. Whatever it was, she'd started to associate it with him. It was clean, fresh and strangely alluring.

'I only came in for one,' she said, knowing it sounded awkward. But Robyn was conscious of not really wanting to end up in a drinking circle and contributing to a bill she might not be able to afford.

'Well, have two.' He smiled. 'You'll need one to have with dinner.'

'I wasn't planning on having dinner.'

'Really?' He stared at the menu in front of her. 'I was going to recommend the spicy shredded chicken with the rosemary mashed potatoes.'

She'd been looking at that on the menu. Could this guy read her mind?

'You've had it before?'

He gave a sorry sigh. 'I've tried most of the things on the menu in here. This place isn't too far from my apartment, and let's just say I can get by in the kitchen, but am not exactly a connoisseur chef.'

She gave him an amused glance.

'Eggs,' he said quickly. 'I can definitely do eggs. But…' he held up his hands '…eggs aren't exactly dinner.'

He leaned across the table towards her. 'Go on. I don't want to eat alone. Let me buy you my favourite shredded chicken.'

It was the easy way he said those words. A wave of recognition swept over her. This was a guy that had never really needed to worry about money. She knew without thinking that he'd never needed to consider his bank balance before purchasing something. She knew he'd never stood in a store counting up the change in his pockets to see what he could actually afford.

He'd never talked about money in front of her. But Robyn had been at the opposite end of the poverty spectrum for too long. When she saw a patient, their financial position was one of the first things she considered. Dependent on what country she was in, did they have medical insurance? If she was back in Scotland, what kind of home did they live in? Was it damp? Did they eat regularly? Were they dressed properly? Poverty affected so many aspects of people's lives, with direct links to their health. While that was recognised everywhere now, at heart, not everyone considered it on every occasion. It was the reason she'd aced the programme application. They'd told her that. Few had been as thorough as she was, directly linking health inequalities to both ends of the financial spectrum.

They hadn't asked about her financial circumstances in the interview. She'd worn clothes from a charity shop in Glasgow in one of the wealthiest parts of the city. She knew she could fake it like the best of them. But nothing would change what ran through her veins. And she didn't want it to change.

Which was why her fingers twitched and she subconsciously pulled back her hands on the table. Away from Avery. It wasn't a deliberate act. It was as if her body had gone into protective mode.

'I have to go,' she murmured, just as her stomach growled loudly. It was as if her body gave up all its secrets around him. Sabotaging her.

'You can, as soon as you eat something.' He leaned back, putting space between them, to separate the fact they'd just looked much more intimate with each other than they really were.

'I know I can't tell you what to do. I have a female best friend. I know much better than to do that, and also that it's a battle I would lose anyway. And I certainly don't want you to feel unsafe in any way.' He took a deep breath. 'Robyn. You're a colleague. I hope at some point you'll call me a friend. You look tired. I know it's stressful coming to a new place. After all the arrest calls you dealt with recently, you must be running on adrenaline. Let me buy you dinner. No pressure at all. I get the feeling you've not had a chance to make friends in San Diego yet, and I want you to enjoy your experience of working here.'

As he spoke, his voice lyrical and calm, the tension started to dissolve out of her muscles. This must be how he did it with the patients. The easy manner, the relaxed and reasoned point of view.

He'd told her she couldn't leave until she'd eaten something. But the decision was hers. She knew that. And the

shredded chicken had been exactly what she'd been looking at on the menu.

She couldn't remember feeling relaxed since she'd got to
San Diego. She felt as if she hadn't had time to draw breath.
Robyn closed her eyes for a few seconds. She'd come into
this bar because she liked the atmosphere, the music and
the scent of the food.

Did she really need to be so uptight all the time?

She opened her eyes. Avery was looking straight at her.
She pressed her lips together for a moment then nodded.
'I'd love to try the shredded chicken,' she said.

Relief swept over his face, he waved to one of the nearby
waitresses and gave their order, settling back on the cush-
ions in the booth.

'When are you working this week?'

Robyn took a sip of her beer. 'I only have another two
shifts. I came straight into twelve days in a row. It was an
initiation of fire, but things seem to be more settled now.'

'I'm glad you came in here tonight,' he said. 'You know
the chocolate you like?'

She was surprised he remembered and she nodded,
slightly confused.

He broke into a wide smile. 'I'll show you a small store
in the next street. It's one of the few places that doesn't sell
UK chocolate at exorbitant prices. The guy that owns it has
Scottish grandkids.'

'Really?'

He nodded. 'He comes from Aberdeen. When he talks,
I can make out about one word in ten.'

Robyn laughed. She looked up as the waitress passed
with loaded plates, heading to another table.

She groaned. 'The smell in here is just heavenly.'

Avery nodded. 'Agreed. Like I said, I come here all the time.'

Robyn bit her lip, wondering if she should ask the question that was playing on her mind. 'You live around here?'

'Yeah, I've got an apartment I used to share with Serena not far away. We shared during our training, and then afterwards for a short while.'

'Ah, this was the friend you mentioned before. The one who moved in with the love of her life? So, she's moved out?'

He nodded. 'Place sure is quiet now. And, of course, the dishwasher broke as soon as she left. Serena was methodical about the dishwasher, always loading and unloading it. Every time I touch it, the thing breaks. I swear it hates me.'

'You clearly don't pay it enough attention.'

'Don't you start.' He wagged his finger at her and rolled his eyes.

'Must be kind of expensive to live here,' Robyn said, her brain hoping she'd sounded casual. Maybe she could ask the hospital administrators about renting in this area?

'It's not too bad,' said Avery easily. 'There are much more popular parts of the city. We were lucky, we scored a place that actually has a view of the marina. It's not right on the marina,' he said quickly. 'But I can see it from the windows. It's a two-bath, two-bed apartment so we each had our own space. So, it worked out fine. I'll probably ask around in a while for another roommate.'

She gave a thoughtful nod. Of course, he would. And when he looked for a roommate, he wouldn't want one that would only be around for six months. He'd want someone who planned to stay. And she was clearly losing her mind since she had not a single clue how much an apartment would be to rent in San Diego on a monthly basis.

'Have you seen much of the city yet?'

She shook her head. 'Not with the working hours, but I'm hoping to get around in the next few days.'

'You need to try the old town trolley. They do a tour, and you head to the other side of the marina to Coronado. Get out there. The beach is gorgeous. There's a beautiful hotel, and, despite what some people say, it's not just a military base.'

'Sounds fantastic. I've seen the other side of the marina when I've been running in the morning, and been curious. Just haven't had the time yet.' She gave a sigh. 'And I imagine the view when the trolley crosses the bridge is amazing.'

'It totally is.' Avery breathed in. 'I love my city. Even when it's packed with avid fans and conferences.' He held out his hands. 'There's a whole host of tours comes around the Gaslamp district seven days a week, several times a day. But I like that people come here and visit.'

'It's my first time in the US,' she admitted. 'I was hoping for huge shopping malls and outlets to buy running clothes for five dollars, but what little I've seen looks like normal prices.' She could feel heat rushing to her cheeks and wondered if she sounded like some kind of cheapskate.

But Avery smiled. 'You've just not found the outlet malls yet. I can show you. All of my international friends stock up as soon as they get here. My favourite was my friend who wanted to take home not just the sneakers, but the boxes too, and was livid when he realised he'd need to buy around three extra suitcases just to get them home.'

Robyn laughed. 'Well, I'm only looking to replace the

running clothes and trainers that I have. I'm not looking for a supply for the next five years.'

The waitress appeared and set down their loaded plates. The smell of the spicy shredded chicken and rosemary mashed potatoes was delicious. Robyn put her nose close to the plate and sucked in a breath before picking up her cutlery. Her first taste was pure comfort.

Avery was watching her. 'You like?'

She nodded and smiled.

'Thank goodness. Imagine I'd just recommended something you hated.'

She shook her head. 'I'd actually looked at the menu and considered it. I just wasn't sure I wanted to stay too long.'

'I can walk you back to the hospital, if you're worried?' he said automatically. She looked up straight into his green eyes and almost caught her breath. There was something strangely hypnotic about being in this place with him. The dimmed lights, the background noise. The food and beer aromas, and the way his arms were positioned on the table, framing his upper muscles and broad chest. He was like a regular movie star. And when he flashed those perfect white teeth? No wonder they called him Mr Sunshine.

She felt oddly self-conscious. Her hair was pulled back in a ponytail band and she'd pulled on a summer dress in dark green. There was nothing wrong with how she looked, but she wished she'd put on a bit more make-up and a darker shade of lipstick—just paid a bit more attention to her appearance. It was stupid to think like that because she was sure Avery didn't care. But all of a sudden *she* cared. And she was having a hard time acknowledging that she did.

Her first reaction to his offer was to automatically say no. But something was stopping her. It would be dark by the time they finished their meal, and although the walk back to the hospital was fairly well lit, she would welcome the company until she was more familiar with the area. But was that the only reason?

'Thanks.' She smiled at him, before she could contemplate things any longer.

'No problem,' he said easily. 'Is there anything else you'd like to see around San Diego in the next few days?'

Her brain wanted to make an excuse, tell him she didn't want to trouble him—she'd find her own way around. But something about this was nice. Was welcomed. She shook her head. 'The sightseeing trolley, Coronado, and the shopping outlet seems enough for now. But if I think of anything else, I'll let you know,' she joked as she continued to tuck into her chicken and mashed potatoes. 'What I really need to do is try and get some sleep. My room is driving me nuts. I swear I hear reversing delivery trucks as soon as I try and close my eyes.'

Avery paused for a moment and then took a visible breath. 'Why don't you move into the spare room at my apartment, Robyn? I swear to you it's quiet. There are no reversing trucks on the high floors.'

Robyn was stunned and wasn't quite sure what to say at first. All her brain could focus on at first was the thought of sleep.

She really needed to rethink her bank balance. The money she was earning as a doctor now was reasonable. The programme also covered some expenses. But Robyn couldn't rethink twenty-five years of constantly counting every penny, finding ways to cut costs, and always wondering when the next disaster would happen.

Two months ago, she'd funded a new boiler for her parents back in Scotland. They could never have afforded a replacement on their own and they'd need it for when the weather grew colder again. She'd likely need to help them over the winter with the rising heating costs too. Would she be able to do that if she rented a room in Avery's apartment?

'How about I show you around it and you can see what you think?' he asked.

Robyn automatically nodded. 'Sure, that would be great.'

That would also give her time to think. To sort out how much she could afford and think of everything she would say if it was out of her price range—she might actually just tell him the truth—or, if she wasn't sure about renting a room with someone she worked with. It might make things a little…odd.

'Want another beer?' Avery asked. He had a grin on his face. It was clear the invitation had been easy for him, whereas it was making her brain spin in circles.

Robyn shook her head. 'Two's plenty. I'm a bit of a lightweight when it comes to alcohol,' she confessed. 'Even though I'm from Scotland and it apparently runs through our veins.'

'Should I report you?' he joked.

'Too late,' she said. 'I'm a lost cause.'

'I wouldn't say that.' His lips had curled into a smile and the words hung in the air between them. 'Come on, then. I'll show you my place.'

'Now?'

'Why not? It's not far from here. I've got a spare room. It's furnished and has air conditioning. There's a bed in there. Seriously—' he held up both hands '—nothing untoward, but if you're honestly finding it that tough, and you need proper sleep at night, you're welcome to stay at mine.'

Robyn found it hard to answer. Partly, because her brain was going to other places. But also because finally getting uninterrupted sleep would be pure bliss. She'd honestly considered finding a cheap hotel for the night just to get some peace.

She licked her lips. She couldn't pretend she wasn't attracted to Avery and would like to live under his roof... preferably in his room, with him. But that wasn't the offer. Was she offended?

She took a final sip of her beer, clearing her throat and smiling. 'I'd love to get some sleep.'

Voices in her head fought to be heard. How much did she really know about Avery? She was prepared to consider living with him, but why was her first thought mild offence that there was no other implication to his offer than platonic friendship?

Because, deep down, she knew she would be entirely safe under his roof. Nothing would happen unless she invited it. No one at Paz Memorial had a bad word to say about this guy. And she understood that.

They walked out onto the street and she followed him as they threaded their way through the crowds.

'You might find that I sleep for a week,' she admitted as they crossed at a walkway.

He shook his head. 'You've only got two more shifts, then, if you need to catch up on some sleep, that's entirely fine. Sleep as long as you like.'

Her mood brightened. 'Air conditioning.' She sighed.

He nodded. 'Air conditioning. I might even stretch to some Scottish candy bars.' He raised his eyebrows.

He was joking, and she laughed, while her skin tingled.

'Promises, promises,' she said.

He took her into the entrance of a high-rise building. The lobby was plush. The elevator took them almost to the top floor, and when it opened there were only two doors.

She'd been looking online at apartments and usually there were four on each floor. But as soon as Avery opened the door to his place, Robyn knew it was bigger than the average apartment.

It had light wood floors, and white walls. But the focal point was the huge windows. On one side, they had a view of the city, on the other, she could see the marina. The kitchen and sitting room were open-plan. Again, the space was the thing that captured her attention. Avery pointed in one direction. 'Serena's room and bath were down there. Mine are at the other end of the hall.'

'Wow, you mentioned the views but I wasn't expecting this,' she said, walking over to the nearby floor-to-ceiling window and just breathing as she looked at the spectacular view of the marina. Sure, it wasn't right next to them, and there was another high-rise partially blocking the complete view, but it was still pretty special.

'They are nice.' He tilted his head to one side. 'Even if you have to squint to get the full view.' He was teasing again and she reached over and gave him a gentle shove.

'I'm surprised you haven't been deluged with people from the hospital asking to stay here.' A tiny thread of dread started in her brain. Maybe the price was just too outrageous?

He gave a sigh and pressed his lips together. 'I haven't really told anyone I was looking for a roommate yet. But since Serena moved out, it's been quiet around here.' He held up one hand. 'Not that she was noisy. But sometimes it's nice to get in at night and have someone else to talk to.'

Her stomach gave a little lurch. She got that. Loneliness frequently echoed around Robyn. She knew at times it was of her own making—she'd found dating hard since her sting in medical school. Or maybe it wasn't the dating that was hard, but more the trusting that came alongside it. Robyn had been so keen to protect herself and her heart that she'd kind of shut herself off from any potential suitors. Maybe it was time to take a breath and rethink?

'Go and have a look about—see what you think,' said Avery.

She could sense an element of anxiety in his voice. Did he honestly think she wouldn't like this place? She didn't need to see another thing before saying yes. All she had to consider was the price.

She gave a nod of her head and padded down the hall and into a white-walled bedroom with a couple of bright prints on the wall. The bed was large and looked freshly made up. The door to the bathroom was open and it revealed white vanity units, a walk-in shower and toilet. The room she had at the hospital was less than half the size of the bedroom in here, and that included the tiny bathroom. This place was luxurious in comparison. The air conditioning was delightfully chilly. She could actually have sunk down into the delicious bed and wept.

She walked over to the window that looked out over the city. San Diego was a vibrant place, but this high up there was no noise. She pulled down the blind in preparation for a good night's sleep.

Her heart quickened in her chest as she walked back down to meet him. 'I love it,' she said without hesitation. Then, before she could think too hard, she asked the big question. 'How much?'

Avery hesitated. 'Actually…' His voice tailed off.

'Actually what?'

He pressed his lips together. 'How about we just split the utilities?'

She frowned and held out her hands. 'But what about the actual rent?'

He shook his head. 'I've got some special circumstances here. Without going into details, let's just say I don't have to pay actual rent.'

Her frown deepened. 'Is this a friend's place? A relatives? Are you just house-sitting?'

'Something like that,' he replied non-committally.

She didn't want to pry further when he clearly didn't want to talk about it. 'How much are the utilities?'

He gave a number she could easily manage. She sighed in relief and walked back over to the window. 'This is for real, isn't it? You aren't just fooling me into thinking I'm actually going to be able to sleep?'

He smiled. 'I'm not fooling you. You can move in to-night if you want.'

Robyn moved over next to him and touched his forearm. Her mood had never been brighter. 'In that case, better get your muscles out. I'm going to need some help heaving my stuff over here.'

His eyes twinkled. He looked as happy as she was, and almost relieved, which was something she could think about later.

'Your wish is my command,' he said with a grin.

CHAPTER FOUR

THE LAST FEW days had been...strange. Avery was definitely avoiding Serena because she would be able to tell he was feeling antsy in a heartbeat and would grill him within an inch of his life. He wasn't sure he could take a Serena grilling right now, or what it might reveal.

Robyn had jumped at the chance to move in, and hadn't asked too many more questions about the rent. He hated the fact he hadn't been entirely truthful with her about who really owned the apartment. But he just wanted to get a better feel for how things were between them both, before he revealed a secret that could impact on his personal and professional life.

Sharing the apartment with her was...nice. More than nice, to be honest. He was conscious of the electricity in the air between them, but was determined not to act on it, and he really liked having her around. He loved her accent. It held his attention and pulled him in. He loved the way she dropped Scottish words into the conversation without thinking and he had to hold up a hand and ask her to back up and translate them. So far, he'd learned the meaning of crabbit, drookit, aye and fankle. He planned to use all of these words at some point over the next few days.

He wanted her to be comfortable in his place. And she had been. That first morning, he'd actually had to go and knock her up in the morning. That made him smile, and then groan, once he realised what Serena would say when he revealed that Robyn had moved into her old room.

Unfortunately, their scheduled time off had been cancelled after a number of colleagues all came down with a mystery virus, so the city tour had to wait a bit longer.

Extra hours working was making a lot of the staff look tired and be extra cranky. He was relieved they'd managed to get Robyn out of her hospital room in time to let her get some proper sleep. He'd spoken to the unit manager the other day, mentioning about nursing and medical staff working more hours than they should, and ensuring those were noted, and that everyone would get the time back once the rest of the sick staff returned to work.

Robyn had just finished with a patient when he heard her pager sound. She answered immediately and her forehead creased. 'I'm not quite sure what you're telling me. Is this a surgical patient?'

She took her notepad from her pocket and scribbled a few things. 'Yes, yes, of course, I'll come and see her. Wait? What? Has she coded?'

Within a few seconds, both Avery's and Robyn's pagers sounded. She didn't even wait for the message. 'It's the ER,' she said to Avery and started to sprint down the corridor.

He followed on her heels, wondering what on earth he was heading into.

It only took a few minutes to find out. Their patient was in the resus room and the staff looked slightly stunned. One of the surgical doctors was in the room. As soon as they came in, he spoke rapidly. 'This is Mabel Tucker, she's twenty-five and was one of Toby Renfro's patients. She had an open splenectomy around eight weeks ago after a road traffic accident and recovered well. She presented today with severe shortness of breath. Her oxygen sats are in the low eighties.'

Avery exchanged a glance with Robyn. 'Another PE?'

'Likely,' she replied. It was hard to believe they'd been called down to a second patient in such a short time with the exact same condition.

These circumstances were different. Throwing off any kind of clot—including a pulmonary embolism—was a risk after the removal of a patient's spleen.

Avery looked at the monitor. Pulseless electrical activity. Not good. He knew exactly what this meant. If this twenty-five-year-old young lady had a pulmonary embolism it must be large and would likely be fatal.

He watched Robyn weighing the situation up. She did this in the blink of an eye. 'Get me the senior cardiac consultant on call,' she said to one of the ER nurses. 'Continue cardiac massage,' she said to the second.

The anaesthetist, Flo, ran through the door. She was a few minutes later than everyone else and had a small smear of blood on her upper scrubs. Robyn looked at her directly. 'Female, twenty-five, previous splenectomy, likely pulmonary embolism. Can you intubate for me, please?'

The anaesthetist drew in a breath and moved to the top of the table, getting to work. 'Let's do an echocardiogram and try and confirm this,' Robyn said as a healthcare support worker wheeled over the machine that was in the corner of the room.

'Avery, prepare me thrombolytics.'

He moved across the room, opening one of the emergency drug cupboards and locating what he needed.

Robyn stayed completely calm, pausing the cardiac massage for a few moments to allow Flo to complete her intubation, then again when she had the transducer in hand to perform the echocardiogram. Time meant everything right now. He knew that Robyn would direct the medicine to be administered rapidly. But rapidly for this drug meant over fifteen minutes. Cardiac massage would need to continue all that time.

'Is someone with Mabel?' he asked as he finished preparing the drug.

One of the ER staff nodded. 'I've put her husband in the relatives' room.'

Avery nodded, his gaze fixed on the screen of the echocardiogram machine as Robyn placed the transducer to look at the heart. There were several signs she could look for to try and confirm the presence of a pulmonary embolism, and it only took her a few moments to find one.

'Sixty by sixty sign, along with a dilated right ventricle,' she said clearly, turning to Avery and holding out her hand for the medicine. Both were signs of a pulmonary embolism.

He saw a trickle of sweat run down her brow. She looked amazingly calm, but he could only imagine how she was actually feeling.

'Dr Shad is on today,' came a call from the doorway. 'He's on his way down.'

Avery moved over next to Robyn. 'I'll do this,' he said, connecting the drug to the cannula in Mabel's arm. 'Fifteen minutes?'

She nodded.

'You concentrate on everything else,' he said in a low voice. 'You're doing great.'

He saw it. The tiny flare of panic in her eyes. It vanished just as quickly as it had appeared. He wondered how some of the other doctors who'd started just before Robyn would have coped in this situation. All of them were capable and competent. But this? This was something else. He was pretty sure that at least a few of them would have panicked. A few might even have decided to call the arrest. Mabel's chance of survival was less than ten per cent. Nearly all of the people in this room likely knew that already.

He couldn't help but admire her calmness and tenacity. 'Can someone call up to Cardiac Theatre on the fourth floor and tell them to ready the emergency theatre?' Robyn asked.

Avery kept his eyes flicking back to the large clock on the wall as he administered the medicine slowly. Another nurse had swapped in to take over the cardiac massage. It was amazing how quickly it tired out anyone performing the massage.

The surgical doctor who'd been there when they arrived appeared back at the door. 'I've let Toby Renfro know. He's currently in Theatre, closing as we speak.'

Robyn gave a nod. She signalled to the nurse performing cardiac massage. 'Let's give it a few seconds to see if anything's changed.'

It was unlikely. The medicine wouldn't go through the veins in the normal way. The blood supply around the body right now was entirely dependent on how well the staff member performed the cardiac massage. After a few moments Robyn shook her head. 'Continue,' she signalled to the nurse.

Avery could almost see the relief emanate from her as Dr Shad walked through the door. 'Report, Dr Callaghan,' he said in a precise but calm manner.

She did. Sticking to essential facts. Dr Shad gave a nod.

'How many minutes?' he asked Avery, looking at the medicine Avery was currently administering.

'It's been ten so far,' he replied.

Dr Shad nodded thoughtfully. 'Halt,' he said clearly to the nurse performing massage. Silence fell across the room as all eyes went to the cardiac monitor. Nothing changed.

'Call upstairs. Let's do a pulmonary embolectomy and try and give this young woman a chance. Everyone, prepare.'

This was why Avery loved his job. The anaesthetist unplugged her equipment and put it at the head of the bed. One nurse climbed up on the bed, ready to carry on with cardiac massage on the transfer. Another was on the phone, giving instructions upstairs. Dr Shad signalled to Robyn. 'You and I will scrub as soon as we get upstairs.' He turned to the surgical doctor. 'Tell Dr Renfro to join us whenever he is free.'

As the cardiac monitor was placed at Mabel's side, Avery took a breath. 'Dr Shad, no one has had a chance to talk to Mabel's husband yet.'

Dr Shad nodded and walked around, taking over the medicine administration from Avery. 'Apologise to him on my behalf. Bring him up to the fourth floor, make sure someone is looking after him, then join us in Theatre.'

Avery nodded, sure that his expression was just as surprised as Robyn's was.

He didn't usually assist in Theatre—although he'd done a rotation in there and was capable. He didn't ask questions—just assumed that Theatre had the same sickness problems as everywhere else. Robyn was also looking a bit shell-shocked. While all doctors on their programme would learn and assist in Theatre, it was usually around three months into their rotations. Robyn was only weeks into her placement.

Avery took a breath as the trolley holding Mabel swept out of the room and straight into the nearest elevator. He knew there would be a team waiting for them already on the fourth floor.

Tom Tucker was rigid in the chair in the relatives' room. He jerked as Avery opened the door. Avery hated this part of his job, but knew it was absolutely essential. This man had already experienced the recent trauma of his wife being in a road traffic accident and needing the emergency removal of her ruptured spleen. Last thing he needed was more trauma.

Avery sat down next to him. 'Tom, I'm Avery Smith. I'm one of the nurses from the cardiac unit.' Tom sat a little straighter, obviously wondering why someone from the cardiac unit was talking to him.

'Mabel is very sick,' said Avery carefully. 'We think she has a clot in her lung. It's stopped the air getting to her lungs properly, and her heart has stopped beating.'

'I saw you,' said the man, his voice monotone, as if he were in shock. 'I saw you and a red-haired woman working on Mabel.'

Avery was cursing in his head. He knew exactly how this had happened. Someone hadn't actually escorted Tom to the family room, and instead had simply pointed him in the direction of it. It was possible to see what was happening in the resus rooms if the curtains and doors weren't shut—and they hadn't been in Mabel's case because it had literally been all hands on deck.

'The red-haired lady is Dr Robyn Callaghan. She's one of the best doctors I've ever worked with. She gave the very best care to Mabel.'

He waited a moment, letting his words sink in with Tom. 'We've given her some medicine to try and break up the clot, but so far that hasn't worked. Our doctor, Dr Shad, has taken her up to Theatre to try and remove the clot from her lung.' He was always careful with the words and terminology he used around relatives. The last thing they needed in a crisis situation was not being able to understand what they were being told.

'Dr Shad's not her doctor,' said Tom mechanically. 'Her doctor is Toby Renfro.'

Avery nodded. 'Dr Shad is her doctor now. A clot in a vein is generally dealt with by a cardiac or vascular specialist. Dr Renfro is a surgeon. But he knows of her condition and we're hoping he'll join Dr Shad in Theatre.'

Tom breathed deeply for a few moments, then his eyes turned to Avery. 'Am I going to see her again?'

Avery swallowed. He was always honest with patients and relatives unless there was a specific reason not to be. He could only continue to be honest now.

'I hope so, Tom, I really do. Her condition is very serious and the survival rate is small. All I can tell you is that she's in the right place and has the best people looking after her.' He waited a few moments then touched Tom's arm. 'I'm going to take you up to the fourth floor where the theatre and cardiac unit is. Would you like me to call someone for you so you're not waiting alone?'

Tom nodded. He handed his own phone to Avery. 'Stephen is Mabel's father. Can you tell him, please?'

Avery nodded, took the phone outside and found a quiet space. He knew he was breaking Stephen's heart as soon as he got him on the phone. Stephen immediately agreed to come to Paz Memorial and wait with his son-in-law.

Avery wanted to get upstairs as quickly as possible. He wanted to get into Theatre—something he rarely did. But

Dr Shad had asked him to look after Tom first, so that was what he would do.

They took the elevator to the fourth floor, where Avery showed Tom to a comfortable waiting area and spoke to the other staff. They were well equipped to look after Tom, and Stephen when he arrived, so Avery was waved away.

He headed straight to the changing rooms, switched his scrubs and searched the board to double-check which theatre they'd been assigned. He headed into theatre five, where the nurse in charge gave him a nod from the theatre table. 'Scrub,' she said.

The theatre was extremely quiet. All eyes were on the machines around the theatre table. A nurse on occasion was still standing and doing massage when instructed. But even from his slightly blocked vantage point, Avery could hear the occasional ping from the cardiac monitor. It sounded as though Mabel's heart was trying to function. It just wasn't in any kind of rhythm.

When he finished scrubbing Avery held out his arms for a theatre gown and sterile gloves. He moved around the table, finally getting a proper view. Dr Shad and Toby Renfro were working side by side, talking in low voices. A thin catheter had been threaded through one of Mabel's veins and there was an extremely large clot in her lungs. At this point they were concerned that the clot might disintegrate into smaller clots and do even more damage to her heart, brain and other vital organs.

Robyn was right alongside the two experts. Her hands weren't shaking and she was using a retractor to hold back a portion of Mabel's skin. The charge nurse, Belle, who was holding a retractor at the other side, nodded to Avery. 'Take over from me,' she said, letting his hands replace hers.

As soon as she stepped back, he saw Belle wobble. He kept his hands perfectly still but turned his head. 'Belle?'

She took backward steps until she was leaning against the theatre wall. It was clear it was propping her up as she snapped off a glove and pulled down her face mask. She was deathly pale, her neat pregnant belly just visible underneath her layers.

The anaesthetist pressed a buzzer near her. 'You should have said something,' she scolded.

Belle shook her head. 'I'll be fine. I've gone from one surgery to another without stopping. I just need to eat something.' She gave Avery a weak smile. 'I was never so glad to see you.'

The door edged open and a cautious head peeked inside. 'Do you need something?'

It was one of the theatre orderlies. Avery didn't hesitate. 'Can you assist Belle out of here, make her sit down and feed her, please?'

Mack had previously worked in the army medical corps and was great at his job. Mack's eyes went over to the far wall and widened with shock. 'Done,' he said. He moved swiftly across the theatre, put an arm around Belle and practically carried her back out.

'Time check,' said Dr Shad.

'Thirty-one minutes,' said Flo, the anaesthetist, clearly.

The interrupted cardiac massage had been ongoing for a long time. They all knew it wasn't realistic to keep this up for an extended period.

'There!' said Toby to Dr Shad. 'We've got it.' The clot was clearly visible in the proximal pulmonary artery.

Avery kept watch as they spent the next few minutes using a variety of methods. Removal of some of the clot, with further direct use of thrombolytics to reduce the size of it. It was the most delicate of procedures. Avery found himself first holding his breath, then meeting the gaze of Robyn, directly across the table from them. Everything about this event today had been full on.

Even the procedure now was different from normal. The wound in Mabel's groin was much wider than normal, probably because her circulatory system was so shut down it had been hard to access the vein. Avery's back ached from leaning over the table, so he could imagine how awkward it had been for Belle, with her pregnant belly and fatigue.

Robyn's blue eyes were steady. But he was getting to know her a little better every day. He could see the hint of panic there. She hid things well.

But she shouldn't have to. Even though this was modern day, sexism was still rife in the health services. He met it by being a male nurse, instead of opting to be a medic. Robyn had the opposite issue. Women were not the weaker sex, but tell that to their male counterparts, who seemed to find it easier to gain promotion across all fields in medicine.

He smiled at her underneath his mask, knowing she probably couldn't tell. But moments later little crinkles appeared at the outer edges of her eyes. She was smiling back.

'Got it,' said Dr Shad, his hands seeming like the steadiest hands on the planet as the catheter was slowly withdrawn. All eyes went to the cardiac monitor, which seemed to spring into life. A few blips with gaps in between, followed by slow steady noise. Blip. Blip. Blip. Avery had never been so relieved in his life.

The theatre wasn't jubilant. Everyone knew how serious things still were for this young woman. There was also the added trauma of the prolonged cardiac massage, plus the chance of her brain being affected by the potential lack of oxygen circulating in her system. No one would know the truth of that until Mabel woke up.

Dr Shad was meticulous. He closed and stitched the wound, had a long conversation with Flo and Toby about immediate plans for Mabel. She would be moved to Cardiac Intensive Care and remain ventilated for the next few hours, with assessment from all three doctors in six hours' time.

Avery could see Robyn following every word. The appreciation of their attention to detail and patient care was evident in her eyes. Some senior physicians would leave all the follow-up care to their more junior colleagues. But Dr Shad had never been like that, and Avery knew Toby was exactly the same. He was a caring and meticulous surgeon. It was part of the reason he approved of his best friend loving him. They were a perfect match.

'Mabel's husband, Tom, and her father will be in the waiting room. Who would you like to speak to them, Dr Shad?'

Dr Shad answered straight away. 'I'll talk to them. I'll apologise for not talking to them beforehand and give them an overview of what's happened.' He glanced down at Mabel. 'The next few days will be crucial, as will the next month for Mabel. She's beaten the statistics today, and we'll have to do our best to ensure she continues to have the best chance of beating them.'

'I'll come with you,' said Toby. 'I know the family well. They may want an explanation from me too.'

Dr Shad nodded appreciatively and completed Mabel's wound, allowing Flo and the newly arrived team from Cardiac Intensive Care to take Mabel around and get her connected up to all the equipment that would be needed for her care.

As the rest of the team exited through the doors it was only Avery and Robyn that were left. He stripped off his surgical gown, gloves, mask and hat, taking a deep breath at the relief of some air around his skin.

Robyn did the same, stuffing her disposable garb into a nearby disposal cart, and pulling her scrub top from her chest. She moved over and leant against the flat theatre wall. Avery knew she would get instant relief from the cool wall.

'Belle,' he said quickly. 'Give me two minutes until I check she's okay.' He looked around at the rest of the theatre. 'And I'm not normally in here. I'll need to check the procedure for preparing the theatre again.'

'No need,' came a voice from the door, as one of the regular theatre team came in. 'Leave it to me.'

'Are you sure?' asked Avery.

The guy put his hand on Avery's arm. 'Go and have a seat for five. Everyone's talking about what just happened in here.'

'Thanks,' said Avery and gestured with his head to Robyn. 'You coming with me?'

It seemed natural to ask her. They'd done everything else together, and if she was surprised she didn't say, but her lips gave a soft smile and she nodded. They washed their hands again and made their way along to the theatre staffroom.

Belle was sitting in a corner, surrounded by food. She held up her cup and a cookie as they walked in. Her colour was much better and she had her feet up on another chair.

'Mr Sunshine, I could have kissed you when you walked into that theatre today.'

Avery walked over and kissed the top of her head. 'Well, I'll kiss you instead. I'm just glad you're okay. You should have told someone you didn't feel well.'

She blew out a breath. 'I know. I felt a bit light-headed when we went in. But it was such an emergency and no one else was available. I got caught up in the adrenaline of it all. I didn't have time to run about and find someone else.'

He sat in the chair next to her, picked a cookie from the bag, then handed it to Robyn. 'How many weeks are you now? Twenty-eight, twenty-nine?'

Belle gave the broadest grin. 'I love how you always remember. Twenty-nine.'

'Maybe it's time to take a breath now and then.'

'Oh, don't worry. You set Mack on me. Have you any idea what he's like? He says if he'd known I'd gone in there, he would have come and hunted me out anyway. He'd already reminded me to eat.'

Avery nodded approvingly. 'In that case, I'm glad I set Mack on you. He has your back. That's what you need.' Avery leaned forward. 'Seriously, I know everywhere is short right now. I can ask if I can stay and cover here today if you need to go home and rest.'

Belle gave a laugh and slapped his arm. 'Avery Smith, you hate Theatre!'

He shrugged. 'I know,' he admitted. 'But if you need cover, I'll do it.'

She shook her head. 'I have more staff coming on duty in an hour, and all the surgeries are covered for today. We should be fine. But I appreciate the offer.' Her gaze flicked to Robyn, before she added, 'Not everyone would make it.'

She nibbled at her cookie and then spoke to Robyn. 'And you had an initiation of fire today. I promise you, we're not usually like that. I run a very refined theatre in these parts,' she joked, 'even if my past star student didn't pick it for their permanent job.'

'Thank you,' said Robyn, and Avery looked at her in surprise. It was the first time he'd ever heard a shake in her voice.

'Let's go,' he said smoothly. 'I'm glad you're feeling better, Belle.'

He stood up and held the door open for Robyn, waiting until they were halfway along the corridor, then taking a quick look up and down. No one else was around. He opened the nearest door, touched Robyn's elbow and indicated to her to come inside.

If she was surprised, she didn't show it. In fact, she willingly stepped inside the linen and scrub closet then put her hands over her face.

Avery froze for half a second, then did what his instincts told him to do, and wrapped his arms around her.

She started to shake and he knew she was crying. But instead of trying to fill the silence with a whole lot of words, he just stayed there, holding her, and letting her cry.

One of his hands rubbed her back, just the way his own mother had done for him years ago.

After she stopped shaking he bent his head and whispered in her ear. 'What's wrong? You did great today.'

For a moment she said nothing. He just felt her breathe, the rise and fall of her chest next to his. Then she lifted her head. Her blue eyes were red-rimmed. Her eyes were glassy, smudged with eyeliner that had run. Her hair was escaping around her face, tiny pink spots on her pale cheeks. It was the most vulnerable he'd ever seen her. 'Did I?' she asked, her voice angry. 'Mabel could have died today. If I'd been left with her, she *would* have died. I should have been more decisive. I should have acted quicker.'

Avery put his hands on her shoulders and pushed her

back a little so he could see her entire face. 'You did act decisively. You did a cardiac echo in the middle of the resus room on a patient who'd arrested. You made the clinical decision she'd had a PE and took it from there.'

She shook her head. 'But I should have made the call quicker. By the time we got upstairs too much time had passed. What if Mabel is brain-damaged because we took too long to get the clot out of her lung?'

'You had an anaesthetist intubate on scene. Mabel had the best chance of oxygen circulating around her system. First line for a PE is always a clot-buster drug. Even at rapid delivery it should be fifteen minutes.'

He could still feel her body tremble beneath his palms. 'Thirty-one minutes,' she murmured.

He tightened his grip a little on her shoulders. 'Don't focus on that. We have a responsibility to time the start of any arrest.' He shook his head in bewilderment and smiled at her. 'Robyn, you did good. Dr Shad will tell you that. He was impressed by you, I could tell. Do you know how often a more junior doctor gets invited into emergency theatre? Never.'

'But everyone's off sick,' she said, throwing her hands up.

'He didn't know that,' Avery said. 'He asked you to come up because he considered Mabel your patient, as well as his. I know this guy. He didn't invite you into his theatre lightly.'

'Really?' For the first time since they'd come in here, he could see a spark of hope in her eyes.

'Really,' he repeated. He took a deep breath. 'Robyn,' he said slowly. Then, before he even thought about it, he was tracing a finger across her brow, and then down her nose. Her head moved automatically, responding to his touch.

Her gaze connected with his. Neither of them spoke.

But Robyn, almost in slow motion, rose onto her toes and wrapped her arms around his neck.

The first brush of lips was tentative. But that lasted mere milliseconds. The next touch was definite. Sure. Without a single doubt.

The length of her body was pressed against his. He could feel every curve. His hand ran down one side of her body, tracing the outline of her waist and hips. Her lips were soft, matching him in every way.

He inhaled deeply, sensing the remnants of that spicy perfume he'd first noticed on her. His mouth went from her lips to her neck and to her ears. Her hair tickled against his skin, her breathing quickening.

His body was reacting to hers, and he stopped for a second, conscious of exactly where they were. She sensed his reaction, and took a deep breath, letting him rest his forehead against hers. She smiled up at him.

'Well, that came out of nowhere,' she said huskily.

'Not exactly.'

Her blue eyes seemed brighter. She leaned back, keeping her gaze locked on his, then stepped back completely. 'We have to go back along to the unit.'

He nodded, adjusting his scrubs, knowing he wouldn't be leaving this linen closet for the next few minutes. Robyn bit her bottom lip and reached behind him, grabbing a clean set of scrubs. 'I'm going to head to the locker room and shower,' she said. 'After the ER and Theatre, I think I need to freshen up.'

He gave her a nod and smile, particularly when her gaze lowered. 'See you in five?' she asked.

'Absolutely,' he said. Robyn laughed as she walked out of the door.

Avery leaned back against the scrub trolley. What on earth was he doing? He'd always had his own rules about dating colleagues. His family life was complicated enough without letting his work life get complicated too. He was still standing there when there was a sharp rap at the door, followed by a recognisable laugh.

'You decent?' It was Serena's voice.

He groaned. 'Would it make a difference if I said no?'

'Not at all,' she said as she pushed the door open and stood in the doorway, grinning. 'Toby told me what happened and I came to find you. No one knew where you were.'

He leaned his head back. He knew exactly what was coming next. Serena had that gleam in her eye—the one that appeared whenever she was about to tease him relentlessly.

She put a hand on her hip. 'But then, by some weird co-incidence, I saw Robyn ducking out of here and into the changing rooms, and I thought—' she put her hand under her chin '—wait a minute...'

'Stop,' he groaned again.

'Not a chance.' Serena's grin was broad. 'I thought, wait—' she mocked shock '—could my good friend Avery, possibly, by any chance, be in a *linen closet* with the feisty red-headed doc he's been lusting over?'

'I have not!'

She clicked her fingers and shook her head. 'Nope. Too quick. The man doth protest too much.'

He narrowed his gaze. 'Isn't that supposed to be the lady?'

'Who cares?' she declared, throwing her hands in the air. 'Spill.'

'Absolutely not.'

She folded her arms and stood across the doorway. 'I'm

patient,' she said steadily. 'I can stand here all day.' She patted her stomach, 'And you can't push past me because I'm a pregnant woman.'

'Stop being smug.' He pointed at her belly. 'And I don't want my godchild to hear you trying to bully me.'

Serena raised her eyebrows. 'What my child is hearing is their mom sorting out their single, sad uncle Avery and helping him find his happy ever after.'

Avery rolled his eyes. 'You were never this unbearable before you met Toby,' he joked.

She pointed to her face. 'What you mean is, I was never this happy. Now, don't try and distract me. Robyn had a very interesting look on her face when she left this linen closet. Want to tell me why?'

Avery was instantly interested. 'Why? What did she look like?'

He could tell Serena was contemplating carrying on with her teasing, but she gave a sigh and said, 'Happy.'

'She did?'

Serena gave a shrug. 'I don't know her well. But from where I was standing, Dr Grumpy looked pretty happy.'

Avery couldn't help but smile. He hadn't even had time to think about what had just happened between him and Robyn, but the very fact that Serena said that Robyn looked happy made his heart miss a few extra beats.

'She might have moved in,' he said quickly.

'What?' Serena's eyes widened. 'No way. Not even you move that quickly.'

He shook his head. 'It's only just happened, and it's not like that. She was having trouble sleeping in her room at the hospital. I offered her your old room in the apartment.'

Serena opened her mouth and then closed it again. He'd

clearly taken her unawares. She held up one hand. 'But, but—'

'But nothing. We've only been roommates the last few days. Nothing else.'

He moved forward and spoke down to Serena's belly. 'Right, tot, tell your momma to get out my way. Uncle Avery has work to do.'

Serena reluctantly stood back. 'Romance work, or real work?' Clearly still a bit stunned by all this news.

Avery tapped the side of his nose. 'That's for me to know, and you to find out.'

He started down the corridor, heading towards the cardiac intensive care unit.

'You know I will,' came the amused voice after him.

Avery didn't turn around. He didn't want Serena to see exactly how wide his grin currently was. So, he just lifted his hand and waved, as he pushed through the doors to meet Robyn, just as he'd promised.

CHAPTER FIVE

Robyn was buzzing. Her skin and lips were on fire, her brain couldn't stop firing either. Now she was sleeping in a perfectly peaceful apartment, it wasn't noisy deliveries to the hospital kitchen that were keeping her awake.

Yesterday had been one of the best, and one of the worst moments in her personal and professional life. And the weirdest part was, how all those pieces intertwined.

The arrest call had been devastating. Robyn could admit to herself how absolutely overwhelmed with panic she'd actually felt. She'd looked at the young woman lying on the emergency trolley and imagined herself, and every one of her friends, being that person.

There had been a real element of luck involved yesterday. The pulmonary embolism diagnosis had been pure instinct. But she could have been wrong. And if she had been, she wasn't sure what might have happened—except the certainty that Mabel would have died.

Avery had been the calmest man on the planet. The few times he'd caught her gaze she could almost hear him whispering next to her. *You've got this.* His calm nature gave her confidence in her decision-making, and she was so glad he'd been there.

Dr Shad inviting her into his theatre was, for any junior doctor, a dream come true. She'd had to will her hands not to shake, and her brain had tried to absorb every movement, every conversation, every technique she'd witnessed. She'd be processing this for days.

Then, there was the last part. The part that involved Avery Smith.

She was lying in her bed and just thinking about him made her skin prickle. The adrenaline had been running through her system so much at the time. She could remember the total exhaustion hitting her, plus the overwhelming emotions of the day, as she'd walked down that hospital corridor. Feeling Avery's arms around her had first been welcoming, then enticing.

She'd been conscious of the vibe between them—she just wasn't sure she was reading it correctly. Of course, he was handsome. Of course, he teased and flirted. He was nicknamed Mr Sunshine after all. There had been the looks. The atmosphere between them when they'd had dinner. His casual suggestion that he show her around the city. The offer of his spare room. And the building attraction between them now that they were under one roof.

But the one thing she was sure she'd read correctly was the connection between them and the kiss from yesterday. It had definitely been real. It had definitely been reciprocated. She hadn't flung herself at him. It had been a mutual meeting.

They'd both appeared back on the intensive cardiac unit. But all focus had had to be on Mabel and supporting her family. Robyn had had to stop her mind drifting back to the kiss and concentrate on the complicated regime of blood tests and drugs that Mabel would need for the rest of that day, and for the next few weeks. She'd been happy to stay late and take notes. Learning was why she was here.

It had been odd, watching the rise and fall of Mabel's chest following her ventilation, and watching it in conjunction with the beeping monitor proving Mabel's heart was functioning again. Of course, what she longed for was Mabel to be breathing on her own, and sitting up in bed, holding hands with her husband. But that could be weeks. Nothing could be taken for granted.

Nothing.

As they'd both finished last night Avery had hesitated next to her. Others had still been around. Some in earshot. So, he'd said very gently, 'I'll get us pizza on the way home.'

She'd been too surprised to give a response. But he'd just smiled and gone on his way. Home.

The word sent a little flicker of warmth through her body. She'd never really had great feelings of affection for her home with her parents. Their relationship had always been strained, and they'd never been all that interested in Robyn.

But back at the apartment with Avery? It was like living in another world. One where camaraderie existed. She was relaxed in a way she hadn't felt before.

They were both finally on days off for the next few days.

She couldn't remember ever being this muddled up by a guy. She dated. Or she didn't date. There was nothing in between. Never anything casual. It wasn't her style. But Avery didn't know her style—did he?

For the next few hours her brain continued to climb up mountains, then tumble down into valleys. It was ridiculous. She needed sleep. But her brain wouldn't quieten enough to let her sleep.

Robyn groaned and sat up. She might as well go out. She glanced out of the window. It was a beautiful early morning in San Diego. She started most days with a run, but today her eyes were muggy and her muscles ached. She couldn't take pounding the sidewalks today.

Instead, she dressed in denim shorts and a white shirt, tied at her waist. As she grabbed her bag, a vision of cakes in a white box came into her mind.

Avery had been carrying a box when she'd bumped into him that other morning. She'd tried a few bakeries in the Gaslamp District, but there might be another she hadn't found yet. Hopefully it also sold the strongest kind of coffee. She could buy them breakfast before they went out this morning. That would be nice.

She stuck a clip in her crossbody bag for her hair in case she felt sticky, along with her wallet, sunglasses, sunscreen and phone. Some mascara and lipstick later, she walked out.

'Hey.'

She jumped. Avery was sitting on the sofa, dressed in jeans and a T-shirt and giving her his trademark smile.

She glanced at her watch. 'It's barely after seven.'

'I know. If you'd taken much longer I might have got cranky. I need coffee soon.'

'And if I'd decided to have a long lie-in?'

He grinned. 'I would have told you which coffee shop to meet me at, and you would have found me there, dehydrated, cranky, and probably shrivelled from all the heat outside.'

Robyn laughed out loud. 'Well, we can't have that. Makes you sound like a house plant I've forgotten to water.'

He gave her a fake shocked look. 'Are you a house-plant murderer?' He put a burr on his r's, attempting a Scottish accent, and Robyn kept laughing. He held out his hands. 'There's a reason I have no house plants.'

She wagged her finger. 'You're going to have to do better

than that.' She looked out of the nearby window. 'It's going to be a hot one today, isn't it?'

'You bet,' he said. 'Let's just hope the air conditioning can cope.'

She closed her eyes for a second. 'Don't remind me what it's like to sleep in a room with no air conditioning.' She gave him a smile. 'I was going to go and get breakfast for us both.'

He gave a wide smile. 'Well, that's a nice way to start the day. But let's go together. What's it to be? Pastries? Doughnuts? Or eggs? You need to tell me, so I can make sure we go to the best breakfast haunt.'

They left the apartment together and stepped into the elevator. 'Hmm, decisions, decisions… Isn't there a place that does all three?'

'Do you want all three mediocre? Or one out of three that's the best of the best?'

'Eggs,' she said quickly. 'Along with great coffee.'

They left the apartment and walked casually together. It was hotter than usual, and Robyn was already pulling her shirt from her body. He took her to a two-storey restaurant that looked over the marina.

It took coffee seriously. Robyn even got to pick the coffee beans she wanted ground from a huge selection behind the counter, as well as ordering a four-egg omelette with peppers, ham and cheese.

They settled at a table on the first floor, the windows folded completely back, in front of and behind them, to let the breeze flow through the entire restaurant.

Avery had pushed his sunglasses up on his head. The swim-trunks-clad model flashed into her head again and she tried not to smile.

'So, what's it to be?' he asked her.

'What do you mean?'

He pointed across the marina. 'We can do a city tour on the trolley, cross the bridge, spend some time in Coronada, hit the outlet malls, or just wander around and watch the world. You gave me a whole list of things you wanted to do.'

'So, I can pick anything?'

He nodded. As their waiter appeared and set down her fragrant coffee and fluffy omelette, Robyn tried not to imagine this was going to be the perfect day. So far, it sounded that way. But she didn't want to put too much stake in things. It had been only one kiss, after all.

One heart-stopping, mind-bending kiss, so rational thinking was hard.

'Pick anything,' he reiterated.

She took a few forkfuls of her omelette. Perfect. Just the way it looked.

'Okay, so I would like to do all the tourist things and some more sightseeing. But I'd also really like to hit the outlet malls. I have a few things I need to pick up.'

'No problem,' he said with an easy smile. 'Outlet malls it is. There's one we can get a trolley to, and there's a stop not far from here. Looking to get some bargains?'

It was an innocent question, but Robyn automatically started coughing. She took a sip of her coffee and tried to form an appropriate response. 'I'd like some new running shoes to replace the ones I have. I don't need a particular design or label, just something that does the job. Same with running clothes and replacing a few staples from my wardrobe.'

He gave her a curious glance as he sipped his coffee. 'What, you don't want a particular type of designer coat, or bag, or computer? Usually when I take friends to the outlet malls, they want a whole host of designer gear.'

Robyn pressed her lips together for a second. Last thing she wanted was to sound like a misery-guts, or someone who was completely tight-fisted. She decided to go with the partial truth. 'I didn't have a lot growing up, so I don't spend money on things I don't need. I've always tended to wait until something was worn and needed replacing, rather than just splurge on things.'

'You never just buy something for fun?'

'Only in my dreams.'

He paused, before realising she wasn't joking. Robyn was aware of the strange silence between them and tried to fill it. 'My fun is books. I don't need designer bags or shoes or jewellery. If I treat myself, it's generally a book I really wanted and couldn't get in a library or online.'

Avery nodded slowly. He looked thoughtful for a moment. 'Not sure there's a bookstore at the outlet mall, but I'll be able to show you some when we get back. I might have a favourite I can introduce you to.'

The late summer heat in San Diego was rising around them, and Robyn felt a trickle of sweat sneak down her spine. She pulled her white shirt from her skin for a few moments, conscious of Avery's eyes on her.

'Want to go?' he said. 'There should be a trolley in a few minutes.'

She nodded and picked up her bag to pay the bill but Avery was too quick for her—not even asking the waitress, just moving over to the counter, handing over some dollar bills and coming back holding two bottles of iced water.

'I was going to pay,' she said.

'My treat.' His voice was insistent and she was uncomfortably conscious he'd paid for dinner the last time they'd been out too.

They walked to the trolley and Robyn bought her ticket from the machine—when she tried to buy Avery's he wouldn't let her. The trolley arrived quickly and was spacious enough for them to find a seat. It was busy, but not overcrowded, and the journey took around twenty minutes.

The outlet mall was a short walk from the trolley stop and Robyn smiled at the size of it. The buildings were spread out, bright, spacious, with many recognisable designer names across the store fronts.

'Do you need anything?' she asked as they started wandering through the outlet.

'I might pick up a few things,' he said casually.

Robyn got the distinct impression that while Avery didn't mind shopping, he'd only done this to keep her happy. 'Let's just stay here for a couple of hours,' she said quickly. 'How about around lunch time we head back and do some sightseeing?'

He gave a nod, and smiled when she pointed at one store and said, 'Let's try this one.'

It didn't take long for Robyn to find the few items she needed. She was a precise shopper—not the type to browse for hours or deliberate over things. She always knew what she was looking for, and if it wasn't there, then she just moved on.

As they left one store, and headed straight into another, Avery started to laugh at her.

'What?'

He waved his hand. 'I only wish all the females I know shopped like this.'

'What do you mean?'

'You waste no time. When I was a kid, my mother could spend hours in one place, trying on the same blouse in a dozen colours, trying to decide what she liked best.' He pointed to a set of benches outside the store front. 'I would spend most of my time on one of those, generally with a soda or an ice cream.'

'Are you hinting?' she asked.

He looked confused for a second. 'For what?'

'Ice cream.'

'Ah.' He nodded. 'Probably, and I know just the place.'

She walked alongside him. 'I've never been someone who spends all day trying clothes or shoes on. It's not that I never do that—of course I do, if I'm not sure about a size or style. But my friends back home used to call me the scanner.'

'The scanner?'

'Yes, they said I walked into a store, scanned the whole place, spotted a few things I liked, picked them up, tried them on and was ready to leave by the time they'd reached the second rail of clothing.' She gave a shrug. 'I think I used to drive them nuts. They were much more like your mother.'

Avery gave a smile. She could tell instantly he was re-membering something. He hadn't mentioned his parents before. And she felt compelled to ask the question.

'Is your mom not here any more?'

It should have felt more awkward and intrusive than it actually did. And Avery didn't seem upset or annoyed by the question. He gave a sad smile. 'No, not for a number of years.'

'I'm sorry,' she said simply. 'What about your dad?'

'He died fifteen years before my mom. They didn't have a great relationship—he was married to someone else when he met my mother and hadn't told her, so, although I knew him, I didn't get to spend much time with him.'

Robyn gave a nod.

'What about your parents?' he asked.

'They're fine,' she said, although that wasn't entirely true. 'They stay back in Scotland. Both have suffered some health issues.'

'They must love having a daughter that's a doctor, then.' She understood where he was coming from, but Avery had never met her parents, and probably wouldn't understand what they were like.

'I might have gone to medical school and worked across the world, but they don't ever ask, or take, my advice. They would rather listen to anyone else other than me. I can't seem to fight my way out of that "daughter" bubble.'

'You sound kind of sad about that.' Avery was looking at her curiously as they walked along.

'It's complicated,' she said, wondering how much to reveal about her life. 'They don't live in the best area.' She lifted her hand in way of explanation. 'You'll understand that health inequalities are linked to deprivation. It's one big cycle that lots of people can't just break out of.'

Avery's brow creased and she kept going.

'You suffer from poor health that affects your mind or your body, and because of your poor health you struggle to get work. Then because you have no work, your income is reduced, and because your income is reduced you choose a cheaper diet and can't always pay the bills for heating—even when it's very cold.' She let out a big sigh, 'And then, because you're cold, that has an impact on your chest, lungs and the rest of your body. And the cycle just continues.'

Avery's steps had slowed. 'Is there anything I can help with?'

She froze and looked at him. Those green eyes were fixed on her, full of concern. She wasn't entirely sure what he meant. But she also knew she didn't want to find out.

Robyn was so used to playing her cards close to her chest when it came to her family. She'd always had a difficult relationship with her parents, and that made things tougher. She was passionate about the inequalities in health all across the world—that some people had access to healthcare and facilities, good housing and employment, while others didn't. With the most significant factor between the two parties being wealth. It made her want to sit in a corner and weep.

Trouble was, while most with a background in health agreed in principle, not all had the passion that she had. The courage of her convictions had resulted in many challenging conversations—particularly when a lot of doctors also came from privileged positions.

She chose her words carefully. 'I bought them a new boiler a couple of months ago, and I occasionally pay their heating bills for them. They're not always careful about how they spend money.' She gave Avery a cautious smile. 'But when I know that both my parents would rather spend money on cigarettes, and sometimes alcohol, than heating for their home or proper food, it causes a lot of strain between us.'

She could tell he was shocked. He tried to hide it, but Robyn was in tune with how people hid parts of themselves when these conversations started.

'Do you go home to see them often?'

She swallowed. 'Not frequently, and I don't stay with them if I visit. In truth, it doesn't really feel like home to me and it never really did. But I try to help whenever I know there's an issue. To be fair to them, they don't normally ask. This time around my dad had a terrible chest infection that didn't seem to shift for a few weeks, and when I asked about the heating, my mother said the boiler had broken and couldn't be repaired. But if I hadn't asked that question?' She shook her head, 'I would never have known.'

Avery reached out and took her hand, entwining his fingers with hers. 'Families are tough,' he said. 'I know that. And our relationships with them can be even tougher. I won't comment, because it's not my place.' He gave her a stiff smile. 'And my pet hate in life is someone else commenting on a life they're not leading. The old *walk a mile in my shoes* thing, I'm a big believer in that.'

She looked at him with interest.

He tilted his head to the side. 'But later, if we have time, I'd like to take you to a place I work at.'

She gave a nod of her head. 'I'd like that.'

They'd reached the ice-cream store by now and looked in the window at the array of ice creams, sorbets and frozen yoghurts, and stood shoulder to shoulder. She contemplated his words, wondering exactly what she didn't know about Avery Smith. He'd never really spoken about his family before. Since they'd met, he'd struck her as a *found family* kind of guy. That was the general impression he gave around his relationship with best friend Serena. There were a few others that he'd mentioned, and she got the impression he would move mountains for his friends if he could.

She gave a little sigh as she looked at all the names on the ice creams. 'I hate that the world isn't fair. I hate that if you are born into money, a whole array of problems are just wiped out for you—whereas at the other end of the spectrum, if you're born into poverty, especially if you lose your job, or have an accident, it can send you into a spiral that there seems no way out of.'

'Lots of people who are rich have problems too. There's a million things that money can't buy.' He was looking at her cautiously.

'I know,' she said honestly, 'but it can also solve a whole host of issues that are insurmountable for others. I find that if people have money, they don't really understand the other side of the coin.'

There was an awkward kind of silence. She decided to break it. 'I'm just a sci-fi girl at heart. I want to live in the *Star Trek: The Next Generation* world where there's no need for money—where they've eliminated hunger, inequalities and the need for possessions.'

He raised an eyebrow. 'And yet Picard still managed to get into a whole heap of trouble.'

Robyn laughed out loud. 'Yes, he did,' she agreed. She pointed at the window. 'Okay, black raspberry and chocolate chunk is calling to me. What about you?'

His shoulders seemed to relax a little. 'Oh, I'm old school, chocolate mint with chocolate sprinkles.'

Robyn was thoughtful for a moment. 'Hmm, sprinkles, haven't had those in years. Okay, I'm persuaded.'

She had her wallet out before they'd even crossed the threshold of the store and paid for their ice creams before he could offer. 'Finished shopping?' he asked.

She nodded as she looked at her few bags. There were other people all around who were carrying so many bags they looked as though they might topple over. But even though she'd needed every item she'd purchased today, and they were cheaper than normal, she was still the tiniest bit uncomfortable having spent so much.

'I'm definitely done,' she said.

'Good, let's head back to the trolley, and we can join one of the tourist trams around San Diego.' He looked up at the cloudless sky. 'It's a gorgeous day. If we go across the marina, you can see the beach at Coronado, and—' he gave a smile '—I've got an idea for something special this afternoon.'

Robyn gave a nod, and they walked back together. The slight tension between them seemed to ease, but she couldn't help but feel it had been her fault it was there in the first place. Avery was unfailingly easy mannered, but every now and then she saw a little flicker of something behind his eyes.

It was ironic really. She could talk. Her lifetime of pent-up frustrations of spending a childhood at the worst end of the poverty spectrum always threatened to bubble over. She was too passionate about things, had so many lived experiences that had, in turn, affected her life in a whole host of ways she hadn't fully understood until she was an adult. Some of it she was still processing today, and she knew at some point it would do her good to sit down with a therapist to take it all apart.

Most of the time she tried to keep things buried. She wasn't in that position any more. She would never be rich as a doctor—she would never do private practice and would likely return to the UK and work in the NHS—but she hoped to live above the poverty line in a way there had never been a chance to before. Doctors in the UK system weren't paid as well as people thought.

She didn't want to remember being hungry, or wearing shoes two sizes too small. She didn't want to remember not going to birthday parties of school friends because she could never take them a present—no matter how small.

Her library card had been her blessing. A place that was always warm, had electricity, and a world of information. She wanted to go back in time, and whisper in her own eight-year-old ear and tell her that one day she would be in America, she'd be a doctor, and be eating ice cream and visiting beautiful beaches and feeling the heat on her skin.

Her past self would never have believed it.

The journey back to San Diego seemed quicker and they boarded the orange trolley to take them around the city and over the marina.

As they travelled through the main parts of the city, Avery showed her the area where the free clinic he worked in was, and where the soup kitchen was. She knew just by looking that the trolley deliberately stayed away from the poorest parts of the city. She understood it, but it still made her sad. Why shouldn't people who visited San Diego see all of the city—the good parts and the bad? Then maybe they would have a more balanced opinion on how things were, and maybe even consider where they could help. Cities, worldwide, always had the richest and poorest of people, and she knew without doubt she wanted to help everyone, regardless of income or background.

'I'd like that.' She nodded and relaxed back into the trolley seat as it changed direction once again.

Robyn held her breath as they crossed the bridge. The view really was spectacular. The range of boats, from the military vessels to the luxury cruisers, was breathtaking. By the time they reached Coronado, the heat was building.

Robyn rubbed on some sunscreen and handed it to Avery as they exited the trolley.

'Coronado means "the crown city",' said Avery as they started along the sidewalk.

Robyn looked around in awe. It was busy, with lots of holidaymakers, and a real vibrant vibe about the place. They wandered through the farmers' market, trying fresh berries, admiring the brightly coloured flowers available, and sampling a few cheeses.

The white sand beach stretched for two miles. There were ample sunbeds and parasols available for hire, families playing on the beach and in the sea. But as they moved further along, Robyn started to get excited.

'A dog beach?' she asked Avery, a wide smile on her face.

He nodded. 'Yep, there is a designated dog beach, where dogs can be let off the leash. Want to go down?'

'Try and stop me,' she said, moving swiftly onto the sand.

She couldn't help herself, asking owners if they minded, then stopping to talk to every friendly dog that she held her hand out to. There were terriers, chihuahuas, cocker spaniels, Great Danes, French bulldogs, retrievers, Labradors and whole host more.

'Didn't know you were a dog-lover,' remarked Avery, a look of pure amusement on his face. She noticed that more often than not he was down on his knees in the sand, letting dogs lick his hands and jump up on him.

'Oh, I never had one of my own. But I just loved them.'

'So, what would be your dream dog, then?' asked Avery.

'A fox red Labrador,' she said without hesitation. 'Friendly, good-natured dogs, but the red colour makes them just that little bit different.'

He was still grinning at her. 'Will you get one when

you finish your training programme and decide to stay in one place?'

Robyn bit her bottom lip. 'The ultimate dream? Well, it would be to find a for ever home that I could buy by my-self—I don't care if it's tiny, as long as it's all mine, and yes, a dog to come home to.' She held up a hand. 'But my dog would need doggie day-care—and that would likely be as expensive as the house.'

Robyn bent down to pat another dog, who'd appeared at her ankles. 'I should have brought treats,' she murmured.

Avery shook his head as a huge Siberian husky bounded over and jumped up on him. 'Hello, girl,' he said without hesitation, not fazed at all by her jumping up, and rubbing her behind the ears.

'So sorry.' A woman rushed over and called her dog. 'Glenda, come back.' The dog's ears perked up and she ran back to her owner.

'No problem,' Avery said with a wave. He turned back to face Robyn.

'Glenda?' they both said at the same time, then burst out laughing.

Before she had time to think about it, Avery slung his arm around her shoulders. He looked down at her, and she instantly felt a rush. This didn't seem awkward. This felt like the most natural position in the world. 'You seem to have given this a lot of thought,' he said, still smiling.

For a few seconds she was lost. Lost in the sensation of his body next to hers, and the scent of his skin. She couldn't remember ever feeling like this. Of course, she'd dated. But nothing important. Nothing that seemed significant, not even the guy at medical school. Not like this.

That final thought shook her out of her daydream. 'What?' she said as they started to walk along the beach together.

'The dog.' He grinned. 'You've given a lot of thought to getting a dog.'

She reached her hand up to clasp his hand that was on her shoulder. He was as close as he'd been all day, and she didn't want that to change.

'I have. I'm an adult now, and once I get my training pro-gramme finished and have a permanent post somewhere, it's definitely what I want to do.' She put her other hand on her heart as she looked across the beach. 'Imagine coming home to one of these wee faces. Someone that just loves you unconditionally. That is my idea of heaven.'

She was conscious of how the words sounded once she said them out loud. He couldn't possibly know she'd never had those feelings of love and security from her parents, and parts of her insides were cringing—praying that he didn't think she was actually hinting heavily about want-ing a partner to love her unconditionally.

Well, of course she did. But right now, she was talking about a dog.

'It's the hours,' he said, and his words had a touch of melancholy to them.

'Yes.' She sighed in agreement, taking her free hand and sliding it around the back of his waist. 'It's the only thing that puts me off. Our hours can be crazy, and I couldn't stand the thought of my dog pining at home, wondering when I'd be back.'

'You should puppy share,' he said.

'What? What do you mean puppy share?' They were coming to the end of the leash-free beach and made their way back along the sidewalk.

'I have friends who puppy share. They both really wanted a dog. Did crazy hours, so decided to puppy share. They have some doggie day-care too, but it works well.'

Robyn stared up at him. 'Like some divorced couple sharing custody of a child?'

He gave a shrug. 'I don't know, maybe. But I can assure you, they're not a couple. Never have been, and both have their own places. They compare off-duty and holidays and try to do opposite shifts.'

Robyn started to smile. 'I've never heard of that. But it sounds great. Of course, it's years away, but it's something I'll think about later. Thanks for that.' She looked at him, and he slowed his steps.

'No problem.' He bent down and kissed her on the lips as they were walking. It was casual, a momentary brush of lips. But it sent little pulses searing down her neck and chest. In her head she could see how they looked to other people—as if they had been doing this for years. But it wasn't. It was all brand new. And she wanted to savour it. To capture it somewhere so she could remember how this felt.

Her stomach gave a churn. It was like she already knew this would be taken away from her soon. As a rule, good things didn't really happen to Robyn Callaghan.

Her place on the programme had been due to her absolute hard work and constant studying. She'd sweated blood and tears for it.

But this? Nice things. Connections with people. They'd never really featured in Robyn's life, so she wanted to hold onto this with both hands.

And that made her scared. Very scared.

Last thing she wanted to do was act like some love-smitten teenager. If Avery acted like that with her, it would likely make her run for the hills. So, she couldn't quite get over the impact of feeling like that with him, and what she was supposed to do with it?

She could hear voices in her head from staff she'd met over the years. Kind folk, in a variety of hospitals, who'd realised how alone and isolated Robyn really was.

Just run with it. Take it a day at a time. Let things happen.

'I have another idea for doing something special this afternoon. Are you interested?' Avery's warm breath brushed against her cheek.

'Yes.'

'Are you ready to get the trolley back?'

'Absolutely.'

They boarded the trolley and she admired the view again as they crossed the bridge. It was a few stops before Avery signalled to her it was time to get off. He gave her a rueful smile. 'It's a bit of a walk from here.'

'No problem.'

He slid his hand into hers. She could tell they were moving away from the more prosperous parts of the city. The area they walked into was more run-down. Store fronts were closed, some vandalised. Housing was poorer, with broken shutters and roof tiles. The people around them glanced in their direction. If she hadn't been holding Avery's hand, she might have been nervous. But in a way, it was like walking back down some of the streets of Glasgow in the area in which she'd been raised. Her stomach twisted. She knew these people. She *was* one of these people.

Avery led her down the steps of a dilapidated-looking building with a nervous glance at her. He moved inside a cavernous space. It was like an old-style school cafeteria. Mismatched tables and chairs covered most of the space.

They were filled by a whole variety of people who looked as if they were having a hard time in life.

At the other side of the hall a queue had formed.

'This is the soup kitchen.' She looked at him.

He nodded. 'It is. Are you okay that I brought you here?'

She squeezed his hand and smiled at him. 'Absolutely. How can I help?'

He should have known. He shouldn't have doubted that Robyn would roll up her hypothetical sleeves and get to work straight away.

She took to it like a proverbial duck to water and, after the few things she'd said today about deprivation and her relationship with her parents, his stomach was starting to churn with his secret keeping.

Robyn didn't hide her feelings about inequalities. She actively disliked the divide between rich and poor. She was entirely right. He agreed with her.

But that didn't mean he didn't come from a very rich family himself, or have inherited wealth. Even though he kept a low profile, and spent his time working at the soup kitchen, and the free clinic, he wasn't sure that would save him in Robyn's eyes.

The more time he spent with her, the more he liked her. He watched as she easily dished out food to some of the homeless that visited the shelter. She then moved among the clients, sitting and talking to them. She found a new coat for an elderly gentleman, a pair of shoes for another in the donation stacks that were held in the supply room. She even disappeared for a while with another member of staff to dress a young woman's wound that she'd acquired the night before, and wouldn't say where from. Robyn made her promise to return the next day to the free clinic for antibiotics.

Nothing seemed to faze her. He'd had the briefest moment of doubt before he'd brought her here. But it was all without merit.

'Sign me up for regular shifts here,' she said as she slid her hands around him from behind. He was standing in one of the back rooms, sorting through some donations.

He leaned back into her. 'Really?'

'Absolutely,' she said with conviction. 'I wish I'd visited earlier. I can work here during the rest of my time at Paz Memorial.'

He spun around to look at her, putting his arms around her waist. 'I love that you've said that.'

There was a gleam in her eyes. 'I'm curious,' she said. 'You told me you worked here, and at the free clinic. Did you know someone around here that made you want to do it?'

Avery tried not to gulp. He didn't want to lie to Robyn. He'd funded both the soup kitchen and the free clinic, but hardly anyone knew that and, considering her views, he didn't know how to tell her. 'I just wanted to give back,' he said, because it was truthful. 'When I worked as a student I saw a lot of homeless people coming into the ER. There had been a soup kitchen years ago, but it had closed due to lack of funding and volunteers. When this one started, I was one of the first to volunteer, and I've encouraged a lot of others from Paz Memorial to help out. But…' he glanced around '…more than fifty per cent of the volunteers here have nothing to do with the hospital. They've come because they want to. Some were even homeless themselves at some point.'

Robyn gave a slow nod. He could almost see her brain

ticking. 'It's a good thing to do,' she said, 'and I'm very happy to help.'

'Well, in case you weren't aware, you're fabulous.' He whispered the words in her ear.

'Thank you,' she said.

He moved closer, his voice low. 'May I?'

She answered by putting her hand on his cheek and meeting his lips with hers. His lips found their way to her neck and ears. Her hands wound their way through his hair and around the tops of his arms and across his back. 'Maybe we should head back to the apartment,' he said in a low voice.

She pulled apart. 'Maybe we should.' The twinkle in her eye was real. He knew exactly where this could lead.

He slid his hand into hers and led her back through the kitchen, talking to a few volunteers and clients before they left.

He was having a hard time concentrating. He bought pizza for them on the way home and some beers, before finally heading back up to the apartment.

Robyn wasted no time. She appeared a few moments later having changed into comfortable soft pyjamas and sat down on the sofa.

She patted the seat next to her and he put the pizza and beer on the low table in front of them, sliding his arm around her back.

'Good day?' he asked.

'The best,' she agreed, brushing her lips against his.

There was a flash in his head. She was only here for six months, and one month of that was already gone. He knew instantly that he couldn't continue to keep secrets from Robyn for another five months. Not when he knew the strength of her convictions.

Not when he knew how strongly he was coming to feel for her.

Maybe this would go someplace, and maybe it wouldn't. But the last thing he wanted to do was to destroy something before it ever really had a chance to grow.

He would tell her.

He would find a way in the next few days to tell her who he really was, to tell her about his family and why he kept things secret.

She slid her fingers through his hair and he groaned. 'I lost you for a second there,' she murmured.

'No,' he said quickly, turning his full attention onto the woman in his arms. The woman who seemed to fit there perfectly.

'You've got me completely,' he said as his lips met hers once again.

CHAPTER SIX

AVERY HAD SPENT most of the next hours of the early morning thinking how, and when, he could tell Robyn the truth about himself. He had checked on her before he'd gone for a run this morning, and he couldn't fathom the tickling feeling in his stomach at watching her sleep, her red hair spread over his white pillows. It had made him run harder, and for longer, as he'd rationalised everything in his head.

By the time he arrived back, the apartment seemed strangely silent. For the briefest of seconds, he thought she might have found out everything, and left.

Then he heard the shower running, and pretended the panic hadn't existed, and casually loaded a pod into the coffee maker.

When Robyn padded back down the hall with her hair all piled up on her head and wearing a pink T-shirt and denim shorts again, he had the oddest sensation.

Serena and he had apartment-shared throughout their training and afterwards. They'd been comfortable around each other, good friends and completely at home with each other.

This felt entirely different. Something he'd never, ever experienced before.

Those simple steps, and the smile edging around her

lips, along with her still-sleepy eyes sent a message direct to his heart.

He wanted her to stay longer than five months.

It almost took the wind from his sails.

The rational part of his brain tried to tell him off. He didn't really know her. They'd worked together for only a short period of time. She didn't know everything about him.

But somehow, the message from his brain didn't get to his feet. Instead, they crossed the apartment and then he was kissing her.

Robyn threw back her head and laughed, before wrapping her hands around his neck and pressing her body up against his.

He walked her backwards. Back into the room they'd fallen into last night. He traced a finger down her nose. 'You sure?'

She gave him a grin. 'Oh, I'm sure,' and she rolled on top of him, and made him forget all about the conversations they needed to have.

When they finally emerged from his bedroom, Robyn disappeared for a while, coming back holding a stack of books. 'Do you mind?' she asked, gesturing to a half-empty shelf.

He gestured to a shelf that held a similar stack of his own. 'Help yourself.' It reminded him that they'd barely moved in together before they'd moved this relationship on.

'Sorry about the lack of sleep last night,' he murmured.

Robyn moved over and put her books on the shelf, raising her eyebrows at him. She sat back down next to him and smiled. 'We need to chat about rules.'

He set down the tablet he'd been holding. 'Sounds ominous.'

'I might have to restock your cupboards.'

'Phew, I thought you might say I can't disturb your sleep.' He gave her a suspicious look. 'What's wrong with my cupboards?'

She gave a casual shrug. 'I'm a girl of tradition. There's no pasta. No pasta sauce. No emergency frozen pizza. No jam. And definitely no emergency stash of chocolate.'

'Jam?'

'You call it jelly—but that's something else entirely in Scotland. I like raspberry jam on my toast in the morning.'

'You eat frozen pizza? I can make you pizza.'

She shook her head. 'Believe me. As a girl who has been a medical student for years, then a junior doctor, I have bizarre eating habits. You don't want me waking you up at three in the morning because I have a craving for pizza. That's why I need a few frozen.'

He gave a slow nod. 'And emergency chocolate.'

Robyn sighed and held up her hands. 'There *always* has to be emergency chocolate.'

'You're kind of bossy, aren't you?'

For a second she looked worried. 'I try not to be. But if I put my cards on the table, we'll get along better, won't we?'

He leaned forward and touched her arm. 'You think we won't get along?' He was grinning at her, and it only took a second before her pale blue eyes had a gleam in them.

She leaned forward too, brushing her lips against his. 'I think we might get along very well,' she said in a low voice.

He sank his hand into her dark red hair, pulling it free from its band and sending it tumbling around her shoulders. Her hair was always pulled back, neat and tidy at her work—just the way it should be. But loose around her shoulders, it was incredible.

'I hope you never get this cut,' he murmured.

'You like it.' The gleam in her eye had turned wicked. She brushed a strand of her hair across his face.

'Okay,' he groaned. 'Chocolate, pizza, whatever you want.'

She leaned forward and kissed him and then stopped. 'What is this?' she whispered.

'I'm not sure,' he answered honestly. 'I just know I've never done this before.'

She touched him with her hair again. 'You've never done this?' she teased sceptically.

He took her hand and sat it on his chest above his heart. 'I've never done *this*,' he corrected. 'I just know it feels right. And I want to do it. I want to see what happens next.'

'So do I,' she breathed, trying to stop tears from forming in her eyes. 'This connection terrifies me.'

He got it. He really did. 'Let's agree to be terrified together, then.' He smiled.

He was being honest. But he hadn't been totally honest, had he? And he would need to be with her. Part of Robyn struck him as raw—vulnerable even. He wanted to tread carefully with her. They were having this conversation. They were telling each other how they felt. But there was still a whole host of history, or background, of related trauma, of experiences, that every adult brought with them to any relationship.

They had time. They had time to learn about each other together. He didn't advertise parts of his life. He never had. Serena had found out by mistake, but, after the initial surprise, she'd been able to shake off any preconceived ideas. Serena had trained in San Diego, so she'd understood a little of his history. Would a girl from Scotland understand too?

He hoped so. Because he wanted this to mean something.

To be worth it. Because he thought Robyn Callaghan was worth it.

There was something just beneath her surface. A vulnerability that she didn't wear on her sleeve—instead it seemed like armour around her heart.

He wanted to shield her. Protect her. None of which was his business to do. He knew it. He had to let Robyn be whoever she wanted to be.

He just hoped they could be something together.

He stood up and held his hand out to her. 'I get the feeling you're not going to help my sleeping pattern,' she said as she slid into his arms again.

'Nights are for sleeping,' he said. 'Daytime? That can be for something else.'

And she grinned and agreed.

They spent the next few days in their own little bubble.

They had a few beers in local bars, sampled coffee from the best coffee shops and restocked the kitchen to Robyn's standard. She introduced Avery to an orange fizzy Scottish drink, to several chocolate biscuits and mallows he'd never seen before, and lamented loudly the fact no other country sold Scottish square sausage.

Avery wasn't entirely sure he ever wanted to taste it, but smiled and nodded willingly.

On their last day off work together he took her to the place he thought she might love best. The store was tucked away down a thin lane, between two buildings. Not really an official avenue or street. Nonetheless, there was a number of quirky little stores.

The front facing was old painted wood. The sign said, carefully painted, The Book Emporium. It didn't have the traditional wide storefront glass window, instead it was like lots of tiny windows surrounded by white wood—a bit like a chess board.

As Avery pushed open the main door there was a tinkle above them, and Robyn smiled at the metal chime. 'Haven't seen one of these in years.'

He watched as she stepped inside and stopped. She was a book person. He got that.

Robyn breathed in deeply. The smell of books. The thing that some people thought they could replicate in a candle, and absolutely couldn't.

The expression on her face said everything. He'd called this right.

Robyn's eyes were bright as she looked around in wonder. The wonky shelves were labelled, and all different sizes. It was as though someone had bought bookcases from all around the world and hadn't cared about the dimensions. The range of books went from ancient and falling apart, to brand new. She was wearing a bright pink dress today that reached her knees, and her hair was falling around her shoulders. The only concession to the heat outside was a dark green headscarf she'd used to keep her hair from falling onto her face, tying it like a headband and making her look like a modern-day Alice in Wonderland.

A small lady with a tiny dog under her arm appeared from a cupboard near the back. 'Avery.' She smiled. 'Oh.' Her eyes widened. 'You brought a friend.'

He nodded. 'Hi, Annie, this is Robyn—we work together. I thought I would introduce her to the best bookstore in San Diego.'

Annie, with tight curly hair and dressed in a bright pink and green kaftan, set down her small dog, who promptly came over to sniff Robyn. She bent down to pat it. 'What kind of dog is it?'

'No idea,' said Annie easily. 'She won't tell me.'

Robyn caught Avery's gaze. She gave him a careful smile—a secret message that she understood. 'Well, I like her very much.' The dog had hair similar to Annie's—in fact, they weren't that different.

Annie gave her an approving glance. 'That's Peggy. If she doesn't like you, you'll soon find out.'

Robyn gave a calm nod and kept petting Peggy. 'Books are everywhere,' said Annie casually, with a throwaway action of her arms. 'If you need something in particular, let me know.' She wandered off back among the shelves.

Robyn's eyes twinkled and she grinned at Avery as she ran her hand along one of the shelves. She was only just noticing how far back this store went. 'How long have we got?'

'All day,' he said easily. 'There are tables and armchairs near the back if you want to take a better look at some of the books. And a word of warning—Annie sometimes refuses to sell.'

'A bookseller who won't sell?'

He nodded. 'She's very particular. If she thinks a book isn't for you—she'll tell you.'

Robyn glanced over her shoulder to the disappearing form of Annie and gave a little smile. 'Next you'll be telling me she's a witch.'

Avery's eyebrows shot up and he wiggled his hand in a 'maybe' gesture. Robyn sighed and started to walk among the stacks.

Avery settled down in a chair next to books on shipwrecks, military history and ancient Egypt. There was always something new to find here. He'd found an old medical book once that showed a very inaccurate circulatory system, and he'd kept a hold of it, to remember how far medicine had come.

Robyn flitted from section to section, collecting a pile of books on a table nearby. Some romance. A historical nonfiction book. A science fiction. The latest thriller. Then he heard a squeal of excitement and got to his feet.

'What is it?'

She was kneeling on the floor in front of a shelf of children's books, holding one in her hand. It was clearly second-hand, and part of a children's series from years ago.

The whole children's section was beautifully decorated. One of the shelves had a wooden castle outlined in lightweight wood attached to the front of it and clearly hand-painted. One half was pink and purple with remnants of long-detached glitter, and the other half was grey and red with a green dragon billowing fire from one of the windows.

It was a little fantasy world tucked away in the corner of the bookstore to allow young imaginations to go wild. Instead, it had caught an adult, who was young at heart. He loved the fact she'd had no qualms about sitting on the floor and wrinkling her dress to find the book that she wanted.

'Do you know how long I've looked for this?' she said, clutching the book in both hands. 'I loved this series as a kid, but over the years I think my mum gave them all away. I've tried to get them back, with these original covers, and I've never been able to get this one.' She held it close to her chest. 'I can't believe I've finally found it. It must be at least thirty years old. My copy was already second-hand when I had it.'

He looked forward at the dark blue cover with a red lighthouse and two younger kids—a boy and a girl—standing in front of it. He'd had these books as a child too, but had never really fallen in love with the series. His mother had donated them to the local library. A thought probably best kept to himself right now.

'Is that the only one you need?' he asked.

She nodded. 'Some of the ones I've got are really dog-eared. This one is actually okay, especially when you think how old it is.' She stroked the cover and smiled. 'I wonder how many people have read this copy?'

'I wonder how many have loved it as much as you do.' There was something so wonderful about this. The expression on her face at finding something she'd looked for.

The door swung open and the chimes rang out. 'Perfect timing,' said Avery and made his way over to the door. A delivery driver had arrived with steaming coffees and a large white box. 'Annie,' he called over his shoulder.

Annie appeared out of nowhere, bustling forward as if she'd always been there. She gave Robyn a knowing grin. 'He always buys me coffee from that fancy place on the corner.' She picked up one of the coffees, and opened the white box, selecting a cupcake covered in rainbow sprinkles. Her eyes caught sight of the book in Robyn's hands. 'You like that series?'

Robyn nodded enthusiastically, 'I've been looking for this particular book for ten years.'

Annie gave her a curious stare. 'That's probably how long I've had this one in my store,' she said simply. She turned to the pile on the table. 'Also yours?' She thumbed through the selection.

'Yes,' said Robyn.

'You're missing something.' Annie looked thoughtful. 'Give me a minute.' She disappeared among some stacks, stopping to touch one book, before shaking her head and moving on to another. Avery could tell Robyn was intrigued. He'd seen Annie do this on numerous occasions with visiting customers. Whether she was just insightful, quirky, or had an actual gift, he had no idea. He just knew that he liked this woman and found her store inviting.

'Aha!' came the voice. Annie emerged from the stacks looking surprisingly out of breath, and her hair askew. She thumped a book down on top of Robyn's pile. 'The perfect book for you.' She tucked all the books under her arm and took them to the old-fashioned cash register.

'On me,' said Avery in Robyn's head but she shook her head firmly and put her hand on his.

'Absolutely not. Books are the one thing I love to buy, remember.' Annie gave an approving smile and rang up the purchases, putting the dollars in the register and directing them to the back of the store.

Robyn was a bit confused, but Avery whispered in her ear. 'She likes everyone to sit down with what they've bought—to make sure they like them. If for any reason you don't, Annie will swap the books for you.'

'Really?' She looked astonished.

'Really. That's why I ordered the coffee and cupcakes. I knew we would be here for a while.'

He carried the rest of the coffees to the back of the store and handed out the extras to people who were already reading. Robyn followed his lead and set out two cupcakes on their table, and then passed around the box with the rest.

The tables were all different. Some carved oak or mahogany, others pine, all accompanied by a variety of chairs. Robyn's was high-backed and covered in red velvet. Avery's was lower, more like a wingback armchair, and was in dark green slightly worn leather.

Robyn leaned over to examine the stack of books. 'I don't even know what the last book she picked for me was,' she said, before examining the cover and then reading the back. She let out a laugh.

'What is it?' Avery sat forward, naturally curious. From his experience, Annie always picked the perfect books for her customers.

'It's about witches,' Robyn whispered, her cheeks turning pink. 'A modern-day rags-to-riches story of a misplaced witch who falls in love with a secret billionaire.'

She looked happy but shook her head. 'She obviously saw that I'd picked a few romances and she must have heard my whispers earlier.'

Avery was frozen. He knew he was smiling. And he hoped it stayed in place while his guts churned over and over. He'd never told Annie anything about himself. They'd had a hundred casual conversations in the past. He'd been in here with Serena before—but he was sure Serena wouldn't have mentioned anything either.

How on earth could Annie know about him?

'Avery?' Robyn's brow wrinkled. 'What's wrong?' She pointed at the cupcakes. 'Wanna swap a strawberry one for a chocolate one?'

He gave himself a shake. 'The book sounds great. And I'll eat any cupcake.' He took a long sip of his coffee, hoping the caffeine would sort out the mess that was currently his brain.

'What did you get?' She leaned over to look at his book on shipwrecks in the Pacific, and a thriller he'd picked up. It was as easy as that. She wasn't concentrating on the topic of her book any more. He breathed a sigh of relief but his brain was still working overtime.

He knew this wasn't an ideal situation. He'd dated in the past without letting people know his real background. But none of those had been a serious relationship. He'd never invited someone to stay in his home before, while officially being involved with them. This was different. This should have a whole new set of rules. With honesty being first.

Trouble was, in the past he'd kept his family background secret because the name was synonymous with enormous wealth. When he'd been younger, he'd wondered if girls were only interested in him because of the name and bank balance. And he'd certainly met a few like that. But since he'd changed his name, taken up an unknown career and kept his head well out of the limelight, he hadn't let anyone know about his inherited wealth.

Robyn had already made her feelings clear on wealth, inequalities in health and all the associated impacts. At times she even seemed angry about those things. Avery knew he would need to approach this subject cautiously. He didn't want to spoil anything between them. Not when things appeared to be going so well.

'I'll read this after you,' she said, tapping the thriller. She leaned back in her chair and took a sip of her coffee. 'This is a great place,' she said happily. 'I could spend all day in here.'

She nodded behind her at a man with bags around his feet and books all over the table he was sitting at. 'It looks like some people do that.' She bent forward, whispering, 'Please tell me that he doesn't read all the books and put them back?'

Avery shook his head. 'Annie wouldn't even care if he

did. But people generally only come back here after they've paid for their books. And she's serious about swapping them. If you start something, and don't like it you can bring it back.' He gave another smile as he remembered something. 'There was a kid a few years ago, bought one book, read it, then brought it back. I think he kept swapping them out and ended up reading the whole series.'

'Annie didn't mind?'

'She didn't mind. She knows how the family were fixed. That's just the kind of person she is.'

Robyn was thoughtful for a few moments. 'It's a wonderful philosophy. But how does she keep her business afloat?'

Avery looked around too. 'She has a gift. A gift for people. Tourists love her and spend money in here. The locals wouldn't go anywhere else. She's able to balance things.'

Robyn stared at the table, her eyes focused on her books for a bit. 'Wish I'd known her when I was a kid,' she said softly.

Avery took a moment. He knew this was an opportunity to tell her. But he wasn't sure he should take it. 'You had a tough time as a kid?' Even asking the question made his heart ache a little. His mother might have broken away from her family, but he knew that he'd still lived a life of privilege.

'Some parts of Glasgow weren't so nice. The community—the neighbours generally were. And lots of families were in the same situation that we were. But it's draining. It gets you down. Never having money means that every single thing you do has to be weighed up in your head. And even as an adult, it's difficult to unlearn that behaviour—I'm not even sure I want to.' She took a deep breath. 'I have a salary now and some savings. But it always feels like it could be snatched away with no notice. I often wonder where I'd be if I hadn't managed to get the exam results I needed.' She shuddered—she actually shuddered. And that simple act brought home a whole host of emotions to Avery.

'Do you have friends from school who still stay there?'

It was the wrong question to ask, because he could see the wave of sadness that immediately crept over her face. 'Some. Not really friends though. One girl from school still stays in my street. She had three children and works part-time in the bookies.'

'The bookies?'

'Bookmakers. The betting shop.'

'Ah.'

'She's happy with her life. There are some families that never want or try to get out of the cycle that they're in. It's not up to me to decide that they're wrong.'

'You just wanted something different for yourself.'

'Absolutely.' She said the word with conviction. She took in another deep breath, picked up her cupcake and peeled back the wrapper, nibbling at the edges.

'How do you feel about going back to work tomorrow?'

Robyn rolled her shoulders. 'I'm ready for it. I'm looking forward to it. These last few days off have been...' she seemed to search for the word as her eyes locked with his '...nice,' she finished.

'Nice?' Avery was fairly sure his eyebrows had just reached the ceiling.

She laughed, and it was a sound he loved to hear. 'Well, more than nice, but we're in a public place. Decorum is required.'

'Are you sure?'

She leaned her head on one hand and said the word again. 'Absolutely.' Then she laughed and changed position. 'How about some home-made pizza tonight—can we go and grab a few things to make it?'

Avery nodded as he cleared his table and deposited their rubbish in the trash, stacking the books in his arms. 'Sure, there's a place just around the corner. We can get everything we need there.'

She walked out by his side and he was conscious of Annie watching them. He gave her a casual wave, but she didn't respond as she normally did.

Instead, she gave him a careful glance, then turned back to her shelves.

CHAPTER SEVEN

IT SEEMED THAT the gossip pipeline in Paz Memorial worked very well.

'You've moved in with Avery?'

'When did that happen?'

'What's his place like?'

'How on earth did you manage to land Mr Sunshine—you're not exactly Miss Happy yourself, are you?'

The last comment was made by a particularly acerbic nurse who'd already decided she didn't like Robyn, and Robyn didn't much care. She deadpanned her. 'I guess I just knew exactly what he *did* want, then, didn't I?'

She turned on her heel and walked away before her cheeks flamed. This chatter had better die down. She had a job to do, and patients to treat. She didn't relish being part of the hospital grapevine. It wasn't something she was used to.

Rounds were busy. A colleague was sick again, so she was covering the cardiac ward, and Cardiac Intensive Care. And, of course, she wanted to see Mabel Tucker again.

As she pushed open the door to the unit she could see Tom, Mabel's husband, by her bedside. Mabel was sitting up in bed. The ventilator was gone, but she was still wearing an oxygen mask, and her colour was pale.

Other things hadn't changed. Mabel was still surrounded by machines, still connected to things that monitored her heart rate, blood pressure and oxygen levels. There were two IV stands and a syringe driver slowly feeding fluids and drugs into her system. Mabel wasn't out of the woods yet.

But Robyn was just happy to see her breathing for herself. She wondered if Toby or Dr Shad had explained to Mabel how lucky she was to be alive. But of course not. The last thing Mabel would be feeling right now was lucky. That was a conversation for far in the future.

Tom was holding a tablet up and talking in a low voice to Mabel. As she moved closer she could see it was a photo of a cottage somewhere. 'We could try staying here,' he was saying, 'Or I found one near a beach, or another at a lakeside. Something to look forward to,' he said as he swallowed slowly, and even though Robyn's first instinct was to tell them that would need to be months in the future, she realised that he needed something to look forward to, as much as Mabel.

'Sounds lovely,' she said as she held out her hand and introduced herself. Of course, Mabel would have no idea who she was. She'd hadn't been conscious the whole time that Robyn had worked on Mabel. But Tom had been. She saw the flash of recognition in his eyes.

He grasped her hand tightly and shook it firmly. 'Thank you,' he said. 'I wasn't sure if you were just an emergency room doctor.'

'It's confusing down there,' said Robyn reassuringly. She held out her hands. 'But I mainly work here, on the cardiac floor. I've been off the last few days, and wanted to check in and see how things were going.'

'Your voice.' Mabel was frowning.

Robyn nodded. 'I'm from Scotland. I've got quite a strong accent, I'm afraid.'

Mabel looked at her, almost accusingly. 'I remember it.'

Robyn paused and nodded slowly. 'I worked on you for quite a long time and I went with you to Theatre. My voice is pretty distinctive.'

She was being careful. Most patients remembered nothing from major cardiac events. But, occasionally, some did. Robyn had never been sure if they were true memories, or pieces of information they'd been given just patched together. But her first thought was that it must be quite disorientating.

She pulled up a chair and sat down at the bedside. 'How are you feeling, Mabel? It's so nice to see you.'

As she sat down she noticed Tom's hands had a slight tremor. 'It's nice to see you too, Tom.'

'Mabel's dad was asking after you. He'll be sorry he missed you.'

'I'll be back in, and around for the next few days, so I'll keep an eye out for him to say hello.'

She turned back to Mabel, noticing the slight hitch in her breathing and her extremely poor colour. She looked anaemic. Robyn made a note to check Mabel's blood results. The medicines Mabel had been given to break up the clot in her lungs, and to stop another forming, could cause bleeding in other areas of her body. It was something that medical staff had to keep a close eye on.

A thousand thoughts flashed through her brain. If they would stabilise Mabel's blood levels. If there would be lasting impacts on her health. If she would ever be able to go on and have a family. If she'd struggle to find life insurance now.

But in that blink of an eye, she pushed them all from her mind.

It was a miracle that Mabel was still here. Still breathing. Still fighting.

'Are you hoping to get some time away and recuperate somewhere when all this is over?' she asked them both.

Mabel wasn't enthused. 'I can't think about anything like that right now.'

Tom looked pained.

'But hopefully you'll start to feel a bit better each day. You've had a traumatic experience. It will take time, and maybe some counselling, before you get over this. When you feel ready, a break away might be nice for you both.' She kept her words light and open. 'Do you want me to explain anything today, or do you have any questions?'

Mabel shook her head. Robyn understood. Mabel really wasn't ready to process any of this. She'd gone from one disaster—the car accident with its repercussions—to another that had almost taken her life.

'I was supposed to be starting my grade-school job.'

Tears glistened in her eyes and Robyn reached over and squeezed her hand. 'And you will. When you're ready. Life's thrown you some hard challenges. You need to find something positive to focus on, one step at a time.'

Mabel blinked. 'Like what?'

Robyn nodded. 'So, I'm not you, but if I'd had something similar happen, I'd feel like you do. I'd want to eventually get back to my job. But I can't do that straight away. So, what can I do? Well, I can try and get out of bed with some help and sit up for a few hours to help my back and posture. I could look for a more comfortable cushion than the one that's currently on my sofa. I could ask my partner to get me the next book in a series that's out this week, that I've been looking forward to. Oh, and the chocolate shop around the corner has a chocolate of the week. I'd make sure someone got me one of those every week.'

She sat back. 'It's hard, and only part of these things are under my control. I need a bit of help from my friends.' She pointed at Tom, 'Or family. But at least I'd feel as if I'd got a little control back, and was making some choices that were mine.'

Mabel looked thoughtful for a few moments then gave a tiny, but definitely wicked, smile. 'Or I could guilt one of my friends into giving me their password for a streaming service that I haven't subscribed to yet, and has a new series I want to watch.'

Robyn held up her hand and Mabel gave her a weak high five. 'I think you're getting the hang of this.' She smiled.

As she stood up to leave she turned back. 'I'll be back around later. We can chat again then if you want to.'

Thank you, Tom mouthed silently at her.

Robyn's heart gave a little skip. After feeling under the microscope for her personal life this morning, it was good to do the job she should be doing, and just be a doctor.

Her day continued well. She spent some time on rounds with Dr Shad. She was learning a lot from this man. He was generous with his time and expertise. She then shadowed one of the specialist cardiac physiotherapists, to see how best they encouraged both breathing exercises and physical exercise in patients with cardiac failure. It was part of the process she'd never really had time to concentrate on, and she welcomed the chance.

She was walking back to the nurses' station when one of the support workers gave her a shout. 'I've got a patient asking for you.'

'You have?' Robyn couldn't think who that might be.

'A Mr Hal Delaney? He's been in and out of here three times in the last month.'

Robyn nodded and sighed. 'What room is he in this time?'

The support worker gave a wicked grin. 'Well, the super-duper room is being used by another private patient, so he's had to make do.'

'Make do where?'

She pointed. 'Second room from the bottom.'

Robyn made her way down the corridor just as Avery came out of another room with a worried expression on his face.

'Hey, what's up?'

'I've got a young guy with cardiomyopathy. He's getting rapidly worse, so I was just going to find someone.' His brow creased. 'Where are you headed?'

'You know that guy—the first one we met at the arrest? He's back in again. He's asked to see me.' She paused. 'Want me to put him off, and come and see your patient instead?'

Avery shook his head. 'No. I'm going to find Dr Shad. The young man's normal doctor is on maternity leave, but I think I'm going to get our expert to take a look.' He blinked, 'No offence.'

She smiled brightly. 'None taken. Let me know how it goes. I'll be interested to hear how Dr Shad handles things.'

He reached over and touched her arm. 'Listen, there's something I need to talk to you about later. Away from here.' He glanced over his shoulder. 'Somewhere quiet, where it's just you and me.'

'Are you okay?' She felt instant concern. This wasn't like Avery. He looked so serious.

He nodded, the serious expression not leaving his face. 'Tonight, we'll talk tonight,' he repeated.

She held his gaze for a few moments, wondering what on earth was wrong. Another member of staff came up behind them, so she straightened her green shirt and put a smile on her face. 'In the meantime, I'll go and talk to Mr Delaney, who likely hasn't been following instructions he's been given. Seems to be his formula.'

Avery disappeared down the corridor. He seemed a little off and she wasn't quite sure why. Maybe he was just worried about the young guy.

She pushed open the door to the private room and, sure enough, Hal Delaney was sitting on the bed, a cross expression on his face.

'Mr Delaney,' Robyn said, keeping her expression serious. 'You asked for me? What brings you into hospital this time?'

'Chest pain,' he said quickly.

She walked over to the bedside. 'Any chest pain right now?' She noticed he was on an infusion of glyceryl trinitrate. She unwound her stethoscope from her neck. 'Mind if I have a listen to your chest?'

He shook his head and breathed in and out as she listened at the front and back of his chest. As she was listening the door behind her opened. She caught sight of a pair of dark trousers and shiny shoes. But no white coat.

'We're in the middle of something,' she said without turning around.

'See, Hal, she's trying to throw me out again.' There was an edge to the voice and she knew before she lifted her head who it was.

'Mr Paz, you seem to make a habit of walking into rooms where patients are being examined.'

He gave a fake laugh.

'Can I help you with something?' Her voice could cut steel and she knew it.

Hal coughed. Another symptom. He shook his head. 'It's okay.' He waved his hand.

She wondered about unconscious coercion. Because Hal knew Mr Paz through business, did he feel obliged to let him stay? Or were they really close friends, and this behaviour was normal? Were they, perhaps, more than friends? Robyn had no idea what to think, but she knew she had a patient to look after.

'If you're fine with Mr Paz staying, then we need to have a chat about what I heard. There's a definite degree of heart failure.' She noted his blood pressure on the monitor and looked at the level of his infusion. 'We need to review some medicines for you. Let me check your ankles too.'

She pressed her fingertips gently into his ankles to see if they left a depression. They did. Another sign of cardiac failure.

She sat down next to the bed. Mr Paz cleared his throat but she ignored him. Didn't he like his doctors sitting down? She didn't care. She wanted to be on the same level as Hal when she spoke to him.

'Sometimes after a major cardiac event—like the cardiac arrest you had—a heart can go into a degree of heart failure. What we need to work out is—is this a temporary thing while your heart still recovers, or is this permanent, and needs to be managed? Have you had a chest X-ray since you came back in?'

He shook his head. 'They ordered one. It's later today.'

'I'll also order a cardiac echo so we can see the heart muscles, the valves and the flow of blood through the heart.'

She glanced sideways at Mr Paz, before connecting her gaze with Hal's. 'Any issues with your waterworks?'

It was a potentially embarrassing question, but he'd allowed his friend to stay, and Robyn needed to ask.

'What?'

'Do you ever have trouble passing urine?'

'Er…no. Why?'

'Because one of the things I want to do is start you on a low-dose diuretic. It will make you pee more. So, I need to ask the question, because if you have kidney, bladder or prostate problems, we might need to insert a catheter.'

'I don't think you'll need to do that,' said Mr Paz, followed by a strained laugh.

'I might,' said Robyn matter-of-factly.

Mr Paz's face reddened. The man really didn't like anyone questioning him. 'No, you won't,' he said stiffly.

Robyn bristled. She wouldn't stand for the man in charge of the hospital she worked in, needlessly questioning her medical expertise in front of a patient in need of care. He'd better be prepared to show her his medical qualifications if he wanted to continue like this.

She tipped her head to the side and pasted a smile on her face. 'Perhaps you would like to step outside and discuss this further?'

'Wait!' Hal raised his hand and Robyn turned around to face him.

'Leo, leave my doctor alone. I like her. And you know I don't normally like doctors. I think if you don't step aside, our Scottish girl will leave you lying in a corner somewhere and I don't want you to feel obliged to fire her. So, leave her alone.'

By the time he'd finished talking he was breathless.

Robyn checked his oxygen saturation monitor and detached an oxygen mask from the wall, switching the dial up to five litres and sliding it over his face.

'Don't worry,' she said smoothly. 'We'll get you sorted.'

He squeezed her arm. 'I asked my chef to make you something special. For you, and the rest of your colleagues.'

She gave him a smile. 'I'm going to get the nurse to come in with a new medication for you to take, and we'll get those other tests carried out.'

She gave Mr Paz the briefest of nods as she walked past him.

Somehow, she knew he was going to follow her out of the door.

'Dr Callaghan,' he said as she walked down the corridor. His voice was a bit nasally. She had the horrible temptation to either ignore him or ask if he wanted a referral to an ear, nose and throat specialist. But of course, she did neither, because she was an ultimate professional.

As she went to turn around Avery came back out of the room he'd been in before, this time with Dr Shad. 'Robyn,' he started and then stopped.

Dr Shad looked up. 'Dr Callaghan.' He nodded in a friendly manner, then noticed Mr Paz in the background. 'Mr Paz, what can we do for you?'

'I want to talk to Dr Callaghan actually, but it might be better talking to you, Dr Shad. You are, after all, one of our experts.'

Robyn could see the immediate creases in Dr Shad's brow as he tried to make sense of the situation, but as she turned back to Mr Paz he had a curious look on his face. He was staring intently, but not at her. He was staring at Avery, and as she turned to look at Avery she realised that he, too, had a curious look on his face.

It was only for a second, because as soon as she'd finished her turn towards him, Dr Shad had stepped up to her shoulder. 'I am one of your experts, Mr Paz, but Dr Callaghan does an excellent job. Is there something you wish to discuss?'

She could almost feel the defensive vibes flowing from Dr Shad. This man had her back. Avery would too, but she sensed movement behind her, and realised with a sinking feeling that he'd headed back down the corridor. She had the oddest sensation of something important happening that she should have been able to put her finger on, but couldn't.

Leo Paz had started talking. Or rather, he'd started whining. He had such an unfortunate manner for a chief executive. She couldn't imagine that he won any favours with the rest of his board. Dr Shad cut him off abruptly and held up a hand.

'I will not, and cannot, discuss Mr Delaney's care with yourself without his permission.' He stepped around Mr Paz and pushed open Mr Delaney's door. 'If you will give me a moment,' he said over his shoulder, making it abundantly clear that Mr Paz shouldn't join them.

Obviously slighted, Mr Paz turned back to her. 'That man in the corridor, who was he?'

Her skin prickled. She knew exactly who he meant. But all her natural defences had kicked in. 'Dr Shad? I would have thought you already knew him.'

'Not him.' He waved his hand angrily. 'The other man, with the dark hair.'

He was describing Avery only as a man—not as a nurse, even though Avery had stood a few metres from him, clearly wearing a nurse's uniform. She found it curious that he hadn't actually identified him. Avery had worked here longer than her, but then, maybe Mr Paz didn't normally walk the corridors of his hospital.

'I don't know who you mean,' she said calmly.

'Yes, you do, he called you by your name.' Colour was building in Mr Paz's cheeks. There was no use keeping quiet. He could ask Dr Shad, and she was sure he wouldn't have picked up the vibe that she had.

'That was Avery Smith,' she said, with no further explanation.

Dr Shad opened the door behind them, with Mr Delaney's electronic chart in his hand. 'I've spoken to Mr Delaney. He's agreed we can discuss his case with you, and is very complimentary of the care provided by Dr Callaghan. I've looked over her findings, test requests and decisions today and agree with everything so far. Can I ask why you wish to discuss one of my doctors?'

Mr Paz had opened his mouth a few times, obviously trying to take over. But Dr Shad was a determined individual, and once his diatribe had started, there was no way he was stopping.

'I... I wanted a second opinion on my friend's care. I thought he should be seen by a more senior and experienced physician.'

'Are you unhappy with the way I run the cardiac training programme, Mr Paz?'

There was a confused moment of silence. Dr Shad continued. 'Because if you are unhappy about the way I train those on the programme, I expect you to tell me.'

Mr Paz tried to gather himself. It was clear he'd wanted to start throwing his weight around but now regretted it.

'Dr Callaghan is an excellent physician and has provided some of the best emergency care. We are very lucky to have her in our service. She excelled in her previous studies—'

'She complained about a medical student.' Mr Paz cut Dr Shad off. Her skin prickled. Something had changed. She'd wondered if he'd been trying to catch her out before. Complain about her care, or her manner, but now? This had changed tack. Now, he seemed determined to pick fault with her, personally. Why was that?

She remembered the rude medical student, who apparently hadn't changed since she'd encountered him. Lia had told her he was related to Mr Paz, but since she hadn't heard anything else about it, she'd put it out of her mind.

'I complained about a medical student,' she conceded, before looking Mr Paz in the eye, 'because he was rude, overconfident, and lacking in clinical skills. He has some learning to do, and, because this is a teaching hospital, it's my duty to give feedback on those who require more supervision.'

Colour flooded into Mr Paz's face. 'Frank is an excellent student, and he will be an excellent doctor,' he exclaimed, clearly annoyed.

Robyn didn't flinch. He didn't intimidate her. Being brought up in one of the most deprived areas of her city meant that she'd been exposed to a lot, and knew exactly how to stand up for herself. 'Frank...' she used the name with purpose '...still has a lot to learn.' She gestured to the door. 'Would you allow him to care for your friend Hal?'

She felt Dr Shad's hand gently grip her white-coated arm.

'Mr Paz, I suggest we talk later,' Dr Shad said smoothly. 'Dr Callaghan and I have tests to arrange for Hal, and have to review his care. Once my clinical duties are completed, I will come and find you to discuss this further.'

Robyn found herself being turned around and guided back down the corridor and into a side office.

As soon as the door closed she didn't wait to be invited to talk. 'He's ridiculous. And I—' she put her hand on her chest '—was very reserved.'

Dr Shad gave a gentle laugh. 'You were, and I agree. He was ridiculous. But I didn't want to get into things with him right there. His nephew is just about to have his placement revoked.'

'No?' Robyn was truly shocked. Medical students frequently did things wrong, it was part of the learning. She'd known of a few who had quit in the past—when they'd realised being a doctor wasn't for them. But she'd rarely heard of anyone having a learning placement revoked. It was the ultimate no-no.

She shook her head. 'What on earth has he done?'

'Exactly what you witnessed before. Talked dismissively to female staff, discharged patients without the authority to do so, and been arrogant, rude and disrespectful. I'd suggest that his learning ability is not where it should be.'

'I'm shocked,' she said dryly.

Dr Shad rolled his eyes. 'And I still have to tell Mr Paz about his nephew. Can you go and complete your work on Mr Delaney, and come back to me if there are any issues?'

She nodded her head. 'Of course.' There was a swell of pride in her chest. That Dr Shad had her back, and that he trusted her decision-making. San Diego had been a good choice for her. In more ways than one.

She continued her work and hurried down to the cafeteria to grab some lunch. She was late, so most of the good choices were gone. A coffee, a peach, and a sad-looking salad were what she took outside to the central courtyard. She could do with being surrounded by greenery for five minutes.

'Hey.' The voice behind her made her jump. Avery. For the first time since she'd known him, he didn't look great.

'You okay?' She wondered about earlier, but maybe he'd disappeared because he was sick.

He sighed and sat down opposite with a can of diet soda. He leaned his head on one hand. 'I need to tell you some things. But not here. It's not the place.'

A horrible feeling crept down her spine. 'Secret wife? Secret love child?'

He gave a half-smile. 'None of the above.'

'I've broken a rule in the apartment and you have to throw me out?'

'Not a chance.' He was almost smiling, but she could still see sadness in his eyes.

Her stomach somersaulted. 'Are you sick?'

He reached over and put his hand over hers. 'Not sick. It's nothing like that. But we need to have a chat. I don't want to do it here. I want to do it somewhere private. We can talk tonight.'

'You're worrying me.'

'I'm sorry. I don't mean to. I just need to tell you some things. I should have told you about them at the beginning.'

Robyn's head was spinning. She didn't know what to think. Was the happy little bubble she'd finally found about to burst?

Her page sounded to let her know that Hal's test results were ready. She stood up and gathered her rubbish, then bent forward and kissed him on the cheek.

And as she did so, she had a moment of realisation. She loved him. She really did.

She probably had for the last few weeks, but had been so busy guarding her heart that she hadn't let herself admit it.

But now, when there might be something wrong between them? It was like a spear in her heart. She didn't want to lose a love she'd just found. He said he wasn't sick, but that might just be an excuse. Her stomach squeezed. She couldn't bear the thought of Avery being ill. She really did love this guy. He'd captured her heart in a way that no one ever had.

Robyn had never had a connection with anyone else like this. Someone who genuinely respected her, and didn't try and change her mind about things. He accepted the way she was, how passionate she was about her job. The moment he'd taken her to the soup kitchen had cemented the place for him in her life. He got her. He really did.

'It will be fine,' she said, reaching over, cupping his cheek and looking into those green eyes and meaning every word.

She hurried back to the doors, taking one last look over her shoulder. Avery was staring at his hands. What on earth could he tell her that would make him feel like that?

Every cell in her body told her she really didn't want to know.

CHAPTER EIGHT

HE KNEW THIS day was just going to go from bad to worse. Some days were inevitable. And some were entirely of a person's own making. Just as his was today.

As soon as Leo Paz's eyes had set on him, he'd known his anonymity was over.

Maybe not instantly—but the flicker of confusion in his uncle's eyes was enough. Avery had always known working here was a risk. It was part of the reason he'd changed his surname to something he'd hoped would be forgettable. The surname Paz would have drawn attention to him straight away.

It was probably always inevitable he'd be exposed, but he'd hoped by the time people in the hospital had learned he was part of the Paz family dynasty he would already have proved himself a good nurse, a hard worker and a respectful colleague.

He still hoped that might happen. But right now, he urgently needed to find the time to be straight with Robyn.

It seemed that Leo Paz had already fixated on her. Robyn had no idea what his uncle's wrath could be like. But Avery did. He'd witnessed as a child, first hand, what it had done to his mother.

To make matters worse—and it could only happen in the

worst kind of story—it turned out the medical student that both Robyn and Avery had spoken to was also a member of the Paz family. From what Avery understood, that arrogant guy was likely to be his cousin.

He'd never met him before—couldn't have picked him out of a line-up if he'd been paid. But that was irrelevant. His mother had two brothers and two sisters. So, it had to be a child of one of his uncles or aunts.

This was why keeping secrets was never fun. He'd been blessed that Serena had never said anything. Though she had warned him this was a secret that would inevitably find its way out. And she'd been right.

His uncle usually never set foot on any of the wards, or in any of the departments. Avery could count on one hand how many times he'd seen him in the hospital during his nursing training and afterwards. Usually, it was whenever there was a new department opening and press was involved. Leo liked press attention, but these things had been easy for Avery to avoid.

His phone rang and he froze when he recognised the number. His family attorney. They only spoke on brief occasions, usually when Avery had to sign paperwork.

He was an older man, who'd been friends with Avery's mother and took care of all her family business on her behalf. Avery trusted him, and he knew Avery had trained as a nurse, changed his name, and worked at the Paz Memorial. There was only one reason he would call.

'Sam?'

'Avery, we need to talk.'

He sighed. 'Should I be worried?'

There was a long pause, then Sam finally said, 'I promised your mother I'd have your back. And I do.'

* * *

Avery Smith rarely got angry. No, Avery Smith never got angry. But Avery Paz? Oh, he definitely got angry.

He heard the shouting from the end of the corridor. This was a hospital, and someone was actually shouting.

He started jogging down the corridor. This couldn't possibly be good.

Robyn's voice was low, her accent so thick he could barely make out all the words. He knew she was talking but he couldn't hear properly because of the shouting by his least favourite medical student who was centimetres from her face.

The set of her jaw told him everything he needed to know.

'You think you can ruin me? You think you can badmouth me? I will destroy you! Who are you anyway? You think I can't find out who you are—where you come from? I won't just destroy you, I'll destroy your family too. I'm rich enough to do it!' Frank Paz was ranting.

Staff were coming out of rooms. Looking to see who was causing such a hullabaloo in their unit. But Avery got there first. Just in time to hear the reply from Robyn. 'This is your final warning. Step back from me and get a hold of yourself.' He heard her suck in a breath before she added icily, 'And if you threaten my family again, I'll break your legs. You stuck up piece of—'

Avery stepped between them, put his hands on his cousin's shoulders and pushed him back firmly. 'You heard the lady, back away and stop shouting, please. This is not the time, or the place.'

'You!' Frank seethed. 'You measly nurse. What do you know? I'll ruin you too. Because of your complaining I'm getting my placement revoked. I'll speak to my uncle. I'll get this overturned and I'll get the two of you fired.' There was pure venom on the young man's face.

Avery's heart sank. He hated that he was related to a person like this. It reminded him exactly of why he didn't want to do what he was going to have to do.

Avery straightened his back. He easily towered a few inches over his younger cousin. 'How many times have you been reported to your supervisor?'

Frank blinked.

'How many times?' Avery repeated. He glanced over his shoulder to check Robyn was okay. She was clearly raging, but was catching her breath. 'Dr Callaghan reported you once, and I backed up her report because it was entirely true. A placement would rarely get revoked over one report. I can only imagine that there have been a multitude of reports about you for it to have reached this stage.'

He shook his head. He knew people were watching. At least he'd managed to stop his cousin shouting and disrupting the place. But everyone was waiting for what would come next.

'You, you're just a nurse. What do you know about anything? This is nothing to do with you. I can get you sacked in a heartbeat,' Frank reiterated.

'Stop it. You're embarrassing yourself now. Take a look at your own behaviour. It seems that money can't buy good manners or a bit of humility.'

'Like you'd know.'

Avery bit his tongue. He could say something. He could wipe the smile off his cousin's face. But he wouldn't do that. It wasn't the kind of person that Avery was. And he wanted to have the conversation about his wealth with Robyn in private.

'He would, actually.'

It seemed fate had decided on a different path for Avery today.

He turned around to face his uncle.

'Avery Smith?' Leo Paz said with his eyebrows raised. 'Or Avery *Paz*? It seems that someone has changed their name. Now, that has to be a deliberate act. Why would you do that? So you could spy on how the hospital is being run?' He turned to face his other nephew. 'Your cousin here does know about money, Frank. He owns a fifth of this entire hospital. He could literally buy and sell you if he chose to.'

'I'm going to leave now,' Avery said calmly to his uncle— even though he felt anything but calm. 'You can speak to my attorney.'

He turned to Robyn and held out his hand. 'Let's go.'

Her brow was wrinkled and she looked completely confused. 'What?'

Avery reached and took her hand, leading her down the corridor. He stopped briefly at the nurses' station. 'Can you let Dr Shad know we've had to leave?'

He put his hand at Robyn's back as they walked down the corridor. He could sense her breathing quickly. He wasn't quite sure where to start.

Her footsteps were slowing. He knew immediately they weren't going to get very far, so he steered them down the stairs and into the cafeteria, grabbing two coffees and taking them to the seating area outside.

He sat down opposite Robyn and she looked him clean in the eye. 'Explain.'

He breathed. At least she was giving him a chance to

speak. 'Leo Paz is right. My name isn't Avery Smith. Leo was my mother's brother. He's my uncle.'

She blinked. 'And that rude medical student is your cousin?'

'He must be, but I've never met him before. My mother was estranged from most of the family, apart from her parents while they were alive. I think I met them all when I was a baby—but obviously I can't remember that. I've had no contact with any of these people in my memory.'

Robyn looked even more confused. 'So, Leanora Paz?' She held out her hands.

Avery nodded. 'The hospital is named after my grandmother. I don't remember her—or my grandfather either. He built the hospital as a memorial to her.'

'And you chose to come here of all places to work—why?'

He took a breath and wondered how on earth to explain this. He put his hand to his heart. 'Because it's in here. I have connections here that I've never been able to tell anyone about. My mother died here. I have huge memories of the time we spent in the cancer unit. As for the family? I know that some of them judged her way too harshly.'

He ran a hand through his hair. 'I've already told you my father was married to someone else when he met my mother, but she didn't know. I understand that my grandfather and grandmother were upset when she became pregnant, but they still loved her. They accepted me as their grandson. But her siblings weren't so forgiving or gracious and after my grandmother died they treated her very badly. She was estranged from them for most of my life, and she didn't want me exposed to their toxic behaviour. I've not been able to freely use the name I was born to. But this hospital is widely renowned. You know that. That's why you're here. And it's why I'm here too. I wanted to work in the best. I wanted to be part of something my mother's father created. And even though I couldn't tell anyone who I was, I wanted to honour my grandmother's name.'

Robyn's colour had steadily drained. 'Exactly how rich are you?'

Avery put his head in his hands. 'Don't do this, Robyn.'

'Why? I want to know. You've kept this from me. You've lied to me. You know how I feel about inequalities in health for people. You know I grew up with barely any money or chances. You can't even imagine what that's like.' Her hands were shaking.

'How much money do I have? I don't actually know—and no, I'm not lying to you. The apartment we're living in? I own the whole building. This hospital? Because I'm an only child, I inherited my mother's entire share. As Leo said, I own a fifth of this place. The free clinic I work at? I own that. The soup kitchen I help at? I own that too.'

Her eyes widened in horror and she shuddered. 'You own the whole apartment *building*?'

He nodded. 'The only people that knew who I was were my attorney, Sam—who was my mother's friend—and Serena.'

'Serena knows?'

He nodded. 'She found paperwork in the apartment when she was looking for something. She realised I'm part of the Paz family. But she's never asked me a lot of questions about it. She promised not to tell anyone else.'

'Your whole life is a lie.' Robyn spoke in a kind of far-off voice.

'Please, Robyn.' Avery leaned forward and took her hands, but she flinched and pulled them back. 'What happened between us wasn't a lie. I've never felt like this about anyone before. This is what I wanted to talk to you about. I wanted to be honest with you before, but it just never felt like the right time to bring it up. I might have been born into a wealthy family, but I try not to use the privilege it brings.'

'By buying an apartment block?'

He shook his head. 'It was my mother's. I inherited it. But I have bought things. I bought the clinic, and the shelter. I try to help people where I can. I work at the hospital under the radar. I don't want to rub my privilege in the face of others. I try to live within my means. I don't own expensive cars, and I don't wear designer clothes.'

'But you still don't get it.' Robyn shook her head. 'You can't. You don't know what it feels like to go into a store and have to decide whether to buy deodorant or tampons because you can't afford both. You don't know what it feels like to wear shoes that are so worn they let in water constantly—or are too small but you don't have enough for a bigger size. You don't know what it feels like as a child to turn down every party invite because you can't buy a present.' She blinked back tears and he knew just how strongly she felt about all this.

'I didn't choose the life I was born into, Robyn. Just like you didn't choose yours. I try to be responsible. I chose to train in a profession I know would have made my mother proud. I work as much, and as often, as I can.'

She was shaking her head. 'But all those conversations we had—when we talked about elderly care. You mentioned the lack of provision for them, and how poor care can be for the elderly. But you are sitting there with how much in the bank?'

He leaned back and closed his eyes for a second. 'That's just it, Robyn. I can't help every single person on this planet.

No one would have the finances for that. But I can help people locally. That's why I set up the free clinic and the soup kitchen. I pay the salaries and buy all the equipment needed. Take care of all the bills. I help where I can.'

She stared at him. 'But that must just scratch the surface.'

He nodded. 'I agree.'

Robyn stood up suddenly. 'I can't do this. I just can't. I can't be with someone who lied to me the way you have. Don't even dare try and say you didn't lie. Hiding the truth from me is the same as lying. And I can't get my head around this.'

'What?'

She pointed at him. 'You. You lied to me. You kept this from me. Did you think I wasn't good enough to know your secret? We've worked together closely for weeks. I moved into your place. We slept together! When would I have been trustworthy enough to tell? Or would that have been never?'

She started to shake. 'Everything between us has been a lie. Was how you even felt about me true—or was that all a lie too? Because how am I supposed to know for sure?' She started to pace, shaking her head as she spoke, and putting her hand on her chest as if it hurt. 'You know how I feel about this. You know how I feel about people being at opposite ends of the social spectrum. The privilege that comes with wealth and how it's all too often abused.'

She shuddered. 'How did I not see what was right before my eyes? You even look a bit like your uncle, and your cousin. I knew there was something off about Frank, and I just couldn't put my finger on it. It was the familiar traits. I can't believe I didn't see it before. I must be blind.'

She was ranting now and he didn't know how to stop her. He just wanted to make himself heard. To try and get a moment to tell her he was sorry, that he loved her.

'Look at the way they treat people,' she muttered. 'The entitlement. I can't do this. I just can't do this. I just can't be with someone with all that privilege.'

'You don't want to know me, be with me, just because I have money?'

He understood he hadn't been upfront with her, but he couldn't honestly believe that the fact he'd inherited money would mean that Robyn couldn't even consider having a relationship with him. She wasn't even giving him a chance to say anything else. The woman he loved was prepared to walk away from him for the simple reason that he had money.

She hesitated. And he could see it in her eyes. For Robyn, that was true. Fundamentally, she didn't believe she could be happy with someone who was rich. It was as basic as that.

'I can give it away,' he said instantly. And he meant it.

His wealth had always played on his mind. It was why he'd kept his attorney to deal with so many things. He had foundations. He had scholarships in place to help under-privileged kids go to college or university. He signed the paperwork, but kept a distance from it all. He'd been conscious of staying under the rest of the family's radar. He didn't want to be involved in the family drama and infights that had caused his mother so much pain.

'It won't make a difference,' said Robyn sadly. 'You were born into wealth. You have a totally different outlook on life than I do. You can never really understand how things are.'

'Then teach me,' he said without a shadow of hesitation.

A tear ran down her cheek. 'I can't,' she said simply. 'I can't be that person for you. I don't want your pity. I don't want to be the poor girl, rescued by some rich guy.'

'I'm not trying to rescue you, Robyn. I'm trying to love you.' He put his hand on his heart. 'I've never felt like this before. I love you, Robyn. I don't want anyone else. I've never been happier since I met you. Please give us a chance.'

The tears were flowing freely now. 'I can't, Avery. Your uncle is probably going to fire me now, and throw me off this programme. Your cousin will likely get to continue as a medical student. Wealth and privilege can buy so much. I can't let myself be involved with you. I have to be true to myself, about my beliefs. I have to be able to look at myself in the mirror.'

'And you can't do that if you're with me?' He was starting to feel annoyed now.

She looked him straight in the eye. Her words were shaky. 'The way I feel right now? I don't think I can. I need some space. I can't be with you any more, Avery.'

She turned and walked out of the door.

He wanted to chase after her. He wanted to tell her to stop. To take her time. To give him another chance. But he knew she wasn't ready to do that.

His heart was breaking. But he also felt a flicker of anger and frustration that she refused to see him. The person she'd worked alongside, in the wards, in the soup kitchen. The person she'd lain next to in bed each night. She couldn't see that Avery any more. She could only see the dollar signs he represented. And it horrified him.

He took a deep breath.

His brain told himself to stay where he was. To let her walk away without going after her. To give her the space that she'd requested.

But when he got back home to his inevitably empty apartment a few hours later it still felt as if his heart had been ripped out of his chest.

He wasn't sure he would ever recover.

CHAPTER NINE

BETRAYED. THE WORD swam around in her brain and stayed there.

There was no other word she could use. He'd listened to her. He'd heard how hard she'd had things as a child. He knew she still budgeted—that she thought carefully about every single purchase.

And he'd still kept his billions secret from her.

Did he think she was in it for the money? Was that how Avery treated everyone he dated? It seemed odd to her he'd kept his wealth a secret from everyone.

She understood families argued and fell out. She understood families were estranged, and she could almost understand him wanting to work incognito at one of the most renowned hospitals in the US.

But she couldn't forgive him not telling her about the apartment block, or the free clinic, or the soup kitchen. He didn't just volunteer at the last two places. *He owned them.*

Packing up her things had literally taken minutes. Everything was thrown, crushed or crumpled into her cases and some shopping bags. She just wanted to get out of the apartment building as quick as she could.

It wasn't until she was back at the hospital in her tiny, noisy room that she realised something strange. The apartment block had a penthouse upstairs, and two much bigger apartments on the floor beneath Avery's. If he owned the place, why didn't he stay in one of those?

Was it all part of his ruse to keep his identity hidden?

The more she thought about it, the more confused she became. How had he managed to avoid his uncle Leo all these years? Her brain started putting pieces of the puzzle together. Now she realised why he'd disappeared that time in the ER the day they'd met. The same on the cardiac floor when Leo Paz had come to visit Hal Delaney.

His uncle was truly horrible. So was his cousin. Could she really blame him for wanting to keep his distance from people like that?

She sat on her bed, looking at her belongings. Everything bought and paid for by herself. She was proud of who she was, what she earned, how she managed her money, and still afforded to help her parents. She couldn't cope being swamped in money—and that was what life would be like with Avery.

It just wasn't for her. Even if he'd been truthful with her from the beginning, she wasn't sure she could have been with him. She could have kept his secret. But would her brain have got around how he managed to live with all that money in the bank?

She shuddered. She'd often thought, *How the other half live*. But Avery *was* the other half. He had wealth and privilege. He'd never known hunger, being cold, wearing clothes that were too small for him, or having to worry about paying for something.

She couldn't imagine spending her life with someone like that. How could he possibly understand the experiences she'd had? And while some people from deprived backgrounds might dream of finding a handsome billionaire, it had never, ever been something she'd wanted for herself.

Whenever she'd come into contact with those from a rich background, it had never gone well for her. The impact of that first rich boyfriend, who'd used her in medical school, treated her like a plaything—or, worse, someone to pity—had damaged her more than she'd ever admitted. Being dumped when someone richer and better connected had come along who could help him with his career had made her feel more useless than ever.

Had Avery felt like that about her? Hot, angry tears spilled down her cheeks and she couldn't stop the sobs. She'd told him more about her life than she'd told anyone before. The thought that he might actually have pitied her, felt sorry for her, made her feel physically sick with humiliation. The handsome man who'd made her heart flutter, who she'd actually thought was falling for her, the way she was falling for him, might only have been with her because he felt sorry for her?

She couldn't bear it. Not for a second. Who even was the genuine Avery Paz? She'd thought that she'd known him, thought they were connected. But now she could see she hadn't ever really scratched the surface. She'd only known what he'd let her know, and most of that was a lie.

She couldn't handle this. She wouldn't be made to feel like this. Used. Lied to. Worthless. She changed her clothes and walked up to the cardiac unit. Mr Paz was likely out for her blood now. If her career was about to be ruined because she'd dated his nephew, Robyn Callaghan wasn't going down without a fight.

Avery's phone rang again. His attorney. He answered. Sam didn't waste a single word. 'My office. Now.'

Avery made his way across the city. He considered changing his clothes, but what was the point? So he turned up at Sam's office in the wrinkled T-shirt and jeans he'd pulled on when he'd left the hospital.

Sam had a number of folders on his desk. 'Sit down,' he instructed.

Avery sighed and ran his fingers through his hair. His throat was dry and, as nice and loyal as Sam was, this was the last place he wanted to be right now.

His silver-haired attorney looked up. Sam was handsome. Some joked he was a Richard Gere lookalike, and Avery often wondered if there had ever been anything between Sam and his mother. At this point in life, he'd probably never know.

Sam turned around to a small glass-fronted refrigerator behind him—not too unusual in a hot city like San Diego. He pulled out a can of Avery's favourite soda and sat it in front of him. 'Buckle up.'

Avery blinked, surprised that Sam remembered, then popped the seal and took a drink.

'I always knew this day would come. I warned you against working at Paz Memorial, but you were determined. It was inevitable that your uncle would discover you at some point, so we are prepared.'

'We are?' Avery was surprised.

'Of course.' Sam turned around a letter. 'I've been sent a number of requests from your uncle's attorney, the Paz family attorney, and the attorney of your aunt Marie.'

Avery shook his head. 'Why?'

'I can summarise. Your uncle wants to sue you for corruption, trespass, illegally spying on his business, gaining information by nefarious means, and a whole host of equally ridiculous things. He wants your share of the hospital and will try any means to get it. The Paz family attorney wants to know your intentions, and whether you intend to be involved in Paz Memorial, and if you want to assume your seat on the board. Your aunt wants to know if you will go and see her.'

Avery sat back, stunned.

Sam nodded. 'The list from your uncle is actually much larger. He also wants possession of the free clinic, and soup kitchen. Claims you have funded them by stealing equipment and—' he raised his eyebrows '—food from the hospital kitchen.'

Avery folded his arms. He was beginning to see where this was going. 'And the rest?'

Sam flicked through some files. 'Wants to sue you for your nursing licence, claiming malpractice, and dismiss you, and another person—a Ro—'

'Robyn Callaghan,' Avery cut in. He stood up. 'No. He can come for me all he wants. He can't go for her.'

Sam's eyebrows shot up. 'Who is she?'

Avery wasn't sure how to answer. His head was swimming. He'd spent the whole walk here still simmering with anger. Of course, he'd been wrong not to tell Robyn his secret. He should have told her as soon as he'd realised how he felt about her. But he was also annoyed that she hadn't stopped to take a breath, to see him, and not his money. He'd even wondered if maybe it was better she'd walked away, if she couldn't see past her prejudices and give him a chance. But now? No. No way. As soon as he knew his uncle was coming for Robyn, he was ready to go to war for her.

He could do this. He could see her again. He could give her the opportunity to cool down, and then sit down again together to discuss their relationship. That might all take time. But for right now? Avery would do everything he could to protect her. 'She's…she's someone… I love. She's a great doctor and does incredible work. He can't touch her.'

Sam looked him in the eye. 'This is America. Dubious claims are made against doctors all the time.'

'They came for my mother before. She wanted me away from all this. This is the exact reason I've always kept away from my family. They won't go for Robyn. Tell my uncle I'll meet him tomorrow.'

Sam shook his head. 'Not a good idea.'

'I don't care.'

'You should. I promised your mother I'd look out for you.'

'Then look out for me. Come with me.'

Sam held his gaze for the longest time. 'I won't let you do anything foolish, Avery. You have that mad look in your eye.' He gave a sad smile. 'I recognise it. Your mother used to get it when people made her angry. It wasn't wise to stray into her path.'

'Then you'd better make sure the path is clear.'

Things weren't any better in the hospital. Robyn had barely taken a few steps into the unit before she was surrounded by staff.

'Is Avery really a member of the Paz family?'

'Is he a billionaire?'

'Why on earth is he working here if he's a billionaire?'

'Why did he even bother training as a nurse? He doesn't need to work for a living.'

'Did you know about this?'

'Yes, yes, I don't know, I don't know, and no. I had no idea,' Robyn answered as the questions were thrown at her.

A hand fixed on her arm. Serena, her eyes laced with worry. 'Where is he?'

Robyn stared at her. 'I don't know. I left the apartment. He's probably there.'

'I've already been there, and to the clinic and the soup kitchen. He's not at any of them.'

Robyn shook her head. 'I don't know, Serena, and right now, I don't care. He lied to me. He knew how I felt.'

'I don't imagine for a second that he lied to you,' she said quickly, her pregnant belly looking larger than the last time Robyn had seen her. 'He just didn't tell you. That's different. And he was going to tell you. He wanted to tell you.'

Robyn's skin bristled. He'd obviously talked about her to Serena. She didn't know if she liked that. Serena looked around at the still gossiping staff.

'You're not supposed to be working today, are you?'

Robyn shook her head.

'Then get out of here. You won't get a moment's peace. Take a walk. Go to the marina. Have a cocktail. Anything but hang around here.'

Robyn glanced around. People were staring at her. She and Avery were clearly the talk of the place. All of a sudden she felt swamped. Serena grabbed her arm again. 'Come on, I'll get you out of here.' She peeled Robyn's white coat from her shoulders and folded it over her arm, walking her to the stairwell, down the stairs and out to the main entrance. She stuck her hand in her pocket and handed over fifty dollars. 'You can pay me back later. Go and get some space.'

It was like living outside her own body. The last few hours seemed like a blur. As soon as Robyn walked out of the air-conditioned hospital and into the intense heat of the San Diego day, she knew she had to find somewhere cool, and away from spying eyes.

Her brain was whirling again. Had he outright lied to her? Maybe not, maybe he'd just answered questions carefully.

She'd thought earlier about seeing a counsellor about her past feelings. Now, she knew she needed to. Avery wasn't like her first boyfriend who'd let her down so badly, or like Frank and Leo Paz. He didn't have the arrogance. Or the fickle outlook on life. She should have seen those things for herself. It really was time to unpick the damage her past had done to her. She had prejudices of her own that she needed to accept and deal with.

Her thoughts flicked back to the soup kitchen. The pride in Avery's eyes. And his interactions with the elderly patients in the ER. His patience and tactful care. This was the Avery she knew.

Her feet seemed to take charge. And before she knew it she was back in the Gaslamp district and pushing open the door to The Book Emporium with a jingle of the metal chimes announcing her arrival.

She didn't even glance at the shelves, just made her way to the back of the store and sat down in the same red velvet high-backed chair she'd sat in before. It took seconds before Annie's fluffy little dog started sniffing around her ankles and she picked it up and sat it in her lap. 'Hi, Peggy,' she murmured as she started to pet her. 'I think I need a hug.'

She jumped as a steaming cappuccino appeared in front of her, and, in a big whoosh, Annie sat down in the chair opposite. Her kaftan today was a mixture of yellows and oranges. There was absolutely no missing her.

She looked at Robyn curiously, but there was something else in her eyes. As if she knew everything already.

'What happened?' she asked.

Robyn didn't look up. She kept her eyes fixed on Peggy. It seemed safer. 'Oh, nothing,' she sighed. 'I found out the man I love is a secret billionaire, who chose not to tell me, even though he knew how I'd feel about it.'

'Why does his bank balance matter?'

Robyn looked up now. 'It matters because he didn't trust me enough to be honest with me.' She gave a little sigh. 'And I have issues. I grew up at the other end of that spectrum. I had a bad experience with a man once, and it's coloured how I feel about certain things.'

'Did you have a bad experience with Avery?'

'No…and yes. How do I even know if anything was real between us?'

Annie spoke quietly. 'Avery Smith is one of the nicest people I know. Kind, generous and handsome too.' She eyed Robyn carefully. 'He doesn't usually bring any girlfriends here. So, you must have meant something to him. What's not to like?'

'But that's just it. His name isn't Avery Smith. It's Avery Paz.' The words Annie was saying were pinging around her brain, falling into line with the thoughts she'd just been having on the way here.

'Ah.' Annie gave a knowing nod.

'You knew?'

'I guessed a long time ago. Avery looks very much like his mother, who used to bring him in here as a child.'

'But he never told me.'

'Because it probably wasn't appropriate. What if you were some kind of secret gold-digger?'

Robyn was horrified. 'I'm not!'

Annie shook her head and gave her a wry smile. 'Okay, you're not a gold-digger. Good. So, let's go back. What did you just say to me about Avery?'

Robyn creased her brow. 'I can't remember.'

'Well, I can. You said, *"the man I love".'*

Robyn sat back in her chair as if someone had just knocked the wind out of her sails. It was ridiculous. She'd already realised that she loved Avery, but she'd never said the words out loud to someone else. 'We're not suited,' she said quietly.

'You're not suited because your brain won't allow you to be suited,' said Annie without hesitation. 'Why is it so insurmountable that you both grew up at either end of a financial spectrum? You can learn from each other.' She looked away for a minute. 'You know that Avery works in the soup kitchen and free clinic.'

Robyn groaned. 'Avery *owns* the soup kitchen and free clinic.'

'Great.' Annie smiled. 'But Avery still needs to grow into his own skin. And you can help him do that. You can do that together.' She emphasised the final word.

Robyn shook her head. 'I don't think I can. It's just too much.'

Annie looked solemn. 'Avery has started so well. He's a Paz. And he's clearly been avoiding his family for good reason. But now, it's time for him to take back his name. You have to help him embrace that. He can do more good from the inside than he can from the outside.'

Robyn breathed. Trying to understand all of this.

'You have to decide,' said Annie. 'You have to decide how

much you love him, and if he's worth the risk. Only you can do that.' She leaned over and lifted Peggy from Robyn's lap.

She started to walk away, then looked over her shoulder. 'And you should do it now.'

CHAPTER TEN

THEY'D JUST PULLED up outside the hospital in the car.

Avery was trying to get ready for this meeting. Sam's face was steely as they exited into the warm San Diego air.

'Avery!'

He recognised the shout before he even turned around. Robyn was running across the street towards him, her hair streaming behind her, and her eyes red-rimmed.

Before he even had a chance to acknowledge her, she had both her hands on his arms. 'What are you here to do?'

Sam shot a look at him. 'Robyn?' he asked.

She nodded and Sam took a second, taking in her un-kempt appearance. Her shirt was half out of her trousers, her skin gleamed with sweat, and her hair was everywhere. He smiled. 'He's here to save your skin,' he said simply.

Robyn shook her head. 'Whatever it is you think you need to do, you don't,' she said firmly. 'Your uncle is a bully. It's time you stood up to him. Don't do anything because of me. I can look after myself. I love you, Avery. I can be a doctor anywhere. But here? This is your place, your home. Take it back. Take it back from the people who made your mother's life hell.'

Her face was flushed, her beautiful blue eyes sparkling with love and warmth. Avery couldn't believe the sight in front of him. He ran his hand up the side of her cheek.

'Robyn Callaghan, I will not let my uncle come for you. I will not let him take from you what you've worked so hard for.' He held up his hand. 'I don't need any of this. I just need you.'

She wrapped her arms around his neck. 'You've got me, I promise. But fight, Avery. Don't give up anything that's rightfully yours. Be the person you should be. Be your own kind of Paz.'

His stomach clenched. She was right. He could do this. He could fight back against his uncle. And he would do it with Robyn by his side.

He held out his hand towards her. 'Are you ready to fight alongside me?'

She lifted her eyebrows. 'Was I born in Scotland?' She slid her hand into his. 'Let's do this.'

He'd finally put on a suit. He wanted to face his uncle on equal terms. Sam was by his side. And now, so was Robyn.

His uncle had three attorneys. None of whom were familiar to Avery.

Sam started by casually throwing a few papers across the desk. 'The ridiculous claims? Are just that—ridiculous. Threatening Avery's nurse registration, and the registration of his colleague, Dr Callaghan, is a low, cheap shot.' He looked Leo Paz in the eye. 'But, as Julia always warned me, not surprising.'

Avery jolted at his mother's name. Sam was clearly not prepared to play nice.

One of the other attorneys leaned forward and spoke a huge amount of legalese. It all sounded very impressive, but barely understandable. Avery picked up parts, from the sublime, to the ridiculous. Having to prove who he was. Objections to his mother's will that left everything to her only child. A list of all his assets that they had 'found' and now wondered how he had acquired them, and if they were actually family inheritance.

Sam was unperturbed, even though the man droned on for more than twenty minutes.

Eventually, Sam stood up.

'What are you doing?' Leo demanded.

Avery stood up too. 'We're leaving. There are more family members than yourself. You're not in full control here, and you seem unable and unwilling to talk. This is a waste of my time.'

Leo leaned forward. 'If you leave, I'll have your friend thrown off her training programme in the next hour and her visa to work here cancelled.'

Robyn moved first. She looked at Leo. 'Try it,' she said steadily. 'I believe Avery is entitled to a seat on your board. He'd like to take that up.'

Leo shook his head. 'You can't do that.'

Avery nodded to Sam. 'File the paperwork, Sam. I've some other things I need to do.'

He took hold of Robyn's hand and pulled her out of the conference room.

He looked her in the eye. 'You do realise what happens next, don't you?'

She gave him her steadiest smile. 'I stand by the man I love, fighting for what he knows is right.' She tipped her head to the side. 'I also need to move back into your apartment. Sort out my shifts at the soup kitchen and clinic.' She pressed her lips together for a second. 'Arrange to find a counsellor, and see if my time in the programme can be extended for longer than six months.'

'That's quite a list you've got.'

She nodded as she slid her hands up around his neck. 'It is. But I have someone to help me. Someone who showed me who he really was, showed me what mattered to him, before I got blindsided by my prejudices. I just needed the space to realise that. Well, that, and a cuddle from a very particular dog.'

'You went to the bookshop?'

She whispered in his ear. 'I don't know if you realise this, but Annie might be your number one fan.'

'She is?' He grinned at her.

'Oh, she definitely is. But then, she has good taste. Who can blame her?'

Avery hesitated. 'This might be hard. I might need to lean on you. The Paz family can be tough to face.'

'They don't know you yet,' she said encouragingly. 'They don't know what you have inside. Your clinical expertise, your knowledge of systems, your philanthropic nature, or how big your heart is.'

'And are you willing to be by my side?'

'Try and stop me.'

He bent and kissed her. 'I love you,' he said.

'I love you too.' She kissed him back, then straightened up and looked over her shoulder. 'Now, go get 'em.'

EPILOGUE

'WHAT TIME IS IT?' Robyn asked, anxiously sweeping things into drawers.

'Relax.' Avery smiled, his large presence filling the smaller part of their original cottage. 'They're not due to land at Edinburgh airport for another few hours.'

Robyn looked around. 'Do you think they'll like the place?'

Avery put his hand around his wife's shoulders and turned to face the back half of the cottage. The wide windows opened out onto a glen, complete with a running stream, gentle slopes, sheep and goats. Their extension and renovation had taken around six months and there were still little things to finish. 'How could anyone not like this place?' he answered simply.

Robyn sighed and put her head on her husband's shoulder. 'I'm just worried they'll think we should have stayed in San Diego.'

Serena, Toby, and their two-year-old daughter, Faith, were coming to stay for the next fortnight. They'd never been to Scotland and were anxious to spend time with their friends.

After a lot of soul-searching, and once Robyn had completed her programme, they'd both decided to leave San Diego. Avery still had his place on the hospital board, where he kept a very close eye on a much more subdued Leo, and, like many people nowadays, attended the meetings by connecting virtually. The soup kitchen and free clinic were still functioning, and Avery had even bought The Book Emporium after Annie had sadly passed away after a short illness, and installed new staff to run it.

Peggy, however, had come to Scotland with them. Both were working at a hospital in Edinburgh, a twenty-minute drive away.

'I have something to show you.' Avery smiled.

'Oh, no.' Robyn wagged her finger. 'You're up to something. What is it?'

He lifted up his tablet and turned it around. 'I think it could be time to expand this family. Peggy needs a friend.'

Robyn let out a gasp and leaned forward, glancing at the tired-looking dog in a basket, with a host of little wriggling puppies at her belly. 'Are those red Labradors?'

He smiled. 'They are. And one of them can be ours.'

'Really?'

He nodded. 'You told me just after we met that this was your plan. A house, a dog.' He gave a laugh. 'And I didn't give you much of a say in the first dog. So, it's only fair that you get to pick the second.'

Robyn breathed in. She couldn't stop the broad smile on her face, or the feeling of her heart expanding in her chest. 'How old are they?'

'Five weeks right now. We can collect ours in another month. There's three girls and three boys. We can meet them before you decide which one you want.'

Robyn threw her hands around his neck. 'Sometimes I think I've got the best husband in the world.' She kissed him on the lips.

'Only sometimes?' He quirked one eyebrow at her.

She raised her own eyebrows and kissed him again. 'Well, that just depends on whether we come home with one puppy or two,' she teased.

'Persuade me,' he said, his eyes gleaming.

And so she did.

* * * * *

COMING SOON!

We really hope you enjoyed reading this book. If you're looking for more romance be sure to head to the shops when new books are available on

Thursday 11th May

To see which titles are coming soon, please visit

millsandboon.co.uk/nextmonth

MILLS & BOON

MILLS & BOON®

Coming next month

THE BROODING DOC AND THE SINGLE MUM
Louisa Heaton

Daniel couldn't stand still. He tried to. But his mind wouldn't let him settle. He felt as if his body was flooded with adrenaline and this was either a fight, flight or freeze response.

Most likely flight.

I thought about kissing her.

That was what he couldn't get out of his head. He'd been having such a fun time. A relaxing time. Playing football with Jack. He'd used to play football with Mason all the time, so the opportunity to play with Jack and remember what it had been like had been awesome! In a way, it had been almost as if Jack was his son. He'd been helping to guide him. Showing the little boy that he was interested in him. That he wanted to spend time with him. That he was important.

And then Stacey had joined them.

Penny had never joined in their football games. She'd always watched, or used the time that Daniel was with their son to get a few jobs done around the house. Daniel hadn't minded that. It had given them a little father-son bonding moment.

So when Stacey had joined in he'd been amazed, and then delighted. They'd had a fun time. It had been relaxing, the three of them together. Nice. Easy. So easy! He'd almost not been able to believe how easy it was for him to be with them.

And then the tackle.

They'd all gone for the ball at once and somehow tumbled into a tangle of arms and legs. And he'd landed on top of Stacey. Not fully. His hands had broken the fall, and he'd tried to avoid squashing her. But she'd been lying beneath him, red hair splayed out against the green grass. Her laughter-filled eyes had looked up at him, there'd been a smile on her face and he'd been so close to her!

He'd felt her breathing, her chest rising and falling. Her softness. Her legs entwined with his. Their faces had been so close. Mere inches away from each other! And the thought had risen unbidden to his mind.

What would it be like to kiss her?

Continue reading
THE BROODING DOC AND THE SINGLE MUM
Louisa Heaton

Available next month
www.millsandboon.co.uk

OUT NOW!

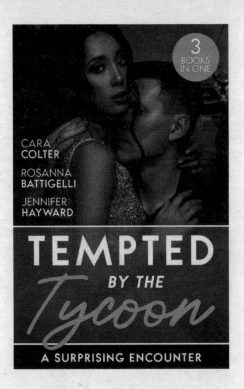

3 BOOKS IN ONE

CARA COLTER

ROSANNA BATTIGELLI

JENNIFER HAYWARD

TEMPTED
BY THE
Tycoon

A SURPRISING ENCOUNTER

Available at
millsandboon.co.uk

MILLS & BOON

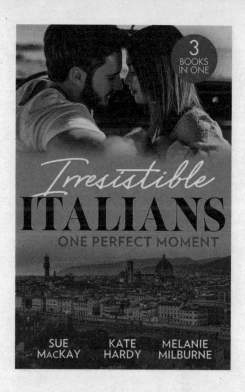

LET'S TALK

Romance

For exclusive extracts, competitions
and special offers, find us online:

- **facebook.com/millsandboon**
- **@MillsandBoon**
- **@MillsandBoonUK**
- **@MillsandBoonUK**

Get in touch on 01413 063 232

MILLS & BOON

THE HEART OF ROMANCE

A ROMANCE FOR EVERY READER

MODERN

Prepare to be swept off your feet by sophisticated, sexy and seductive heroes, in some of the world's most glamourous and romantic locations, where power and passion collide.

HISTORICAL

Escape with historical heroes from time gone by. Whether your passion is for wicked Regency Rakes, muscled Vikings or rugged Highlanders, awaken the romance of the past.

MEDICAL

Set your pulse racing with dedicated, delectable doctors in the high-pressure world of medicine, where emotions run high and passion, comfort and love are the best medicine.

True Love

Celebrate true love with tender stories of heartfelt romance, from the rush of falling in love to the joy a new baby can bring, and a focus on the emotional heart of a relationship.

Desire

Indulge in secrets and scandal, intense drama and sizzling hot action with heroes who have it all: wealth, status, good looks…everything but the right woman.

HEROES

The excitement of a gripping thriller, with intense romance at its heart. Resourceful, true-to-life women and strong, fearless men face danger and desire - a killer combination!

To see which titles are coming soon, please visit

millsandboon.co.uk/nextmonth

JOIN US ON SOCIAL MEDIA!

Stay up to date with our latest releases, author news and gossip, special offers and discounts, and all the behind-the-scenes action from Mills & Boon...

 @millsandboon

 @millsandboonuk

 facebook.com/millsandboon

 @millsandboonuk

It might just be true love...

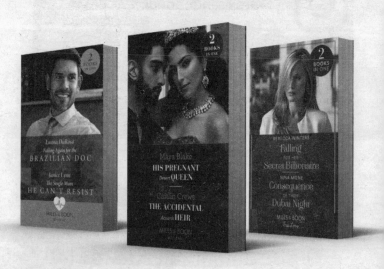